WESTERN

Rugged men looking for love...

The Texan's Journey Home
Jolene Navarro

A Faithful Guardian
Louise M. Gouge

MILLS & BOON

DID YOU PURCHASE THIS BOOK WITHOUT A COVER?
If you did, you should be aware it is stolen property as it was reported
'unsold and destroyed' by a retailer.
Neither the author nor the publisher has received any payment
for this book.

THE TEXAN'S JOURNEY HOME
© 2024 by Jolene Navarro
Philippine Copyright 2024
Australian Copyright 2024
New Zealand Copyright 2024

First Published 2024
First Australian Paperback Edition 2024
ISBN 978 1 038 93909 8

A FAITHFUL GUARDIAN
© 2024 by Louise M. Gouge
Philippine Copyright 2024
Australian Copyright 2024
New Zealand Copyright 2024

First Published 2024
First Australian Paperback Edition 2024
ISBN 978 1 038 93909 8

® and ™ (apart from those relating to FSC®) are trademarks of Harlequin Enterprises
(Australia) Pty Limited or its corporate affiliates. Trademarks indicated with ® are
registered in Australia, New Zealand and in other countries.
Contact admin_legal@Harlequin.ca for details.

Except for use in any review, the reproduction or utilisation of this work in whole
or in part in any form by any electronic, mechanical or other means, now known
or hereafter invented, including xerography, photocopying and recording, or in any
information storage or retrieval system, is forbidden without the permission of the
publisher, Harlequin Mills & Boon.

This book is sold subject to the condition that it shall not, by way of trade or
otherwise, be lent, resold, hired out or otherwise circulated without the prior consent
of the publisher in any form or binding or cover other than that in which it is published
and without a similar condition including this condition being imposed on the
subsequent purchaser.

All rights reserved including the right of reproduction in whole or in part in any form.
This edition is published in arrangement with Harlequin Books S.A..

This is a work of fiction. Names, characters, places, and incidents are either the
product of the author's imagination or are used fictitiously, and any resemblance to
actual persons, living or dead, business establishments, events, or locales is entirely
coincidental.

MIX
Paper | Supporting
responsible forestry
FSC® C001695
www.fsc.org

Published by
Harlequin Mills & Boon
An imprint of Harlequin Enterprises (Australia) Pty Limited
(ABN 47 001 180 918), a subsidiary of HarperCollins
Publishers Australia Pty Limited
(ABN 36 009 913 517)
Level 19, 201 Elizabeth Street
SYDNEY NSW 2000 AUSTRALIA

Cover art used by arrangement with Harlequin Books S.A.. All rights reserved.

Printed and bound in Australia by McPherson's Printing Group

The Texan's Journey Home

Jolene Navarro

MILLS & BOON

A seventh-generation Texan, **Jolene Navarro** fills her life with family, faith and life's beautiful messiness. She knows that as much as the world changes, people stay the same: vow-keepers and heartbreakers. Jolene married a vow-keeper who shows her holding hands never gets old. When not writing, Jolene teaches art to teens and hangs out with her own four almost-grown kids. Find Jolene on Facebook or her blog, jolenenavarro.com.

Books by Jolene Navarro

Lone Star Heritage

Bound by a Secret
The Reluctant Rancher
The Texan's Journey Home

Cowboys of Diamondback Ranch

The Texan's Secret Daughter
The Texan's Surprise Return
The Texan's Promise
The Texan's Unexpected Holiday
The Texan's Truth
Her Holiday Secret
Claiming Her Texas Family

Visit the Author Profile page at millsandboon.com.au for more titles.

Strength and honour are her clothing;
and she shall rejoice in time to come.
—*Proverbs* 31:25

This book is dedicated to Jesus Alfredo "Fred" Navarro for his persistent belief in me until I believed in myself.

CHAPTER ONE

LYRISSA RUSHED OUT of the crowded restroom as she dried her hands. She hadn't wanted to leave the boys alone for a second, but some things just couldn't be avoided. Especially after being in a car for more than twelve hours. They were back in Texas and so close to the ranch where she grew up. Port Del Mar might live too much on gossip for her liking, but her father's ranch was always safe.

They just had a few miles left and hopefully she wouldn't run into anyone. This new situation was going to have stories flying along the shoreline and her father didn't deserve any of it. Once again, the train wreck of a woman who called herself Lyrissa's mother had rammed straight into their lives without any thought of others. Deeann Herff Martinez had torn apart their family for the sake of finding her own happiness.

She pulled the scrunchie off her wrist and tried to wrestle her curls back into a ponytail. The humidity and coastal air were not her friend. She hadn't wanted to waste time in front of a mirror with the boys waiting.

Buc-ee's was one of the best convenience stores in Texas, but still. She had told them if they stayed at the fudge counter then they would each get to pick a flavor when she returned. It was still hard to comprehend that she had two brothers, eight-

and five years old. They were the only reason she had allowed her mother back into her life.

Of course, that had proven to be a huge mistake—not her brothers, but her mother. Dee was and would forever be a party girl first and foremost in search of an easy high. Why did Lyrissa think this time would be any different?

The sad part? At forty-five, Dee was still looking for the big score and next hit. This time, the woman had abandoned her two young sons and stolen everything of value from Lyrissa's apartment and wiped out her checking account. At least Dee hadn't been able to access Lyrissa's savings, not that it was much.

She was resigned to the fact that her mother would never change, and it would be up to her to make sure her brothers had a safe place to live.

Her neighbor had told her to call the police and turn the boys over to Child Protective Services, but she couldn't do that. The one time her mother had taken her when she had left the ranch, Lyrissa had ended up in the custody of CPS until her grandmother and father had been contacted. As a nine-year-old, she had been terrified that she would never see her father or grandmother again. She had just wanted to go home.

Her brothers didn't even have a home. But they had her now… She stopped. Where were they? Fear seized her lungs.

They were gone. Frantically scanning the large store again, she gazed from person to person and in between. The Texas-size truck stop was clean, well-lit and huge. It was filled with a mix of tourists and locals but there was no sign of the boys.

Had Bennett, the eight-year-old, taken his little brother back into the bathroom? *Breathe.* She needed to find an employee to check for her. As she leaned over the counter to get the attention of one of the candymakers, a gentle touch on the back of her shoulder caused her to jump.

"Ma'am?" A deep Texas drawl, cool and confident, ran along her nerves.

She turned and saw both boys. She took a deep breath with immediate relief. *They're safe.* She clenched her hands to her chest so she wouldn't grab her brothers and startle them.

They wouldn't appreciate the uninvited affection. Bennett had perfected the sullen look mixed with an air of boiling rage. Ray-Ray, younger by three years, was impossibly shy but wanted to trust her. He reminded her of a puppy that had been kicked too many times. The tears in his big brown eyes pulled pieces of her heart right off. His expression warned her that he could burst into sobs any minute.

"Lyrissa?" That voice.

Pull yourself together, girl. The question in the man's voice brought her gaze up to his. He was tall, dark and good-looking. Had to be a little over six feet. And well-built. His large hand gently sat on Bennett's shoulder. Not too tight, but firm enough to make sure the boy didn't run. His golden-brown eyes stared at her.

Reno Espinoza. Her heart sank. Of all the people to meet on this little side trip into town, why did it have to be him? When she had left Port Del Mar eight years ago, that had included standing him up for the homecoming dance. Had she at least sent him a text saying she couldn't make it? She hoped, but probably not. She had been humiliated and in too much of a rush to leave town.

Meeting his gaze, she expected judgment or resentment. But she only saw a genuine concern. The warmth and softness of his gaze was at odds with the hard jaw and wide mouth. Evidence of the Indigenous warriors who were his ancestors. His thick, dark hair was a casually tossed mess, just like in high school.

With a sigh, she attempted a smile. He was one of the Espinoza kids. It was a well-known fact that they were the nicest family in town. Reno was the youngest and had the reputation of being the party boy, the one and only wild child of the bunch. He was famous for always wearing a smile and having fun in any situation. But that was when they were teenagers.

Reno was a grown man now, very grown. A loud rumble of thunder shook the building. Ray jumped and the older boy put an arm around him, pulling him closer. She needed to focus and get the boys to the ranch.

"Hey, Reno." She nodded, then looked back at her brother. "What's going on, Bennett? You were supposed to stay at the fudge counter. Both of you." Her gaze slid to Ray.

"He didn't mean it. Please don't get mad." Sweet Ray-Ray was already pleading for his brother.

Reno's eyes went wide for a second. "So, they *are* yours?" He looked at Bennett, doing the math. *Great*. She scanned the area. Rumors and stories, true or not, spread fast in these parts. Actually, the faster they flew, the further from the truth they grew.

Of course, when it came to her mother, there had been more truth in the gossip than Lyrissa had liked. In Port Del Mar, her mother's shadow was overpowering. She had been guilty by association for most people. The rumor mill was going to have so much fun with this.

"Yes. They're mine. They're my *brothers*."

Confusion clouded his face. "I didn't know you had any brothers."

A very unladylike snort escaped her. "Join the club." She rubbed the bridge of her nose. All she wanted was to get to her father's house and hide under the quilt her great-grand-mother had made for her sixteenth birthday. At least she hadn't taken that one with her to Missouri, or it would be gone too. She turned back to her newly found brother. "Bennett, what's going on?"

"Nothin'." He rolled his shoulder but couldn't dislodge Reno's hand. "This guy's just being a jerk. He needs to leave kids alone."

Reno gave her a slanted smile, obviously not offended by

the comment. "I don't think the beef jerky and Dr Pepper accidentally fell into the pocket of his hoodie." He looked back at Bennett with one eyebrow raised.

She gasped. "You're stealing?"

The eight-year-old shrugged. "I was hungry. It's overpriced. You said you don't buy sodas."

She dropped down on her haunches and tried to look him in the eye. He had a talent for staring right over her shoulder as if she didn't exist. "If you were that hungry, you should have talked to me. Stealing is never okay. We're almost home and you can have a full meal."

His gaze cut to her. "Not my home." Hostility burned, covering up the hurt caused by their mother. "Mom said stores like this mark everything way up because they know half of it'll be taken. It didn't hurt anyone."

Ray-Ray eagerly nodded as he stepped in front of his big brother, his eyes wide. "She said that they didn't mind if kids took stuff, it was…" He looked up at his brother.

"Charity," Bennett offered. He shrugged. "They'll just right it off as a donation."

She closed her eyes and took a deep breath. The reality of her mother's problems had become clear to her long ago. Alcohol and drugs changed a person. It took control and had to be the center of attention. There's no telling what the boys had been exposed too. It shouldn't surprise her that she had taught her sons to steal as a way of life. The woman had stolen everything from her own daughter and from the church where Lyrissa had worked part-time.

It was less than twenty-four hours ago that the church had called to say that they had Dee, her mother, on video, walking out with all the petty cash that had been in Lyrissa's desk. Her mother had used her keys to steal from the church. Who did that?

Lyrissa had rushed home to find her apartment and checking account stripped clean. Only the boys were left behind.

She reached out to take Bennett's hand, but he pulled back. Ray-Ray pressed himself closer to his big brother, looking at her with fear in his eyes.

After only a few weeks of knowing each other, the boys were still reserved around her. Asking them to trust another adult was too much. All they knew was a mother who had walked out on them. They hadn't been blessed with someone like her father. A man whose compassion and unconditional love was an anchor in the worst storms.

He had always welcomed Dee back into their lives. No questions asked. Lyrissa had made a promise to herself to never be in that situation. Loving someone who only wanted a good time had to be fun at first, but it only led to heartbreak and misery. But the moment Dee knocked on her door with the boys, Lyrissa had welcomed them into her small apartment.

She was too much like her sweet father, foolishly optimistic. Where did that get her? Instead of reconnecting with the woman who never acted like a mother, she was now responsible for two young boys.

She was already messing it up.

And here stood Reno Espinoza, witnessing it all. This was why she never had gone into town the few times she had visited her dad and grandmother.

People knew her mother. It was so embarrassing, being the daughter of the town drunk. They looked at her father with a mix of pity and disgust. How could he love a woman like that? They had always eyed Lyrissa with suspicion.

All they saw was Dee.

Back in high school, after the pastor's gentle *intervention* that day, she knew she'd never be more than *Dee's daughter*, no matter how hard she worked to prove otherwise. She had begged her father to take her away. To start over somewhere fresh. But his mother-in-law needed him to run the ranch and Dee might come back. As much as she loved her father, she prayed to never be like him.

He had finally agreed to call his cousins and arranged for Lyrissa to finish her last year of high school in Dallas.

She hated and loved her father for his loyalty and capacity for forgiveness. But this was too much, even for the sweetest man she knew. Now, she was bringing home two boys who carried her father's name but weren't his blood. And they were caught stealing their first day in town.

She was in over her head.

Hand out in front of the boys, she stared Bennett in the eye. "Give me everything you put into your pockets. And listen to me. Our mother has an illness. You know stealing is wrong. Don't ever try to justify it again. You are my responsibility now and there will be no stealing, lying *or* cheating."

Heat spread up her neck and over her cheeks as she stood and looked at Reno. "Thank you for bringing him to me."

"You're heading to your dad's? He didn't say anything about—" he glanced at the boys "—you coming home. Does he know?"

Why did her family have to be such a mess? People in the store were starting to stare. Before the sun set, rumors would be everywhere. "I just called last night. We've been on the road all day. Thank you for bringing him to me and not..." She sighed. "Thanks. We need to be going."

Reno reached over and took the items Bennett had taken. After placing them in a red basket he carried, he looked back at her. "Let me get these as a welcome-back-to-town gift and to let you know all is forgiven for leaving me high and dry for homecoming." Giving her a charming smile, he winked.

Heat climbed up her neck. *Great, my whole face will be strawberry red soon.*

She took a few deep breaths, but she knew there was no stopping the scarlet splotches. "I..." Not knowing what to say, she bit her bottom lip. So, she hadn't sent a text.

It had been the Wednesday before the dance that the pastor had accused her of stealing. In her humiliation, she had figured Reno wouldn't want to be seen with her. Even though he had just been a sophomore and she'd been a senior, he had been a varsity player in their small school and was loved by everyone. It was clear she had been a pity date for him. Her best friend—who happened to be one of his sisters had probably made him. Now he caught her brothers stealing. *Please God, let the ground open beneath me.*

He leaned in closer to her, his forehead wrinkled in concern. "Sorry. If I had known that would make you uncomfortable, I wouldn't have said anything." Sincerity had replaced the teasing glint from earlier. "Did you know that Belle De La Rosa confessed and returned the money after she heard you had been blamed?"

Her mouth dropped open. "Belle?" That family might have had it worse than Lyrissa. At least she'd had her father and grandmother in her corner. Those kids had been all alone after the death of their mother. "I didn't know."

"She felt awful." He laid one large hand flat on his chest. "Really, no hard feelings." He gave her a genuine smile and squeezed her arm before dropping his hand. With a gentle nudge of his elbow, he winked again. The charmer was back. "Another underclassmen might have been scarred for life. Thankfully, my resilient personality protected the fragile teenage boy's ego from harm. My sisters all agreed it was good for me. Humbling."

He glanced at the boys, then grew serious. "Please, let me buy these for you to prove there are no ill feelings and send you out to your father with happy bellies. Your dad is one of my favorite people, you know." He guided them to the side doors to check out.

"Mine too." Her father deserved to be respected and she loved that Reno saw him for the kind human he was.

"What about the truck?" Ray-Ray asked.

She stopped. Dread knotted her stomach. "What truck?"

"Mama took mine, so Benny gave this one to me." He pulled

a mini metal truck from the front pocket of his jacket and held it out to her.

"Ray-Ray," Bennett said between gritted teeth. "I gave that to you."

"But she said no more stealing." The sweet boy looked at his older brother in confusion.

Reno took the truck and tossed it in the basket. "Anything else, guys? Come clean now or suffer the consequences."

"What's that?" Ray-Ray looked between the two adults.

"It'll be up to your sister, but it usually involves chores no one wants to do. Mucking stalls, shoveling manure into a compost bin, and there is always the old pulling weeds from the pastures."

Bennett rolled his eyes and crossed his arms.

Ray-Ray shook his head. "That doesn't sound fun. What's manure?"

"Lyrissa? Lyrissa Martinez?" A woman with unnatural red hair touched her arm. "I thought that was you. Hi, Reno."

She hugged him, then turned to Lyrissa. A well-manicured hand rested on his arm as if staking a claim.

Madilyn House. Her throat went dry. The inadequacies she had grown up with surged into her system. *Maddy.* Why did she complain to God about seeing Reno? This was so much worse.

As nice as Reno had been, Maddy was the opposite. In school, the girl had taken every opportunity to put Lyrissa down. She was the one who had blamed her for the church's missing money.

She would never make the mistake of coming to town, ever again. Small town homecomings were not her thing. The past was better off forgotten.

RENO STIFFENED AT Maddy's possessiveness. Ever since she'd returned to help her mom with the flower shop, she had made it clear she was interested in him. He had told her as gently as he could that it was a big no from him, but since he wasn't dating anyone else, she didn't think he really meant it.

Being nice was sometimes a huge pain. With a sigh, he shifted his attention to the two boys standing next to Lyrissa. He knelt to be eye level with them, then rested one arm across his knee. The move also dislodged Maddy's hold on him. *Two birds. One stone.*

She was being nosy, and he didn't want to give her any more information about Lyrissa and her brothers. He nodded. "As a welcome-to-town, I'm going to get these for you. Why don't you also go ahead and pick up your favorite chips."

Ray-Ray glanced at Lyrissa, then gave him a shy grin before turning to pick out a bag. Bennett shrugged as if showing any gratitude would make him weak. Lyrissa had her work cut out for her with that one.

"Which ones are plain? I like plain." The little boy looked up at Reno.

A moment of panic blurred his vision. He had not been prepared to read. All the bags had the same design. He blinked then forced a laugh and rubbed the boy's shoulders. "It's the start of a new adventure. Be brave and grab one. Then guess what flavor it is."

Ray-Ray grinned and nodded. Muscles he didn't realize were tensed relaxed. He had been caught off guard. He had spent his life pretending he could read, and no one had caught on yet. Surprise attacks were the worst. Making sense of all the lines and shapes seemed so easy for everyone else.

Needing to get away from the situation, he stood and grabbed a couple cups of fruit. "It was good seeing you, Maddy. They're running late. They need to beat that storm rolling in." He placed his hand on the back of the smallest one's shoulder and moved them away from the town gossip and toward the register at the other end of the store.

The woman didn't take the hint. She stood in front of Lyrissa, not letting her pass. With a big friendly smile that didn't hide the excited glint in her eyes, she forced Lyrissa to interact with her.

Maddy wanted to be the first to get a juicy story, so she'd have something exciting to talk about. It didn't matter if it was all true or not or if it hurt someone. "So, it's not Martinez anymore? I hadn't heard you got married."

Her smile tight, Lyrissa shook her head. "I didn't."

Maddy looked between the boys and Lyrissa. "Your dad didn't say anything about being a grandfather. That's so weird. When my oldest brother had his first, everyone in town knew about it." She chuckled. "They were so excited about being grandparents."

Stepping around her, Lyrissa held her forced smile. "They're my brothers."

Mouth opened, Maddy was wordless for a moment. "Oh. Well, that would explain why your father isn't bragging. I just..." She waved her hand as if to gather the right words, and the spark in her gaze burned brighter.

Reno needed to intercede before this meeting spiraled into even murkier waters.

"Maddy." He gently took the hand of the younger brother and moved around her. "Lyrissa and the boys have been in the car for hours and want to get to the ranch. You can talk later." He glanced at Lyrissa. Her smile was softer as she nodded to him and walked around Maddy. How had he forgotten how stunning she was? She wasn't the stereotypical beauty. *Pretty* was too tame a word.

Her thick curls were dark with streaks of fierce red that the scrunchie couldn't contain. But it was her eyes that made his breath seize in his chest. They were a bold green with shattered flakes of gold surrounded by thick black lashes. To an outsider, she had the look of a fiery warrior, no matter how much she wanted to blend into the background and disappear.

Back in school, she had been at war with her looks. His sister had said no one really knew the real Lyrissa. She had always intrigued him. Over the years, that type of curiosity usually got him in trouble.

"Y'all want to get out to the ranch, right?" He gave everyone his best smile and guided the boys around Maddy. As they made their way to the cashier, Reno tossed a few of the BBQ sandwiches in the basket. "You can't come to Buc-ee's and not get the chopped."

Lyrissa stiffened. "Really, Reno. This is too much."

Her skin was pale. It looked as if she might be sick. He sat the basket on an available counter. As the girl started ringing up the items, Lyrissa fumbled through her purse.

He rested his hands on hers. "Let me do this. And don't worry about Maddy. She just returned home after a divorce and is not in a good place."

She glanced over her shoulder, then at the boys. They were hanging back.

The youngest blinked at them as if he weren't sure they wouldn't leave him here. Reno's sister Savannah and Lyrissa had been good friends. He knew too many of the details of how hard Dee Martinez had made her daughter's life. This new situation with the boys and her mother must have rubbed her nerves raw. And now she was back in the town she wanted to escape.

She leaned in close, keeping her head down. "What kind of lesson will this teach the boys if I let you—"

Reno shook his head at her. "Don't. I remember being hungry all the time at that age. When I lost my dad, it helped when others saw me. They've lost their mom."

"Your father died. Their…our mother made horrible, selfish choices."

"Yeah. But losing a parent shakes up your world, no matter how or why they left. Let me do this. It makes me happy and lately I haven't had a lot to be happy about." *Ugh. Too much personal information.* Now why did he go and say that?

And in a second, the self-pity in her eyes turned to concern. "What happened?"

Great. He had wanted her to stop feeling guilty and now she was worried about him. He wasn't sure if this was better or worse.

He put his smile back on. Complaining was something he never did. His family had already been through too much because of him.

She shook her head. "Sorry. It's none of my business."

"It's okay. No big secret." He shrugged then added a handful of candy bars to the growing pile of food. He could share the parts of his life everyone knew already. The real secrets he had kept to himself had been buried far too long to say them aloud now.

"I'm just wallowing in a little self-pity. My sister and I started a construction business, and it was going great, but she fell in love and they moved away. I mean, I'm happy for Savannah getting her happy-ever-after, but I'm feeling a little left behind. She considered you a good friend. So, helping you helps me feel better. See, totally selfish." He made sure to give her the grin that his sisters said gave him his irresistible dimples.

"Sorry. I haven't spoken to Savannah for over a year. Where is she?"

Not wanting to get into it, he shrugged and gathered the bags. "Come on. Let's get y'all to the ranch." He could get her and the boys to the safety of the ranch. That was the least he could do for her. He smiled.

No one needed his bad mood to make things worse.

CHAPTER TWO

LYRISSA'S STOMACH WAS in knots. She just wanted to get out of town and hide on the ranch. As they walked toward the first set of sliding doors, they opened.

Reno followed them. She stopped next to the red carts and shopping baskets. The camping chairs and fire pits lining the glass wall caught the boys' attention. Thunder rumbled through the air. The clouds billowed as they threatened the earth with a heavy downpour.

A few people hurried by, going into the store. One of them called out a greeting to Reno.

Lightning flashed and a strong wind warned them to move to shelter.

Her skin felt too tight for her body as she scanned the parking lot. "It's probably better for you if you're not seen with us." She glanced at the boys. "You know Maddy is going to start some wild rumor. I really appreciate your help. Thank you."

She took her youngest brother's small hand and went out the sliding glass doors.

The sky opened and heavy raindrops fell hard. Lyrissa fumbled for a small umbrella in her backpack and when she opened it, the wind flipped it inside out. She adjusted it and used the wind to pop it back in place. "Come on." She would not cry. "We can make a run for it."

The small boy shook his head and looked down where the water was gathering. "My socks'll get wet. I hate wet socks."

Reno and she looked down at his feet at the same time. Heavy tape barely held together his sneakers. Should she go back inside and buy him a new pair? Before she could make a decision, Reno picked him up and carried him like a football. Pulling his Carhartt jacket over to shield them from the rain. He nodded to Lyrissa to lead the way.

"Really, you've already helped too—"

"Nope. The longer we stand here, the wetter everyone gets. Where are you parked?" He shifted Ray-Ray and the boy giggled.

With a reluctant nod, she put an arm around Bennett to pull him under the umbrella then jogged to her car. Each step slashed the quickly rising water.

She used the key fob to unlock the doors and handed the umbrella to Bennett. Reno slid Ray-Ray into the back seat. Water dripped from his hair and into his eyes.

She pulled her wallet out and took out a ten. She hated being a charity case. "Let me pay at least part of—"

"Nope."

The strap of her purse slipped, and she adjusted it. She wrapped her thin jacket closer. "Thank you." She nodded to the boys, hoping they understood.

"Thank you for keeping my feet out of the water." Ray-Ray's tentative grin melted her heart.

"You're very welcome. Once you get settled into the ranch, we'll have to get you some boots."

Ray-Ray smiled bigger. Stepping back, Reno closed the door and jogged back to the storefront. Reno had always made everyone around him smile. It was a gift he had. She pushed the wet strands of hair off her face and glanced at the rearview mirror. "Ready to go home?"

Bennett crossed his arms and glared at the truck parked next to them. Ray-Ray nodded. "I like Texas."

"You're going to love the ranch." She hoped she was right. Her father had told her God had a plan and it would all work out. She hoped it was true, but she had seen it go wrong so many times before that it was hard for her to have her father's kind of faith. Maybe one day she would.

RENO WATCHED AS Lyrissa and her two brothers pulled out of the parking lot. He wasn't sure why seeing her had hit him so hard. Yeah, she had stood him up, but he hadn't mooned over her or anything. Life happened and they moved on.

So why did seeing her stir up his insides in a weird way? With a deep sigh, he shrugged it off and turned back into the store to get his coffee. With the boys and Lyrissa's return, he'd gotten distracted and forgot his whole reason for stopping.

He shook his head, trying to get the extra water off. This would have been a good day to wear his hat. After wiping his boots on the oversize welcome mat, he went back into the store.

It didn't take long for Maddy to reappear. "I noticed the age of that oldest boy. The math is not hard to do. Is he yours? Did you know about him?"

He dropped his head and stifled a groan. He poured a packet of sugar into his coffee, then a touch of cream, and stirred the hot liquid. Maddy was a gossip.

In school, she had been the kind to stir up drama then sit back and watch the fireworks like it was a personal performance for her entertainment. Avoiding her had always been his plan of action. He had never understood people who were entertained by others' suffering. She stood next to him, sipping her coffee like she had all day to wait him out.

He and Lyrissa hadn't had that type of relationship, but it wasn't any of Maddy's business. "They're her brothers. Have a good day. I need to get to work." With the rain, he wouldn't be going out to the jobsite, but she didn't need to know that. He walked past her.

She followed. Of course she did. She had an agenda.

"Y'all were dating when she took off all of a sudden. It was the middle of her senior year and *poof* she just left. We were just sophomores. So, was she pregnant? That's why she left, isn't it? It makes sense."

Maybe to get away from gossips? "Nope. She went to stay with her cousins in Dallas." Why was he even engaging in this conversation? He pulled his wallet out of his back pocket then nodded to Maddy's coffee and fresh fruit cup.

"Oh, you didn't have to do that. Thank you." She followed him through the sliding glass doors. "So, she stayed in touch with you. Did you know she had a baby? Is he yours?"

"Those are her brothers." But the facts weren't important to Maddy if she thought she had a good story.

"No. I don't think so. We would have heard if her mother had more kids. Those boys are hers. Why is she lying? That Wimberly girl came back into town with Adrian's kid. That blew everyone out of the water. He was going to be sheriff and now they live in Canada."

She put her hand on his shoulder. "Reno, you're a nice guy. Be careful. She could totally be here to ruin your life. It would be just like her. That kid kind of looks like you."

"Maddy, stop. Those two boys are her mother's sons. They have enough to deal with. Leave it alone. She left because someone lied to the pastor and told him she had stolen money from the church."

Eyes wide, she stepped back as if he had yelled or lifted his fist at her. "I did see her with the offerings. I just reported what I saw. Don't be mad at me. I'm on your side. She's always been trouble. Be careful."

"Bye, Maddy." He was profoundly grateful that his work truck was on the opposite side of the monster parking lot.

The rain had pulled back into a drizzle as he made his way

along the sidewalk. He should have said more, but no matter what he said, Maddy was going to start a line of rumors that had no truth.

Without a conscious thought, he looked to the spot where Lyrissa's Mazda had been parked. There was something on the ground. He narrowed his gaze. It was a wallet. He stepped closer. It was the one she had pulled out when she had tried to give him money. It was drenched in rainwater.

He picked up the worn leather wallet and flipped open the silver latch. It was well made but well used too. The insides were still mostly dry. On the top was her driver's license. He closed it then tucked it inside the pocket of his jacket. Her father was on his list of people to check on later this week.

Mundo Martinez just got moved up. He couldn't believe the youngest was named after Raymundo. Dee hadn't been home in over ten years, so the boy wasn't his.

And now Lyrissa was bringing Dee's sons to the ranch and Mundo was okay with this?

He didn't know many men who would take in their ex-wife's children from other relationships. Mundo was one of a kind and the nicest man he had ever met. The problem with being nice? People take advantage.

Was Lyrissa going to drop the boys and run back to her life in Missouri or was she at least going to stick around long enough to make sure the boys were settled?

He should call his mom. She was great at helping people who were in over their heads. Not that Lyrissa gave any indication that she wanted help. The times she had visited the ranch in recent years, she never came to town. It was a clear message that she wanted nothing to do with the people of Port Del Mar.

The wallet would be easy to slip into the mailbox at the end of the road. A text to Mundo would ensure she got it. There was no need to hand-deliver it to her.

Not one single reason.

CHAPTER THREE

"STOP MAKING THAT weird noise," Bennett snapped at his brother.

"I'm not making a weird noise." Ray-Ray opened his mouth wider and made another nonsensical sound. "*Mmmmmoowt.* Stop looking at me."

"You're such a baby. You wouldn't know I was looking at you if you weren't looking at me."

Ray-Ray yelled and swung to hit Bennett.

"Boys. Stop." The pounding of the rain echoed the pounding behind her eyes. But she took a breath as they fell silent. She was in over her head. She had been an only child and had no clue how siblings interacted. The Espinoza family was the only one she had ever been around, and they certainly didn't act like this.

Was this normal for brothers or had their mother left deep psychological scars? That was a ridiculous question. How could they not be scarred? Tomorrow, she would investigate therapy.

She snorted. They all needed some good counseling. There was no way the path of destruction left by her mother didn't affect them all. Her father claimed that God had him and his faith was all he needed, but really?

Then again, there had to be something to it. When she had called him not knowing what to do, he immediately and without hesitation told her to bring them to the ranch. These were his ex-wife's children from other men, and he told her to bring them home. That was a man speaking from a heart of gold.

Everyone in town was going to see him as a fool. Maddy crossed her mind. Or they'll say she's a liar, and that the boys are really Lyrissa's own.

People annoyed her. Her father was too kind. Too forgiving. The world chewed up and spit out people like him. Her mother definitely did.

And here she was, bringing more of her mother's drama to her father's doorstep. She should take the boys to her grandmother's house. They might not be related to her father, but they were her grandmother's grandsons. Mew-Maw had always worried about not having anyone to continue the family ranch.

Maybe the boys were God's gift to her grandmother.

She glanced at the dashboard clock. Her brain was in a fog. Going without sleep for this long was not conducive to clear thinking. Home was so close.

Once on the ranch, they would come up with a plan together. Hopefully, it wouldn't include coming back to town, ever.

She turned right into the entry. The once-white fence leaned as if too tired to stand. One strong wind would take it down. The main post for the front gate wasn't in any better shape. Why hadn't her father told her he needed help? Of course, she hadn't asked.

Her dad's house, the old foreman's place, came into view. It was closest to the front gate. The main house where her grandmother lived was a little farther down. The biggest barns were in between the two. She had spent her childhood wearing out a path between the houses and barns. It was the best part of her childhood.

This was exactly the stability the boys needed after the chaos wrought by their mother. Hoping they would love it as much as she had, she glanced in the rearview mirror. Ray-Ray's face was pressed against the glass.

"Look, Benny. Cows. Oh, and there's someone riding a horse." Benny didn't seem impressed by Ray-Ray's excitement.

The rain had stopped. "That's your grandmother." It was hard to see it was a woman well into her sixth decade, with the long yellow rain slicker, but her grandmother loved riding out in all sorts of weather. When her father worried, Mew-Maw would laugh and say the more challenging, the more alive she felt. Just because she was closing in on seventy didn't mean she had to stop living.

Lyrissa dodged the biggest potholes, but it was impossible to miss them all. Her little car would be covered in mud. Not getting stuck would be a blessing. "She likes to ride one of the horses to check the mail," she told the boys.

That had them quiet as they stared at the horse and rider. That was encouraging, so she went on. "Your grandmother is excited to meet you. I call her Mew-Maw. We'll visit with my dad, but I think we'll be living with her."

"She's not our real grandmother." Bennett crossed his arms and swung his gaze away from the window.

"She's our mother's mother. That makes her your grandmother."

He frowned. "But I thought we were visiting your father's ranch."

"Our family is complicated. It's our grandmother's ranch. It's been in the Herff family for seven generations. We make nine. My father lives here to help her. He loves his mother-in-law and working on the land. Our mother wanted to live in the city."

"Apparently in all of them." Bennett's sarcastic words were too bitter and cynical for his years.

"Where she goes doesn't matter anymore. This is your home now. It's a forever home and no one is going to take it from you.

I'm so glad you're here now. They are too. There're only a few days of school left, so we'll get you registered for next year."

"School?" Ray-Ray perked up. "I want to go. I'm old enough?"

Bennett scoffed. "School's stupid."

The road ahead of them would be rougher than the road under them now. The three-bedroom, one-bath house she grew up in came into view. The roofline over the old porch sagged in a sad smile. But the man standing on the top step wore a huge grin. He waved and came toward them carrying a huge umbrella like a walking cane. Her father, Raymundo "Mundo" Martinez, acted as if he had been waiting for this day his whole life.

As he came down the steps, thunder rumbled and rain started to fall in huge, heavy drops again.

Her heart tugged at the sight of her daddy waiting for them. She pulled up to the side of the house, then cut the engine and turned to face the boys behind her. "My dad is the sweetest, kindest human you will ever meet. Please treat him with respect."

Before either boy could reply, her father had the back door opened, angling the colorful umbrella to block the rain. "Hey sweetheart! So sorry about the rain, but I'm happy you're home. Look at these two fine young men. Welcome. I'm excited to show you the place. This is your home too, you know. Have you ever been on a ranch?" He helped Ray-Ray out of his seat belt.

"No, sir," the shy boy said with a small grin. "Do I need boots and a hat? I don't have 'em."

Bennett snorted. "We're not staying. Our mom will come and get us." He hadn't moved to get out.

Her dad nodded. "This is a good place to wait for her. I'm glad you're here. She grew up on this land and knows it well. In the meantime, we can get to know each other. Love my daughter to pieces but always wanted a couple of boys too."

His smile went even wider. "This will be great, you'll see. God has a plan and purpose for each of us. Let's get you out of the rain. I'll show you to your room."

Did God have a plan? She sighed. Now was not the time to question her father's faith. "Dad. I think it's best if we move in with Mew-Maw. The house is bigger and—"

"Stop right there. You said you were coming home. This house might be smaller, but it's a good home. You and the boys will be staying here. Your room is here, and they can have the loft. It's been waiting for them before I knew they were here. God knew." His eyes shined with emotion. Lips pressed tightly together, he smiled and nodded. "The three of you belong here."

With a heavy sigh, she pulled herself out of the car, and went around to open the trunk. Her father was nice but also one of the most quietly stubborn people she knew, only after her grandmother.

"Looks like we'll be staying here, boys." There was no way she could tell her father no. Not after that speech.

He took them to the porch at a run. She grabbed the few bags they had and followed. Her father believed what he just said—she knew he did—but she was having a hard time coming to grips with God's plan for her.

Earlier this week, she was on track and had a clear purpose. Now her life was being derailed by their train wreck of a mother. If God was in control, then how did this happen to her and the boys?

On the porch, she stopped and looked back over the front pastures. A warm hand gripped her shoulder. "Sweetheart. It's all going to be okay. I'm thrilled you're home. Right now, you don't see it, but I promise God has the perfect path that is just for you if you stay faithful and open to his will."

"I was on a great path, Daddy. Until she flew in and destroyed it. But this time it's not just me." She looked at the two innocent boys left behind and couldn't hold the question back. "How can this be God's will?"

He pulled her into his arms and pressed his forehead to hers. "Right now, everything looks ugly and you're hurting. Your mother has been lost for a while now. That's the danger of free will. My heart aches that you've been hurt by her again. But we'll get through this, and you'll be stronger on the other side."

With a sigh, she kissed his cheek. He stepped back and took the two worn duffel bags from her. He turned to the boys and smiled. "Come on, boys. I'll show you to your room."

He was opening the door when they heard a truck approach the house. "Is it Mom?" The hope in Bennett's voice broke her heart. They all turned.

"Nope, not yet. It's a good friend of mine. You know him, Lyrissa. It's Reno Espinoza. I wasn't expecting him till later this week."

The well-worn work truck stopped behind her car and Reno jumped out.

"It's the man from the store. The one who caught us stealing." Ray-Ray sounded too happy for that statement. She groaned.

"Stealing?" Her father frowned.

"Hi again, Reno," she yelled in hopes of distracting her father.

"Hey!" Reno jogged to the porch as he pulled something out of his jacket. "Mundo, *como esta*?"

"*Bien*, I'm good. Thank God for the beautiful rain and bringing these fine boys to the ranch."

"We had the pleasure to meet in town. I told 'em they'd be needing some boots and a good hat." He ran his hands though his wet hair and pushed it back. "I could have used mine today." He laughed. The kind of laugh that spread joy and made everyone within hearing distance join him. Golden-brown eyes sparkled. Someone this happy all the time didn't take life seriously, Lyrissa thought.

"This was dropped in the parking lot. Thought you might get worried when you found it gone." His eyebrows wiggled a couple of times. "Or you left it behind so I would follow you." With a wink, he reached toward her. She stepped back. It was dangerous to be too close to him. The proverbial flame that drew in the moths seeking warmth and light.

It was her wallet. He was trying to give it back to her. His hands were large and strong, the fingers graceful despite—or maybe because of—the dark golden brown of his work-worn skin. They looked warm to the touch. As warm as his golden-brown eyes and smile. She jerked her head to the side to look away from him.

She looked in her purse as if she needed to check if hers was missing. Obviously, it was. With a deep breath, she took it from him as if they were handling explosives.

Warm fingers brushed hers. She cleared her throat. "I didn't even realize it was missing. Thank you." She made the mistake of studying his face and their eyes locked. The Espinozas were a beautiful family and Reno was...

"What's this about you catching the boys stealing?" Her father's voice broke her train of thought and the staring contest.

Shaking her head, she took a moment to center herself. She was tired. Any feelings or attraction she had for Reno was just her brain not functioning at full capacity.

She needed to get the boys settled and a good sleep. All this messing about would clear out and she'd be fine. For now, she would just keep her distance. Tucking her wallet in her purse, she stepped as far away from his warmth as she could.

He would be leaving in the next few minutes.

RENO WATCHED AS she pulled away from him. Apparently, as far as she could get. Had he done something to upset her? He shook his head and turned to Mundo. "There had been a misunderstanding. But we straightened it out. Lyrissa did promise the boys that there would be a full meal here."

Lightning streaked through the sky and thunder shook the foundation of the house. "Yes. Yes. Let's get y'all inside." Her father waved his hand to the door.

She quickly turned away from him and reached for the door.

"Reno, join us." Mundo clapped a hand on his back.

Lyrissa froze and glanced at him in a panic. So, she didn't want him to stay. "Thank you, sir. But I need to—"

"I won't hear any excuses. With this weather you won't be working on the Carter's barn. You might as well come in and get something to eat."

"Is that our grandmother? Is she a real cowboy?" Ray-Ray yelled from the railing, barely out of the rain. He pointed down the long drive. The lone figure covered head to boot in a yellow rain slicker was running a horse full-out toward the house.

With a big grin, Mundo joined the boy. "That there is your grandmother. Lyrissa calls her Mew-Maw. Stubborn woman. I told her I would get the mail. She's the most real cowboy you'll ever meet."

The gray horse came to a sliding stop at the base of the steps. The tall figure swung a leg over and dismounted. She moved up the steps and the horse followed. Lyrissa's dad pulled Ray-Ray back.

Throwing the reins over the porch railing, Edith Herff, the sixty-eight-year-old matriarch, dropped the hood of her rain slicker. She turned and stared at them, hand on her hips. "This rain can't seem to make up its mind if it's coming or going. The forecast said slight chance of drizzle. Being a weatherman must be the easiest paycheck ever. If I was wrong that many times, we wouldn't have a ranch at all."

She pulled off her cowboy hat and shook the rain off. Her silver hair was pulled back into a thick braid. "These must be my new grandsons. They look strong." She grinned. "It's been some time since we had any male children in the family. Shame you've been gone so long. But you're here now, that's all that matters. That youngest is the spitin' image of my daddy. I'll have to show you the pictures."

"Hey, Mew-Maw." Lyrissa stepped forward. The boys looked as if an alien had just popped out of a flying saucer. "This is Bennett and Raymundo. He goes by Ray-Ray."

"The little one's named after you?" She squinted at her son-in-law.

"Appears so."

"Well, that girl of mine is something else." She shoved her hat back on. "Hello, Reno. Don't think there'll be much outside work done today." She eyed Lyrissa then winked. "Are there other things that you're interested in? Maybe something new that just showed up on the ranch?"

"Mew-Maw! I dropped my wallet in the Buc-ee's parking lot and he was kind enough to bring it out so I wouldn't worry." Her gaze darted across the pastures, looking everywhere but at him.

"Aww. Such a good boy. Your momma raised you right." She patted Reno on the arm.

"There's a horse on the porch?" Bennett looked at them as if they were from another world and he didn't understand the language.

"Well, where else should I put him? The barn's way over there and I don't want him standing in the rain."

"Can I touch him?" Ray-Ray asked.

"Sure. Come here. I need to get the mail out of the bag anyway."

The boys tentatively followed her to the far end of the long porch, staring in awe at the big gelding.

Her father opened the door. "I have *papas* and huevos rancheros on the stove, ready to be eaten. Ya'll come in when you're finished with the horse."

"What's that?" Ray-Ray asked.

"Some really good stuff and the real reason I braved the storm to come over." Reno rubbed his stomach. "Mundo's potatoes and eggs wrapped up in a tortilla is the best. Well, second best. No one compares to my mom's."

Her father laughed as they entered the house. "That's the absolute truth."

The cabin was modest. The front living area had a sofa and two rocking chairs with stuffed seating. A large fireplace filled one wall. There was a TV in the corner, but other than the evening news, Reno had never seen it on.

A hallway led to two bedrooms with a bathroom in between them. "Your room is ready for you," he told Lyrissa as he went down the two steps into the dining room and kitchen area.

To the left was a spiral staircase that led to a large loft and an unfinished bathroom. It had been like that for years. When Reno had asked if he wanted to finish it out, Mundo had said there was no reason. Years ago, Mundo had dreamed of his wife coming home and a couple more children. Reno couldn't imagine how this must feel for the man.

Lyrissa glanced at him then. He should leave. He didn't belong here. The last thing he wanted was to make her uncomfortable in this very private family reunion.

Before he could make an escape, though, Edith came in behind him with the boys and they blocked his exit. He was trapped.

LYRISSA NEEDED TO get over herself. There was absolutely no reason for her to be acting this way around Reno. He was her father's friend.

Mundo moved to the cabinet and pulled down paper plates. "Reno, don't think about leaving. We need to talk about that bathroom upstairs. I finally have a reason to make it a working restroom. These two will need it as soon as possible. I knew God had more children for me to raise, but I didn't see how it would happen." He shook his head. "I shouldn't have doubted." Her heart squeezed at her dad's joy over this unexpected curveball in his life.

"Lyrissa, why don't you take the boys up and show 'em their room. There is a double bed on one side and a set of bunk beds on the other, so they can pick which one they want. Reno, can you take a look?"

Still standing at the entrance of the kitchen, the man looked like he was planning an escape.

"Please stay, Reno." Mundo asked in a soft voice.

Ray-Ray was already halfway up the stairs when he stopped and looked up in awe. "Really? We get a room just for us?" He turned to her dad.

Lips tight, her father nodded. He blinked then smiled. "Especially for you. It's been waiting."

He bound up the last steps to the top then stopped and gasped. "Benny, it's huge. We each get a real bed. All our own." The unbelieving tone in his voice broke her heart. Where had they been staying?

Bennett had one hand on the railing but just stood there. Reno came up behind him. "Come on. Your brother's going to get first pick if you don't hurry."

With an obvious swallow, he nodded and moved up the staircase.

Reno followed with Lyrissa close behind. Ray-Ray was on the top bunk, bouncing. "Benny, this is fun."

"You shouldn't pick that one." Bennett sounded older than his years. "You could fall."

The little one scrambled down. "I'm careful. We could make the bottom one into a fort. That would be cool. We can hide in there."

As Ray-Ray climbed over all the beds, Reno went into the small bathroom that divided the loft into two spaces. "Your dad asked if I could finish it out." He turned around and leaned on the doorframe. "It has most of what's needed. There are a few items to be bought. A little framing and detailing. The last thing will be connecting to water. I've worked with a guy in town who can do the plumbing. He's good and fair."

Ray-Ray bounced off the bed and ran to Reno, then poked his head into the bathroom.

"We get our own bathroom too? I don't want to ever leave." He darted to the other door behind the bathroom and opened it up. "A closet! It's like a secret room. This is the most greatest place ever."

"Don't get used to it. We won't be staying." Bennett got up from the double bed and stood by the railing, looking down into the kitchen. He pulled the hood of his sweatshirt up and crossed his arms.

"But they said it's our home," Ray-Ray said.

"Yeah. We've heard that before and it never happened. People lie."

"Bennett." She wanted to put her arms around him and pull him close. But he wouldn't welcome her comfort. She stood next to him and mirrored his stance at the railing. They both watched her father fixing their plates and setting the table. He was whistling.

"I know you've no reason to trust me or my father. But this is your home. No matter what happens. You are Herffs and there is nothing you can do to change that. You're stuck with us."

He shrugged and she knew it was going to take so much more than a few words to make him feel safe.

Reno came over and patted the sullen boy on the shoulder. "Come on down. You can ponder life and mope later. The food is on the table."

It didn't take long for everyone to settle around the old farm table. The wood was worn from decades of meals being served. Her father had them join hands for a prayer. The boys wiggled a bit but kept their heads bowed. With an *amen* he passed the tortilla basket around. Mew-Maw took a few bites while she flipped through the mail to separate the envelopes. Then she froze. Her green eyes came up and she made eye contact with Lyrissa, then her son-in-law.

She cleared her throat. "There's a letter from Dee." She held it out to her father. Everyone went quiet. Eating had stopped.

His hand shook as he took the envelope. As if expecting a bomb, he carefully opened it. After a reassuring smile to the boys, he looked down and silently read the letter. It was one page.

Lyrissa's stomach twisted. What new ways could her mother hurt the man who loved her so much?

He looked at the boys then at her. Moisture pooled on the bottom lid of his midnight eyes. He shook his head as if denying something. Everything in her readied for the worst.

Standing quickly, he knocked his chair back. It crashed to the ground, and he didn't seem to notice. The letter was crumpled in his fist.

She reached out for him with one hand and covered her heart with the other. What in the world had the letter said to get this reaction from her father? Something was wrong. In everything they had been through, her father had never cried. Never had an angry reaction. Whatever was in that letter had brought tears to his eyes.

"Daddy?"

Next to her, Reno stood. "Mundo, is there anything you need me to do?"

The urge to take his hand overwhelmed her. She couldn't reach her father. As if reading her mind, he wrapped his warm fingers around hers and gently squeezed. It shouldn't have comforted her, but it did.

"No. No" Her father looked at Bennett and made a muffled cry. He cleared his throat and stepped back. "I need a moment. Sorry." He rushed to the back door and into the storm.

CHAPTER FOUR

STUNNED, LYRISSA LOOKED at the fallen chair. Its carved legs pointing at her. The slam of the door echoed in her head. Not once in her whole life had she seen her father that upset.

She moved her gaze to her grandmother, then blinked, not sure what to do. The other woman jutted her chin to the door. "Me and the boys will finish up our meal then go out front to check on the horse."

The boys. All day she had reassured them how nice her father was. They looked at her but didn't seem too fazed by the outburst. Of course, growing up with Dee's drama, this was commonplace. "I'm going to check on Dad. Y'all enjoy your food."

Reno righted the chair. She walked out the back and scanned the area for her father. Dee wasn't even here, but still managed to ruin her father's happiness.

The screen door squeaked behind her. It was Reno. With an easy and relaxed posture, he joined her. Hands in his pockets, he stared at the sky.

"Never seen Mundo react to anything like that before." His expression was gentle. "Do you mind if I check on him with you?"

Her immediate response was yes, she minded. This was a

private matter. But the genuine concern in his face stopped her. Reno had been here for her father more than she had over the last few years.

With a quick jerk of her head, she kept walking to the barn. The rain had stopped. The smell of parched soil given a long drink floated around her. Fresh air filled her lungs. She wanted to stay and linger here.

Rainy days had always been her favorite on the ranch. But she didn't have the time. Nope, her mother had crushed the pleasant day from miles away.

"Any idea what the letter said?" Reno asked.

"With my mom, there's no telling. He's usually happy to get any word from her, so I don't know what could have caused this kind of reaction."

She glanced behind her to the house. "Maybe it's something to do with the boys. But when I called and told him about them, he was surprised but immediately told me to bring them home. He handled it with his usual calm attitude. What could be worse than learning about them?"

"He doesn't get ruffled easily and I've never seen him over-react. When he's upset, he goes there." Reno pointed to the stables. The large door was open, and lights were on.

The stables full of horses, hay and leather had been her sanctuary growing up. It had been a place to go when being in the world had hurt too much.

The tall man beside her stopped. "You know what. You're here. You should go. I'm not any good with…" He waved his hand in front of his chest as if stirring a pot.

"Feelings?"

He shrugged. "Emotional stuff. I'm good when someone needs a laugh or to forget their troubles. But your father seems really upset. I just wanted to make sure he was okay. You should go on without me."

Reno turned away from her.

Her stomach knotted. Fear of whatever was in the letter

made her nauseous. "No. Don't go. I can't imagine what she told him. I haven't been around much. He might talk to you about the news she gave him. I don't know what he needs."

"Okay." With a sigh, Reno turned back and reached the large double door before she did. He slid it a little farther open, then held it for her while she walked into the old, familiar space.

"Dad?"

Rustling came from the tack room on the right side of the corridor. He stepped out with a caddy of grooming supplies in one hand and cubes of alfalfa in the other.

With an uncharacteristic grunt, he shook his head. "Go. Don't think I can talk about it right now." He turned his back to them and headed to the back stalls.

His jaw was rigid, there was so much pain and anger in his eyes. She went to him and put her hand on his arm, stopping him.

He looked away. "Are the boys okay?" he asked. "I didn't mean to scare them."

"They're fine. Mew-Maw has them." She moved in front of him, trying to make eye contact. "Daddy, what did that letter say?"

His tongue went over his bottom lip, then he pressed his mouth into a hard straight line. Moving to the left, he broke contact with her and went to the blue roan mare tied at the double post in the open grooming area.

The only sounds were Reno's boots on the century-old brick and the shifting of the stalled horses. Reno came up behind her, placed his hand on her shoulder. His presence created a conflict inside her. There was a tension she didn't like but also a calming reassurance that her father trusted him. Then again, her father loved her mother to a fault.

"Mundo, is there anything we can do?" he asked in a voice much calmer than anything she could manage. "I've never seen you this upset."

Putting the caddy down, her father remained silent. He shook his head. Then he went to the head of the horse and talked to her as he ran his hand under her jaw and down her neck.

She stood by helplessly as she watched the hands that raised her with love and gentleness shake. He moved from the front of the horse to the mare's side. He brushed her from the top of her shoulder down to her hooves.

"Daddy, you're scaring me. I know Dee. If you're protecting me, don't. We talk about everything, right? Why aren't you talking to me now? I've never seen you this angry."

He stopped and braced an arm on the horse's back. "When you were ten and your mother took you without telling me, I was this angry. I tried everything, then the police finally called. I was livid but she cried and asked for forgiveness. She promised me she would never take you again. I believed her. Just when I start thinking she can't do anything else to hurt us, she goes and proves me wrong."

Lyrissa's heart dropped to her stomach. She wanted to scream at the frustration of seeing him like this and not being able to make it better. "Daddy, please tell me what she's done this time."

He leaned into the mare, pressing his forehead against her. "She...she..." He stepped back and brushed the mare's hind-quarters with quick, jerky movements.

The lack of information was strangling her. She moved forward, but Reno reached for her hand and held her back. He nodded his head, suggesting she give her father space.

Her father grabbed a hoof-pick and a hard brush from the caddy and moved to the horse's front. He lifted a leg and worked on the inside of the hoof.

After a moment, he started talking again. "I tried to intervene with you. I really did. Once the addiction took control, I knew her actions hurt you. I knew. I worked hard to stand between you and the addiction. I thought if I prayed hard enough and stood on truth, she would come back… I would have the woman I loved back. I loved her and I loved you. I didn't know how to balance that. You had to be protected so I let her go and hoped she would find her way back to us. I never wanted my children to suffer."

"I'm fine, Daddy. You were always making me feel safe and loved. I know you loved her. You've always said grace costs us nothing to give. You made sure to teach me that forgiveness releases the bitterness from our hearts. I'm not sure I'm there but you're my hero, Daddy, and I want to be more like you."

"It's not me you should strive to be but our Savior." He shook his head, and it dropped in defeat. "What if the price of grace becomes too much and it costs the well-being of the innocents? You're not unaffected by your mother's choices. The boys…" A soft straggling sound cut off his words.

The heartbreak and doubt tore her heart apart. He had always been so steadfast in his faith.

Moving to his side, she put a hand on his sagging shoulder. "The boys were out of your control. You can't blame yourself for that. But we have them now. They're safe."

She wanted to cry at the pain she saw in her father. The suffering her mother's addiction had caused them all. Her lungs were tightening. "Daddy, what's in that letter that changed everything?"

"I should've done more, but I put it in God's hands. It was a cop-out and I'm just weak."

She looked at Reno. Maybe he knew what to do.

"Mundo." Reno's voice was thick, but he had a dazzling smile on his face. "You just need to get it off your chest." He pushed his still-damp hair back. "Hey. Do you know what a rabbit needs after getting caught in the rain? A *hare* dryer."

She turned and glared at him and mouthed *What?* He shrugged his shoulders as if he had no other options. She groaned.

It was a mistake including him in this, but then again, she should have learned by now that relying on other people was a waste of time.

RENO WANTED TO slam his head against the old brick wall. He never handled emotional situations well, but really? A pathetic dad joke? He sighed and tried to ignore Lyrissa's obvious and justified irritation.

He cleared his throat. "It might help if you share what's in the letter."

"I didn't read the whole letter. Stopped at the second line. It all went blurry. I can't even speak the words." He stepped back and pulled the crumpled ball of paper out of his pocket.

Jaw gritted, he handed it to Reno. No clue what to do, he instinctively took it from the older man. Mundo wanted him to read it. Swallowing, he tried to get enough oxygen in his lungs to speak.

Mundo kept his gaze on the horse. The man's only daughter looked at Reno, waiting for him to start speaking. He had already disappointed her once today.

As he slowly unfolded the wadded-up paper, his mind raced. He took more care to smooth it out. *Now what?*

The horses shuffled as if they were also getting restless waiting for him. Heat pushed against his skin.

"Read it, Reno," Mundo said. "Read it aloud so Lyrissa will know that she's been right to cut her mom off. She's been right every time she's told me to let her go and move on."

"I don't want to be right, Daddy." Her voice was small, as if she was eight years old all over again.

"I thought if I gave her enough grace, she would come back but…" He swallowed hard and turned to Reno, lifting his chin. "Go ahead. Read it, Reno."

Maybe this time if he tried hard enough and really focused he wouldn't let down one of his favorite people. This man didn't deserve this kind of pain.

Pulling the paper straight, he tried to flatten it. The lines and shapes of the letters floated. Reno was going to be sick. He closed his eyes and took a few breaths. But when he looked at the paper again it was still gibberish.

At this point, he usually made a joke and either faked his way through reading aloud or passed it off to someone else without anyone being the wiser that he couldn't read.

Reno squinted at the paper. "I…uhm…forgot my contacts today." He handed the letter to Lyrissa. "Sorry. Would you read it?"

A frown crested her forehead. "When did you start wearing glasses?"

His stomach churned. That was the problem with people knowing him his whole life. He hated lying and people didn't usually challenge him. He stood in silence until she finally took the letter. Her hands shook. He was a complete heel forcing her to read the letter from her mother.

As soon as she looked down, she read. "'My dearest Raymundo. I'm so sorry that I'm just now writing this to you. It's eight years too late. Bennett's birthday is September nineteenth. If you count back the months, you'll know he's… yours.'"

Lyrissa's voice cracked and she looked up at her father. Mundo had his hand on the horse's neck and face buried in her mane.

"Daddy?"

He nodded without looking up. "Go on. That's where I stopped."

"Okay." She took a deep breath. Reno moved closer to her. None of them had known about the boy who was Mundo's son and Lyrissa's brother. He wasn't sure how to help them with this revelation, so he stood next to her and put one hand on Mundo's back.

She continued reading, tears trailing her cheeks.

"'I know what I've done is wrong.'" A very sarcastic snort

escaped Lyrissa before she went back to reading. "'But I have
to take the time to find myself and make it right. Then I'll
come back for the boys and fix everything. I thought having
the boys would help me, but I know now they are better off
with you. I know I said the same thing when I called you to
come get me in California, but I wasn't ready. The thought of
going back to the ranch made me feel trapped. When I realized I was pregnant, I thought maybe it was a chance for me to
have a do-over, because I messed up so much with our daughter. She's one hundred percent you and I wanted this baby to
be mine. So, I kept him and didn't tell you that we had another child. Benny is your son. Little Ray-Ray's father is history, and we're better off without him. I wanted to give him
a good strong name. You're the best man I know so I named
him after you.'"

A soft sob came from Mundo. The kind of noise someone
makes when they are trying to hold everything inside and it's
too much. Lyrissa heard it too. She stumbled over the next
words.

Reno wanted to take the paper and rip it to shreds. But it
wouldn't make this go away. All he could do was stand next to
Mundo and put his arms around the man's shaking shoulders.

"Do you want me to read the rest?"

Her father nodded without raising his head.

"'Nick is different than all the other men. We have a plan
to make everything right. We have a perfect business venture.
I just needed the money to become a full partner with him.
Please tell…'" She paused, then took a deep breath.

"'Please tell Lyrissa I will pay her back for everything with
interest. I'll make a donation to the church. I figure a good
church supports those in need. It's for a worthy cause. I…'"

Lyrissa closed her eyes and tilted her head back. "How
can she justify stealing from the church using my key?" She
looked back down.

Reno wanted to reach for her and offer to read the rest of

the letter. He hated his brain sometimes. Why couldn't he just learn to read? "I'm so sorry—"

She held up her hand, her jaw set. "I've got this. There's not much more."

"'Please, tell the boys that I love them. Once the business is making a profit—and I know it will—I promise I'll come to the ranch. Hopefully next summer. It will be a really fun time, I promise. I love you and always will. Give Lyrissa my love, even though I'm sure she hates me. I'll fix this—I promise I will.'"

Mundo wiped his face. Reno stood back and gave him room to move to Lyrissa. Her mouth was open and her eyes wide. All the signs of being shell-shocked were on her face.

"Daddy, is it true? How can Bennett be yours? She hasn't been to the ranch since I was in the sixth grade. This doesn't make any sense."

Mundo put one arm around her and pulled her into his barreled chest. He laid his cheek on the side of her head and stroked her back.

"It was after you went to Dallas. She called me in mid-January. She was in a real bad place. She was living on the streets, trying to get to shelters but kept being kicked out because of the drinking. She said she was going to end everyone's misery and called me to say goodbye. I told her to hang on and I'd come get her. I was so afraid of what I would find. But she was in the shelter waiting for me. She was clean and wanted to put the past behind her. She said the hope I gave her saved her life."

"Oh, Daddy. You never said anything."

"I didn't even tell your grandmother. I didn't want to worry y'all. It was winter so we had some downtime. I just said I needed to take care of some business. I thought that might be the time to bring her home. You know, hitting rock bottom and all that." He hugged his daughter tighter.

"But she didn't come home with you."

"She wanted to get her life in order before facing her mom. You know they've had a tough relationship. Edith had always been harsh. I rented an apartment for six weeks. That was the time she asked for and I would visit on the weekends, checking in on her. She was doing great." He looked at the ceiling. "She said she was ready to fix herself and be the wife and mother we deserve."

"How long did it last?"

"About five weeks. In February, she stopped answering my calls and when I went out there, she was gone. No note. Of all the selfish, self-destructive things she's done, why would she get pregnant and not tell me? That boy should have been here on the ranch from day one."

The horse shifted her ears, sensitive to her dad's raised voice.

Lyrissa said, "I stopped trying to figure her out long ago. It's easier to say I don't have a mother. It might be wrong, but we've got the boys now and we just need to move forward without her."

Reno patted Mundo's shoulder then gripped it. "She's right. You've got the boys. They have your last name. I don't think any court in the country would say she was a fit mother."

A heavy silence filled the air. Reno scanned the barn. There was more work needing to be done here than Mundo had let on. He had said the front fences needed some attention, but it was much deeper than a few fence posts. "Once I finish the last job, we can sit down and make a plan for your place. You know I do more than fences."

"Oh, I can't afford a full-time ranch hand."

"Good. I'm thinking a part-time gig would work out for us both."

"Aren't you taking the exam to be a firefighter?" Mundo asked.

Reno shrugged. "Maybe. I haven't decided." He had already tried twice and failed. The physical part he had passed with flying colors. The written part might end his dreams. Being a handyman wasn't a bad career choice for him. With his sister gone, he didn't want to run the construction company alone.

Mundo checked the last hoof then patted the mare's shoulder. "I'm going to take her out. Y'all head back to the house. Thank you for following me out and letting me process the news." He looked at his daughter. "I'm okay. This will all work out for the best. I always wanted more kids." The corner of his mouth quirked. "Not how I imagined, but it's good." He looked at his watch. "Give me an hour. I'll be back in the house ready to talk to the boys."

Mundo unlatched the lead from the post and walked past Reno. He paused and gripped his shoulder for a mere second. "I see your struggle. You're a good man. Have faith in yourself."

The hooves clicked on the brick walkway as they went out the back doors. Lyrissa came to stand by his side. "What did he say to you?"

How did the man have the heart to lift Reno when his world was crumbling? "Just some words of encouragement."

"That's my dad for you. So, you're the town's handyman and want-to-be firefighter? I always thought you were going to leave Port Del Mar and do heroic deeds."

A dry laugh, more like a *humph*, was his first response. "Yeah, well I changed my mind." He turned to head back to the house but paused and waited for her. "Are you okay? This has been a rough few days for you."

"Oh, you know. It's what one is used to if Deeann Herff Martinez is your mother. When can I get off this roller coaster?"

His heart dipped a little. There were no words. She had every right to hate this town and get back to the life she had created for herself in Missouri. He didn't like the silence. "So, your dad said you just finished your master's degree in special education. He's immensely proud of you. Do you have a job lined up in Missouri?"

"I did. It was temporary while I finished my master's. I ran the youth and special needs programs for a church. It was a small community and perfect for me at the time."

"With summer about to start, you probably have to get back."

She shook her head. "Did you miss the part where my mom used my key to clean out the cashbox? They have her on video. They understandably asked for the keys back and they already have someone else to run the programs. She was my intern, so it worked out for her." She sighed. "I can focus on the boys, and I have résumés out. The next few weeks, I'll send more. Location doesn't matter to me as long as it's not here or anywhere close. I'll use the summer to make sure the boys and my dad are good."

The rain started again. With jackets pulled over their heads, they ran for the back porch. "I've always loved being in the rain." Her laughter rumbled through him like the thunder that rattled the landscape.

He wanted to stop and soak it in. It wasn't good of him to be having fun on such a rotten day for her and Mundo. He reached the screen door and opened it for her. Together, they shook off the water and laid their wet jackets over the back of the rocking chairs.

She turned away and lifted the lid on a wicker storage box. Facing him again, she had two towels. Without warning, she used the soft blue towel to wipe his face. The gold flecks in her dark green eyes danced. "How is it fair that you even look good caught in the rain while I look like a drowned rat?"

"Rat? You look more like a lost mermaid." He couldn't contain his smile. "You think I'm good-looking?"

With a chuckle, she shook her head. "It's no secret in town that everyone thinks you're good-looking, so don't go getting

any ideas. You're not my type. I prefer reading to partying."
She stepped away and toweled off.

The light mood evaporated, and his heart went a little heavy.
Someone else who wrote him off as shallow and only good
for entertainment.

With a sigh, he followed her into the house. So much for
clicking with her. He misread the situation as usual. Putting
a smile back on his face, he joined her family.

LYRISSA WAS LOSING her mind. It was all the stress with her
family. That was it. Otherwise, she would have never had the
wild feeling that she should move closer to Reno. He was the
opposite of everything she wanted in her life.

Okay. So, he was cute in a very unreal way. Hollywood
would take him up the minute he knocked on the door. But
then, everything in life came too easy for him. His carefree
smile was evidence.

He was nice and all. His family was one of the best. A
very functional family. He was the wild child of the group
but there wasn't a hint of the dysfunction that ruled the house
she grew up in.

And now, she had two brothers to add to the mess. They
needed her. Her father and grandmother needed her. No time
to get all weird around Reno Espinoza.

In the house, they found her grandmother on the sofa. The
boys had pulled out all the games that had been stored in the
TV cabinet.

"Oh, good. You're back." Her grandmother stood. "I need
to get going. Forgot how much energy young ones have. They
also have lots of questions."

"Thank you, Mew-Maw," Lyrissa said. The boys had pulled
out all her father's favorites. She wasn't sure if the games were
age-appropriate for them.

"How's your father?" Mew-Maw stepped closer and lowered her voice. "What has that daughter of mine done now?"

She glanced at the boys. "She hates me so much she's kept my grandsons from me."

"I don't think it has anything to do with you. It's all her."

The older woman let out a dry laugh and the boys looked up from the chess pieces and stones they were playing with. She waved them off. "Don't mind me, boys. Go back to your thingies there."

She shook her head. "Lyrissa, take my word for it. She hates me. Told me so many times. The last time I told her she was out of my will. The ranch and every last speck of dirt on it was going to you and your father. Oh, man. She was furious. That was the last time she came to the ranch."

Shock rocked Lyrissa. "When did you do that? Does Daddy know?"

"Of course. I had to tell him so he wouldn't be blindsided. The ranch and most of my accounts are going to you. I love your father, but he has a weak spot for your mother. If he thought it would help her, he'd give it all away. So, I can't trust him when it comes to her. But you have a strong head on your shoulders. You won't let her take advantage of you."

Lyrissa had to laugh. "Really? You do realize she stole everything from me and walked away, leaving me with two brothers?"

"Oh, posh." She walked to the door and put her hat on her head then slipped her rain slicker on. "She used the boys to con you. You won't let that happen again. Hey, boys. I'm heading out. Y'all come over to my house tomorrow."

Ray-Ray jumped up and ran to her and threw his arms around her leg. "Bye, Mew-Maw. I always wanted a grandma and you're the best."

With a scowl on her face, she patted his back. "Easy, boy. You'll knock me over. And I don't know about being the best. I'm good with horses, not so much people. But I'm glad you and your brother made it home. This is where you belong." She nodded at Bennett. He still sat on the floor at the coffee table with a game of chess and Go scattered over the tabletop.

He didn't look as eager to have a grandmother. Now that she knew the truth, she could see her father in the boy. How had she missed it earlier? Her grandmother was right. He had the look of a Herff, but his eyes were all her father's. The shape and color.

Mew-Maw chuckled and squeezed Ray-Ray's shoulder before dislodging him. She pointed at her skeptical grandson. "That one is one hundred percent Herff. It won't hurt to smile, boy." With one last goodbye she went out the door.

Ray-Ray grabbed Lyrissa's hand and pulled her to the coffee table. Then ran to the perpetually smiling Reno. Leaning against the doorframe, he looked too comfortable in the middle of this mess of her life.

Ray-Ray picked up a thin pamphlet and handed it to Reno. "We want to play this game with the astronauts. Right, Benny? This one looks cool."

"That's a chessboard my father bought when we visited NASA. We have several boards with different themes. He is a serious player." The memories of all the nights playing with him brought a smile to her lips. "Have y'all played before? He would love it if you would play with him."

Taking Reno's hand, Ray-Ray tugged on it. "Do you know how to play? If not, read us the directions. I want to play chess with our grandpa. Benny can't read. Well, he can but he stumbles over the—"

"Stop talking. I can read. I just don't want to," Bennett snapped at his little brother.

Ray-Ray sighed and looked up at Reno. "You'll read them to me?"

Reno looked at the pamphlet in his hand and a flash of panic burned in his eyes before he laughed. "You know what I like doing?" He tossed the chess booklet on the sofa and sat on the floor next to Bennett. "Making my own rules. We don't need to read someone else's."

That was twice in less than an hour Reno had laughed off reading something aloud. Was she just seeing signs of a learning disability because she had just studied that topic for almost two years, or was Reno hiding the fact he couldn't read?

She didn't recall it being an issue in school, but they never had classes together. Not that it was any of her business. She had enough of her own issues.

"If you're going to play with my dad, you will have to know the agreed-upon rules. He takes chess and Go very seriously." She lowered herself to the ground on the opposite side of Reno and crossed her legs. "I'll teach you the game. We'll start with chess since it's easier to learn."

Reno's eyes went wide. "Chess is the easier game?"

"Yep. We don't need the book. It's all up here." She tapped her head. "My father would love that y'all learned."

As she set up the chessboard and went over the moves, she noticed Bennett intensely studying every word and action, but if she made eye contact, he would sit back and look away. He didn't want her to see how much he wanted this.

Okay, she could pretend he didn't care. For now.

That was the attitude she should adopt with Reno. She would just pretend she didn't care and he wouldn't notice her weirdness.

Across from her, Reno was so relaxed and had both boys laughing at his mistakes. He made it okay for them to miss a step or make a wrong move. Probably because he was still a kid at heart.

She had loved her mother so much. Just one smile from her would light up Lyrissa's world. But that joy brought so much pain, eventually. Big smiles were good for a moment but couldn't be counted on in the long run.

That was the thing about people who never took life seriously. They were fun to be around. Until real problems interfered with their fun. They couldn't be counted on when they were needed.

CHAPTER FIVE

THUNDER SHOOK THE HOUSE. A bolt of lightning flashed so brightly through the windows, Reno was blinded for a moment. All the lights went out.

Ray-Ray whimpered. Reno stood. "Do you know where your dad keeps the flashlights or candles?"

She reached for a drawer under the coffee table. "Here's two small ones." She turned one on and handed it to Reno. She sat the other on the worn wood. "The big lights are on top of the refrigerator. There is also an old hurricane lamp on the mantel. It should have oil in it. I hope he's in the barn and not outside."

He didn't need to see her to know she was worried about her father. It was heavy in her voice.

Lyrissa struggled to stand with Ray-Ray clinging to her neck. Moving to them, Reno gave her his hand to help her up. Before she was stable on her feet, she broke contact. He fought the need to reach out again to support her. Instead, he shoved his free hand in his pocket.

In a few steps, she put distance between them and grasped for Bennett's arm. The boy nearly stumbled when he backed into the coffee table to get away from her.

Reno handed the second flashlight to Bennett and they followed him into the kitchen. Another flash of lightning lit up the dark sky.

Her phone vibrated. It was her father. "He's going to stay in the barn until it's cleared out."

Reno nodded. "Good. That's the wisest move. This kind of storm can be dangerous."

She nodded then licked her lips.

Instinct told him to take her in his arms and reassure her. That was a huge no go, so he settled with a weak "We'll be safe in the house."

Armed with flashlights, they went back into the living room. With her free hand, she lit the hurricane lamp. The soft light glowed, illuminating her when she faced him. Her arm held the small boy close to her chest. "He wants us to go ahead and share the good news." She tried smiling but it was tight.

Reno tilted his head. "Good news?" He studied her. "Oh, news in the letter?"

"Yeah. That one."

"Is it about Momma?" For the first time, Bennett didn't even try to hide his obvious interest.

"Yes. Let's sit down." She sat on the edge of the sofa. Bennett willingly sat close to her. Reno put the lamp in the center of the coffee table then pulled up the rocking chair, so they were in a tight circle.

"Well?" Bennett's one word dripped with impatience.

"Okay. So. Your mom. Our mom had a very big surprise for Dad. It's the best surprise ever."

She pulled her lips in, then looked up to the ceiling. His heart went out to her. How did she tell one brother that he was her father's biological son, and the other wasn't?

The silence grew heavy as the boys stared at her. Anticipation bubbled from every pore.

"The best surprise ever? Really?" Bouncing on his knees, Ray-Ray leaned forward in excitement.

Her gaze sought his. Once again, she was silently pleading for his help. He wasn't going to let her down this time.

With a careful grin, Reno looked at each boy. "It *is* the best surprise *ever*." He leaned in and scanned the room as if he had a big secret. "Mundo always wanted more kids, and your mom knows this. In the letter she granted his wish. She told Mundo that he is legally your father. His name is on both of your birth certificates. He didn't have a clue until he got the letter. He was so excited to find out he has sons he didn't know what to do and had to go outside."

Ray-Ray leaned closer, his eyes gleaming. Bennett crossed his arms and narrowed his eyes.

"You have a father now. He happens to be Bennett's biological father. And Ray-Ray, you have his exact same name. Raymundo Jesus Martinez. You have the same name as him because she wanted you to have a real father and she knew Mundo was the best."

Bennett gazed skeptically between the two adults. "That doesn't make any sense."

Not knowing what else to do, Reno nodded. "I know. It's wild, right?" Was he getting in over his head? He looked to Lyrissa for support. She pulled Ray-Ray closer to her and nodded at him to continue. She wasn't ready to take over.

Faking confidence, Reno smiled. The boys had been lied to enough. But how to handle this very complicated truth in a way a child would understand? How much truth was too much?

With a big sigh, he gave himself a bit of time to organize the words. "It can be super confusing. But here it is." Leaning forward, he held out his hands as if explaining the next play in a football game. "There are a few different types of fathers. One—a biological father. That's the guy who knows your mom and you get your DNA from him. Then there's a real father who raises you. He's there for you whenever you need him. He takes you to school, goes to your events and gives you advice. Sometimes the biological father and the real father are the same man. But it's not always the case. What matters is that from this day on and forever, Mundo is your real father. He's the man who will raise you and will call you both sons."

Ray-Ray jumped up. "I prayed for a father. I did but I want my mom too. Why can't we have both?"

Lyrissa reached out for him and pulled him back into her lap. She wrapped her arms around him and held him close. "Our mom lives in a world of her own making and doesn't always do the right thing for the people she loves."

"Like taking all your stuff without asking?" Ray-Ray asked.

"Yep. She makes decisions that we don't understand. I know from my own experiences that Mundo is the best father you can have. Mom is unpredictable. She wanted to keep you to herself for as long as she could, but I'm thankful and so is our dad that she wanted you to come to the ranch. That's why she finally told him the truth."

"Why didn't she tell him or us before?" Bennett's voice was low and dripping with suspicion.

They all turned to Lyrissa. Reno could see her heart breaking.

She took Bennett's hand. "Honestly, I don't know. What I do know, she has given you and our father a great gift today. She's given you a father who I promise will never leave you. I'm your big sister. We are a forever family."

Ray-Ray had tears in his eyes. He laid his head against her chest. "Promise? Because I always wanted to belong to a family with a house and a bed and a dog. Do we have a dog?"

Lyrissa chuckled. "If you ask real nice, I imagine you can get a dog."

She kissed the top of his head. Bennett shifted to the side and looked out the window.

Reno slid to the other end of the sofa and put a hand on the boy's shoulder. "You okay, Bennett? It's a lot to take in." He looked down at the small hands and tight fists.

Bennett wipe his nose with the back of his hand. "There's

been a couple of guys that mom said we could call dad." He shrugged. "They didn't stick around. Which wasn't a bad thing. They...weren't nice." He hesitated over the last words.

Lyrissa pulled him closer to her other side. She had her arms wrapped around both boys, trying to hold them all together. "This is not the same thing. He is your legal father, and he wants you here in his life. He had a bedroom waiting for you."

"He did." Ray-Ray's eyes were wide and full of wonder.

Bennett pulled away from her and moved closer to him.

His heart fluttered at the sign of growing trust. "Bennett, listen to me. Those other men were not the same thing at all." He nudged Bennett with his shoulder. "I lost my dad when I was a young kid like you."

Ray-Ray popped up. "Was he your real dad or your biological dad?"

With a soft laugh, Reno nodded. "He was both and when I lost him, I thought I had lost everything. My sister's friend—" he nodded to Lyrissa "—your sister—had a cool dad. I would follow my sister here and hang out with Mundo. He always made the time to talk to me. I still find reasons to come over once a week. There is not a man who would love being your father more than Mundo."

The back door slammed.

Ray-Ray jumped up from her lap. When Mundo walked into the living room, the small boy hurled himself at his new father. "Are you really my dad forever? No takebacks?"

A large, calloused hand came around him and held him close. "I am." Mundo ran his free hand through his wet hair. His voice was raw. He nodded to Bennett, who sat stiffly on the sofa, arms crossed.

"I pray you can open your hearts and allow me to make up for lost time."

Reno's skin was too tight. The family needed time together and he needed to breathe. He stood. "I need to get to the firehouse. Volunteers are needed to clear roads and check on people. Y'all have a good evening."

If he stayed, he would start imagining being part of this family too, being a real part of Lyrissa's life. But she made it clear her life was not here and even if it was, he was not her type.

LYRISSA BIT BACK the plea for Reno to stay. With her dad on the sofa next to Bennett and Ray-Ray on his lap, she followed Reno to the door. "Thank you for everything. It's been an overwhelming day. You helped us get through it." She tilted her head. He really had.

"I'm always here to bring a smile. That's what I'm good at." He stood on the porch and for a second just studied her.

Self-conscious, she tucked loose strands behind her ear. "Well, I appreciate it. Be careful out there."

She stayed on the porch until he was out of sight. It would be so easy to get mixed up with the charming Reno Espinoza again. Not that they even made it to their first date the last time, but still.

Her father's laughter came through the door. What was she thinking? She had a family with major healing ahead of them. There was also the matter of finding a job. One as far from Port Del Mar as possible. Mooning over Reno was just avoiding the real issues.

As soon as her father and brothers were settled, she would be gone.

CHAPTER SIX

RENO DODGED A large rut, but hit a smaller one. The Herff Ranch drive really needed work. All the effort and money had gone into keeping the production part of the ranch working. It wouldn't hurt to spend a little time on the aesthetics.

He had planned to come out Friday, but he'd finished the other job a day early. So here he was. Next to him sat a welcome dinner from his mom. She had asked him to drop it off. It was a good reason to be here.

And he was a big old liar. When his mom asked if he had the time to take it, he jumped at the chance to come back out. What he should have said was that he had to do a bid on a kitchen and bath extension on another ranch. He rescheduled.

Construction wasn't as fun now that his sister was gone. She loved detailed woodwork. He was good at putting things together but didn't have the creative eyes she had. And when it came to the bookkeeping, he really missed her.

Now that she was gone, he should just go back to being a ranch hand. Before starting the business with his sister, he had worked full-time at the Wimberlys' ranch. He was good at that.

It didn't look as if his dream of being a firefighter was ever going to happen. There was no way he'd pass the written exam.

His mother would be happy. She hated the idea of him being a first responder. She didn't even like that he volunteered.

His big brother was in law enforcement and a few years back he had been shot in the line of duty. It had brought Bridges home, but his mother also used every opportunity to encourage them to find another line of work. Tapping her chest, she would tell them how much her heart worried.

He grinned. She was small, with the heart of a warrior. But she wasn't above emotional blackmail to keep her children safe and close by.

Before he brought his truck to a complete stop, Lyrissa ran out from behind the house, waving at him. He jumped out of the truck. "What's wrong?"

"I can't find the boys. Mew-Maw and Dad went into town. The boys and I went to check on the stock tank. They wanted to come back to the house to get something to eat. They're not here. I went to the barns. Buster, the horse Ray-Ray was riding, is back at the barn with all his gear on. Reno, they don't understand all the dangers on the ranch."

Her gaze darted around the yard. "I should have come back with them, but I wanted to check on the… Ray-Ray!" She sprinted to the large side gate. The youngest boy was running to them. His face was red, and wet with tears.

"Benny is stuck. We…" He couldn't get any more words out. Reno was right behind Lyrissa. She fell to her knees in the muddy pasture and pulled Ray-Ray to her.

"Take a breath." He put a hand on the boy's shoulder. "Where's Bennett?" He had his phone out, ready to call dispatch if needed.

The boy rubbed his eyes and took several breaths. "We wanted to help Mew-Maw. Before getting a snack, we rode along the fence lines like she told us about. We wanted to help."

Lyrissa cupped his face, using her thumbs to wipe at the tears. "Is he with the horse?"

Ray-Ray nodded. "We…we slipped into a huge crack in

the ground. It was muddy. I landed on the top side. My horse jumped up and ran away. Benny's slipped down on its back. He told me to...to stay on the top and he went to help the horse. It was on its back and couldn't stand up."

Worst-case scenarios ran through Reno's head. A panicked thousand-pound animal with hooves was a dangerous situation for an experienced horseman. A small kid with no knowledge was not good.

"Can you take us to him? How far away is he?"

Ray-Ray pointed in the direction he came from. "I went through a gate and climbed a fence."

"He's in the bottom fifty. There's a washed-out ravine on the edge. A four-wheeler would be the fastest way there." Her words were rushed as she ran to the barn. Reno picked up the small boy and followed her.

At the largest barn, she reached inside the door and tossed him a key. "You know where we're going?"

She reached for her brother. "You take the single. It's faster." He nodded as he handed Ray-Ray over to her.

"I'll follow with him in the Coleman. It'll be safer."

He didn't hesitate. Time could make all the difference for Bennett in a situation like this. Helmet on, he didn't look back. As he went through the gates, he left them open.

Once in the last pasture, it didn't take long to spot the horse. All four legs were in the air. Deep grooves were slashed into the soft dirt around him. His head was to the side. He was breathing heavily from exhaustion from the struggle.

Reno's heart squeezed as he scanned the area for the boy.

He eased to the edge of the grass line. "Bennett?" He kept his voice low and steady. The horse tried to lift its head.

"Reno?"

Relief flooded his system at the sound of that sweet voice.

"Where's Ray-Ray? Is he okay?" The ragged voice came from under the horse.

"Yes. He found us. He's safe with Lyrissa. They're on a slower ATV. Are you okay?"

There was a narrow ditch under the horse. Bennett must be there. "I tried to help Smokey get—" a sob interrupted his words "—up, but I slipped and fell in. He reared then landed on top. I'm flat in the mud." His voice broke. "I'm sorry. We wanted—" Sniffles stopped him this time.

"I know this is scary, but I need you to relax. I called the firehouse. They have equipment that helps rescue big animals. You'd be amazed how many times this kind of stuff happens out here. We're going to get you and Smokey out, but I need you to stay calm and be still. Can you do that?"

"Yes."

"Benny?" Ray-Ray had jumped from the larger ATV and was running when Lyrissa caught up to him and picked him up.

"Shhh. We are going to get him up. But we don't want to spook the horse." She cradled his head against her shoulder. Her eyes went to Reno, silently pleading for good news.

"He's in a crevice under Smokey. He doesn't seem to be hurt, just trapped." He didn't need to mention what could go wrong. "I called it in. One of us needs to be at the house to lead them out here. They have the gear to pull up the horse. If we go down in the muddy slope we could just make it worse."

She nodded, then hugged Ray-Ray. "The firemen are coming to help. We need to go meet them so we can show them how to get here. Okay?"

Nodding, he leaned away from her. "Benny?"

"Yeah." The voice was a little shaky, but Reno was impressed by how well the kid was doing. "I'm good. I got a comfy little spot. I just need someone to help get Smokey so I can come out. Reno said the firemen are coming with trucks."

Lyrissa patted the small boy in her arms. "Ray-Ray and I are going to meet the firemen. Then I'm fixing a big lunch for everyone."

Once they left for the house, Reno lay on his stomach and studied the area. He talked in a low, soothing voice to help keep the boy and horse calm.

Time crawled. Finally, the rumbling of the big rescue truck sounded at the pasture gate. "They're here. We'll have you out soon." He prayed that he spoke the truth.

He knew everyone in the crew except one young guy. But Reno was focused on getting Bennett out and didn't do more than give the teen a passing glance. They discussed the problem and the best way to get the horse up without risk to the boy. With expertise, they gently maneuvered the large straps under the horse.

Lyrissa and Ray-Ray were back, but they stayed on the ATV. About twenty minutes into getting everything in place and checking for safety, another truck approached them. It was Mundo and Edith. They wanted to help, but he told them the best way to help was to stay out of the way.

The crew started pulling the horse up and Reno slid into place to grab Bennett as soon as he was clear. The horse was on solid ground, shaking but standing.

With Bennett in his arms, Reno came up the slippery slope with the help of one of the guys. Another group of first responders were carefully removing the wide yellow straps from the dazed horse.

"That was amazing." With a laugh, the teen slapped Smokey on the rump.

Startled and stressed, the horse reared and twisted. Reno saw a flash of hoof before he turned to shield the boy with his body. The impact knocked him to the ground. The horse jumped over him and ran. Someone was yelling at the teen. Apparently, his name was Devin.

"Are you okay?" he asked the boy cradled under him.

"Yes?" The small voice lacked confidence. Standing, Reno adjusted the boy's weight. Pain shot through him, and his sight went blurry. *Oh man, I'm going to faint. Not cool.*

Lyrissa's heart stopped the moment that teenager slapped Smokey's rump. It didn't matter how gentle a horse was; everyone knew to not startle them when they were in flight mode.

Watching the horse rear up on its hind legs then lunge and kick out toward Bennett's small form stopped her heart. She knew she would never be fast enough to protect him. But Reno was. He had shielded her brother with his body and took the blow.

When he stood up so fast, all the tension had flooded from her limbs. The relief had been overwhelming, but short-lived as Reno crumbled back toward the ground.

The crew surrounded Reno. One of the EMTs brought Bennett to her and said he was good, but they needed to take Reno in. Edith loaded the boys into the truck and took them to the house while she and her father followed with the four-wheelers.

She prayed it wasn't a head injury. It had happened so fast. She wanted to stay and make sure he was going to be okay, but for now all she could do was focus on the boys.

They needed to address the fact that they thought it was a good idea to go out to the pastures by themselves. She knew they were scared. So was she. And guilty for letting them out of her sight. Now Reno was in trouble, and it was her family's fault.

She prayed all the way back to the house.

Her father sat them all down at the kitchen table and talked calmly about the day. In all the excitement of the boys moving in, they had forgotten to establish rules and expectations.

So, a list was made and hung in the kitchen. The boys kept asking about Reno. There was a great deal of guilt to go around.

"I'll call his sister." Gathered at the table, not eating the lunch she had made, everyone stared at her as she spoke with Resa.

"A broken clavicle and dislocated shoulder caused him to

pass out. The doctors are discussing if he needs surgery. There is no indication of a head injury."

"That's good." Her throat was so tight it was hard to speak.

"Reno's worried about Bennett. He keeps asking for you too. Can you come and reassure him you're all okay?"

She glanced at her father and grandmother. Mundo nodded. "Go. We'll keep the boys."

It didn't take her long to cross the bridge and enter the hospital.

Room number in hand, she tried to steady her breathing. Each step closer to his room tightened her nerves. She wasn't sure why she was having a hard time breathing.

Taking a deep breath, she tapped on the door to his room. His mother opened it with a wide smile. "*Pásenle. Pásenle. Como esta?*"

Lyrissa nodded at the invitation. "I'm good. *Muy bien*. Thank you."

His mother, barely five feet tall, stepped back then leaned in closer to her and whispered, "He is asking for you. He is also heavily medicated so he's not making much sense." She made her way to the side of the hospital bed.

The room was full of people. His oldest sister, Margarita, and her husband stood on the other side of the bed with Resa. If she remembered correctly, she was a midwife. His brother, Bridges, was in some sort of law enforcement uniform. There were a few people who looked familiar, but she couldn't place them.

A couple of kids sat in the window playing a card game. There wasn't much room left. Reno was in the center, asleep. A sling was over his left shoulder and supported his arm.

"I'm sorry. I'll come back later. I brought these for him." The boys had picked out snacks to give him. She had grabbed a couple of magazines—one about coastal fishing and the other about cows and horses. She laid them at the foot of the bed then backed away, moving toward the door.

"Oh, no, no, no." His mother stopped her. "You stay. Some of us were leaving." She waved her hands around.

Reno opened his eyes and groaned. Everyone in the room stopped midmovement and looked at him.

"Lyr…issa?" His voice was thick and rough.

"She's right here." His tiny mother pulled her to the side of the bed, forcing his sisters to move out of the way.

He blinked, then searched the room as if lost. She was standing on the side of his uninjured arm, so she reached out and laid her hand over his. "Reno. We can't thank you enough for protecting Bennett."

"Ben… Bennen." His long lashes went down. Had he gone back to sleep? Then they opened wide and he blinked rapidly. "Bennett? Is…" His words slurred but she was pretty sure he was asking if her brother was okay.

"Not a scratch on him, thanks to your quick move. He just needed a good shower to wash off the mud. You saved him. Thank you."

"You good? Was worried." His lids went down again.

Leaning forward, she smiled at him and pushed back an unruly curl from his forehead. "I'm great. All is good on the Herff-Martinez home front, thanks to you."

"You're lovely. So pretty." He mumbled some other sounds, but his mouth didn't seem capable of forming legible words. His grin was lopsided as he reached out to touch her face.

Stunned, she didn't move. Was he actually flirting while banged up in the hospital?

"Easy, boy." His brother was on the opposite side of the bed. Extending his tall frame across the bed, Bridges eased Reno's good arm back to his bedside.

Reno frowned. "Want to…" More random sounds came from his lips. "Pretty."

There were a few soft giggles around the room.

She wasn't sure what to do. "Reno, I brought a couple of magazines, and the boys wanted you to have good snacks."

He lifted his hand again and cupped her face. "You the best." Narrowing his eyes, he shook his head. "I... I..." His gaze left hers and went around the room. "Why you all here?"

His mother stepped forward. The worry was still in her face. She covered his right foot with her hand. "You were hurt. We're here to make sure you have everything you need."

He glared at her. "I'm not a baby." Turning back to Lyrissa, he winced, obviously in pain, but then gave her a wide, goofy grin. "I have a sec..." He closed his eyes. "Secret."

Opening them, he leaned forward. "Come here," he slurred.

With trepidation, she moved closer. He flung his good arm out and wrapped it around her neck. "Only you to know." The words ran together.

"Hey, champ." His brother intervened again. "No mauling your guest." He pulled his arm off Lyrissa and gently pushed him back into the pillow.

"But I love her." That came out way too clearly.

A cold sweat broke out over her whole body. She looked around the room at the amused faces. "We're just friends. Really. I have no idea why he is saying these things."

"I say these things because they are the truth." His head rolled back, and his eyes closed.

Heat climbed up her neck. *Please let him fall asleep.* "On that note, I think it's time for me to go."

His hand reached out and touched her fingers. "Sorry." He looked around. "I need paper...pen."

One of his older nephews grabbed his backpack and pulled out the supplies he needed. "Thank you, Coop." Struggling to hold the pen, he stuck out his tongue. "I can't spell good."

"*G-o-o-d*," a small niece offered. A few chuckles filled the room.

He squinted one eye at her. "Not what I meant, but okay." He went back to focusing on his note. "There." He handed it to Lyrissa.

Bridges went to take it and Reno pulled back. "Nope. I'm

doing this…with…without my family. You do everything for me. I'm tired of being an Es… Espa." He grunted. "I am a grown man and I don't want to be an Espino…za. That's a hard word. I was in the…fourth grade before I spelt it. *Reno* is easy." He nodded then closed his eyes. "I'm just Reno from now on."

His mother put a hand to her chest. "*Mijo*, what's wrong? I've never heard you say such things before. You could spell your name in first grade."

"Nope. Maddy and Crystal wrote it for me. They took my spelling test too. I can't spell or read." He pressed his finger to his lips. "Shhhh. Don't tell. It's a secret 'cause I don't you to be diss…dissa…p…p…worry. Don't worry."

Lyrissa looked from him to his mom. The poor woman had tears in her eyes. Resa went to her side and wrapped an arm around her shoulder. "Mom. Don't let anything he says worry you. He is heavily medicated and doesn't know what he is saying."

"But all this about reading and spelling makes no sense. He passed all his classes."

"Mom. We'll figure it out later. He's going to be okay."

"Okay," Reno said, louder than needed. "Ever since trapped in the box you worried about me. No more worry. No more. I'm…" He blinked as if he forgot what he was saying. He held up the note. "This is for you. Only you." He glared at his brother.

Bridges lifted his hand in surrender. "I was only trying to save you from yourself. I'm thinking you might regret whatever is in that note once the painkillers wear off, little brother."

Reno blew out a hard puff of air. "I don't need you or you or you or you." His gaze went around the room. "To save me. Here." Once again he handed the note to Lyrissa.

With a weak attempt at a smile, she took it from him. She had always thought the Espinozas were the perfect family. Apparently, there were some undercurrents in the calm waters. She really didn't want to be here.

Looking at the note, she bit her bottom lip. Maybe once the drugs wore off, he'd forget he gave it to her. That would be for the best. No need to embarrass herself or him.

"Read it. Please." His gaze was so earnest as he watched her. The room was dead silent.

The back of the page was facing her. If she didn't turn it over, she would not have to deal with any of his drug-induced secrets.

"What do you say?" he asked, his voice clearer than before.

"I don't know." It was all she could offer.

He blinked. "You don't know? That's not an ans…answer. Yes or no?"

"What did you ask her?" Bridges put all of his authority as an officer and older brother into the short question.

With an exasperated sigh, Reno flopped back onto his pillow. The pain brought his right hand to his left shoulder.

Gently, she laid her hand on top of his. "This is not the time to talk about it. Focus on getting better than we'll talk. In private."

His mouth opened and he scanned the room and if surprised that they had an audience. He leaned forward. "Right." He nodded. Then he closed his eyes. "Bennett's safe?"

"Yes. Thank you for saving him. If there is anything we can do to repay you, let us know."

"No. He's a good kid…just wanted to help with ranch work."

"I know. I'll check on you later. Bye." She stepped away before he could say anything more. A quick trip to the hospital had turned into a complicated mess.

She rushed out of the room. She knew she was being rude, but she didn't want anyone to ask her questions about the note.

Once she was alone in her car, she took a deep breath then turned the paper over. *WIL U MARY M?*

Her heart stopped. Why would he ask her that, even in a drug-induced state? It was so far from anything she knew how to handle. This was not real. He wasn't in his right mind. Once the meds wore off, he'd have no memory of this.

She wouldn't bring it up, saving both of them from the humiliation of this bizarre question.

On another subject, it was obvious his family had no clue he was dyslexic. It wasn't uncommon for an undiagnosed student to figure out strategies to hide it. They didn't understand there was help. Without being exposed to learning disabilities, they would just think something was wrong with them and work to hide it.

Apparently, no one in his family had dealt with it so he had been on his own and solved the problem the best way he could. This was her area of expertise, but after so many years of hiding it, she worried he would not be open to letting her help him.

There were so many ways dyslexia presented. She knew she could assist him, if he'd accept it.

She looked at the note, then carefully folded the paper and put it in her bag. She was nowhere close to being his type and he was the last person she would want in her life. It didn't matter, anyway. She would be leaving soon. He wasn't serious about wanting to marry her. She knew firsthand people were not reliable when on drugs, any kind of drug.

She thought back to their first day here and how Reno had stepped in and helped. She shook her head. Really, where had that proposal come from?

CHAPTER SEVEN

SWEAT BEADED RENO'S forehead and it wasn't from the heat. The Martinez house loomed before him. If the gossip from his siblings, nephews and nieces were to be believed, he had made a total fool of himself in front of Lyrissa.

They loved reminding him how he had pulled her over and declared his undying love. He swallowed. They had to be exaggerating. *Please, God. Let them be tall tales with little to no truth.*

They said he also had declared he remembered everything about the day he was trapped in a box on the fishing boat. And because he was on a roll to clear out all his secrets, he admitted he couldn't read or write and had cheated to get through school.

Lyrissa had been there to hear it all. Slamming his head against the steering wheel, he let out a groan. He was going to have legal papers drawn up that none of his family members were ever allowed to be around him in a hospital until he was fully aware.

Not that it mattered now. Every secret he had worked so hard to keep hidden from his family over the years was out. His mother kept crying. Apologizing for being neglectful and missing the signs.

Leaning back in the truck, he closed his eyes and prayed.

Prayed for God's wisdom and peace. The past week had been all about trying to get the smile back on his mother's face.

He hated that she felt responsible for any of his faults. That had been the whole reason he had hidden them for so long. She didn't deserve to cry another tear in her life.

Now he had to face Lyrissa and try to put all the toothpaste back in the tube. She had no interest in him, and he knew that. He valued her friendship and didn't want it to be awkward or weird between them.

Plus, the idea that she now knew he couldn't read or write was downright embarrassing. She had a master's degree in education, and he barely got out of high school. Yeah, she'd really want to hang out and have deep conversations with him.

His favorite things to talk about were ranch stuff, movies and fishing. She was probably one of those people who preferred the book over the movie. He reached for the key to turn the engine back on and back out before anyone saw him. One more week would be good.

"Reno!" Ray-Ray launched out of the front door, waving and jumping. Bennett, much more aloof, followed.

Caught. He turned off the engine, opened the door and stepped out, remembering not to use his left side.

"Reno!" Ray-Ray turned to look behind him. "Dad! Reno's here!"

The small boy ran to Reno and stopped a foot away. "Can I hug you? Is it hurt bad? It was so scary to see the horse go up and knock you down. But you twisted like Spider-Man and saved Benny." He spun his little body then threw his head back with his hands clutching his chest. "Then you passed out. I was so scared. Are you better? Dad said we couldn't go to the hospital. That you needed to rest. I made you a drawing. It's in the house."

"Whoa there, boy." Mundo braced his hands on the shoulders of Ray-Ray and laughed. "As you can hear, Ray-Ray has been very worried about you." His smile dimmed a little. "It was a traumatic day for him and his brother."

"I'm okay," Bennett grumbled. He eyed Reno with curiosity but hung back with his arms crossed. "Are you okay? That horse was big."

Reno went to one knee. "My shoulder took a little hit and needs to rest a bit, but I'm good. You and your brother were so brave. I'm proud of the way you stayed cool the whole time under the horse and told your brother to go get help. It's okay if you need to talk about it. When I was younger, I was once trapped in a fishing boat box all day. I didn't know if I would make it home. Sometimes, I still have dreams about the darkness and the waves. So, if you get scared, it's okay to talk to your dad or sister." He knew how hard it was to hold it in and suffer alone.

"He can talk to me too." Ray-Ray jumped up and down.

"That's good advice, Reno." Lyrissa joined them. The morning sun kissed her skin and reflected the red streaks in her dark hair. For a moment, he forgot to breathe. She was so beautiful.

He stood, making sure to fill his lungs. That thought had to be banished from his head. Today was about convincing her that anything he said in the hospital had to be forgotten.

With one smile from her, the songbirds sounded happier. He was still on painkillers. To make sure he didn't say anything stupid, he kept silent.

Lyrissa knelt in front of Bennett. "Being brave doesn't mean you don't get scared."

With a nod, Reno agreed with her. "I'll give you my number. You can call or text anytime. Nighttime can be the hardest. If you don't want to wake anyone, I'm always up late." He held the boy's gaze until he got a nod. "I was sent to deliver a homemade meal from my mother's kitchen. It might include brownies. Anyone want to help me take it in?"

Ray-Ray lifted his hand. "Me! I want to help."

Laughing, Mundo patted him on the shoulder. "Come on,

son. We'll take care of it." With Lyrissa's father guiding the boys, the containers were taken into the house.

"Thank you. Not just for saving him, but for opening up and giving him someone to talk to. I understand you don't talk about the time you were trapped. Savannah had told me the story back in high school. All those hours lost were terrifying for them. They had thought it a blessing you didn't remember." She pulled her lips in then glanced at him through her lashes. "But you did remember. You were four?"

He nodded. It had become a habit to keep it buried and not talk about it when others retold the story from their perspective.

"Were you in the box the whole time?"

"Yes." His mouth went dry. Clearing his throat, he thought of what words to use. This was hard but it was better than talking about his attraction to her. "The inside was rough wood with the smell of wet towels and saltwater. There was a thin crack of light. The waves made me sick to my stomach. I was afraid the men on the boat would be mad at me. Somewhere in my brain, I thought they would throw me overboard. Probably something to do with the stories my older siblings told me. I prayed that I would be good and never make my mother mad or sad if God took me home to her." One corner of his mouth pulled up. He'd forgotten that part.

"You pretended not to remember to keep everyone happy?"

He shrugged then touched his left shoulder. "I guess. Whenever anyone brought it up, my mother would cry and hug me so tight I couldn't breathe."

"I'm grateful you said something. Keeping that kind of experience buried had to be hard. I wouldn't want that kind of burden for Bennett or any child. Thank you for sharing with him."

"I'm glad I could help. On the other hand, now my mother is back to tearing up every time she sees me. I had to get away. Plus, I wanted to talk to you."

There. He said it. Now he just needed to form the next words. They were all jumbled, just like when he tried to read or write. He hated it when words played hide-and-seek in his head. What was wrong with his brain?

She glanced at him then turned away. Swallowing, he tried searching for the right words. He had already embarrassed himself enough. Just a simple apology. But he should say what he was apologizing for. That's where it was foggy.

"Lyrissa—"

"Uhm. Reno—"

They spoke at the same time. He adjusted his sling as they both gave an awkward chuckle. "Well, I guess that establishes that we both know each other's names."

With a grin, she looked at him then cut her gaze to the pasture on the other side of the drive. A herd of Herefords grazed peacefully. Bringing her gaze back to him, she smiled unnaturally.

He opened his mouth and jumped in. "I hear from not-so-reliable sources that I might have made a fool of myself. I hope anything I said didn't make you uncomfortable." Now he was studying the cattle like his life depended on them. His skin had never felt so hot.

"You were on some pretty strong painkillers. Do you remember any of it?"

"Not a bit. And I mean that." He grinned. "It's not me pretending to avoid making you unhappy."

"There was something I really wanted to talk to you about, but I don't want to offend you."

He blew out a puff of air. "I'm pretty insult-proof. You can say anything. Please." He laid his good hand over his heart. Her taking the lead in the conversation would be so much easier than him trying to muddle through.

"Before the accident, I noticed you used some classic strategies to avoid reading aloud. In the hospital you admitted to not being able to read or write."

His nerves pinched his stomach. Maybe letting her take the lead had not been the rescue he thought. His muscles locked in place. "I can. Sometimes it's harder than other times."

"I hope I'm not overstepping, but do you or have you ever been diagnosed with dyslexia or dysgraphia?"

He just stared at her.

She bit the corner of her mouth. "Okay. I'm assuming not, since your mother was surprised by your comment. Is this why you haven't taken the written exam to be a firefighter?" She relaxed her face and tried to smile. Then she blinked a couple of times. This time she allowed the silence to hang between them.

"I don't see letters backward." Taking a deep breath, he shook his head. "I've never even heard the term *dysgraphia*. It was just hard to read or write. I can, but…" Did he tell her the truth about the exam? No one wanted to look like an idiot.

She leaned closer to him. "It's so much more complicated than backward letters. You know my specialty is working with neurodivergent students. I might be able to help. If you want me to." She held her hands up. "But like I said, it's completely up to you."

"What if we find out I'm not neurodivergent, just stu—"

"Stop. Without going any further, I can guarantee you have a solid—if not high—IQ. You figured out how to pass your classes. You speak two languages fluently. You solve problems quickly even in stressful situations. What some people don't understand is that neurodivergences just help us understand that some people have a different way to process information. Even the way they think and behave can be different."

She looked him straight in the eye. "Not wrong. Different. With support and strategies, their ways of thinking and seeing information can be a great advantage."

He raised his eyebrows.

Her voice had gotten louder. Straightening her spine, she took a breath. "Sorry. I get passionate about this and might go overboard. But the one thing I want you to know is you're in no way less than. Just different than. And that can be a good thing once identified. Your quick thinking saved my brother. If you want to be a first responder, I want to help you get there."

He tried to process everything she just said. It was overwhelming, but one thing he understood was she thought he could pass the test. "Okay. The thing is, I did take the written exam and I failed. Twice. The second time more than the first."

"On the second test. Did you get in your head?"

"What do you mean?" His chest hurt. It was strange talking about this with someone. After a lifetime of pretending it wasn't a problem, it was hard to put his doubts and struggles into words.

"Did you go into the second test doubting your ability to pass? Were you afraid you were just wasting time and money?"

A dry laugh escaped. "I did waste time and money. What's the point? I'm a good ranch hand. I'm going back to that as soon as my shoulder is better."

"You were focused on your fear instead of what you knew." She stepped closer and touched his arm. "I can help. That's what I'm trying to tell you. Let me help. Together, we can get you to pass that test. If that's what you want."

His breath was coming in short pants, like he'd ran five fast miles. Could this really happen? "You think I can pass the test?"

"Yes." She stepped closer and placed one soft hand on his shoulder. "You keep adjusting your sling. Is it hurting? We should sit." Her gaze moved up until it met his. They both froze.

The world faded away. Her face was clear and sharp. He glanced at her lips.

Yeah. He had said everything his family accused him of.

It was all in his heart, but his head knew there was no point. He leaned closer. His mouth was dry. She didn't pull away.

A hammer pinged his brain. What was he doing? She would

never be his, even for a brief time. The best he could hope for was friendship and he was about to mess that up too.

Stepping back, he lost her touch. A part of him screamed to step back into her circle but the practical side won. "Sorry. It is hurting."

He hadn't even noticed he was messing with his shoulder. She pointed to the porch. He nodded and they walked up the stoop.

Settling into one of the old rockers, he became uncomfortable again. It wasn't his shoulder this time. Should he mention the hospital and beg her to forget anything he had said? Had she noticed he almost kissed her?

"Reno. I really hope you accept my help, but we also need to talk about the other thing that happened at the hospital."

His heart jumped three notches. *No.*

It was his problem, not hers. He should just jump in and take the lead. "They said I gave you a note, but no one knows what I wrote. A little painkiller and I started making things up." He gave her a grin, but this was what he dreaded most. "I'm sure it was gibberish." *Please let it be gibberish.*

She crossed her arms and sat back in her rocking chair. Her gaze was on the land around them. With a big sigh, she turned her head. "The thing is—"

"Lyrissa!" Ray-Ray banged the door open. "Mew-Maw fell down. She was yelling at Momma on the phone. And then—."

SHE DIDN'T WAIT for Ray-Ray to finish. Reno was right with her. In the kitchen, he went to his knees next to Mew-Maw. Using the counter, she supported herself when the blood stopped flowing to her legs. Her grandmother was limp on the floor. Her head was in her father's lap.

"They were yelling at each other then she just collapsed like in slow motion." Worry was etched in every line of her father's face.

Reno placed his fingers on her throat. "Call 911." He counted. "Her pulse is good. Edith, can you hear me?"

She turned her head and groaned. Lyrissa's heart jumped in relief.

"Did she hit her head when she fell?" Reno asked as he gently checked her.

"No." Her father's attention was fully on his mother-in-law. "I had time to break her fall. I was moving to take the phone because the yelling got louder."

Dispatch answered. It was Izzie. Lyrissa made herself focus on giving her the information. But she couldn't take her gaze off Reno and Mew-Maw.

"Edith?" Reno's voice was gentle but firm as he touched the weathered cheek.

Her eyes blinked. "What?" Her blue gaze was unfocused.

She was awake. Lyrissa breathed for the first time since coming through the door.

"Can you tell me where you are and the last thing you remember?" Reno asked.

"I'm in Mundo's house. About to have dinner with my boys. Dee called." She closed her eyes. "That girl is going to be the death of me. I can't believe the things she said."

She was getting upset again. Reno redirected her. "It's okay. Focus on Lyrissa and the boys." He pointed to her. Ray-Ray was holding her free hand. "They're all good."

"Yes. Those boys should have been here as soon as they were born." Her voice went up. "Lyrissa, are you talking to her?" She was yelling again. Fighting Reno and her father as she struggled to get up. "Why am I on the floor?"

"You passed out. We need to make sure you're okay." Reno took her hand. "She called 911."

"Hogwash. I'm fit as a fiddlin' frog." She pointed to Lyrissa. "You had better not have called the ambulance, young lady. I don't need no one making a fuss over me. And it cost too much money."

Bennett moved a chair close to her, and Mundo helped Reno get her into it. She waved them off. "Girl, hang up that phone."

Lyrissa ignored her. She turned away so she could focus on the call. "Yes. She's alert. Thank you, Izzie." She slipped the phone into her back pocket. "The ambulance is already halfway here. She said if you don't want treatment, you have to sign a refusal form."

"I'm not going to be taken out on a stretcher like some old feeble person. Why did you call them?" She glared.

"I asked her to." Reno winked at her grandmother as if they were partners in crime. "A distraction from you lying lifeless on the floor."

Mundo moved to the counter and gave Lyrissa a look like she was the one who had to handle the older lady's stubbornness.

With a sigh, she went to one knee and took her grandmother's hand. "Mew-Maw, you were unconscious. I didn't want to waste time if it was a stroke or your heart. The boys were scared."

The older woman softened and patted Ray-Ray's hand. "They think because I'm old, I'm going to just drop dead. I promise you boys, it's going to take much more than your mother's shenanigans to do any real damage to this old bird."

Mundo slid into the chair at the front of the table. He gave a pointed look at his daughter.

Lyrissa nodded and sat next to her grandmother. She knew a fight was coming. "We'll make an appointment with Dr. Villa as soon as his office opens."

"I ain't going to no doctor either. They just find things wrong with you and order drugs. Then they make you come back all the time."

Reno smiled at her as if all was great. "You know you're not going to the doctor for yourself," he said as his gaze met Lyrissa's. "It's for your family's peace of mind. They have enough to worry about."

Edith crossed her arms and harrumphed. "They'll want to start me on drugs. I ain't doing it."

Lyrissa wanted to beat her head against the wooden table. "Stop being so stubborn." There was a vehicle pulling up to the house. "That's the ambulance. I'll go meet them."

Reno stood as if going with her.

She pointed to the chair he had been sitting in. "Sit. I've got it." After their encounter on the porch, keeping distance between them was the best choice. She did not look at him as she left.

Right now, she was too fragile to deal with any of those weird feelings.

Brenda and Joe were at the door, and she led them to the kitchen.

Reno had everyone laughing when Lyrissa walked in with the paramedics. Even Bennett couldn't hide a half grin. Reno was in his old familiar role of jokester. Lyrissa gave him a quick glare then focused on her grandmother.

Did he ever take anything seriously?

Brenda checked on Edith as the older woman grumbled through the whole routine about people treating her like a cracked egg.

Smiling, Brenda explained what she was doing and what they were looking for. True to her word, Edith refused to go to the hospital and signed the form.

"Mew-Maw, first thing in the morning we're calling to make you an appointment. No arguments."

"I'm not a child." The woman crossed her arms over her chest. "Y'all wasted your time coming out. Sorry they bothered you."

"It was no bother, ma'am," Brenda said with a smile.

As Lyrissa walked the pair out, Reno was going to the back door. What was he doing now?

Coming back into the kitchen, she didn't see Reno. She was about to ask her dad where he went but stopped herself.

She didn't care. Or at least she shouldn't care. This was her not caring.

"Are you hungry, Mew-Maw?" She needed to take care of her family and not think about Reno.

It started working and then he walked back in. A wrapped plate in his hand. "We almost forgot the brownies. It's a lot of food. I hope it's okay that I called a friend of mine. I'm doing work in their kitchen. They could use a good homemade dinner so I went ahead and invited him and his wife over. I hope it's alright?"

Heat climbed up her neck. Was he serious? "I don't think—" Her father cut her off.

"Sure!" Mundo smiled. "The more the merrier. Looks as if your mother sent over enough to feed an army."

The frustration she was feeling just moved to borderline contempt. "You invited someone to come over, now?"

He held her gaze and grinned. "Yep. Should be here in about fifteen minutes. He happens to be a neighbor of sorts. You know him. Victor Villa."

She blinked. "Dr. Villa?"

"I think you're right. Yes. He is a doctor. Anyway, he's bringing his sweet wife too." He went to the stove and turned it on.

"She's a neurologist." Lyrissa took the top pan and opened it. All the anger was gone and just a hint of worry remained. She blinked a couple of times. He must have called Dr. Villa outside. He knew her grandmother would never agree to go in. "Thank you."

The urge to cry was ridiculous.

Edith harrumphed. "Well, I like Beverly and Victor, so if you're going to sneak in a doctor, they're good ones. Boy, get a couple of plates and set the table for them." Edith gave directions and stopped grumbling now that guests were coming.

Lyrissa grabbed a tortilla and gave him a pointed look.

"After dinner, we're setting up a schedule to go over reading strategies."

His smile faded. "Okay. But don't get frustrated when you discover how pointless your mission is."

"If you come with an open mind don't be surprised if you find yourself doing things you didn't think you could do." It was her favorite part of her job.

She needed to be very careful, because she was starting to see him in a whole new light, and it wasn't good for her heart.

There was a knock at the door. She put her smile firmly in place. Time to entertain.

CHAPTER EIGHT

LYRISSA GLANCED AT her watch. Her father and grandmother would soon be home from her doctor's appointment. Lyrissa had been on the phone longer than anticipated. But it was for a worthy cause. The boys would be enrolled and start school in the fall, and she had a summer job. Perfect for building her résumé. Her life was getting back on track.

While she was on the phone, Reno had arrived and took the boys to the barn. Stepping through the partially open door, she scanned the space for them. She squinted against the drastic lighting shift. She didn't see much, but it was too quiet. Where had they gone?

Today was the third round of lessons. The topic of her hospital visit never came up and she liked it that way. It was too awkward. He probably had no memory of it, and she was happy not telling him. There was no way he meant to ask her to marry him.

He was already embarrassed by his reading skills. She didn't want to make him feel worse.

The boys' favorite horses were still here so they hadn't gone riding. A giggle came from the far end of the barn, followed by someone shushing.

Placing each foot with care, she moved to the back of the barn. With a tilt to her head, she listened for any other sounds.

In the far-left corner, she saw the bottom of boots. All three of them were on their bellies halfway under a platform with hay. Bennett and Ray-Ray were on one side of the ladder that went to the loft and Reno was on the other side.

Not sure what was going on, she waited.

"I got one!" Bennett's excitement was clear.

"Be gentle." Reno's voice was low and soothing. "We don't want to hurt them."

Bennett scooted backward. Once he cleared the edge of the platform, he sat up. A black-and-white kitten was in his arms.

"Come here, kitty, kitty," Ray-Ray whispered. "I'll be a good friend."

"I think I can reach her," Reno said.

Bennett turned and saw her. His eyes filled with excitement for the first time since she met him. "We found kittens. Two. This one is black-and-white. The other's orange."

The kitten hissed and tried to get away. Bennett held on tight. Behind him, Reno handed Ray-Ray a small orange fluff-ball. It immediately snuggled closer to the little boy. "It likes me," he whispered to the purring kitten.

She had to smile. "I can hear purring from here. I think the black one wants to go back to its hiding place."

"She's just scared." He held out a piece of cheese and the kitten stilled then ate it. "She needs to learn she can trust me." He scratched her ears. "I'll put her back. Then she'll know I won't hurt her." He went back to the platform and hung out under there for a while.

"Can we keep them?" Ray-Ray was stroking his now-sleeping kitten.

This was not good. "Uhm. Cats belong in the barn. Dad strongly believes they have a job on the ranch, and they won't do it if they're pampered in the house."

Ray-Ray looked as if he was about to cry. Reno dropped

to one knee in front of the little boy. "You should ask Mundo. He might say yes."

"Ask Mundo what?" Her father entered the barn.

Lyrissa jumped, hand over her heart. Reno laughed. "You look like you got caught doing something you're not supposed to do."

"Benny and I want to keep the kittens," Ray-Ray said, charging in without any tact.

Mundo frowned. "Nope. They belong in the barn. You can visit them. We'll need to catch them and the momma cat to take them in to the vet. Make sure they're healthy, and we don't get overrun with barn cats. But they do not ever come into the house. They're happier out here."

Ray-Ray hugged his closer.

Before more tears could fall, Reno stood. "What did the doctor say?"

With a snort, Mundo shook his head. "All the tests just proved she's healthier than most women ten years her junior. They said it was probably a vas—" He sighed. "I can't remember, but I wrote it down. It's caused by extreme emotional stress. The blood flow to the brain stops and you pass out. It's a way for the brain to reboot and get the blood flowing again. So, they advise she—" He glanced at the boys. "Well, I guess you can figure out what—or better yet, who—she should avoid."

"Daddy, I'm so sorry." She hugged her dad. Ray-Ray was watching them intently.

"Did Momma make Mew-Maw sick?" he asked.

Mundo walked over to him and put an arm around his shoulder. "Your Mew-Maw's temper made her sick. Yelling and screaming is not good for the body, mind or spirit. Do you want to go visit her? She went to tend her garden. Which means pulling weeds. She says it settles her."

"We should go help her." He smiled up at Mundo. "Bennett! Daddy wants us to go help Mew-Maw in her garden."

"Do I have to? I want my kitten to get used to me," Bennett yelled as he went back under the platform.

Ray-Ray hushed his brother. "Daddy says yelling is bad for you. But working in the garden and helping others makes you strong." He looked up at Mundo. "Right?"

"Couldn't have said it better myself," Mundo chuckled. "Bennett, get out from under there. We need to leave so these two can get on with their date."

"No! It's not a date," she protested. Heat climbed her neck. The thought of dating Reno was more exciting than it should be. Was she begging to have her heart broken?

She couldn't look at him. His smiling, charming face would be her downfall. He'd be all nice until he was bored, or something better came along. "Daddy, there is nothing between Reno and me."

THE BULLET-FAST DENIAL hurt his pride and his heart.

It also answered a question he had been tossing around in his head. The answer would be no if he asked her out. *Note to self. Don't ask her on a date.*

Of course, her answer would be no. She was trying to teach him how to read. Who wanted to go on a date with a guy who couldn't read the menu? He just always ordered the same or waited for others to order so he could copy them.

"We're friends." She looked at him, worry etched in her face. "Right?"

And he would do anything to make her happy, so he gave her his best smile and agreed. "No dating going on here."

"I'm just helping him with some of the chores around the ranch. I'm cheap labor. We're just friends, so don't get any ideas."

"Yep. Just friends." He would always be in the friend zone with Lyrissa.

Her shoulders relaxed and took a deep breath as if the weight of the world was lifted from her.

"Well, that's a shame." Mundo frowned.

Great. Reno made one person happy and upset the other. This was not a good day for him. They stood in silence as they watched Ray-Ray put his kitten back. Then the trio of Martinez males went to the big house to help Edith with the garden.

He didn't feel like doing a lesson today. He wanted to work in the garden too.

"I'm so sorry." Lyrissa broke into his thoughts. "I should have let Dad think we were dating. It would be an easy way to explain all the time we're spending together. But I don't want to lie to him." She stuffed her hands in her jean pockets.

"No worries, teacher. Are we going out on horseback today or going to the beach?" He shifted and looked around. He still wasn't comfortable with her teaching him to decode the written language. It forced him to sit in the horrible, vulnerable place he hated. His whole life had been an exercise in covering it up. Now, he was exposed and raw.

"Today I have a few things I want to try that require sitting and some sort of table. I do want to stay outdoors. The front porch swing work for you?"

At the end of their first lesson, she had told him he was a kinesthetic learner. His body needed to be moving for maximum learning.

He had never heard the word before. But apparently, mixed with dyslexia, a traditional school setting was not a good fit.

It made sense. He had just thought he preferred outdoors and working with his hands. The lessons she did with him were more like games.

"Lead the way, teacher." He held the barn door open.

"Thank you for keeping an eye on the boys. You've really helped with their adjustment."

"They're good kids."

"I totally agree. Let's go through the kitchen so I can pick up my supplies."

Once settled into the swing, she introduced new strategies

to see how he responded to those. About forty-five minutes into the lesson, he read a line without stumbling.

His eyes went wide, and he looked up at her. "It worked." He moved his finger along the rose-colored transparent filter and continued to read. He paused over one word and couldn't get it. With a grunt, he leaned back in the swing.

"Don't get frustrated. You've done great today."

He scoffed.

"You're an amazing man. Don't let this one thing define you." She gathered the papers and filters. "I think we should stop for the day. Brain work takes a lot of energy."

"You're the amazing one." He leaned forward without thinking. "The phone call earlier. Was it good news?"

She raised her head then froze. Their faces were less than six inches apart. If one of them leaned the slightest, they could be kissing. Five seconds. Five years. He had no sense of time or space. It was the two of them and she was not moving away.

Afraid she would bolt, he held perfectly still and waited.

She blinked but didn't move. "Uhm. The call? Yes. It was the school. They confirmed the boys' paperwork was complete for school next year and I got the part-time summer job with the special ed department." Her eyes moved but then came back to him. "It's perfect for my résumé."

Résumé. That's right. She was leaving. Did he just shift closer, or was it her? It was her. He was pretty sure he hadn't moved.

"You smell really good." Her eyes went wide. Jerking back, she slammed her lids shut. A guttural groan escaped passed tightly pressed lips. "Did I say that aloud? I didn't mean it. I mean, you do smell good. But I didn't mean to say it. Is it a new cologne or shampoo? Okay, I'm going to stop talking now."

He tucked a loose strand of hair behind her ear and gave her a lopsided grin. For the first time, he had hope. Maybe she would say yes. "We could go on a real date. No deep lifetime commitment. Just a fun date." He searched her face for any hint of agreement and held his breath. *Please say yes. Please.*

No would probably be the smarter answer for both of them. Once again, it was the wrong place and time. But his stupid heart wanted a *yes*. It wanted to spend real time with her.

If they didn't take a risk now, it would never happen. She leaned toward him. He could feel the echoes of her heartbeats. He could see a *yes* hanging on the edge of her lips.

[faint text from previous page showing through]

CHAPTER NINE

A CAR COMING down the driveway broke the trance she had fallen into.

Whoa. She had been so close to…to kissing him? Saying *yes* to a date with Reno? Her heart raced as if she had just run a mile at a full-on sprint.

Shaking her head, she stood and turned to the car that had just parked in front of the house. People didn't just drive out to their place. The driver was talking to someone in the seat behind them. The back door opened.

Deeann Herff Martinez adjusted her large, floppy hat and sunglasses, then looked around before stepping away from the car. The car backed up and left the way it came.

Leaving the woman who gave birth to her standing alone in the drive.

No. She was not allowing that woman to create havoc. Rushing down the steps, she blocked Dee from stepping foot on the porch.

"Oh, my beautiful Lyrissa." Her mother came forward and went to hug her, but Lyrissa put her hand up and stepped back. "Don't come any closer."

A warm hand gently touched her back. Turning, she found Reno. He wasn't looking at her. He was staring down at her mom.

"Deeann, what are you doing here?" His always friendly voice was uncharacteristically stern.

Her clear, green eyes darted back between the two of them. "Who's this good-looking fellow? Do you have a sweetheart here in Port Del Mar?"

"No. You—"

"Baby girl. I know you're mad at me and you have every right to be." Dee batted her lashes as the tears built up. "I thought I was helping everyone. It was going to be grand for us all. But Harrison turned out to be a con artist and a bad influence. He had me making bad choices. You know I lose myself and make horrible decisions. I'm so sorry." She moved toward Lyrissa again, but Reno gently stepped between them. Not completely in front of her, but enough to hinder any attempt of Dee's to reach her.

Her mother made a pathetic whimpering sound. "I came home to beg your forgiveness. And to see my baby boys." Tears welled up in her big green eyes. "I *am* so sorry for the hurt I caused." She fisted her hands against her chest. "I know I messed up. This time I want to make it right."

Lyrissa put her hand in Reno's. He squeezed it, reassuring her that she wasn't alone. "Mom, you have to leave. You're not welcome here."

Her mother let the tears fall full force now. "Oh, baby girl. Please don't do this to your momma. I don't have anywhere to go. Harrison took all the money. He left me with nothing after I gave him everything. I trusted the wrong person."

The heat started at Lyrissa's chest. Did her mother even listen to herself? "I've trusted the wrong person too. But not again. You stole everything from me then abandoned your sons. You can't just walk back into our lives. Go find a way to start over somewhere else. Not here."

"What about my momma? What happened while I was on the phone with her? Mundo's not returning my calls. Is she okay?" Her chest moved with each heavy breath and panic filled her eyes. "He always answers my calls. What's wrong?"

Her father had stopped communicating with Dee? That was a first.

If her father didn't want to talk to Dee, then there was no way she'd allow her to stay on the ranch for a minute more. "She passed out because you upset her. That's what you do. You hurt people and I'm not going to allow you to hurt the people I love anymore. Leave, now."

"I'll take her to town." Reno stepped closer to Dee. "I'm Reno Espinoza. I'll take you to my mom's until you figure out where you're going next."

"No." It was a whimper. "This is my home—"

"You left us a long time ago." Lyrissa pushed down every bit of emotion and stared at the woman who had caused so much damage to her family. "Go get help. Professional help."

She hit her chest. "I'm still Gavin and Edith's daughter. I belong here as much as you do." She pointed at Lyrissa. "Your dad was just a ranch hand when I started dating him and...." She took a deep breath and patted her hand against her chest. "Sorry. You can't imagine how upsetting this all is."

Dee looked at Reno and smiled. "You were just a boy last time I saw you. I didn't even recognize you." Turning to Lyrissa, she nodded. "I'll go visit Mrs. Espinoza and text your dad. He'll come pick me up. He always does. I'm going to make this right, baby girl. I promise."

Lyrissa's stomach twisted and acid burned her throat. She didn't even bother to point out that promise had been made more times than she could count.

Reno put his hand on Dee's elbow. "That's my truck." He gently led her away.

Dee paused and looked back. Tears still soaked her fake lashes. "I'll be back for dinner. I love you."

Lyrissa held herself straight as Reno opened his passenger door. She would be gone before—

"Momma!" Ray-Ray came running around the corner of the house and flew past Lyrissa.

No.

He flung himself at his mother. Wrapping his arms around her, he buried his face in her stomach. "I told Benny you would come back."

Spinning around to see where he came from, she found different degrees of devastation on the faces of her father, Benny and Mew-Maw.

RENO FROZE. THIS *was not good.*

"Oh, Ray-Ray. Benny. I'm home. Come give some love to your momma." One arm went wide while she held Ray-Ray close to her. Bennett stood alone, not moving. His face, a hard mask. There was so much hurt and distrust radiating from the boy.

Mundo's jaw flexed. His eyes narrowed as if not sure what he was seeing. Edith was at his side. Her hand wrapped around his bicep. None of them moved forward.

"Mundo?" Dee's voice was smaller now. "I'm home."

The older man stood straight and shook his head. "This is not your home. Not anymore." He reached for Bennett and pulled him close. "What are you doing here?"

"I wanted to see my babies. Thank you for taking care of them. I—"

"You are not taking my sons anywhere. They're home and they'll stay here until they're old enough to decide for themselves."

Dee blinked as if not understanding. "But you said you'd always wait for me."

"That was before you stole from our daughter, abandoned our sons. The ones you've hidden from me. And before you pushed your mother to an unhealthy state. You are no longer welcome in my home."

Reno stepped forward. "I was about to take her to mom's."

Edith walked to the front of the truck. "She can stay in her old room in the main house. Until we can all calm down."

"Edith?" Mundo turned to his mother-in-law. "Are you sure you want to—"

"She's my daughter. She needs a place to rest." The older woman stood straighter. "This is temporary. No drinking or anything else. You will be up early with me and do whatever work needs done."

"Of course, Momma." Dee rubbed her sleeve under her nose. "Thank you."

"I'm doing this for your boys. And your daddy. Also, to make some of my wrongs right." She shook her head. Decades of regret filled her eyes and she looked older than she had in the morning.

Reno's jaw hurt from the tension. Lyrissa and her family didn't deserve this kind of drama. "Are you sure, Edith? My mom always has a room ready for anyone who needs it. To give you all some time." For what, he wasn't sure.

"No. She can stay with me. But one misstep and you're gone. If you do anything to hurt my family—" she pointed around her "—you'll be off this ranch forever."

Dee hugged Ray-Ray tighter. "I missed my boys. I missed all my family. Hitting rock bottom made me realize how much I love you. I'm so sorry."

"Actions speak louder than words, Deeann. So, show us. Come on." She walked to her daughter and picked up the one small travel bag. "Let's get you settled at the main house."

Dee held the hand of her youngest son, and paused as they passed Bennett. "Benny, will you come with me?"

He stepped closer to Mundo and wouldn't make eye contact with his mother. Mundo put an arm around his shoulder.

After a few long seconds of silence, she nodded and picked up Ray-Ray. "You have to tell me everything you've done on the ranch."

He nodded but stared at his older brother. Confusion was stamped all over his young face.

"It's okay, Ray-Ray," Bennett told his brother. "It's going to be alright."

A knot twisted Reno's heart over the older boy giving his brother permission to be with their mother despite his own pain. They stood in silence as they watch the trio go.

Mundo hugged the boy. "You are a good brother and you're right. All will be good. Is it okay if I take one of the horses out? I need to clear my head and spend time with God."

"Of course, Daddy." Lyrissa went to him and wrapped him in a tight hug. "I tried to get her to leave before y'all saw her. I'm so sorry."

"It's all good, cowgirl. We'll get through this. We're in God's hands. Bennett, do you want to go with me or stay?"

The boy's troubled gaze darted between his sister and father.

Reno tapped the hood of his truck. "I thought I'd take these two to my sisters' bakery. How does that sound?"

Sister and brother both nodded.

"That's a great idea. Your sisters' pastries make everything better." Mundo patted Reno's shoulder. "Thank you, son. You've been a blessing to my family."

"I've learned more from you than I had in all my years in school. Which might not be saying much, but it means a great deal to me. You're a good man, Mundo, and a great father."

Mundo grabbed him and pulled him in for a full-out hug, slapping him on the shoulder. "Thank you." With that, he turned and went back to the barns.

The air was heavy. Reno had a job. He had to bring back the smiles. "Y'all ready for the best sweets in the world? We need to get to town before they sell out of everything."

Should he tell a story or a joke? What did they need right now to deal with today's pain? He sighed. Today was an accumulation of years of broken promises and hurt. He was at a loss how to make it better.

Silence filled the cab of his truck as they passed the city limit sign.

CHAPTER TEN

THERE WAS A muffled sniff from the back seat. Bennett was trying to hide the fact he was crying. Lyrissa's heart was twisted with guilt and the unfairness of life.

"Bennett?" She turned around and reached over the seat. "Hey. That was a rough scene back there. It's okay if you're upset, angry, confused or all the above. This is a safe place—you can talk to us. You know you can tell me anything."

The silence hung heavy in the air as they gave him space to speak. He adjusted his position so he was looking at them instead of the passing landscape. "Is she going to make us leave?" His voice was low and shaky.

"Oh. No, sweetheart. I've got you enrolled in school. Dad is on both of your birth certificates as your father. Something we're all grateful for. This is your home. For as long as you want."

Reno nodded in agreement. "If she leaves, she can't make you go with her. She would have to go to court, and I don't see her doing that. And no judge would take you away from a stable home."

"Why did she come back now?" Bennett asked. "How can she show her face after what she did? Then pretend to love us. We shouldn't have left Ray-Ray with her."

"I don't think she pretends to love us. It's the addiction. It's loud and demands all her attention. It lies to her, and she turns around and repeats those lies as if they're truth. I wouldn't have left him alone with her either. He's with Mew-Maw. And Dad is on the ranch. She might be our mother, but we don't have to trust her."

"But she is our mom."

Reno tapped the top of the steering wheel and glanced in the rearview mirror. "She is. God has known from the very beginning. He won't let you go. You also have two great siblings you can count on. And a grandmother and father who will do whatever it takes to protect you."

He eased past a slower car whose occupants were sightseeing. "I lost my dad when I was very young, and your father filled that gap for me. Your mother might not be the kind of mother you need, but there are other women in your life who will fill that role. Women you can rely on to have your best interests at heart. Families are a mix of people we are related to and people who come into our lives as we need them, if we pay attention."

He was messing this up. Life was so much easier if he was just expected to make people smile. "Does any of that make sense?"

"No." Bennett huffed and flopped back against the seat.

He glanced at Lyrissa. Oh no. She had tears in her eyes. She didn't cry. What had he done? "I'm sorry."

"No, don't be." She smiled at him and waved at her face. "Ignore this." Not a huge, laughing smile, but a sincere, gentle curve of her lips. "You're right." She looked back at Bennett.

"I had other women who stepped in and guided me as any good mother would. First Mew-Maw. She's tough but she'll always be on your side. Trust her. I also had my best friend's mother. Reno's mother. Ms. Espinoza. She's the one I think of when I think what a mother should be. All of Reno's older sisters are outstanding role models. We can learn what not to do from our mother, but we can learn how to love from others. You'll get to meet a couple of his sisters today."

Reno parked in front of a colorful storefront on the corner of a strip. People filled the chairs and tables, which were arranged under a colorful awning. "They have so much love to give they had to open a bakery to let it flow over to the whole county."

He was right. His family was a cornerstone in the community. Her family, not so much.

OPENING HIS DOOR, he paused. Everything felt unresolved. They had allowed Bennett to talk about the reappearance of their mom, but Lyrissa hadn't really said anything. "We told Bennett this was a safe place to talk about what happened. It is for you too. I also know you hate coming into town. How are you doing?" He resisted the urge to reach out and hold her.

She chuckled. "I was so ready to get off the ranch I didn't even think about the people I might see in town. You know what? I'm not going to let the gossip and judgment stop me from doing something I want to do."

She reached across his cab and took his hand. "I forgot I had more friends than enemies in Port Del Mar. I allowed them to take up too much space in my brain. I'm looking forward to seeing your sisters again." Turning away from him, she studied the ocean across the street. Her throat worked as she visibly swallowed. "As for my mom? I'm so angry and scared. It's complicated and I'm not sure what to do."

She shook her head and looked at her brother. "When I saw her standing there, I just wanted to get her off the ranch before she could see any of you. I thought if I could keep her far away, I would be protecting you from getting hurt. I don't trust her. I don't think I ever will. But my dad, our dad, has forgiven her over and over. As much as I love him, I resent his forgiveness of her actions. I'm afraid to be like him or that I might be like her if I let myself have fun."

Now holding Bennett's hand, she squeezed it. "If you're confused and hurt, it's okay. So am I." She turned to Reno. "Thank you for offering to take her to your mother. I'm not sure if that would have been fair to your family, though."

"My family can handle anyone or anything."

"People are starting to stare. We should go in?"

"I'm hungry." Bennett took off his seat belt.

"Okay, get ready for lots of questions. They've noticed how much time I've spent at the ranch and have been sending out scouts to gather information. Since your visit to the hospital, they've turned up the heat. Bringing you here will be a total free-for-all." He put his hands on his steering wheel. "What was I thinking? This was a bad idea. Let's go somewhere else."

His sister Josefina opened the glass door and waved at them, then lifted her hands as if to ask what the holdup was.

Lyrissa laughed. A lightness began in her chest she wouldn't have thought possible. "I think it's too late. If you drive away now, it will look so much worse. The whole pack will be after you. I don't think you could return home."

Bennett's eyes went wide. "How many sisters do you have? You can stay with us. We have an extra bed upstairs. You can have the big one."

"I might have to take you up on that. I have my mother, five sisters and a brother. All older. All but two live in town. Three of my siblings live on the same street as my mother."

"Do you still live with your mother?" Bennett sounded horrified.

"I live in an apartment over the garage."

Bennett raised his brows. Great, now he was being judged by an eight-year-old. "You know, it's not unusual in our family to live with multiple generations. My mom's getting older and—"

"It's okay. We're also multigenerational on the ranch." She looked at Bennett, chin down and her brows raised. "Come on, let's go. Reno is procrastinating."

"That is probably true," he agreed with a chuckle.

Josefina held the door open for them. "Come in. You're just in time, *mijo*. We need a man's opinion and now we have two. It's good to see you again, Lyrissa. This must be Bennett. Hi. I'm Josefina." She hugged Reno then Lyrissa. "Can I hug you? We're huggers unless otherwise told." She grinned and opened her arms.

Bennett dropped his chin but stepped into her hug.

"Follow me." The whimsical seating area was a mix of fairy-tale tea party and traditional Mexican flare. Two of his nieces were behind the counter. They waved and came around to hug him and greet his guests. "So, Tio Bridges is turning an eye away from child labor laws."

Nica, Josefina's daughter, rolled her eyes, but had a big grin on her face. "We tried that, but a family-owned business doesn't count."

His sister swatted at him. "Stop that. The girls are hardly here part-time. With Resa's wedding, we're shorthanded." She went through the back doors. "All hands on deck. You're coming, aren't you?" She glanced at Lyrissa as she held the swinging door open.

They stepped into a dreamland of pies and fancy cakes. Reno had grown up with his sisters' baking brilliance, but this was on a whole new level. "Has Resa or Enzo seen this?" They were the happy couple getting married next weekend. They were both low-key when it came to events and parties.

Margarita, his oldest sister, popped up from behind the sweet monstrosity. "*Mijo!* We're having a difference of opinions about the groom's cake and pie bar."

"Pie bar?" His gaze went over the twenty different pies sitting on a menagerie of pedestals.

"We are also having a lively debate about the wedding cake." Josefina moved to the side of the table that held four different wedding cake tops. From glass swans to a cowboy couple, each a different style.

"No. We are not discussing the cake. I have decided and it's done."

"You cannot make a seven-layered cake with a carrot cake–cream cheese mix."

"I can and I will." They kept arguing.

He mouthed *sorry* to Lyrissa and Bennett.

She giggled.

He cleared his throat to get their attention. And he had been worried they were going to grill him. "I don't understand," he said carefully. "Shouldn't Resa and Enzo be the ones to decide?"

Margarita threw her hands up and rolled her eyes. "You would think so. But she says she just wants a simple cake. She also wants a carrot cake and cheesecake. She says that as if that is a thing. Do you know how hard it is to make a carrot cheesecake that has the right level of moisture? To top it off, it must feed three hundred people." She rubbed her head.

"That is why I say we just make the top for her and the rest one of our nice traditional flavors."

"Have you tasted my carrot cheesecake?" She cut a big slice, grabbed three spoons then marched over to him, Lyrissa and Bennett. "Here." She handed them each a utensil. "Try this."

They all did as were told. His eyes went wide. He was used to the wonders his sisters created but this was... He swallowed. "This might be the best thing I've ever eaten."

Bennett nodded as he went back for a second scoop.

"I agree. I would have never imagined putting a carrot cake and a cheesecake together. This is...incredible." Lyrissa took another spoonful.

Margarita looked angry. He wanted more cake, but he stepped back.

"See." His oldest sister waved her hand around. "If I make just the top with this a few people will get it. Then we have three hundred other people upset because they hear about this cake, but I didn't make enough for everyone. That is not something I would do."

The sisters were in the middle of a staring contest. Risking their wrath, he stepped between them. "You're both right. Have you talked to Mom?"

In unison, they sagged. "No," his sisters said at the same time. "She already has too much on her plate, so we said we had this covered."

"I agree that when people come to an event hosted by the Espinoza family, they know they are going to be fed well. It's more complicated, but what about a small traditional cake then cupcakes instead of a traditional seven-layer cake?"

"Oh. We can use fancy tulip liners and make them look like flowers. That's a great idea." Margarita rubbed her hands together. "We'll have to get a couple of stands. Wood painted white, four tiers."

"That'll work." Josefina nodded. "We would need less pies." She looked at Reno and Bennett. "Enzo is also not much help. He says he prefers pies to cake. I ask which pies. He says all. I try to corner him. Pecan? He says yes. Apple? Again, he says yes. Cherry? Chocolate? Yes and yes. You know what he said next?" She looked at them like they were the ones causing problems. Trying to be agreeable, they shook their heads. Reno would laugh aloud if it wouldn't upset his sister more than she already was.

"He says he also likes chocolate peanut butter pie, key lime, coconut cream, banana cream, strawberry and lemon meringue. Then he nodded his head and said 'I like all those.' He tells me to pick the one I want to make, and he'll be happy. What am I supposed to do with that?"

"So, we decided to make a pie bar. We were going to do ten, but I think with the cupcakes we should cut it back to five or three. Enzo is not going to be able to eat all of them anyway."

"Will you sample the pies and vote on the ones you think will make Enzo happy?"

With a hand on Bennett's shoulder, he tried to get his most serious face on. "It sounds like a tough job. But we've got this."

Bennett grinned. "I like your family's problems."

He laughed and he looked up at Lyrissa. She was smiling but it looked sad. He'd do anything to make her happy. But that wasn't his job. He focused on the pies.

His sisters were talking about the wedding to Lyrissa, but he didn't understand half of it. After a sample of each pie, he talked over the pros and cons of each slice with Bennett. It was serious stuff.

Margarita handed him a notebook and pencil. "Just write down the ones you like in order." She paused. "Oh. I'm sorry. I didn't… Do you…"

"It's fine. I'm good. Bennett and I got this. I know my numbers." He winked at her. Ever since they found out his secret, they had started acting like he was a helpless kid all over again.

"He's been doing great." Lyrissa filled the awkward silence.

"Oh, I'm sure he has. He is obviously super smart to be able to hide it so long from us. But I'm sure that's not the only reason you've been spending so much time at the Herff Ranch."

And there it was. "I've been working as a part-time ranch hand. There's a lot of work that needs to be done."

Josefina joined them. A sly grin on her face. "Could be that we'll have another wedding to plan soon? You laid it on pretty thick in the hospital, baby brother." She wiggled her brows.

"Stop. You look ridiculous. You're a mother." He wouldn't allow his sisters to embarrass Lyrissa. "Just because you're taking credit for Resa and Enzo doesn't make you matchmakers."

His oldest sister leaned a hip on the worn farm table and looked at Lyrissa. "You know he always had a thing for you, but under all that charm and swagger he's pretty shy."

He rolled his eyes. "That's enough. We came to pick up some sweets for the house. Their mom is back on the ranch, and we came to town to get the best pastries around. A few empanadas and cookies. We don't need unsolicited advice."

She opened her mouth, but before she could get any words out Nica came through the swinging doors. "Mom. We're out of pecan pie in the front, and someone wants a slice. Do we have any more?"

"Yes. I'll bring it out." She picked up a pie and headed for the door. "So much to do and not enough time to get it all done." She paused with her back to the door. "Maggie, we'd be smart to have someone who's not family watch over the pie table." She pushed through the door.

"Josie does have a good idea every now and then." As far as he knew, they were the only ones ever allowed to call each other by those nicknames. His sisters were great people, but they exhausted him.

"We just came by for the goods. Are there any empanadas left?"

"No. We ran out about an hour ago. I have a pumpkin and strawberry already mixed for the morning. I could throw some together if you can wait."

"Oh, please don't do that." Lyrissa shook her head. "You have so many other wonderful treats. We'll save the empanadas for another day."

"Okay." She reached over and squeezed Lyrissa's hand. "Is everything okay? Is your mom in a good place?"

His heart slammed against his chest. This was the reason she hated coming to town. His sister had only good intentions, but still.

"We don't know yet." She nodded to Bennett. "We came into town to give her space to settle and for us to…be okay with it. She's staying with Mew-Maw in the main house."

"That's good. If there is anything we can do to help, let us know. You spent so much time with Savannah growing up, you're an honorary Espinoza." She leaned in with a smirk. "And another Espinoza might have a crush on you."

"Will you stop?" He had known this was a bad idea. "You do realize that you make people extremely uncomfortable?"

He couldn't believe that his sister was actually saying these things aloud.

"Oh, hush you. You would help her in a heartbeat."

"I would, but you're making more out of it than you should. You think you're being clever or cute. Well, you're not." He shoved his hands in his pockets.

Lyrissa patted his arm. "It's okay. She's just being a big sister. I always wanted one."

"Well, now you have two. Be careful what you wish for." Margarita laughed at her own joke. "There is something you can do for us." She held her hands up. "Feel free to say no, but we do need someone to keep an eye on the dessert table during the reception. Restock if needed. You wouldn't have to stand there all night. There might be someone who wants to get you on the dance floor. If you say yes, well, we would all be thrilled."

"Yes. To helping with the pies and cakes. No to dancing."

"What? You wouldn't want to dance with me?" He cleared his throat. That sounded way too high-pitched.

"That's not what I meant," she stammered.

He laughed. "Sorry." They needed to leave. His sisters had him acting like a child.

Lyrissa swatted him. "Now who's making this weird and awkward. Let's check to see what we can take with us."

He was coming to realize that dating Lyrissa would be a lifelong wish come true, but one look at her unamused face told him it was never going to happen.

"Y'all are both weird." Bennett grinned at Reno. "You should just date and make everyone happy. And I vote for the chocolate peanut butter pie. That would make me very happy."

If he had his way, he'd want to make the whole Martinez clan happy. They deserved it. But like so many of his other wishes and desires, it was beyond his capabilities.

CHAPTER ELEVEN

LYRISSA'S ROOM WAS full of light as she swayed side to side. In the mirror, the skirt swirled around her. She didn't wear dresses often and it made her feel pretty. She had been at Resa's bachelorette party when she confessed to Josefina that she didn't have anything to wear to the wedding. Which immediately prompted everyone to move from the kitchen where they were wrapping mason jars with ribbons to Josefina's closet, where they made her try on several dresses.

She almost teared up at the memory. It wasn't just Reno's sisters. She had been surrounded by cousins, coworkers and friends. She had never felt like she belonged anywhere. Until now. The place she ran from. Why was it so different this time?

Reno was right. She had been the one to keep people out. Last weekend, they pulled her in and didn't let go. Tears burned in her eyes. *Nope. Not getting emotional or attached. Refocus.*

Holding the soft material, she swirled again. The bold floral print of pinks, yellows and greens was not anything she would have ever tried on.

"Oh, baby girl. You're beautiful." Her mother came up behind her, laying her hand on Lyrissa's shoulder as they made eye contact in the mirror. "You're the best of your father and me."

Stuffing back a sigh, she smiled at the woman who had given her life and her biggest heartbreaks. "Thanks. You look nice too."

Every time they talked, her mother cried. At first, she saw it as manipulation. Now she wasn't so sure. Her mother seemed to be really trying and not pushing herself into the family.

There was so much pain, but she couldn't let her mother's unresolved issues ruin her family's life. She went to her dresser on the other side of the room and pretended to get something.

Dee sat in the chair at her desk. "I hear you and Mom are going early to help set up. That's very nice of you." She plucked at something on her skirt. "Your dad is taking me. I was thinking of not going, but Mundo loves to dance. I promised your dad I wouldn't drink. I promise it to you too."

"Don't worry about making promises, Mom. Just do the right thing. I'm not worried about others. I've decided that people not in my circle won't be allowed to keep me from being happy with the people I love."

"What? Everyone loves you. Just like they love your father. There are so many gossips in Port Del Mar, and they don't want me to be happy." Tears threatened to fall again. "Your dad is talking to me again and that's all that matters. I don't want to mess it up." She smoothed her skirt. "I have something to give you."

Without another word, she disappeared. On her way out, she passed Mew-Maw.

"What was she doing?" her grandmother asked.

"I'm not sure. She said she has something to give me." Lyrissa didn't have a good feeling. "Any ideas what it might be?"

"With that girl, I have no idea." Her grandmother was wearing a denim skirt with a white blouse, tall boots and lots of turquoise jewelry.

Dee came in with a box. She held it out to Lyrissa. "When I saw these, I hid them so Harrison couldn't pawn them too."

Tears were falling. "I'm so sorry. If you never forgive me, I understand."

Taking the box, she lifted the lid. It was her great grand-mother's necklace and wedding ring. It had more sentimental value than monetary. She thought they were lost forever. What was she supposed to say to her mother? Thanks for returning something she stole?

"I know you didn't trust me with them, Mom, but see? I took care of them." The silence was heavier than the elephant sitting in the middle of the room.

A knock on her doorframe saved her from spilling the heated words that were boiling under the surface. A very dashing Reno stood there, in a tux.

"I'm sorry. Do I need to come back?" He hesitated. "Or should I remind you that we need to leave now?"

She put the box on her dresser and grabbed her clutch. "We need to leave. They'll be waiting and you have pictures to be in." Without making eye contact, she rushed past her mother.

"Lyrissa?" Dee's voice carried all the hurt of someone who's been betrayed. How did her mother always manage to see herself as the victim?

"Not now, Dee." It was petty, but she knew it hurt her mother when she called her by her name. She kept moving forward and headed straight to Reno's truck.

On the porch, she stopped. His truck wasn't there. The door opened behind her. She turned. "Where's your truck?"

"I thought we would look too good to be in that old work truck, so I borrowed Mom's SUV. She's with Margarita and didn't need it." He shrugged.

Mew-Maw stepped out behind him, laughing. "You borrowed your mom's car to take your girl to a dance. Does that make me the chaperone?"

Lyrissa glared at her grandmother. "Stop it. Reno and I are just friends. Why is everyone giving us a tough time about that?"

"Maybe because we all see something you're denying." Mew-Maw winked at Reno as if they were in on a joke together.

He opened the back door and helped Mew-Maw in the vehicle. "I'd say it's more likely that we're your chaperones. Someone needs to keep you out of trouble."

"Oh, I could use a bit of trouble. Keeps one young." She climbed in and clicked her seat belt.

Reno moved to the front passenger door. "Your carriage awaits, my lady." He bowed. "You look beautiful, by the way."

Heat climbed up her neck. "Thank you. You look rather dashing yourself."

They all settled in, sitting in silence as he drove the SUV off the ranch.

"Everything okay?" Reno asked.

"Sweetheart." Her grandmother's voice was uncharacteristically soft. "It's okay to be mad. She had no right to take a thing from you. But then to present Granner's jewelry as if it were a gift?" She clicked her tongue.

If she attempted to talk, she would cry. *Please Lord, remove this bitterness from my heart.*

"Is that what happened before I interrupted?" Reno glanced at her. The concern in his eyes was her undoing.

She nodded. "I don't understand why or how she is the person she is." She looked back at her grandmother. "You've been a solid rock for me. Daddy has always been there for me and for her. He never calls names or is harsh in any way. What happened to her? It scares me. She's my mother. What if…" Some fears were just buried too deep to unearth. "What happened to make her this way? I want to understand."

Her grandmother leaned forward and patted her shoulder. "She was such a sweet child, but stubborn. A true daddy's girl. We always butted heads. When I complained about her attitude, Gavin would laugh. He said we were too much alike."

"But I've never seen you drink, and you would never steal

from anyone, especially your family or the church. She didn't learn it from you."

Her grandmother stared at the passing landscape. "When Gavin was killed in the accident, I lost my partner. My best friend. *My rock.* We lost the person who kept us balanced."

Her gaze went to her hands where she was twisting her wedding band. "I'm old-school, you know. Raised by a Texas rancher who was raised by a Texas rancher. This land can be harsh, and you got to be tough to build a home here."

"But you've never given me anything but love and support." Lyrissa reached out her hand. The work-worn, leathered skin of her grandmother grasped her in return.

"I'm happy to hear you say that. But I didn't react to his death with the grace that Reno's mother did at the loss of her husband."

"My mother had my older sisters and Bridges. A lot of the burden fell on his shoulders to keep the family together." His gaze shifted to the rearview mirror for a moment, then went back to the road. "I was too young to understand or appreciate it at the time, but it might be the reason I learned to hide any problems I had. I didn't want to upset anyone. If they were happy, then my world was safe."

Her heart twisted at the thought of a small Reno who believed his value was making others smile. She longed to hold his hand, but nope. No. She turned to her grandmother.

"Mew-Maw. This is not your fault."

"I gave her three days to cry." She tapped her chest three times. "That's what I said. Three days. Then we had a ranch to run. Life didn't take a break for death. She was fifteen and I denied her time to feel her grief."

"Oh Mew-Maw. You denied yourself too."

Her grandmother nodded. "Yes. When you came home this time with my grandbabies that I didn't even know about?" She shook her head. "I broke. I couldn't take it. I went to Pastor Rodriguez for help."

"Really? You always said—"

"Posh." She waved her silver-and-turquoise-covered hand at Lyrissa. "I repeated what my grannie and daddy told me. And it is a bunch of hogwash. Look at Reno and his family. They've suffered tragic losses and tough times. I wanted to know how they did it. Pastor Rod has been immensely helpful. One of the first things he gave me was this little book on the seven stages of grief. Do you know anything about it?"

"I do. And it's not only a process we need to get through the death of a loved one, but any major loss." She sat back. The epiphany of her own grief swamped her mind. Her mother wasn't dead, but somewhere in her early childhood she had lost the mother she had loved and trusted.

Some of the anger dissipated. It was okay to grieve the mother she had lost. It was okay not to trust Dee or expect any motherly reactions from her. She had her brothers, her father and Mew-Maw. They were her family and loved her as much as she loved them.

Reno nodded. "You're going to come through this and be stronger. So will the boys with family support."

"And counseling," Lyrissa said, agreeing. Determination replaced anger. "I'm grateful she brought them home. I am not going to let her take them away. Even if it means I have to stay in Port Del Mar."

"Oh, you don't need to worry about the boys," Mew-Maw said with a reassuring firmness. "Your father has that under control. He has a lawyer drawing up paperwork. She isn't getting a free pass from him any longer."

"Really? Why hasn't he talked to me about this? I was surprised when Dad didn't let her move in with him." Lyrissa shook her head then grinned at her. "It was a total role reversal. It was the first time I saw him stand up to her and tell her no. That gives me hope more than anything else."

"Holding her accountable is the only way she has a chance of getting better. Your dad sees that now." Mew-Maw flopped back against the seat. "If I hadn't been so hard on her after the death of Gavin, I might have a different daughter."

"Or not," Reno said. "Never seen redoing the past done successfully, even in fiction." He grinned. "But you have today. You have God, and you have each other. That's one life lesson my mom made sure each of her kids understood. *Mi familia.*"

"And tonight is about celebrating that." Warmth snuggled in around her. And for the first time since stepping back into Port Del Mar, gratitude hummed in her heart.

Mew-Maw snapped her fingers in the air. "Dancing. You're saving one for me. And my beautiful granddaughter." She clapped with childish joy.

Shaking her head, she looked at Reno. She knew without a mirror that her cheeks were red. "You don't have to dance with me. I have two left feet."

He winked. "So, we'll only turn to the right. You owe me a night of dancing." He whispered it low and soft as if making a promise...or a threat.

Reno parked the SUV by the back door of the bakery. It didn't take long to load up the pies and cupcakes. The aroma made her mouth water. Reno looked at her with a knowing gaze. "I don't think they will miss one or two."

She put her hand up. "Don't you dare tempt me. You're a bad influence, Reno Espinoza."

"I'm good at everything I do." He winked and she groaned.

Mew-Maw laughed. "Come on, you two. Stop flirting and let's get the pies set up."

Reno joked around with Mew-Maw. Once they arrived at the Painted Dolphin, she found Elijah, the owner. He directed them to the tables set up for the desserts.

Josefina was putting the last touches on the wedding cake. "Remind me to never again insist on making the cake for a wedding when I'm also a bridesmaid. I'm too old for this."

She placed the last tiny sugar flower on the side of the round top cake. It was exquisite.

"You'll forget by the time the next wedding comes around," Reno told her.

"You're the only one left, baby brother. So, I guess I don't have to worry about it."

"What? You're my first choice for best man. Or do you think I'm not getting married?" He took the spoon out of the extra icing and licked it. "Hey Lyrissa, want to lick the spoon with me?"

Josefina took the spoon from him. "I'm going to hit you over the head with this if you don't behave. So sorry Lyrissa that you got put on babysitting duty for my brother."

"What?" Reno pressed his hand to his heart in an overly dramatic move. "No. You got it wrong. I'm on bodyguard duty."

The DJ was setting up and doing sound checks.

"This is a great song. Dance with me." He held his hand out to Lyrissa.

She glared at him. "Don't you have prewedding duties too? What time are you supposed to be there?"

He shrugged and pointed to his sister. "I figure when she leaves, I leave."

Josefina was arranging the cake top over the tower of flower-looking cupcakes. From there, she joined Mew-Maw and helped her with the tea, lemonade and water station.

"Come on. One dance?" He gave Lyrissa his big, puppy dog face with that bottom lip sticking out.

Shaking her head, she put the last pie on a short pedestal. It really was pretty with all the spring flowers in mason jars and yellow ribbons. "Why am I surrounded by people who don't take life seriously?"

He looked hurt. Closing her eyes, she took a deep breath. "Sorry. I'm just on edge with Mom and—" She looked at the dessert table. "Your sisters are amazing, and they trusted me to set this up. Please let me focus. Find something useful to do."

With a sigh, he put his hands in the pockets of his black pants.

His sister walked by. "See? I told you he needed a babysitter."

"You people are way too uptight for your own good. When you get the chance to laugh, do it. Laughter is always an excellent choice." The smile was back on his face, and he started dancing in place.

"I'll dance with you, cowboy." Her grandmother put her hand out.

"Mew-Maw, don't encourage him."

He winked at her as he spun her grandmother into a Texas Two-Step. When the song ended, he took his sister's hand and made her dance with him. She was laughing.

Her grandmother joined her. Gripping her shoulders, she laid her head against Lyrissa's for a brief second. "It's okay to have fun. He's right, you know. Laughter is a good choice, and you need more of it. Don't let your mother take the joy out of life. Reno wants to see you smile. He's a good man. You should give him a chance. I've seen how he looks at you and how hard he works to make you smile."

Past the dance floor, the horizon was endless where the ocean met the sky. "I'm kind of tired of people who just want to have a good time."

"Oh, sweet baby. My heart aches to see you happy."

She made sure to give her grandmother a big cheesy grin. "I know you mean well, but I have a bucketful of worries before I even think about dating."

"I spent my whole life working hard and not making time to laugh or cry. I lost my best friend and then my daughter in the process. Don't miss the opportunity to find joy because you're caught up in the past or worried about the future."

Lyrissa pulled the container full of glass pie covers out from under the table. "Right now, our job is to cover the pies so we can go to the wedding." And she prayed her mother didn't have too much of a good time. This would be her first social event in Port Del Mar in years.

"I just don't want Mom to embarrass the family. The Espinozas are such good people."

Laughter floated from the dance floor. Reno spun his sister around several times. Her head was back as she laughed.

Her grandmother nodded. "Your father and I will have your mom. If something happens, hopefully we can de-escalate before anyone notices. Make sure you enjoy yourself." They stood side by side and watched Reno with his sister. "There's nothing wrong with having fun. Your mom just uses it to hide. Reno's not like that. His love for life is real. Give him a chance."

Josefina swatted at her brother's chest and stepped back. She looked over at them. "Are y'all all set?"

"Yes," her grandmother answered. "It's going to be a beautiful night."

Reno looked straight at Lyrissa. "It's already more beautiful than I imagined."

Words like that would lead her heart to cave. It would only end in heartbreak. There wouldn't be any happy endings for her in Port Del Mar.

"Do you have Mew-Maw?" she asked him. "I'm going with Josefina to the wedding so I can help with all the children. They have a small herd to get down the aisle."

She ignored the disappointed look that flashed in his eyes. She smiled and pushed on, not giving him time to say anything to change her mind. "I'll see you there." She followed his sister to the parking lot.

RENO LOVED SEEING his family happy. Resa's wedding had been as special as she was. Weddings and babies brought out the best in all his siblings.

He missed his sister Savannah, but he knew in his gut she had done the right thing by leaving with her husband. If it wasn't for Lyrissa, he'd feel very alone.

But she was leaving too. By the end of summer, she would be moving on to make a life somewhere else.

One of his nieces asked him to dance. No way would he ever say no to his siblings' children. He had to enjoy them; he wouldn't be having any of his own anytime soon…or possibly ever. That soured his good mood. This was not a time for those ugly thoughts.

It was a popular opinion he was too much of a kid to want to settle down. It was a false opinion, but he wasn't doing anything to prove them wrong.

"*Tio*, I want a wedding just like Tia Resa's," the eight-year-old said as he led her around the dance floor.

Enzo's family ranch had been covered in fairy lights. They led to the barn where his sister and Enzo Flores promised to stand by each other for the rest of their lives. And it wasn't one of those trendy fake barns. The working barn still had a couple of horses in the stalls.

Now the party had moved into town at the Painted Dolphin, with a dance floor on the large deck looking over the water.

"It was beautiful," he agreed. She went on in more detail. He scanned the area for Lyrissa. He spotted her grandmother.

Mew-Maw had taken the opportunity to make a deal with Enzo's father about borrowing one of their bulls. Reno had to grin. That woman would use her last breath to make the ranch better.

The Painted Dolphin was on the most popular pier in town. They even had a pirate ship docked right next to the large deck of the restaurant. The ship was set up for the kids to play. Bennett and Ray-Ray were both over there, having fun. Bennett had become fast friends with his brother's oldest son.

On Monday, he would be going to summer camp with his nephew. Cooper had invited Bennett to go home with Bridges and his wife tonight. It felt good to see the boys settle in and make connections in the community. He was proud that they were fitting in with his family.

The song ended and his niece ran off to join her cousins. He scanned the area for Lyrissa again. They were going to dance tonight, and she was going to smile. If he did his job right, he might even get to hear her laugh.

She didn't have to tell him how worried she was about her mother coming tonight. Her family was so focused on the unpredictable Dee, Lyrissa was often forgotten and left on her own.

Not that she asked him to worry about her. She made it clear that the friend zone had very strong barricades that he would not be crossing.

There she was. His heart lightened and his smile widened. She had returned to the pie table. Handing a plate to someone, she smiled, but it was her polite I'm-a-good-person smile. Not the one that made her eyes sparkle.

As he approached, she pulled a fresh pie from a cooler hidden under the table and removed the empty dish. She looked up and smiled. The same smile she had given the other person. That wouldn't do.

"The boys are having a great time in the pirate ship," he said as a greeting. She worried about them.

Her smile softened as she glanced over to where the ship was docked. The lights strung up the mast were reflected in the water. "That makes me happy. It looks straight out of a storybook. I'm so proud of the De La Rosas. Who would have ever guessed they would own half the businesses in Port Del Mar?"

"Hard work and dedication pays off. They're well respected. It didn't come easy, but they deserve it."

"It also took lots of faith." Elijah De La Rosa joined them. He picked up a plate with a piece of pecan pie and started eating. "God can work wonders when we open our lives to him. Your parents look happy tonight."

She laughed. It was a bit stiff, but he didn't think Elijah noticed. "Not something I would have ever predicted. But the night is still young. She has plenty of time to create a scene."

Elijah turned and scanned the dance floor. "The blessing and curse of a small town. Everyone knows you and everyone *knows* you. Can't hide the skeletons in the closet. Not when they want to come out and play. But like I said, with God anything and everything is possible. I'm a primary witness to that. If you need anything, let me know."

"Thank you."

He took the last bite of pie and nodded. "Have you checked out my pirate ship? It's really cool."

She laughed, a real laugh and Reno marked it in the win column. It was for Elijah but that didn't matter as long as someone reminded her to find joy in the day. Elijah moved to talk to another table. He was always playing host, making sure all was good.

"Come on. Dance with me." Reno held his hand out. "You've owed me since homecoming. And you've been watching your parents all night. You can get a closer look if we are on the dance floor."

She looked at the pies.

"No." He cut off any excuses her brain was forming. "I heard Josefina say that you just needed to keep an eye on the table to restock." He waved his hand over the delicious-looking table. His sisters did know how to feed people. "You just did that. So, unless you want me to get my sisters and tell them you are not having a good time, you better join me."

"Snitch." She tilted her head, hands on her hips. "Are you really blackmailing me with the threat of your sisters to get what you want?"

"Yep." He gave her his most charming grin. He held out his hand. "They can be a deadly force when their baby brother calls on them. But I don't need to ring the alarm, do I?"

With a shake of her head and a lopsided grin, she came around the table with her hand out. "Lead the way, cowboy."

Second point in the win column. He'd take it. He'd never felt lighter or prouder as he led her around the dance floor.

As they moved with the other dancers, he didn't see anyone but her. They were on the third dance when she pulled him back to reality.

"Have you seen my parents?" She was looking over his shoulder, then hers. "They were out here the last dance. I don't see them at any of the tables either."

"It's okay, Lyrissa. Your dad has her. Everyone is having fun. The stars are over us. The moon is full and round. The breeze is cool. It's a perfect night. Relax and enjoy." He spun her away from him then pulled her back. With her head back she laughed. Score three for him.

Her sigh was so heavy it vibrated up his arms. It seemed like a happy sigh. He gave himself another point. As the song ended the DJ called all married couples to the floor. He moved Lyrissa to the side. Most of his siblings gathered and started dancing.

His mother, a widow for most of his life, smiled. "It's good to see my babies settled and happy." She hooked her arm through his. "You're next."

"Mom." He would love to be half of a happily married couple, but he didn't see it happening anytime soon. The wedding coordinator came over and asked for his mother's help with something. The younger couples left the dance floor as the number reached fifteen years.

How would it feel to be part of a couple that faced the day together every morning?

Josefina joined them. Eight years ago, she had returned home from college with a newborn. No husband and he had never asked. She looked out at the couples with longing.

"Hey sis. You okay?" He hated it when anyone he loved looked sad.

"Yea," she sighed.

He didn't buy it for a minute.

He nudged her. "The other day at a men's retreat, old Jose

was asked how he'd managed to stay happily married for almost fifty years. You know what he said?"

She eyed him with suspicion and remained silent. Lyrissa leaned forward. "What did he say?"

Josefina shook her head. "Don't take the bait."

There were even fewer couples now that the number had reached thirty years.

"He told the young husbands, 'I treat her nice. Never went to bed angry. I spent some money on her. Best of all, I took her to Paris for our twenty-fifth wedding anniversary.' The men wanted to know what he had planned for their fiftieth wedding anniversary coming up. He proudly replied…" Reno paused, dragging out the suspense.

Josefina jabbed him with her elbow. "Get it over with."

"He said, 'I'm going to pick her up.'"

Bridges, who had come off the dance floor with his wife, laughed.

"That wasn't funny," his wife and Josefina said at the same time.

His brother grinned at him. "Come on. It was a little funny."

His sister snorted. "I got more important things to do than stand here listening to your dumb jokes."

"*Clever.* The word you were looking for *is clever,*" he yelled after her as she walked away. But she was smiling, so he had done his job.

"I see what you were doing." Her eyes were worry-free as she looked up at him.

He leaned back to get a better look at her. "And what was that?"

"It's okay to let people be sad sometimes. It might be what we need to get over whatever is running through our hearts. But out of love for your family, you have appointed yourself court jester and if you see someone slipping away from happy, you try to reset their course." She lifted her chin as if to dare him to dispute that.

"No comment." He loved that she really saw him, even in a way his family didn't, but it was also uncomfortable. "How about pie? I never got a piece, and you are queen of sweets tonight."

At the table, he picked up his favorite, pecan pie, and she was digging into a piece of key lime when Elijah came over. "Hey, would y'all step over here for a minute? I need to talk to you."

Reno's good mood evaporated at the other man's expression. Elijah was always a great host with an easy smile. This was something serious. Something they weren't going to be happy about. At least he was here to support her.

CHAPTER TWELVE

As SOON AS they were out of earshot, Elijah took a deep breath. "Your mom got upset when someone asked him to dance. There was a little heated discussion. Your dad didn't want it to turn into a scene, so he took her home. Edith picked up the little one. They said the older boy was going home with Bridges's family. Everything is fine and Mundo wanted to make sure you didn't worry."

Any fun she was having was gone. He could see it in the droop of her shoulders.

"Thanks for giving us the message." Reno offered his hand, and they shook.

"No problem." He put a hand on Lyrissa's shoulder. "You know I've been there myself on both sides. If you need anything, let me know. I can connect you to resources. Even if she won't get help, the family needs support."

She nodded. "Thank you."

Once they were alone, he took her hand. "Do you want to go home? I can take you."

"No." Her gaze went past him, at the party going on under the star-filled sky. "I knew this would happen. I hoped it wouldn't, but she hasn't really changed."

"Don't let this ruin a great night. Your father and grand-mother handled it."

Her glare came back to him, hot and hard. "They shouldn't have to handle her." She spun around and crossed her arms around her middle. "I want to be done, but I can't leave them. She needs to go to rehab, but she won't."

"Life's not fair and I'm so sorry you have to deal with this." Staying calm on the outside, he was frantically orchestrating a plan of distraction. "You said you missed the beach. The waves soothe you?"

He held out his hand and waited for her to take it for the second time that night. "It's a beautiful night for a walk on the beach. We can talk. I can tell you jokes."

She quickly shot that down with one hard glare.

He shrugged, not offended. "Or you can be sad. We can be silent, focusing on the texture of the sand and sound of the water. Maybe be still and listen for God's wisdom."

"Just about the time I think you are truly superficial, you throw in a curveball." She looked over his shoulder to the water behind him. "The beach does sound nice."

He took her around the edge of the party and down the pier. They were on the steps to the beach when Bennett found them.

"Is it true?" he asked. "Some woman flirted with Dad and Mom got mad. She got loud which means she was drinking, right? She promised not to drink. Why did you let her drink?"

"Bennett. I don't know what happened other than Dad took her home before there were serious problems."

"Mew-Maw picked up Ray-Ray and didn't say anything to me. They didn't tell me they were leaving. I need to get home. Ray-Ray needs me. I've always taken care of him when she gets like this. He'll be scared without me."

This was one of the reasons Lyrissa and he orchestrated the weeklong camp with Cooper. Bennett had put himself in the caregiver role for Ray-Ray out of necessity, but now there were adults to parent the boys and he could focus on being a kid.

She went to her knee in front of Bennett and looked at him, her hands firmly holding his upper arms.

"You have great plans for the weekend and the following week. We're not going to allow her to derail your joy. You have a family you can depend on. A family that will protect Ray-Ray and you."

His jaw was still tight. He stepped back and one of Lyrissa's hands slipped off his arm. But her other hand found the smaller one and held on, not letting him go.

Reno stepped next to her and put his hand on her shoulder. "Hey. He knows you have plans for the week. Great plans that you've been extremely excited about."

Lyrissa nodded. "Your job is to have fun and at the end of the week, come home and report back if the camp was as good as the hype." She pulled him to her and hugged him.

He was stiff at first but then awkwardly patted her. He wouldn't have done that a month ago.

Cooper came running down the pier. "Hey, Bennett. They're starting a new round. Are you still my partner?"

"I don't know. I'm thinking about going home."

"What? But you're staying the night. What happened?" Cooper came closer and lowered his voice. "Is it what Matt said about your mom? Don't let him get to you. He can be a jerk. I'll talk to my dad and make him leave."

"Don't make a scene. That's what my mom does, and I hate it. I just want to go home."

Cooper came closer and glanced at the two adults before turning his attention to Bennett. "Hey, I get it. Did you know I'm adopted? I'm not really a Espinoza."

"Yes, you are." Reno didn't like that line of thought.

Cooper smiled. "Sorry, Tio. They are but I didn't grow up here. My mom had problems with that kind of stuff too and she started lying a lot. We don't have to talk about it. I just wanted you to know I understand."

Reno had always liked this kid, but he just lifted him up

a level. Bridges would be proud of his son. Bennett didn't look convinced.

"If Ray-Ray needs you, I'll call." Lyrissa squeezed his hand. "I promise. You've been excited about camp. Don't let our mother take that from you. I did that too many times. If you stay with Cooper and go to camp, you'll be showing your brother how life should be lived."

He nodded. "Okay. But you'll call?"

"Yes. I promise."

He gave her a quick hug then turned to Cooper. "Come on, let's go beat them."

Lyrissa watched the boys run back to the pirate ship. Arms across her middle, she looked so alone. He wanted to pull her into his arms and shelter her from all the pain.

He reached out and waited for her to accept his offer. She looked down then glanced up. "I'm not good company right now."

"This is not about entertaining me. You need a friend. Let's walk on the beach since you don't want to go home. Or have you changed your mind? Is there somewhere you want to go?" he asked.

"I don't have anywhere else to go." She sighed and took his hand.

"As long as I'm around, you'll always have somewhere to go and someone to talk to. I've got your back. Always." She had his heart too, but that he kept to himself.

If all she needed from him was friendship, then that's what he would give her.

THE WAVES ROLLED in and out. Her heart followed the rhythm and calmed down. They were far enough away that her breathing finally slowed to a normal level. Why was she letting it upset her? Nothing had actually happened. It was just based on what could have happened.

Even if her mother had perfect behavior, people would be

watching and waiting for the worst. Including her. This was all her family would ever be known for.

"She doesn't reflect who you are. You know that, right?" Reno's gentle voice interrupted the downward spiral she was about to dive into.

She snorted. "In this town? I've been judged by my mother's actions my whole life."

"By some. Yes. But the people who really know you don't hold you up against her. More importantly, God doesn't judge you by your mother's actions."

She plopped down into the sand, and dug her toes in. She stared out into the horizon. Giant clouds billowed above the line that separated Earth from the sky. Dark blue and gold faded as the day slipped away. "My favorite thing about Port Del Mar was the sunsets. It might be the only thing I miss."

With a harrumph, he landed beside her. "Ouch. Good thing I have a tough hide."

It was safer not to respond.

"Hey. Don't let a few people ruin all the good. This is a great little town. Your dad and grandmother are here."

She sighed. He wouldn't understand fighting to fit in. "You have a family that people adore. One's in law enforcement. One is a beloved midwife, and two others own the best bakery for miles. Then there's your mother. She is everything my mother is not. Even you. Mr. Run-to-the-Rescue-and-Ask-Questions-Later. You've always been popular."

He leaned forward, crossing his arms over his bent knees. "Most of us struggle at one point or another. When Dad died, my mother had to raise seven kids on her own. People felt sorry for us. We were seen as charity cases. We were told to smile and be grateful even when it felt people were looking down on us. For some, it was more about showing how generous and wealthy they were. Look at us giving help to the poor Espinoza kids. People made comments that she shouldn't have had so many kids." He shrugged.

That had never crossed her mind. "I'm sorry. From my seat, it looked like you had everything."

He snorted. "On one level, I did. But I was also so worried that someone would figure out my secrets, I could never relax and be myself. I couldn't let anyone see the real me. It somehow became my job to keep everyone smiling."

"You're more than that. What about your happiness?" Heart racing, she reached out and touched his arm. "You're a good man."

Twisting, he looked away. "I'm not so sure. I've been pretending for so long." He turned back to her, and his eyes searched hers. "But with you I feel like I'm closer." His gaze lowered to her lips. *Oh. He is thinking about kissing me.*

Not wanting to give herself time to change her mind, she leaned forward and laid her hand gently on his cheek. She needed to be seen by him. To connect to him.

Eyes closed, she moved forward, and he met her. The touch was tentative at first. As soft as a butterfly landing then moving to another petal. He pressed his lips to hers to move back then came forward again.

She turned to get closer. Her other hand went to his shoulder. This was the closest she had ever felt to another human. Could she just stay here forever, wrapped up in his warmth?

He leaned back and caressed the side of her hair. "You're so beautiful. I'm not anchored to this town, you know."

Blinking, she tried to connect what he was saying to the present moment. Past the way he made her feel. Feelings like that were dangerous. "What does that mean?"

"It means I could leave if I wanted to. I can do any sort of work."

There was no way she heard him right. "Are you saying you would leave Port Del Mar for me?"

"Yes."

"You can't do that. Pleasing other people can't be the reason you do something. And what about being a firefighter?"

"If it's someone you...really like and their happiness makes you happy, then what's the problem?" He shrugged and grinned. His thumb traced her jawline. "It would be good for me too. I'll always be the youngest Espinoza here. I might never pass that test. As much as I want to change the role I've played my whole life, I don't know if people will let me."

Dropping his hand, he gave her space to breathe. Leaning back on his palms, he stared out into the ocean. The reflection of the setting sun was fading. The last bit highlighted his strong profile.

"I'd recommend Houston or Austin," he said. "Somewhere close enough we can come home if they need us."

"Reno. You're moving too fast. I like you, but you're talking about moving away from the only home you've known because of me?" The tightness in her chest made it hard for her lungs to work. "Plans have to be carefully thought out, and groundwork needs to be laid. You can't just decide huge, big life-changing moves on impulse. After one kiss. No matter how great it was."

"So, you admit it was great?" His gaze moved across her face and his smile fell at her serious look. He went back to the safety of the ocean view. His jaw flexed. Was he upset with her?

She reached out and placed her hand over his in the warm sand. "You can't be serious about leaving Port Del Mar and your family."

"Why not? You don't want to stay because you feel people just see your mom when they look at you. Why can't I do the same? My family casts a big shadow too. It's not an impulse. It's been in my head a while now."

"I'm not sure why we're even talking about it. My family is a mess and the last thing I need is any romantic entanglement to bring more drama into my life. I like you, I really do. Can we just spend time together and be friends while I'm still in town?"

He stood and dusted the sand from his slacks. "I'll follow your lead."

He offered to help her up, but his beautiful smile didn't have the same warmth as earlier. Was she overanalyzing and messing up a good thing? He dived in without looking. Was she being overly cautious and methodical?

"It's getting late. Let's get you home." In silence, they walked down the beach to the pier. Music and laughter could still be heard.

Reno opened his truck door for her.

She paused and looked at the lights strung across the patio where the celebration was still going full force. Then back at Reno to thank him for a wonderful night.

Reno was watching his sister dance with her new husband. One side of his face was highlighted with the warm glow, emphasizing the beauty of his features. It left the other side deep in shadow.

Everyone hid parts of themselves. Parts that weren't always easy to live with once they were revealed. She looked at the happy couple who were putting all their faith in love. That was terrifying.

"How do you think they have so much hope?" she asked. "Enzo already had one failed marriage. How do you think he's able to believe it will work this time? How does someone trust again? Like my father taking my mother back over and over." She was babbling and not making any sense. She didn't even understand her own mind.

"Your father is a man of strong faith and loyalty. I don't think he saw the damaged woman you see. He was fighting for the girl he fell in love with. As for Enzo? I don't know. I can only imagine he's seen a dark side of the world as an FBI agent. Coming home and turning his life over to God gave him a new outlook. I don't think it was easy. At one point, my sister thought she had lost him. Now they have everything they want because they trusted God and each other."

She pulled herself up into his truck and buckled her seat belt. He walked around and slipped into the driver's seat. "Reno. Thank you for getting me out of there. I'm sure you would rather be with your family instead of dealing with my drama."

"There was no real damage caused. Everyone was having a good time, and I don't think they noticed any problems before your dad and grandmother got her out of there."

"Only because of Elijah's help. I'm sure he didn't want a scene in his restaurant. That was so embarrassing. If no one noticed tonight, I'm sure they will hear about it tomorrow." She tilted her head back and closed her eyes.

"Elijah is not going to say anything. He's been there. He understands."

"Yeah, I remember his uncle. That man lived to cause scenes."

"You've been gone so you don't know, do you? Elijah is a recovering alcoholic. Everyone in town knew and a lot of people had written him off, including his in-laws. He lost his wife and oldest daughter for a while because of his drinking. He's been clean for about ten years. They've only been back together for a few years now."

"Seriously? Wow."

"He's someone who can help your dad."

She watched the landscape go by without seeing it. "I guess I get so caught up in how my family is so messed up, I see everyone else's as perfect." She sighed. "I'm also worried about the boys. They'll have to grow up in my mother's shadow like I did. There are already rumors about them. Should I stay?" Her brain was at war with her heart. Each answer had flaws, and each had benefits. But it came down to her living in Port Del Mar. The place she dreamed of escaping most of her life. "I can't. Not if my mother's here. I just can't deal with her and her legacy."

"You can get a place over the bridge. You'd be close enough to see the boys but not live with your mom. There are always options."

He was right. She didn't have to live on the ranch or even in Port Del Mar. She could take the full-time job and get an apartment in a town nearby. "I wish I had the type of faith you and my father have."

He laughed as he turned onto the dirt road going to her house, her dad's house. "Letting go of our fears and expectations to trust God fully is hard. My mom and your dad are great role models. You are too. Because of you I was able to find the faith to try for my dreams of being a firefighter again. You have it, you just have to trust."

They sat in silence until Reno sang along with the song on the radio. He winked at her. He made life seem so much easier than it was. How did he do that?

As he approached her father's house, he turned off his headlights. He parked in front of the porch and killed the engine. The phone between them vibrated. He flipped it over.

"It's a text from Elijah." His gaze scanned the screen. "He put a few extra desserts in the back seat. And he said to tell you not to worry. Everything is fine and if anyone—he emphasized *anyone*—needs help, he is just a call away. He wants you to have his number."

The thought of Elijah De La Rosa offering her family help made her eyes burn. She blinked a few times to push the tears back. "That's very kind of him."

Reno tried to get the dessert in the back seat. "Oh man!" He lifted his hand. It was covered in whipped cream and chocolate shavings. He licked the majority of the cream off his fingers. "What a mess." With his other hand, he lifted the brown paper bag by its handles. The Painted Dolphin logo was stamped on the side. He peered inside. "Good news. I only took out the top pie." He licked his fingers. "Bad news. The top pie is a goner. Can I come inside to wash this off?"

She took the bag from him. "Let me have this before you deprive anyone of the good stuff. Come on. I'll see if Ray-Ray is still awake. This is his first night without his brother. He deserves a treat."

He followed her through the dark house. The silence was heavy. "Did you say they made it home?"

"Yes. Dad said he took Dee to Mew-Maw's house. He put her in her old room and brought Ray-Ray home." She liked having Reno in the house. He made it feel so much safer, even with her mother around. She looked at her watch. "He is used to turning in early."

In the kitchen, she sat the bag on the table then turned on the light over the sink. He turned on the water, but nothing came out.

"Oh, sorry." She opened the door under the farm sink and dropped to her knees. "There was a leak and Dad didn't have time to fix it before we left so he just turned off the water." She popped back up, leaned across him and turned on the water. For a moment, they stared at each other. She was so close she could see all the details in his eyes, smell the clean fresh scent of him. Sea salt, leather and bonfires on the beach. She was too close.

Lifting her hands in the air, she took a step backward. "Ta-da! Modern wonders. Here." She handed him a towel then turned away before she kissed him again. "I'll get Ray-Ray. He'll think it a special treat to eat this late and with you."

Rushing up the spiral staircase, she counted to get her heart rate back to normal. She could not kiss him again. Once was a mistake; twice would be a disaster and it wouldn't be fair to him.

She came to the top of the landing and found the beds empty. All of them. The bottom bunk had been slept in. The sheets tossed aside. She checked in the bathroom. He wasn't there.

Leaning over the railing, she tried to stay calm as she called down to Reno. "He's not here. Ray-Ray's gone."

CHAPTER THIRTEEN

"DON'T PANIC. HE could be with your dad." Reno tried to reassure her as she ran for the hallway.

Reno thought through all the scenarios. Did he go to the barns? Or to Edith's house? That's where his mom was. That made sense. He grabbed the heavy-duty flashlight.

"He's not with Dad." She rushed back into the kitchen. "Should I call 911? Seriously, it seems like one emergency after another. I'm doing something wrong." A wild desperation burned in her eyes.

"You haven't done anything wrong. I'm sure he's close by."

A sleepy-eyed Mundo came into the kitchen behind her. "Yeah. He might be at Mew-Maw's. He had wanted to stay with his mother. But I said no. Then he wanted to get Benny and again I told him no. There is a slight chance he went to get his brother. They're used to walking everywhere. I should have slept upstairs with him. I knew he's never been away from Benny, but I thought this was good for him. I'm an idiot." Mundo was looking for something, digging through the drawers and moving things on the counter.

"No more than the rest of us. He needed me and I was hanging out on the beach." Guilt poured from her.

Reno put his arm around her and pulled her close for a second then let her go. He just needed to make contact to let her know he was here for her. "No one is to blame. We thought he was safe in his room. You were going to check on him. That's why we know he is missing this soon."

Mundo looked at the clock. "It hasn't been long at all." He now had a set of keys in his hand. "I'll drive slowly to Bridges's place. You go see if he went to his mom. If we don't find him between those two places, I'll let Bridges know he is missing."

Lyrissa made a whimper.

"Most of the time, kids are close by," he reassured her.

It took him by surprise when she reached up and touched his face. "You'll go with me?"

His heart was pounding. He covered her hand with his and intertwined their fingers. It felt so right. Making sure to smile, he lifted the big flashlight. "I'm ready. Let's go."

Her father headed out the front door. Reno paused at the back stoop. His heart tugged at him to speak to God. "Can I take a moment to cover us all in prayer? Is that okay?"

She squeezed his hand and nodded.

"Lord, we come to you in thanksgiving. We ask that you continue to protect Ray-Ray and all our family. We lift them up to you. Open our eyes and ears so we find him quickly. Let us tuck him safely into his bed. Open our hearts to your wisdom so we may help him with his fears and insecurities. In Your name we pray."

"Amen," Mundo said, then went through the door.

"Thank you. That was perfect." She was searching to the left while they walked. "When is he going to start trusting us? I should have been here instead of avoiding the house."

"Beating yourself up won't help." He scanned along the sides of the well-worn path to the barns with the flashlight. "He's most likely curled up with your mom."

She nodded. "Ray-Ray!" she called out again. A slight panic was on the edge of her voice. She gently pulled him to the barns but didn't remove her hand from his.

"Let's check the barns on the way to Mew-Maw's. He loves the horses." The barn door was open. "It was always my favorite place to hide when things got overwhelming."

He wanted to go back in time and hug little Lyrissa. To let her know she wasn't alone. Flashlight high above his head, he scanned the loft then the stalls to the right. He lowered the flashlight and went deeper into the barn.

Lyrissa was right behind him. "Ray-Ray," she called out.

"Shhhh." They both jumped at the unexpected female voice coming from the last stall. "He's sleeping." Dee's voice was low and gravelly. Lyrissa dropped his hand and rushed to the opened stall.

Reno followed her and found Dee sitting against a stack of hay. Her youngest was snuggled against her chest. One arm around her neck the other around something small and furry. The orange kitten was curled up in his lap. It would have been an adorable scene if they weren't so frightened.

This was not good. He didn't want to startle them with a light in Dee's face, but he really wanted to check her pupils.

"Mom?" Bewilderment filled the one word. Lyrissa went to her knees next to her brother. "What are y'all doing out here?"

There was a deep hollowness in Dee's eyes and voice that had him alert. He eased down to the other side. "Dee, are you okay?" He gently touched her arm. Closing her lids, she sighed. Her skin was normal to the touch. Lips and fingers were a good color.

His own breath came a little easier. He needed to call Mundo but he wasn't sure of the situation yet.

"Momma. Open your eyes. What are you doing in the barn with Ray-Ray? Reno asked if you are okay. Are you?"

There was a long silence. Dee finally lifted her lids halfway and looked at Lyrissa. With a weak attempt at a smile, she nodded.

Then she shook her head. "No. That's a lie. I've told so many lies. I can't do this anymore." New tears followed a well-worn path of wetness. She had been crying for a while. A shaking hand reached for Lyrissa, then dropped.

"I'm so sorry, baby. I'm not okay. No." She looked down and caressed Ray-Ray's hair. "I was going to leave. Walk to town and get a ride. But this sweet baby found me. He said he was looking at the stars, talking to God like his dad taught him. Then he saw me leaving Mom's. He wanted to show me his kitten. I thought about taking him with me."

Her face relaxed and a real smile slipped in for a minute. "I couldn't. Mundo's such a good daddy. I should have brought the boys home to him as soon as I had them." She raised her chin and gazed at her daughter. "Why am I so selfish? Daddy would be so ashamed of me. I was supposed to go with him to Dallas, did you know that? But my friends asked me to go to the movies. I should have gone. He wouldn't have fallen asleep. People said he was drunk, but that wasn't true. He was just tired. I've always been so selfish."

Reno laid a hand on Dee's shoulder. There was so much pain in every word Dee spoke. Lyrissa's expression was tight. Had she known the story behind her grandfather's death? He had a gut feeling the family didn't really have open conversations.

Lyrissa moved closer and smoothed Dee's hair. It was a wild, tangled mess around her face. "Mew-Maw says your dad was the best. You were just a kid. It wasn't your fault. From the pictures I've seen and the stories I heard, he loved you very much. And we both know people prefer drama over the truth. I'm grateful you brought the boys home."

Dee's gaze went over his shoulder. "My daddy built this barn. This is where your father first told me he loved me. I thought the world was perfect that day and I would be all right even with Daddy gone. But it didn't last. Your dad deserves someone so much better than me. I had been clean for two months and tonight because that woman flirted with your dad, I gave in. Just one drink, you know, to take off the edge. I hate hurting."

Her chin fell forward as she studied the sleeping boy snuggled up to her. "I messed it up for Mundo. Why do I do that? I had promised your dad I wouldn't drink. I've made so many promises to him and broke them all. He deserves someone better. So do you and the boys."

Lyrissa's phone vibrated. With a frown, she answered the call. "Mew-Maw?"

"Yes. I'm with her. We're in the barn." Her gaze darted from her mother to him. The vein in her neck pulsed harder. "She's fine. Ray-Ray followed her to the barn. He's asleep in her lap. Will you call Daddy for me and let him know. He's on the road, looking for Ray-Ray."

Blowing out a puff of air, Reno ran his hand through his hair. *Well, that problem is solved.*

He knew that Mundo had a worst-case scenario plan for Dee. Once he got here, Reno could focus on Lyrissa. She might play tough, but no one wanted to face this kind of trauma alone. Nor should they.

Lyrissa nodded. "Okay. I love you too." She slipped her phone in her back pocket. "Mom." It sounded as if she were about to cry. "Mew-Maw found your note. She said to tell you she loves you and she was very worried."

Tears fell down Dee's face. "No matter how hard I try, I always end up making it all worse. I'm tired of being the bad person in the family. You hate me."

"No. Mom." Lyrissa pulled her knees to her chest and hugged them close. The kitten looked up and meowed but stayed in the center of them.

His heart ached to take her in his arms and remove all the pain from her life.

"I never thought it was you, Mom. It's an addiction. It wants to control you. But you're not alone. Please, let us find help for you." She glanced at Reno. Tears were falling. "Should we call someone?"

"Dee, it's a horrible place to feel like you have failed everyone you love. But there are people trained to help you. As soon as Mundo gets here, I think you should talk with him about how you want to get help."

She reached out with her free hand to him. "Yes. Please. You know where I can get help?"

Taking it, he nodded. "The most important thing to remember is you're not alone."

"Thank you." With her free arm, she hugged her sleeping son closer. "He said he loved me, and I was his mommy. He asked me to stay. He promised—" A sob interrupted her words. She swallowed and kissed the top of his head. "He promised to be a good boy if I stayed. But he's already a good boy." Letting go of Reno, she reached a hand out to Lyrissa. "I'm so sorry for embarrassing you. I wanted to be a good mom but I..." She hung her head.

"I love you. I just want you to be sober."

"Dee?" Mundo rushed into the barn, pausing for a second at the stall door. He was out of breath. Reno stood to give Mundo space. He joined her on the ground and pulled her into his arms. He held on to her and Ray-Ray as if he'd never let them go. "Sweetheart, are you okay?"

"No. I'm so sorry Mundo. I'm so sorry." She was sobbing now.

Lyrissa gently picked up the kitten and handed him to Reno. Purring, the orange fluffball curled up against him. Then she untangled Ray-Ray from her mother and lifted him onto her shoulder "I'm going to put him to bed."

Her little brother opened his eyes. "Mommy?"

"I'm right here, baby." She stood with Mundo's help. "Let me take him." She reached for her youngest son.

"My kitty. Please let me keep Butter."

Reno stroked the fluffball. "Butter? You named him?"

He nodded. "Mew-Maw said butter makes everything better. He makes me feel better. Can I keep him?"

They turned to Mundo. He had had a strict rule that cats

belonged in the barns not the house. Mundo looked at Dee. "It's up to your mother. Can he keep the cat in the house?"

With watery eyes, she nodded. "That's a great idea. She can keep you company and make you better while I'm at the hospital getting help."

Mundo rubbed the boy's back with one hand and held on to Dee with the other. "I agree. Butter has a new home. You'll have to take care of him. Like your mommy said, she's been sick so I'm taking her to the hospital."

"Mommy, you said you wouldn't leave," he cried.

Dee wiped her face again. "I'm going so the doctors can help fix me. I'll be back. Your daddy will take me so he can tell you where I'm at. It might be tonight or in a few days. Will you let us tuck you into bed in case he takes me tonight? Your sissy will stay with you."

"I want to go with you." He reached for his mother and hugged her tightly around the neck.

"You stay here and help Mew-Maw, okay? I promise I'll be back." Tears ran down her face. "Me and your daddy will take you to the house. I'll read a bedtime story. Then I have to leave as soon as they let me in so I can get better. I promise…" She took a deep breath. "I really promise that I'll come back. Can I tell you a bedtime story?"

He nodded.

Lyrissa patted his back. "I'll be in the house soon. Do you want me to sleep upstairs with you?"

"Will you? You won't leave? And Reno. Will he stay?" Ray-Ray asked.

His heart melted a little. No one had ever turned to him for support during challenging times. His throat burned. He would not cry. He wouldn't. One corner of his mouth flipped up, but he couldn't get to the other side without it feeling like a grimace.

Lyrissa shot him a quick glance. "I will be by your side all night. In the morning, we will go get Bennett."

"What about Reno?"

He looked at Lyrissa. She gave him a quick nod of approval. "I'm staying right here as long as you need me. In the morning, I'll take you and your brother for breakfast at my sisters' bakery." The kitten touched his face with its soft paw. "And we need to go to the feedstore and get Butter all the house supplies he needs to move from the barn to your room."

"Okay." He reached for the kitten and the orange bundle of fur almost leaped from Reno to Ray-Ray. "He already loves me." He pulled him close and smiled with his eyes closed as he stroked the top of the kitten's head. The purring filled the barn.

Mundo and Dee took Ray-Ray to the house. As soon as they were out of sight, Lyrissa collapsed on the barn floor. Without hesitation, Reno rushed to her side and gathered her to him and surrounded her with his arms. Time had no measure as she sobbed.

He held her close and rocked her. Whispering words of care and support. He wasn't sure what he was telling her. He just wanted to fill the silence with comforting words.

Taking a deep breath, she pulled back and wiped her face. "I'm so sorry."

"Don't be. No reason to apologize." He wanted to pull her back into his arms and hide her from all the pain in her world, but she had made it clear that wasn't his job. "Like you've recently told me. Sometimes we need to be sad. She's finally willing to get help. That's good, right?"

With a sharp intake of breath, she swept the barn with her gaze. Her expression had grown hard as she put distance between them. She was isolating herself. "Where do we take her?"

Reno couldn't take it any longer. He reached for her and pulled her against his chest and held tight. She buried herself deeper into his arms. "Your dad has a plan. He already has a facility researched. He has one in Austin. In her current mental state, he might be able to get her in immediately. She'll be a priority. And she asked for help. That's huge, Lyrissa. As horrible as this night has been, it might be a blessing."

Sniffing, she leaned back. "Really? Daddy will be able to get her in tonight?"

"Probably. He had already spoken to her about it. He loves your mother, but he also knows the facts. If she's going to get better, she'll need professional help. I'm sure that's where he's taking her tonight."

The doors and windows rattled as the wind tried to push through. She stood. "I need to get myself together and into the house. They won't leave Ray-Ray alone and I need to go so they can get Mom to the center." She wiped her face with the top of her dress.

He wished he carried one of those old-fashioned handkerchiefs like his dad did. Or a bandanna. The urge to take care of her was so strong. He reached his hand out but she hesitated and slipped past him.

"I know it's asking a lot, but would you stay? I'm going to be upstairs with Ray-Ray, but I don't want us alone in the house. It's weird, but I...just feel so raw? I'll have to get Bennett in the morning and explain that Mom leaving is a good thing this time." Exhaustion shadowed her voice.

"Maybe let him go to camp. We can—" Before he could finish, her phone chimed.

"It's Mew-Maw." She answered and updated her grandmother. "Do you want me to come over?" She paused, listening. "Okay then. I'll see you in the morning. Mew-Maw, get some sleep. I love you."

Lyrissa hung up then tilted her head back and closed her eyes. "Dad called Mew-Maw. He'll be able to take her tonight. I'm so tired."

"Just like I told your mom. You're not alone. Are you ready to go to the house?"

With a nod from her, he led the way in the dark. He didn't offer his hand again. One rejection was all he was able to handle tonight.

IT WAS TOO MUCH. Lyrissa's emotions were all over the place and it hurt her heart and her mind. At this moment, she understood her mother's desire to numb herself. But that wouldn't help, obviously.

They stopped inside the kitchen. She didn't even remember walking to the house. When he had held her and let her cry, she felt safe enough to fall apart, like he could hold all the lost pieces until she was strong enough to pull them back together. That was dangerous. Holding his hand was off-limits.

"Lyrissa?" He said it as if he was repeating himself.

She blinked and looked up at him. Poor guy. His family was so wonderful. What did he think of hers? "I need to go upstairs." But she didn't move.

"I'm worried about you." He pushed her hair back. It had to be a mess. Wanting to lean into his touch, she forced herself to step away.

He asked, "Do you want your grandmother to come over?"

"No. No. I'm fine."

He raised both brows.

"Okay. I'm not, but I will be. I never gave it thought, why she chose to feed her addiction."

He pulled a chair out. "Here, sit. I'll make tea." Reno put the kettle on the stove for hot water. He pulled her basket of teas out of the cabinet. "Which one do you want?"

How had she ever thought this man was shallow and irresponsible? He'd been the surprising anchor in the wild waves of this life. It was so tempting to cling to him and hold on for dear life.

Her father came down the stairs. Good timing. A great reminder that she couldn't afford a man-made shelter from this storm. Her dad would be focused on her mom. She'd have to take a page from his favorite book. Have faith that God had her and her family would get through this. She stood. "I need to go upstairs."

Her father shook his head. "She wants to stay with Ray-Ray for the next hour. He asked her to read all the books they had up there. When she finishes, I'm taking her to the house to pack a bag."

"What can I do to help?"

"Stay up there with him when we leave. Pick up Bennett in the morning and let him know what is happening."

"Of course, Daddy. I'll do whatever you need. Are you okay?" This man had been through so much and had given everything to his wife.

He hugged her. "Yes. My faith is strong that God has us. This is the first time she's ever admitted to needing help and willing to go to rehab on her own. I don't know what the future holds, but I have real hope." He patted her back then let go. "I'm going back upstairs. You take the next hour for yourself. I know this has been hard on you. I'm sorry we weren't the parents you deserved."

"Daddy." She hated that he ever thought she was disappointed in him.

He kissed her forehead. He glanced over at Reno waiting by the archway between the kitchen and living room. With a nod to the other man, he went back up the stairs to his wife and son.

Reno walked over to her and held out a warm cup of tea. After she took it, he went to the counter and picked up a second cup. She just stood there watching him. Was he real?

He took a sip. "Sit. Drink your tea and let me know what I can do to help."

"You know, when all this started, I was the one helping you. Have you registered to retake the exam?"

"Aww. So, we're going to change the subject. Okay." He grinned at her. "I have. It's in about a week." He was staring into his tea. "It's not easy to ask for help, is it?"

"No. I think we all would rather be the hero than to be the one who needs saving." The silence between them was comforting as she sipped the soothing tea. "Is that why you want to be a first responder? You were great with my mother earlier. I froze. I didn't have a clue what to do, so I did nothing." She wanted to cry all over again. She brought the cup of tea up to her face and took a deep breath.

"I've had training. When something traumatic happens, if you have a plan then your mind will default to that. Your dad had a plan. That's reason he was able to get her moving. He was prepared."

"He was." She was so proud of her father tonight. "She's going to get the help she needs because he never lost faith." She closed her eyes and took another slow sip of her tea. The lemon-balm-and-lavender mix was her favorite. "You don't have to stay the night. Driving back over in the morning will be fine. It's been a long day for you."

"I'm good."

"Oh." She sat up and gaped at him. "Your sister's wedding. They must be missing you."

"Nope. They're good. I texted Mom to let her know I took you home. She said not to worry about coming back to the reception." He laid the phone on the table. "I need to let her know I'm staying here. I'll let Bridges know we'll be picking Bennett up in the morning."

"I feel horrible that you missed any family moments."

He laughed. "Then I must thank you. The only moment I missed was cleaning duty. Which I've done a million times, so I have credit." He took a sip, then his gaze went up to the loft. "What do you want me to tell Mom about why I'm staying tonight? She'll ask and not let it go until I give her an answer."

"That my mom has finally agreed to go to rehab. I don't think the rest is anyone's business outside of our family." Lifting her cup, she took a slow sip. "This is my favorite tea. Thank you. It has helped to calm my nerves and settle my brain."

He reached for her father's bible, which sat on the table. It was here in the hub of the house unless he was meditating in prayer. "My mother has verses for everything this world will throw at you. There's one in Philippians she uses a great deal." He flipped through the well-loved and used leather bible with confidence and knowledge.

"Here it is, 4:8–9. 'Finally, brethren, whatsoever things are true, whatsoever things are honest, whatsoever things are just, whatsoever things are pure, whatsoever things are lovely, what-soever things are of good report; if there be any virtue, and if there be any praise, think on these things. Those things, which ye have both learned and received, and heard, and seen in me, do: and the God of peace shall be with you.'"

At first, she didn't really understand. It wasn't one of the obvious verses that she expected. She took the time to process each word. "That's candidly beautiful. It's like a warning but full of hope all at the same time. God knows the world is a mix of beauty and brutality. It's God who can give us peace in the messiness of life."

They sat in prayerful silence. She finished her tea and stood to take the cup to the sink. "Thank you, Reno. That really helped."

"No problem. Happy I could help. Where am I sleeping? The sofa looks good."

"Are you sure you want to stay? I think you're longer than the couch."

He laughed. "I'm the youngest of seven kids. I can sleep anywhere. Just give me a blanket and pillow and I'm good."

"I can do that." She went to the linen closet and pulled out the extra bedding. Then she went to the sofa and made it up. She snapped the sheet open, then tucked it under the cushion. "Thank you so much for doing this. It's going to be so much easier to explain this all to Bennett with you there. The boys have really connected to you." It was also going to make her feel safer, but she didn't want to spend any time analyzing that.

"I'm glad I can help. Your brothers have become special to me. What I can't believe is your father has agreed to let a cat live in his house."

After fluffing the pillow, she spread the top sheet. "I love the way he let Mom be the hero. It'll help the boys while she's gone."

He nodded. "I hope I can be at least half as good a man as him."

She stopped fussing with the bedding. "What? Do you really think you're not?"

He shrugged. "I feel like I lied my way through life, and no one ever took me seriously. They still don't."

"You thought you were protecting the people you love from worry and stress. You didn't lie, just hid what you saw as flaws. You put your family's feelings above your own. You're a good man, Reno."

The sofa was now a makeshift bed. Hands on her hips, she scanned the room. Not a single thing left to distract her.

Reno stood in front of her. "Lyrissa? Talk to me. What's going on in that beautiful brain of yours?"

She shook her head. "I don't want to think about it. But… what if she changes her mind when it gets hard? It's not going to be easy to undo everything from the last twenty or thirty years."

He took both of her hands and sat her down in the chair. He sat across from her on the coffee table. "*You* will be okay. Is it going to be a happy ending with your mom?" He shrugged. "There is no telling. But she has a dedicated support system. The one thing I know for certain is you have the boys, your father and grandmother, and they have you." There was a longing in his gaze that made her uncomfortable. "I want to be here for you too if you let me."

She sat back and shook her head. "That's not fair to you."

"I can decide that. Are you sure it's not that you're scared to rely on someone else? On me? You think I'm untrustworthy. Too much like your mother?" His eyes held her gaze.

She had to close her eyes to break the intense contact. She wanted to reach out and hold on to him, but he was right. That would take a leap of faith she didn't have the courage for. She settled by touching his cheek with her hand. "I'm sorry I ever thought you were anything like my mother. You are a man of honor and can be counted on. But there is so much up in the air right now. I don't even know if I'll still be here in the fall."

He stood and moved away from her, then sat on the opposite chair. "Life's hard enough. No reason you should have to do it alone."

Breathing easier now that she had more space, she leaned back in her chair. "Can we just sit here until they leave. Then I'll go upstairs."

"As long as you need me and want me here, I'm not going anywhere." He looked around. "Do you want me to put on one of your dad's old records? We can play gin rummy."

"I'd like that." She settled into the oversize chair covered in a quilt made by her great-grandmother. The soft sounds coming from one of her father's favorite vinyls wrapped around her. Tilting her head back, she closed her eyes and took a few deep breaths.

They played a few rounds, but her mind wasn't on the game.

"Hey. You want me to look at the sink? I can have it fixed before your dad gets back."

She curled up tighter in her little nest. "That would be great. Thank you."

He flipped the record then went into the kitchen. She snuggled deeper into her great-grandmother's quilt and shut out the world. Reno made it easy to breathe and forget the stress.

She didn't have the right to feel this comforted with all the wrong going on in her family. Rolling her head to the side, she peeked into the next room where she heard a metallic clink. Reno was under the sink. She grinned. He might be always looking for a good time and finding ways to make others laugh, but he had a heart to serve others.

Comparing him to her mother had been blatantly wrong. One day, he would make a perfect husband for some incredibly happy woman. New tears threatened to fall, but not for her family this time. She knew she had to let Reno go. It was the only right thing to do for him.

It would be wrong to tie such a beautiful human to the train wreck of her life.

CHAPTER FOURTEEN

EVERYONE IN RENO'S truck sat very quietly, each lost in their own thoughts. He cleared his throat. "So, this doesn't mean you shouldn't go to camp with Cooper tomorrow morning."

Lyrissa nodded. "That's true, Bennett. I promise we'll call you if anything major happens. But at this point, there is nothing for you to do. She'll be safe in rehab, getting healthy."

"But what about Ray-Ray? He needs me."

Twisting in her seat, Lyrissa reached her hand out to him. "You're not alone anymore. You both have Daddy, Mew-Maw and me. Even Reno is here. You were excited about the camp. Show Ray-Ray how to carry on with the good things in life. Go to camp."

He gave her a nod but doubt still filled his eyes. She faced forward and discreetly wiped a tear away.

Reno glanced up to check on the boys. In the rearview mirror, they were holding hands. Ray-Ray nodded in agreement. "You wanted to go to camp. You should go. Lyrissa said she'd sleep upstairs with me until you get back."

THESE BOYS WERE too old for how young they were. "It's good that y'all are talking about it," Reno told them. "My brother said we can call him anytime today to let them know. Do what feels right." He found a parking spot on the boardwalk. It was thick with tourists, so they'd have to walk a few blocks to his sisters' bakery. "Ready for the best empanadas you've ever eaten?"

"Can I have a doughnut with chocolate milk?" Ray-Ray asked.

"Yes. But I'm also ordering a few different empanadas. You have to at least try one. They might change your whole outlook on life."

He helped Ray-Ray out of his truck and pointed out someone flying a kite. "Ray-Ray and I can pick up some kites or even try to make one while you're at camp. As soon as you get back, we'll come to the beach and fly them."

The boys were excited and picked their favorite ones that were in the air and guessed how high they were. Lyrissa stepped out from his truck.

With a smile that didn't look at all natural, she joined them. "Just talked to Dad." She stood between the boys and hugged them to her side. "Mom is checked in and she likes the place. He said it's really nice and she has pictures of us that are important to her. He'll be on his way home soon. We should pick up some of their freshly made cuernitos pan dulce."

Bennett gazed up. "A sweet bread?"

"Very good. Yes, it's light and flaky like a croissant. I'll stuff them with my chicken salad."

"We can grab a dessert too," Reno said as he started walking toward his sisters' shop. On the right side of the sidewalk, huge boulders protected the street from the ocean. Below on the sandy beach, families enjoyed the sun and surf. Across the street on his left were the historic storefronts. All the repairs from the last hurricane were complete.

Ray-Ray was walking between him and Lyrissa. It took him by surprise when the small fingers found his. Looking down, he found Ray-Ray watching the beach. One little hand in his, the other in Lyrissa's.

That is not my heart melting. Nope, it isn't. He blew out a puff of air. *This kid.* For the first time in his whole life, he truly longed for a family. Being a father. The only problem was he could only see Lyrissa as the mother.

Bennett walked a few steps ahead, pointing birds out to his little brother.

"Can we feed them?"

"Only if you want to be attacked," Reno chuckled.

Lyrissa shook her head, but she was grinning. "One time I ran screaming from the beach. Hollering that the birds were going to kill me. I'll never live it down."

Someone honked and waved as they drove past. Ray-Ray let go of his hand and waved back. "People are so nice here. I like it. I hope we get to stay."

Bennett looked at them. Worry in his eyes.

"This is our home now. We're family. Right?" His voice soft. "I mean, we're used to moving. It's no big deal."

"It is a big deal. This is your forever family home." Lyrissa looked a little teary eyed.

He tried to think of a joke that would make her smile.

She looked at him, then narrowed her eyes as if she could read his thoughts. "This is good. It's okay to be a little sad. We have each other and God has us."

She knew him too well. He nodded.

The air was humid. But a cool breeze came off the gulf. He loved the Texas coast. Walking with Lyrissa and the boys felt good deep in his core. Anyone who didn't know better would see a family walking and enjoying the day.

His heart longed for this. To be a family with Lyrissa. But she wasn't in the same place as him. *God, what do I do with these feelings?*

Another car honked. He waved without really looking. He got everyone safely across the street and held the door open for them.

"*Mijo*." His oldest sister greeting them from behind the counter. "What a beautiful little family you have here."

He ignored the family comment. "I'm surprised to see you. The wedding kept you up way past your bedtime. I thought you'd have employees covering the shop this morning." He had hoped.

He loved his sisters, he did, but sometimes they were too much. The word *boundary* was not in their vocabularies.

"Oh, I did sleep in. Came in late. Josefina won't be coming in today. I'm taking tomorrow off. Now—" her gaze slipped to the boys "—tell me what brings you in this morning?"

Bennett and Ray-Ray stood close to Lyrissa, almost behind her. "I promised them the best empanadas ever." He leaned over the counter and spoke in a dramatic stage whisper. "They have never eaten them. You were out the last time we were here."

"We'll have to fix that." She went to the back of the store and returned with a platter of assorted pastries. "Come sit in the back booth." After placing the tray of goodies on the table, his sister turned to the boys and hugged each one of them. Holding the oldest for a bit longer, she whispered, "Being the big brother is a heavy burden, but you're not alone now."

Then she wrapped her arms around Lyrissa. "You have always been in our prayers. We don't understand God's timing and there is the slight problem of free will." She grinned. "If people would just listen to their elders, the world would be a place full of grace." She hit Reno's shoulder with the back of her hand.

He kissed his much-shorter sister. "Yes. If the world followed all your words of wisdom, all the people would live in joy and harmony."

"Oh, you. You're such a charmer. Some girl is going to be treated right when you decide to settle down." His sister had the audacity to wink at Lyrissa. "I'm going to the back to make sure your father gets his favorites. We ran out of the cinnamon churro empanadas faster than usual."

"Your sister is amazing." Lyrissa shook her head. "You know how blessed you are, don't you?"

He nodded, even though he took them for granted way too often. "I do. You know they've considered you family since you came home with Savannah after school."

She looked up at him, her eyes full of wonderment. "I was so busy listening to the negative gossip in town, I missed the people supporting me. Their numbers are much bigger than I imagined. I wasted so much time on the wrong people. Does that make me self-centered?"

"Human." He looked to the rustic wood beams above them, the colorful *papel picado* with intricate designs cut from tissue paper brightened the shop. "I think the correct word you are looking for is *human*. We tend to focus on the negative. I must admit I've fallen into the same trap more than once."

She took a bite of a pumpkin empanada and gave a little moan with her eyes closed. "This is so good." Lids opened, she made eye contact with him. "You don't."

"I don't what?" He had totally lost track of what they were discussing.

"Focus on the negative. You always have a smile. No matter what is going on, you're trying to make everyone else laugh."

The doors to the back swung behind his sister. "It's because I focus on the negative that I'm trying to distract the people around me. I hate seeing the ones I love sad. In my world, everyone would be happy."

He'd gotten too good at hiding his real emotions. Buried them so deep, it was impossible to reach them. He wasn't sure he would be able to express them clearly anymore. It was too raw.

She covered his bicep with her hand. Her gaze searched his. "I think we've all underestimated you. Your well runs much deeper than you let your family believe."

He shrugged, not really enjoying this line of questioning. "My family deserve the best and worrying about me is not how they should spend their time."

"They love you."

But he wanted her to love him. That wasn't going to happen. "Who needs more chocolate milk?"

"I do!" Ray-Ray lifted his hand high above his head. "Bennett too."

Needing space, he moved to the large glass front cooler. Fingers brushed the back of his hand. Maddy.

"Reno." She laughed and tucked a loose strand of hair behind her ear. Lowering her lashes briefly, she then lifted her chin and blinked at him. Smiling. "Imagine meeting you here."

He frowned. "At my sisters' bakery?"

"I know that's silly. I was teasing. I'd been wanting to see you. You left the wedding early before I could claim my dance."

"I took Lyrissa home." He glanced at the chocolate milk in the refrigerator. How to grab the bottles and run without being rude.

She was still talking as she blocked the door.

"I loved dancing with you back in the day. We had such a good time. With everything that's happened, I could really use some of the classic Reno fun and forget the past few years."

He tilted his head and studied her. No memories of them dancing came to mind. They had hung out with groups of friends, but he didn't remember interacting with her one-on-one. "I'm sorry, Maddy. Lyrissa and the boys are waiting. The church has an active singles group. Have you connected with them since you came back to town?"

Something harsh flashed in her eyes. Surprised, he stepped back. She followed him and in a gritty whisper said, "Careful you aren't pulled back into her drama. After using you up she'll be gone. Just like in high school. I'm still not buying that oldest is her mother's."

For a moment he was too shocked to say anything. Taking

a deep breath, he shook his head. "We aren't high school kids any longer and I don't appreciate you talking about Lyrissa or Bennett like that. They're important to me."

"You can't be serious." She stepped closer, her voice a harsh whisper. Eyes wide, she stared at him. He moved back. Her hand went to his arm to hold him in place. "Did you see her mom create a scene all because my mom just wanted to dance with Mundo?"

"Maybe she…" He stopped himself from saying anything else. It didn't matter. "Like I said, we aren't in high school any longer. I've got to go."

Her grip tightened. All the years of being the nice guy and putting everyone at ease warred with getting as far away from her as possible.

She wasn't getting the hint and stepped full-on into his space. "Reno, please. You'll end up just like Mundo if you're not careful. He wasted his whole life on a woman who doesn't deserve him. Is that what you want? To look back on a life of regret with wasted time?"

He broke contact and glared at her. "Maddy, pettiness doesn't suit you. But I agree our time is too precious to hang out with negative people. Bye, Maddy." Reno was not going to allow her to take any more of his.

He stepped around her and grabbed two chocolate milks, then walked back to the table without a backward glance. Lyrissa met his gaze. A question in her eyes. She glanced at Maddy. "Everything okay?"

He did what he was good at—smiled. An easy, comfortable smile. "Yep." He looked at the boys. "So, are these the best things ever?"

"I want to eat a hundred of them," Ray-Ray cried.

Reno picked one up. "They have always made a rough day smoother. My sisters claim that my mom gave them secret ingredients. I've tried to watch them, but they always know and wait until no one is looking. I suspect it's a bit of love and hope."

Bennett scoffed. "Those aren't real ingredients."

Ray-Ray wiggled in excitement. "Those are real ingredients."

Lyrissa laughed. "It does make the day feel better and the sunshine brighter. I think you're on to something about the hope."

They made eye contact above the boys. For a long moment, they stared at each other and all the worries crowding his head disappeared. She leaned in close and put her hand over his. Every instinct screamed to move closer.

"Reno, this morning I couldn't have imagined smiling today, let alone laughing. Now I feel hope and love all around me. You do have a true gift."

She reached up and cupped his face. Every muscle locked in place. His lungs froze. Not a single breath went in or out. She dropped her hand and sat back. "Thank you."

After a few slow heartbeats he managed, "De nada."

A longing in him yelled to move in and kiss her. Just one sweet kiss. He sighed. Not the time, the place or the girl.

He was still the guy who made everyone smile. The desire to be more ate at him. He wanted to love her and be loved by her. He was in so much trouble.

For now, knowing he helped bring light back into her beautiful eyes was enough. It had to be.

UGH. SHE DID it again. Where was her self-control? With a shake of her head, she cleared her thoughts. "Sorry. That was weird."

He opened his mouth, but her phone went off. Pressing his lips closed, he leaned back.

She was just saved by her ringtone.

"Mew-Maw?" he asked, recognizing the theme song of *Bonanza*.

With a nod, she answered. "Hey, Mew-Maw." Listening,

her gaze went to her brothers. "Do y'all want to go riding out to the north pasture with Mew-Maw?"

Ray-Ray jumped up on the bench. "Yes! Yes!"

Bennett was much more subdued, but he nodded. "I'd like that."

"We're at the bakery with Reno. So, we'll meet you at the barn in a bit." After disconnecting the call, Lyrissa pulled Bennett close and rested her cheek on top of his head. "Thank you. She needs to spend time with us."

The boy leaned into her for a quick minute and hugged her back. She savored the moment. When she looked up, Reno was giving her a knowing smile.

Bennett tilted his chin as if he hadn't needed that hug and reassurance from his big sister.

Reno patted him on the shoulder. "It's a good start to the day."

The back corner booth was separated a bit from the general sitting area. Reno opened one of the bottles of chocolate milk and handed it to Ray-Ray. "You are sitting in the Espinoza special booth. This is reserved for family."

He looked at Lyrissa. "Speaking of family, my sister works at a clinic that has family counselors and connections to support groups through the church."

Lyrissa nodded. "Mew-Maw used to have the belief that you kept any problems in-house and didn't waste time talking about feelings." She held out her hands to both the boys and they held on to her as if she was a true lifeline. "She has changed her mind and would be willing to go as a family. Will y'all go with me?" she asked the boys. Ray-Ray agreed, not really understanding what was going on.

Reno opened the other bottle of chocolate milk and handed it to Bennett. "Your mother's addiction doesn't just turn her life upside down. It affects the whole family."

Bennett played with the corner of his pastry. "Will she come home?" he asked with his head down.

"Honestly, we don't know. I hope she will, but either way we need to make sure we are okay and living the life God has for us."

Bennett looked across the table at his little brother. "If it helps Ray-Ray, I'll do it."

Lyrissa's heart twisted at the pain they were going through. The desire to comfort them was so powerful it hurt. She wanted to make their world better.

She glanced at Reno. That's why he worked so hard to make the people around him smile. He had a huge heart and loved his people deeply.

The youngest dipped his fingers in the chocolate milk then put his eye against the opening and picked it up like a tele-scope. Reno gently placed the bottle back on the table and gave the little guy a napkin to wipe his face.

"Yep, the five-year-old is over this serious talk of support groups and healing," Reno chuckled. "I totally identify with being the youngest and totally bored with a family discussion."

He glanced at Lyrissa. She nodded. "I think we're done eating."

"Can we get a kite?" Ray-Ray lifted his bottle of chocolate milk as if it were flying.

Gently taking it from him, Reno grinned. "How about we walk across the street to the beach. We can look at the birds and kites before we leave for the ranch."

Lyrissa gave Reno a grateful smile. "Now that sounds like a wonderful idea."

"Great." He stood and helped Ray-Ray out. "Let me get a box from my sister so we can take the rest of the pastries home."

Lyrissa ran one hand through Ray-Ray's messy hair, at-tempting to tame it back into place. "Reno, do you mind going ahead with the boys? I'll take care of the food. I also need to tell your sisters thank you."

"Yay! The beach." Ray-Ray jumped then took off running.

Bennett stopped him and held his hand. "We have to wait for Reno."

Laughing, Reno took Ray-Ray's other hand. But as Bennett opened the door, Maddy got up from her table and made a beeline toward Lyrissa. He paused and looked at Lyrissa, then turned away from her and spoke to someone on the patio.

Through the window, she saw Jazz, Elijah's wife, with their daughter. The boys joined them, and Reno went back in.

Maddy touched her arm. "I know what you're doing. Just like your mom."

Lyrissa blinked. Had she heard her correctly? Was this really happening?

She had her head down and she spoke low. "And if you care for Reno, you won't cling to him and drag him down with your sinking ship."

"Maddy." Reno was at her side.

"Reno." Maddy smiled, but it was tight. "I'm setting the record straight. We all know her mother is a walking disaster who ruined Mundo's life."

Taking a deep breath, Lyrissa placed a hand on his arm and gave him a quick glance.

He got the message. Stopping a few feet away, he put his hands in his pockets and pressed his lips together.

She faced Maddy. "My parents' relationship is between them and God. And Reno is an adult. He can take care of himself."

Maddy clasped her hands in front of her chest and lowered her chin as if being obedient. "I believe it's our duty to speak the truth and hold people accountable. Reno is a good man, and he deserves someone looking after his best interest."

Reno frowned. The expression foreign on his face. He was very unhappy, and Lyrissa didn't like that at all.

Before she could say anything to him, he glared at Maddy. "This is the reason she avoids town." He turned to her with guilt and pain in his eyes. "I'm sorry I brought you into town."

Lifting her chin, she smiled a calm, quiet smile at him. "It's okay. Really."

Looking a little confused, he paused.

Ignoring Maddy, she met his beautiful, warm gaze. "Honesty can be a fickle excuse for people to be mean and rude."

Then she turned to Maddy. Her voice was strong and serene. She lifted three fingers. "*Is* it the truth? Is it kind, and is it helpful? And by helpful, I mean, is it asked for and will it make a difference? I recommend that you take a long look in the mirror and start there. Not that you listen to others, but that's my advice to you."

Maddy leaned back with shock on her face. In the past, all the stabs she had made at Lyrissa had never been returned. In shame and embarrassment, Lyrissa had walked away. Not today.

She didn't need him to intervene. "Is there anything else I can help you with?"

"No, I'm good." Maddy went to her table, picked up her bag and walked out the door.

They stood shoulder to shoulder as they watched the woman leave.

Margarita came through the swinging doors. "These are your father's favorites." She put a white box on the counter. "On the house. Let him know we're lifting him up in prayer and if he needs anything else to let us know. We've got him covered from babysitting to food."

"I will. And I can't thank you enough for all your support. Not just today, but for as long as I can remember your family has been there for me."

"*Para eso esta la familia.*" Margarita said it so casually, as if being a part of the family was a given. There was a huge lump in Lyrissa's throat. She smiled and nodded because words were impossible.

Reno hugged his sister, kissing her on the top of her head. She handed him an empty white box. He went to the table and packed what was left then turned to Lyrissa. "Ready to check out some kites and birds?"

"I am. Looking forward to riding with Mew-Maw and the boys too. You'll join us?" She wanted to bite her tongue. Why did she keep sending him mixed messages? She should make an excuse and take it back. Maybe he would say no.

HE PAUSED. HAD she just invited him to spend more time with her? He grinned. She had. "Love too. Lyrissa, I'm so sorry about—"

She held her hand up and shook her head. "Don't. I've been hiding too long. I have way too many friends in Port Del Mar to stay away. I'm not going to let her make me ashamed of my family."

His chest burned with pride for her. She was so amazing, and she didn't even see it. If she would let him, he would find a million different ways to show her the woman he saw.

For now, he needed to act cool. With a nod, he went to the door but before he could open it, her phone rang again. Concern flashed across her face before she brought it to her ear. His whole body went tight, then she smiled. "Hello to you too."

He released his breath. It wasn't bad news.

"Yes. They did. I told them I'd let them know by Wednesday. Yea, but I have three other offers too." She paused. "I know, right? I had some family stuff come up. But it's nice to be wanted." She listened to the speaker. "Okay. I'll let you know. Thanks for calling."

She put her phone away then headed to the door. He paused before he pulled the door open. "You got a job offer on a Saturday?"

"No. I got it yesterday morning. That was a friend from college. She works in the district and when she heard I was offered the job, she called to encourage me to take it. It's in Missouri."

Rocks hit the bottom of his gut hard. "So, you're going back?"

"I don't know." She shrugged as if his whole world wasn't teetering on the edge of a canyon.

"I have an offer in Dallas and one in San Antonio."

He wanted to ask why she hadn't told him, but that sounded childish. Pressing his lips together, he bit back any pleading to make her stay or at least take the one in San Antonio. That was close enough for a day trip.

She raised an eyebrow in question.

He frowned. "What?"

Her gaze went over his shoulder.

Oh. Right. He was blocking the door. He pulled the door open and waited for her to go through. Clearing his throat, he tried to sound neutral. "What are you going to do?"

Not knowing the turmoil going on in his head, she gave a low sigh. "I was leaning toward the Dallas one. It's my dream job, but after last night I don't know."

"Like we told Bennett. You have some time. Don't rush it and don't let a sense of obligation make you do something that will steal who you are." *But please stay close or let me visit.*

She nodded. "Everyone is full of great advice today. I really don't know what I should do."

Face to the sun, she walked past him.

For a moment he couldn't breathe. She was beautiful. The world should be hers. "Pray and focus on what feels right."

She gave him a weak smile. "I'm just as clueless about that. Ready to get the boys?"

He was ready for whatever she wanted to do. Pointing to where they sat, he said, "Lead the way."

CHAPTER FIFTEEN

AFTER CHURCH, THE ESPINOZA FAMILY had invited her family to join them for lunch. It was loud and welcoming. Ray-Ray couldn't be separated from his new friends. They would be starting kindergarten in the fall with him.

Her heart was overflowing with watching her family connect with the community. They would need all this support when or if Dee came home.

Mew-Maw hugged Reno's mother. Her grandmother stood a good foot over woman. "Thank you for a great lunch. I need to be heading back to the ranch." She turned to Bennett. "Are you going back to the ranch or staying and going to camp with Cooper?"

"Is it okay if I stay?"

Kids, including Ray-Ray, ran though the kitchen again to the back door.

"Of course. Go. Join your friends." He hugged each of them then ran off.

Lyrissa laughed. "I always loved the energy at your home when I visited Savannah. But it seems ever more…"

"Bonkers? Chaotic?" Reno smiled as he tossed an apple to a tall boy who came around the corner.

"Not exactly. You love being surrounded by all your nieces

and nephews." It wasn't a question. It was obvious. He loved being in the middle of his big family. He adored the kids. Someday, he'd be a great father.

His mother laughed. "Most of the time, he runs around with them. It's nice to see him acting like an adult. You've been an enormous influence on him."

"*Mami!*" He was turning red.

Mundo patted him on the shoulder. "Lyrissa has always been the most adult in our family. Too much so. He's been a good influence on her too." He turned to Reno. "Are you sure you can bring her home? If it's too much trouble, I can come back into town to pick her up."

Reno smiled. "I really appreciate her helping with my test. It's the least I can do. I'll bring her home early. I know she has work in the morning."

Her father and grandmother went out the back to get Ray-Ray and say goodbye to everyone. His mother grinned at them. "Y'all can work in the front living room. It will be quiet." She followed the others out.

"Why does it feel like we're being set up?" she asked.

"Because we are. Under all that sweetness, a stubborn streak runs deep." They went into the living room. He looked around, rubbing his hands on his jeans.

She gathered the material and books she brought. "Why don't we go outside? The front porch looks empty."

He nodded but didn't say anything. They settled in on the porch swing, the papers between them. She wasn't used to a silent Reno. "What's wrong? Are you feeling, okay?"

He took a deep breath. "I'm taking the test in a few days. I don't know if I'm ready." He snorted. "I might never be ready."

She leaned over and took his hand. "You've worked so hard. You're more than ready."

An uncharacteristic scowl pulled at his mouth. He leaned back and crossed his arms over his chest. "I've worked hard before and learned it was a waste of time." His tone had a sharp defensive edge to it.

"What happened?" She waited. He looked off in the distance. After a long, silent moment, he sighed. "In the sixth grade we had to write an essay that could be entered into a contest for the local animal shelter. I poured everything I had into that paper. It was about my dog being my best friend after my dad died. I went over that paper so many times. I wanted it to be perfect. I stayed in while everyone else was outside playing. I got to school early and sat in the bleachers looking for every mistake. I found them too. I was so proud I went to class early to give it to Mr. Poole. I knew it was going to win the contest. It would be published in the newspaper."

He looked away, his jaw flexing.

"Reno?" She moved closer and put her hand on his arm.

"He said it could have been a good paper if I had tried harder. He said being lazy with spelling and grammar would stop people from seeing my story. He gave me a seventy and didn't enter it in the contest. Hard work does not guarantee success."

She wanted to pull him into her arms. She also wanted to find that teacher and give him a good lecture about learning disabilities.

Instead, she nodded. "You're right. I misspoke. Learning disabilities can be huge hurdles and you have to work twice as hard to just do the bare minimum. But this time you asked for help. You have strategies in place. Take your time. Use the process that works for you. Believe you can." She reached for his hand. "You've got this. Either way, I'm proud of you for putting yourself out there. The world needs more first responders like you. You deserve the best and they deserve you."

He cupped her face and leaned in. "You do too. You've helped me get closer to my dream. Closer than I've ever thought possible." His throat worked as if he was about to say something that was difficult to get out.

"Lyrissa, let me take you out on a date. A real date and show you what a good relationship could be between us. I want to be there for you."

No. No. No. She tried to smile as she shook her head. "You're a protector. You need someone to rescue. That's what you see in me. My family is a fire you're not responsible for. Your energy and love need to go to someone who can return it. I don't think I can."

She stood before she leaned into him and did what she really wanted to do. Hug him close and never let him go.

"You're ready for your test. I need to go. Bye." *I love you* almost slipped out. It had to be buried. Saying it aloud wouldn't be fair to him. Port Del Mar was his home. His family was here. Her future was far from here.

She rushed down the steps then realized she didn't have her car. He was supposed to take her home. Frozen, she just stood there with her back to him.

"I'll get Bridges." His words were followed by the screen door shutting.

She wanted to say *No, it's alright. You can take me home.* But right now was not the time to be locked in a car with him. It didn't take long for his big brother to come out.

"Hey, hear you need a ride home." Bridges joined her.

Unable to speak, she nodded then followed him to his truck. Once inside, she glanced over her shoulder. Reno stood on the top step, tall and handsome, looking as if he might chase after her.

Was she making a mistake walking away or was she being smart?

The tears started falling. She bit the inside of her mouth to stop any sobbing, but the tears fell anyway. Her throat burned from holding in the yelling she craved to do.

Bridges stopped at her father's house. "Lyrissa, is there anything I can do? Are you okay? Well, obviously you're not. Do I need to have a man-to-man with my baby brother?

He's a good guy but he's not the most mature when it comes to relationships."

She smiled. Poor Reno. Everyone always assumed he was the one who messed up. "I'm good. It's not Reno's fault," she managed to say. "Thanks for the ride." She swung her bag over her shoulder and turned to the house. Then she stopped.

Mew-Maw was sitting on the swing. Was she waiting for her? Had something happened? With a smile, her grandmother stood and waved to Bridges as if letting him know she had it from here. He drove away.

The woman who raised her tilted her head and arched an eyebrow. She opened her arms and waited.

Pulling in a deep breath, she wanted to rush to the porch. But the earth shifted under her boots, making it difficult to move forward. It was like walking through deep sand. It shifted, not letting her get traction. Her entire world was unstable, and she didn't know what to do.

As a teenager, she ran as far away as she could. Was there anywhere far enough to escape a broken heart? The worst part? It was all her fault.

"Mew-Maw." She made it to the steps.

"Hey, cowgirl."

"Why are you here?"

"My sweet child, you're hurting."

"You always said to pull up your boots and move forward. No sense in wallowing. It's a waste of time." She imitated her grandmother's voice and smiled. "You're right. We can't change unpleasant facts, so no point in crying about it." Her shoulders fell.

Mew-Maw took her hand and led her to the swing. "Yeah, well, we've seen how well that philosophy worked with my daughter. I thought we agreed to do things differently. What did that boy do to break your heart? I can lock him up with Brutus. That's one mean bull."

Lyrissa laughed. It was a little dry, but more than she

thought she was capable of today. "No one deserves that, Mew-Maw. Knowing Reno, he'd have him eating from the palm of his hand. I thought you were going to sell that old bull."

"I have a soft spot for that old man. I'm afraid no one else would put up with him. We suit each other just fine." She squeezed Lyrissa's hand. "Tell me what our boy has done."

She shrugged. "I think he loves me."

Her grandmother blinked at her. "Not what I was expecting. His mother called, worried." Her words were slow and measured, as if she was dealing with a skittish foal. "She saw you leave, upset. When she tried to talk to Reno, he wasn't himself. She was worried about you. Men can be clueless when it comes to matters of the heart."

Lyrissa snorted. "I'm pretty sure the women of our family are heartless."

Mew-Maw narrowed her wrinkled eyes. "I'm…"

She leaned into her grandmother and hugged her. "I'm sorry. I'm all out of sorts, but there was no excuse for that. We just don't deal with emotions well."

With a sigh, her grandmother hugged her. "That might be an understatement of the century. I'm so sorry I passed this on to you and your mother."

Tears dampened her shirt. She sat up and stared at her grandmother. "Are you crying?"

The older woman wiped at her face. "Don't be silly. Of course I'm not crying."

Lyrissa caressed her thumb over the work-worn, beautifully wrinkled skin. "It's okay to cry. We're a mess. Reno wanted to start dating. I told him there was no future for us. I can't bring him into this family. I don't think I can love someone the way he deserves to be loved. I don't trust myself or him to not get hurt beyond repair. I mean, look at my parents. I just can't risk that with someone who's so good."

"Oh, baby girl. You're not your mother or your father. Or any other member of your family. Our blood may run through your veins, but you are a child of God first and foremost. You're Lyrissa Herff Martinez. Do you have faith in Him?"

"To be honest, I'm not sure. A month ago, I would have said yes, but I wasn't living in that faith. Now I'm on rocky ground. I want to trust God with everything, but I have certain bits I know I'm holding back on."

"You can't allow your parents' drama to derail you from God's plan. Take hold of your faith and trust in God. Without it, what's the point of life? We can't control what happens to us or the people around us, but we can control our reactions."

"Reno has asked me to trust him."

"Do you?"

Lyrissa shrugged.

"I've known Reno for most of his life. More so as an adult. He's a good man. If you don't love him, then you're doing the right thing. But I fear you do love him and you're walking away from the one man who you can build a real life with. Someone who will stand by your side."

"How do I know which it is?"

"Deep inside, you know. God does not lead with fear. Be still and listen. That's why I ride out so much now, even when I don't need to. I'm so busy making plans and having opinions, I have a tough time listening."

Lyrissa pulled her knees to her chest and rested her head on her grandmother's chest. The older woman gathered the quilt over their shoulders. The love of past generations surrounded them.

"I love him," she whispered.

Mew-Maw nodded. "Then you go get him and let him know."

"What if I'm too late?"

"I don't believe you are."

Lyrissa thought about the note Reno had given to her the day in the hospital. He didn't know he had asked her to marry him, but she had a feeling he had meant it.

Did he still see her in his long-term future? There was so much uncertainty. But together, they would figure it out. First, she had to open up and be honest with him.

The thought of laying all of her heart out in front of him made her a little sick to her stomach. "I don't know if I can do it."

"If you start, I think he will meet you halfway. If he doesn't and you find yourself standing alone, then it's not meant to be. But you will never know if you don't take that first step and reach out to him."

She had to find a way to prove to him that she was in this for the long haul. He had every reason to doubt her. How many times had he stepped closer, only for her to run away?

She got her phone out and texted him. Can we meet tomorrow after work?

No, I've got the test. I'm turning my phone off. Night.

Blinking, she stared at the phone. He had never cut her off like that. Was she too late? *No.* He was stressed over the exam, and she would only make it worse. She would back off and let him focus.

What she needed was a plan to prove she was ready for a relationship with him. And she could handle the uncertainty of a future as long as he was in her life.

Together they could get through anything. She knew that without a doubt. She loved him and he deserved to know that.

Sending one more text, she smiled. Now to make plans and trust God had them.

RENO DOUBLE-CHECKED THE time then the message. 5:00 p.m. at the barns.

I am in the right place at the right time. But the wrong guy again.

Why was he here? He had made a promise to himself not

to let her tie him in knots. Her happiness was all he wanted. Of course, in a perfect world it would be with him.

The horse reached for him out of the half door. He rubbed her muzzle. "I think I lied when I thought we could still be friends." He loved Lyrissa more than he thought possible. Too much to just sit on the bench.

Stepping out of the barn, he scanned the area. What if there was a problem? Fists stuffed into his jeans, he bit his lip. What if there was trouble and he had cut her off?

Sunday night, in an angry fit he had turned his phone off. The test had to have his full focus. As soon as his test was over, he stepped outside and turned his phone on. Seeing all the missed calls had dropped his stomach. But the last text had given him hope. You've got this. Meet me at the barn Tuesday at 5:00 p.m. I have something I want to show you.

Was he at the right barn? What if something was wrong? She hadn't returned any calls or his text in the last hour. He blew out a puff of air. He should have come out to the ranch earlier.

Should he send another message letting her know he was here? Had she changed her mind?

After another long breath in, he went back into the barn. "Looks like she stood me up again, Cinnamon." He rubbed the horse's soft muzzle. He'd check at the house then head home.

He turned to the door then froze. Lyrissa stood there. One hand pressed against the frame. Each breath came hard and heavy and her hair was a mess.

A canvas saddlebag was thrown over her shoulder. "Oh good. You're still here. We had an issue at school. Then on the way home I went to call you. Realized my phone was dead. And my cord—" she took another breath "—wasn't charging."

All doubts left, replaced by concern. He moved to her, his hand lifted to her face. He searched her eyes. "Are you okay?"

Standing, she nodded. "Yes. I had a big plan to…" She

waved a hand in the air. "Well. I was hoping to show you something. Do you feel like a ride?"

He shook his head to clear his thoughts. "That was a huge change of subject." Why was she acting like their last conversation never happened? "I'm always up for a ride. But Lyrissa, I'm confused. The last time we talked, you made it clear you couldn't be more than friends. I know you've counted on my friendship but I'm still a little raw. So, what's this all about?"

She bit her lip. "I know I've been the queen of mixed signals, and you did put yourself out there, only to get rejected. I'm sorry I didn't respond the way I should have. I let fear rule me, but I want a redo. Can we do that? Will you give me the chance to start over? I can't lose your friendship or you." She stood before him, her big eyes shining and asking him for another chance.

And he crumbled. He nodded. "Of course. There's a secret you haven't learned yet. With me, you will always have another chance. I'm not going anywhere."

She smiled, but there was a suspicious glint of moisture in her eyes. "Good. No more talking. Let's get the horses saddled."

It didn't take them long to be on horseback. She pointed her horse to the west, and he followed. They made their way across her family ranch, following a narrow path through the knee-high grass. The creaking of the saddle and the thumping of hooves on packed dirt were the only sounds.

His heart fell into rhythm with his horse and the stress slipped away with each sway. The sun was still high above the horizon and birds glided on the wind. There were enough clouds to break the sun's intensity. They came to a gate, and she opened it with a well-practiced side step.

"We're leaving your ranch?" he asked in surprise.

"Yes. I found this old path as a teenager. I didn't want anyone to tell me not to come this way. So, I kept it a secret." She

smiled at him, the kind that made her eyes sparkle. "I'm sharing my best-kept secret with you."

A pair of huge cranes lifted themselves into the sky. A small
herd of Angus cows grazed in the distance. Tall, golden grass
gently rustled in the breeze.

They followed an overgrown path up a small hill. At the top,
the view before him took his breath away. The Gulf of Mexico
reached as far from the east as to the west. Billowing clouds
hovered over the horizon where the water touched the sky.

"Lyrissa, this is breathtaking." It was a place of peace. He
felt it seep into his bones and banished his last worries.

"It's my favorite place in the world and I've never told anyone about it. Let alone shared it." She dismounted and pulled
the rolled blanket off the back of her saddle and untied the bag.

Stopping about five feet from the edge of the cliff, she
spread a blanket over the ground. She went back to her saddlebag. "I have a few things to eat and two bottles of water."

Worry was stamped in her beautiful eyes when she finally
made eye contact with him. "I've been planning for this since
Sunday night. I don't want you to be mad at me. Your friendship is so important."

The rigidity was back in his muscles. All peace was gone
with one word. When had he started hating the word *friend*?
She sat down and patted the space next to her. "Join me."

The horizon held all his attention. Otherwise, he might
start yelling at her to stop sitting there looking all innocent
and sweet. She had torn out his heart and it still hurt. He
knew himself enough that if he said what he wanted without
a filter, the guilt would eat him alive. So, he bit the inside of
his mouth and prayed as he stared at the clouds shifting and
changing with the wind.

He should just go along and pretend everything was fine.
That way, when he had gotten over himself, they would still
be friends.

"Reno. Please talk to me. Don't pretend everything is okay if it's not. Not with me."

She was right. He respected her too much to give her the same old song and dance. He couldn't sit, though. Not yet. Gaze still fixed on the moving clouds, he took a deep breath. No matter how much pain he was in, the world would keep going. That was a truth he had learned long ago. "I'm tired of being the guy who's always easygoing and fun."

Dropping his gaze, he studied the ground and stuffed his hands in his pockets.

"You are so much more than that guy. Reno, I brought you here to talk to you about our future. I can't see mine without you in it."

As a friend. He shook his head. "I can't do this. I told you that I loved you and I want to build a family with you. You said no and left. Today, I can't go back to just being your friend. Not yet. Give me some time and I'm sure I'll get over it."

There was movement behind him. In less than a minute, she stood next to him, but he couldn't look at her. His deepest feelings were raw and exposed.

He tilted his head back and looked at the endless sky above them. *God, I could really use some help here. A bit of wisdom or something. I'm not even sure what I'm asking for.*

She slid her hand along his forearm and pulled until her fingers were wrapped with his. "Reno, I didn't bring you out here just to talk and hang out and tell you about all my troubles. We've done a lot of that, and you've been there for me through so much upheaval. I also want to be there for you. I know you have your family, but I don't think you really allow them to see you. I want to be your safe space."

She stepped back and pulled something out of her pocket. She took a deep breath and looked down at the piece of paper, then up at him.

"Sit down with me, please." She pulled her bottom lip

between her teeth and just looked at him with those huge, soft eyes.

He sighed. With a nod, he moved to her blanket. He'd give her anything. "Okay." He dropped to the green-and-red plaid.

She sat across from him. "I want to give something back to you." She had the paper in her hand. It was torn off from a larger piece. "This is what you gave me in the hospital."

His stomach twisted and his heart pounded faster. "When I was basically unconscious."

She laughed. "You were conscious. You just didn't have your filters in place." She reached out to him. "I want to give it back to you with an answer."

Swallowing, he took the paper from her and with complete dread, looked down. Yeah, it was his writing. This was so humiliating. He looked at the uneven scrawl of letters. It wasn't bad for a first grader just learning to write. Each letter was wonky but bold. All caps. *WIL U MARY M.* There was a mark after the *m* that he supposed was an *e* but it looked more like a *z*.

He had asked her to marry him. In this crude, primitive writing. He blinked.

On the bottom, evenly slanted letters spaced carefully apart read *Let's date, then ask me again.* He couldn't breathe.

"Reno. I would have said yes, but you weren't in your right mind. So, I thought it only fair to give you time to reconsider the question."

"Do you have a pencil?" He was floating, maybe even flying right off the cliff, and gliding over the ocean.

Stay focused, Bucko. He could hear his dad's voice. His eyes burned at the thought that his dad was here, encouraging and guiding him.

"Are you okay? You read that, right?" There was a nervous edginess to her voice.

He smiled, trying to keep it cool. He doubted he was successful. "You always have pencils or pens or something to write with. Do you have one with you now?"

She stood. "I think so." She wasn't gone long, then came back and sank to her knees. "Here."

He turned the paper over. Very carefully, he wrote the question again. *Lyrissa, will you marry me?*

He looked up. Curiosity and uncertainty along with hope and joy warred on her lovely face.

He cleared his throat. "Before I give this back to you, I should tell you I love you, with all my heart, body and mind. You are my home, and I would love to date you for the rest of my life." He handed the note back to her.

For the longest minute she started at the note. It was cupped in both her hands as if it was the most precious gift. After a heartbeat or two she pulled it to her chest and looked up at him. "I'm so sorry I responded in fear the other day." She took a breath. "Yes. Reno, I love you and would love to be your wife."

The wind came up over the cliff and swirled around them. A bird called out. He pulled her close and kissed her without trepidation or fear. She wrapped her arms around him.

He rested his forehead against hers. "Can we stay here forever? Right here?"

With a laugh, she shook her head. "I don't want to miss the rest of our lives. I love you, Reno."

Before he could respond, his phone vibrated. The world was already intruding. He glanced down. "It's the fire chief. They said they would let us know today."

He hesitated. Did he want to know right now?

She put her hand over his. "It doesn't matter what the results are. You're so talented. If you don't become a firefighter, there are other paths for you. You'll find the right one. And I'll be by your side."

"If I passed then I'd have to stay here. Go through the training. We can live in Port Del Mar or over the bridge. I'm so—"

She shook her head. "No. I've already decided to take the

job here. I need to stay close to my family. Mom is so unpredictable. I would be so worried if I wasn't here for them."

He looked down at his phone with a frown. "Oh no. I waited too long. The call ended."

"Call back." Her smile lit up her eyes. "No matter the news, we've got this. God has a plan if we take the time to listen and not react with fear or pride. I just figured it out. I'm sure you'll have to remind me a few times."

He hit the number and called. "It's Reno. I missed your call."

"Well, son. It is an honor and my privilege to welcome you to…"

Reno didn't hear the rest of the words. He might have blacked out. His dream had just come true. He glanced at Lyrissa, her face blank as she tried to read his expression.

He smiled and she smiled back.

"Yes, sir. I'll see you Monday." He hoped that had been the correct response. His brain was buzzing.

Once he put the phone down, she leaped across the space between them and hugged him tight, knocking him back. "You did it."

"*We* did it. I have a feeling together we can do anything we want."

"I love you and trust you with my heart and my future, Fireman Reno Espinoza."

After kissing her, he pressed his lips against her ear. "Forever and ever. Amen."

EPILOGUE

HE GLANCED AT his watch. Where had everyone gone? He was supposed to be getting married in less than twenty minutes and his best man and little groomsmen were missing in action. His stomach fluttered but not in nervousness. Lyrissa was about to become his wife.

If everything was okay. Okay, so he was a little nervous. He glanced around the study of the old ranch house, searching for his phone. This room was fancier than anything he'd ever been in. From here they would be driving up to Lyrissa's favorite spot.

The Wimberlys owned the largest ranch in the area. They were gracious enough to not only let them get married on the property, but gave the use of their home to get ready in and provided shuttles up to the lookout point. Somewhere in the other side of the large house, Lyrissa was with her parents getting ready. One of her friends from college was standing with her. Her mother had been home for a few months and things had been going well. Mundo and she were even talking about a recommitment ceremony. But maybe she did something.

Lyrissa, the boys, Mundo and Edith—his new family— would all be devastated.

He went across the room to get his phone. The heavy oak

door opened, and his tiny mother slipped into the room. His heart slammed against his chest. Had she come to tell him something had gone wrong? "Is it Dee?"

"What? Oh, no. Everyone is good." The smile on her face calmed him. "Oh *mijo*, you're so handsome. Of all my children, you look the most like your father." She cut across the room and cupped his face. "I'm so proud of you."

"Thank you, *mami*."

"You saved me, you know? All of my kids did. In one way or another. But you, my baby, gave me a reason to get out of bed every morning. Your smile and laughter brought me so much joy in my darkest days. But I never meant for you to take on that responsibility and carry it by yourself. I'm so sorry for that. Please tell me you've released that burden."

He hugged her. "I'll always do whatever to make my mother happy. But, yes, I'm good. In another hour I'll be even better. Do you know where Bridges and the boys are?"

Bennett and Ray-Ray had been so proud and excited to be his groomsmen. They were going to spend the day with Lyrissa. She was going to make sure they were ready then send them over. "The boys should've been here by now."

"They're on the way. I asked for a few minutes alone with you."

"Oh? Is that why Bridges suddenly had something he had to take care of?"

The extra twinkle in her eyes warned him she was up to something.

"*Mami*, what is going on?"

Instead of answering, she opened her little purse and pulled out a box. "I have something I promised your father I would give you on a special day." She looked up at him, unshed tears hovering in her eyes. "I think today is it."

His throat went dry as she opened the lid and pulled out an old-fashioned wristwatch with a leather band. "That's Dad's watch. Shouldn't it be given to Bridges?"

She shook her head. "When you were five all you wanted was

a watch like your dad's. And Bridges loves those fancy smart-watches with his heart rate and steps. But you always wanted this watch. Your dad knew that and asked me to save it for you. And to make sure you knew he'd always be with you. Here."

She held out her hand. "Let me take your old watch off and put on your father's."

His throat was tight as she removed his watch and set it to the side. They stood in silence as she put his father's watch on his wrist. She patted it. "It belongs here."

Unable to talk, he pulled her into his arms. For a long moment they stood there. He took a deep breath. "Thank you. On the day I asked Lyrissa to marry me, I heard his voice."

She stepped back and cupped his face. "Of course you did." She laid her hand flat against his heart. "He's always here."

The door swung open with a lot of energy. Bennett and Ray-Ray burst into the room. "We're here to distract you!" Ray-Ray yelled.

"Distract me?" He grinned.

Bennett hit his little brother on the shoulder. "We're not supposed to tell him that."

He looked at his mother. "What's going on?"

She shrugged with a mischievous grin. "I have no idea. But I have something I need to take care of. Just a heads-up we will be late. So don't worry. Lyrissa is ready. There is just one detail. When I come back, we'll be riding up to the spot. Love you." And she was gone.

He looked at his new little brothers. "What's going on, guys? Is your sister okay?"

Ray-Ray bit his lip and gave a side-glance to his brother. Bennett tilted his head, avoiding any eye contact. "Uhm. Everything's good. There's a surprise, and we were told not to tell you because…it's a surprise."

His mind raced. What kind of surprise would make everyone late?

"Lyrissa said you had pizza." Bennett moved to the table and lifted a lid off a pizza box.

"Freeze! Let's slip a T-shirt over your tuxedo. Your sister will kill me if you get sauce on your fancy duds." He found his shirt and one of Bridges's and covered the boys.

They had devoured one of the pizzas when a slight knock drew their attention. "Come in."

Was this the surprise? The door eased open. He froze, not believing what he saw. Savannah, his sister, stepped into the room. She had been gone so long, without a word. All he had known was his sister and best friend had disappeared from his life for the safety of her new family.

"Savannah?" She wore a pretty sage-green dress, and her dark hair was pulled up with curls falling around her face. She was also very pregnant.

"Hey, baby brother. I hear congratulations are in order."

He rushed her and lifted her into a hug. Well, he tried. Her belly was in the way. "Sorry. Wow. There's so much to talk about. What are you doing here? Is it safe?"

"I called Momma yesterday to let her know the threat to Greyson and the girls was over and we planned to move back home. I want to have our baby boy here. She told me you were getting married."

"A boy? That's great. We can use a few more boys in this family." He shook his head. "I can't believe you're here."

"There's no way I would miss the wedding of my little brother and best friend." She squeezed his shoulder. "Really? Lyrissa? I can't believe you're marrying her. I knew you always had a thing for her. Later, you're going to have to tell me how this all happened. And I can get you caught up with my life. Now introduce me to these fine young men."

He cleaned them up and removed the shirts as he introduced them to his sister. The door opened and his brother and mother came into the room. "Okay. Okay. More talking later. We have a wedding to get to," his mother announced.

He hugged Savannah one more time before she left to join his soon-to-be bride.

Bridges gripped his shoulder. "We have a Jeep at the side

of the house. Once we head out, Lyrissa and her party will follow in a few minutes. Ready to get married, little brother?"

Bennett and Ray-Ray cheered, "Yes!"

Reno wasn't sure he needed the Jeep. It was as if he could float all the way to the spot where she had first told him she loved him.

Chairs had been set up and were filled with people. Pastor Rod stood under a wooden archway covered with greenery and flowers.

The light faded into soft pinks and blues at the horizon, just like the day that changed his life. He walked down the aisle with his mother on his arm. His older brother and two little brothers followed.

With a kiss on her cheek, he sat his mother down in the front row with his sisters. They were all smiling like fools. Then he stood and waited.

When she first came into view, he lost his breath. His Lyrissa was a princess in a white gown. The top was simple and fitted to her but then flared out a little. The skirt was covered in lace flowers.

Music came from somewhere, but he only saw her. Pastor Rod spoke but he just looked into the eyes of the woman he loved. He promised to love, honor and cherish her and slipped her ring onto her finger. She was his. He was hers.

It was over and they turned to face everyone. But he couldn't take his gaze off her. They walked to the Jeep that would take them to the Painted Dolphin to celebrate their wedding.

Bridges drove and they slipped into the back seat.

She cupped his face and kissed him. "It's official. I'm yours."

"And I belong to you, completely." He pressed his forehead to hers and soaked up her presence. The good and the bad ahead of them would be better because she was by his side.

* * * * *

A Faithful Guardian

Louise M. Gouge

MILLS & BOON

Award-winning author **Louise M. Gouge** writes historical and contemporary fiction romances. She received the prestigious Inspirational Readers' Choice Award in 2005 and was a finalist in 2011, 2015, 2016 and 2017; was a finalist in the 2012 Laurel Wreath contest; and was a 2023 Selah Award finalist. She taught English and humanities at Valencia College for sixteen and a half years and has written twenty-eight novels, eighteen of which were published under Harlequin's Love Inspired imprint. Contact Louise at louisemgougeauthor.blogspot.com, Facebook.com/louisemgougeauthor and on X, @louisemgouge.

Books by Louise M. Gouge

Safe Haven Ranch

K-9 Companions

A Faithful Guardian

Love Inspired Historical

Finding Her Frontier Family
Finding Her Frontier Home

Four Stones Ranch

Cowboy to the Rescue
Cowboy Seeks a Bride
Cowgirl for Keeps
Cowgirl Under the Mistletoe
Cowboy Homecoming
Cowboy Lawman's Christmas Reunion

Visit the Author Profile page at millsandboon.com.au for more titles.

There is a friend that sticketh closer than a brother.
—*Proverbs* 18:24

My special thanks go to my wonderful agent, Tamela Hancock Murray, and to my fabulous editor, Shana Asaro. Thank you for all that you do.

Thanks to my beloved great-niece, Elizabeth Chelsey Lawrence, for providing research about cerebral palsy from her youngest son Nikholas's life experiences so I could accurately portray my character Zoey. Thanks to Elizabeth's daughter Clementine for letting me name a character after her. Thanks also to my beloved granddaughter Emmy Santiago Halaby, who gave me permission to use her real-life seizure episodes to further develop Zoey's story. I pray I was faithful to each of you in this book.

Finally, as with all of my stories, this book is dedicated to my beloved husband, David, my one and only love, who encouraged me to write the stories of my heart and continued to encourage me throughout my writing career. David, I will always love you and miss you.

CHAPTER ONE

ROBERT MATTSON SLAMMED on the brakes, then steered his brand-new RAM 3500 into the first empty parking space at the edge of Riverton Park, his eyes laser focused on two women at a picnic table. The dog they were playing with was his cow-herding border collie, Lady, no doubt about it, with her black face and coat and distinctive white heart-shape mark on her chest. How could they dare to bring his stolen dog out in public? He'd demand an answer right before he had them arrested for the theft.

"Siri, call Rex Blake," he ordered. "Hey, Rex," he said when the sheriff answered. "Listen, I found Lady." Pause. "She's with two women at Riverton Park. Can you come over and make the arrest? Great. Thanks." He disconnected the call, shut off the motor and climbed out of his truck, making sure to lock the door, something he'd been doubly careful to do since Lady went missing eight months ago. The sheriff's office was right around the corner, so Rex should be here pretty quick.

The mid-August sunshine bore down on his head, so he put on his weathered Stetson and pulled in a deep breath of fresh air scented with the fragrance of newly mown grass, then moved toward the women to face this unpleasant situation. Several folks waved to him from their picnic tables or Frisbee games. He waved back, mindful that he needed to be careful how he approached these thieves. As he'd learned early in his forty-two years, folks around here looked up to the Mattsons as leaders of the community. As much as he wanted to vent his anger at the women, he needed to set a good example of how to handle an unpleasant and *criminal* situation.

The closer he got to the pair, the more he could see they didn't fit the expected profile for dog thieves. The older woman, maybe in her thirties, was vaguely familiar, and the younger one was just a girl, probably close in age to his own twins' fifteen years. Her jerking movements as she tossed the ball for Lady to fetch, along with her broken laughter when the dog chased it, suggested some sort of disability.

Rob huffed out a long breath. Perfect. Just perfect. His family had always been allies for those with disabilities, so he'd have to be twice as careful not to make a scene.

He approached their picnic table and shoved his Stetson back from his forehead.

"Mornin', ma'am." He aimed a slight smile toward the woman, whose back was now turned, hoping to catch her off guard once she faced him.

"Yes?" She turned around and looked up at him, her pretty face the picture of innocence.

Now who was caught off guard? She wasn't just pretty. She was gorgeous, and her rose-scented perfume wafted up to engage his senses. For some ridiculous reason, his pulse kicked up. Any other time, Rob would have backed off. He had a built-in radar to protect himself from females. Ever since he was a boy, his beloved Jordyn had been his shield against women who regarded his status as the Mattsons' primary heir a prize to grasp at. Since Jordyn's death in a riding accident four years ago had left him a widower, females had swarmed around him like bees, so Rob had been forced to create his own shield, which included keeping his distance and not trusting their motives.

"Did you want something, Mr. Mattson?" The woman gave him a half smile.

How long had he stared at her? And she knew his name. No surprise there because everybody knew the Mattsons. Heat rushed up his neck. He turned his attention to the dog, dug a dog biscuit out of his pocket and crouched down.

"Here, Lady. Come here, girl."

Lady tilted her head and gave him a puzzled look before trotting over to accept the treat. He ruffled her fur and stroked her back and sides, dismayed to feel her protruding ribs. Lady finished the treat, then licked his hand. "That's my girl."

"You know her?" The woman's tone held no guilt.

"Mom?" The girl stepped closer, her ball in hand, a worried frown on her sweet face.

"It's okay, honey." The woman's maternal smile made her even prettier, if that was possible. "Well, Mr. Mattson, you seem to know our Daisy, and she seems to know you."

"She should." Rob stood and towered over her. Unlike most folks, who were awed by his six-foot-three-inch height, she barely tracked his movement with her eyes. "I bought her over two years ago and hand raised her from a puppy. What are you doing with her?"

The question brought an innocent blink from those gray-green eyes. "I… I've been taking care of her." She glanced beyond him with a surprised look.

Rob didn't bother to turn around. Sheriff Rex Blake was a large presence that a man could feel before he saw him.

"Got a problem, Rob?" Rex spoke in his authoritarian lawman voice that no doubt rattled many a lawbreaker's nerves. He watched the woman to see her reaction.

"Yep. Sure do." Rob noticed the woman moving closer to her daughter and putting a protective arm around her. Obviously she couldn't make a run for it. "This woman has my dog I've been looking for since she was stolen last winter."

Rex settled a stern look on the woman, but his expression quickly softened. "Mrs. Parker?"

"Hi, Rex." Her tone sounded guarded. Had she been arrested before?

"Um, Rob?" Rex nudged Rob's arm. "This is Lauren Parker. She's your cousin Will's new paralegal. I met her in his office when I was there on a child custody matter." He chuckled. "You sure you want me to arrest her?"

Rob clenched his jaw so it wouldn't drop open with surprise. Though not too much surprise as he now remembered seeing her across the church's fellowship hall after Will's wedding. In fact, Will had tried to set them up. Fat chance that would happen. Will knew he wasn't interested in dating. "So what are you doing with my dog?" He didn't try to keep the accusing tone from his voice.

"Well, I—"

"I find it interesting—" he refused to listen to her excuse "—that you work for Will and you didn't connect my missing dog to the one you found. We put posters up in every store in town. And don't tell me Will never mentioned the puppies they found out by his place that a DNA test proved were hers. You should have posted a 'found dog' notice."

She stared up at him, annoyance beaming from her eyes. "We found her at a rest stop outside of Santa Fe when we were moving here in May." Her expression softened, enhancing her beauty. "Poor baby was terribly thin and bedraggled...and covered with fleas." She glanced at her daughter, who now knelt beside Lady and held on to her. "We took her to a vet down there and had her checked out, including checking for a chip, but she didn't have one."

"Didn't have a chip? That's a l—" he noticed the startled look in the girl's eyes "—not true. We chip all of our dogs at twelve weeks."

"Well, she didn't have one when we found her." She glared at Rob. "If she had, we would have brought her to you as soon as we arrived in Riverton. We did the best we could to take care of her and even spent money we couldn't afford to pay the vet for treating her."

Ah, there it was. The money thing. "And no doubt you'll want the reward."

She huffed. "Reward? No, thank you. Taking care of her was the right thing to do. And the joy she's brought us more than makes up for the expense." She gazed at her daughter. "Zoey, this man is Daisy's owner. Remember I told you this might happen."

"Yes, ma'am." Zoey's eyes filled with tears, and she held Lady closer for a few seconds. Then she looked up at Rob, and her heartbroken expression pierced his chest. Her mother's actions were not her fault. "You can take her." A humming sound preceded the girl's words, as though she'd had to take a breath and start her vocal cords before she could speak. She opened her arms to release Lady.

It saddened him to hurt this girl, but he had to focus on his dog and get her back to Bobby as soon as possible so his son could resume her training. He bent down and picked Lady up. She rewarded him by licking his face. After all this time, she still remembered him.

"Okay, Rob." Rex clapped him on the shoulder. "You've got this. See you later."

"Thanks, buddy." He turned away from the women to head back to his truck.

"I have her shot records from that Santa Fe vet," the woman called. "Or I can give you his business card so you can call or email him."

He faced her. "Mrs. Parker, you still haven't told me why you didn't know about my missing dog. I'm sure Will's talked about his pups and their lost mother."

She lifted her chin and glared at him. "We consider it unprofessional to discuss personal matters at the office."

He stared at her for maybe ten seconds. Knowing his sociable cousin Will, he couldn't quite picture that. "Yeah, right." He spun around and strode toward his truck, ignoring Lady's wiggling and whimpering as she looked over his shoulder, no doubt already missing the girl who'd been her best friend all summer. That problem would be fixed after Lady spent enough time with Bobby and remembered where she came from.

LAUREN TRIED TO stop shaking but couldn't begin to manage it, even when Zoey sat beside her on the picnic bench and hugged her.

"It's okay, Mom." Zoey laid her head on Lauren's shoulder. "Jesus's got this, so she'll be okay."

As usual, she emitted a little hum before speaking, and her *l*'s came out as *w*'s. Would her fellow students torment her in her new school as they had back in Orlando?

"I know." She patted Zoey's hand. "Jesus has this." She eyed the picnic basket. "You hungry?"

"Not much, but I should eat." Zoey reached for the basket and tugged it closer.

Yes, she should eat. When Zoey went too long without food or water, she was in danger of having a seizure.

Lauren pulled the contents from the basket—sandwiches, chips and iced tea, and left the generic dog kibbles she'd packed. She'd done the best she could for Daisy... Lady, but her money would stretch only so far. No doubt Mr. Mattson would fatten Lady up with one of the healthier, more expensive brands. For that alone, she was glad. For Zoey's broken heart, not so much. But it was too soon to promise a new puppy. Zoey never liked it when she rushed in to try to fix things.

Like right now as she struggled to open the plastic zip bag. But she stuck with it until her uncooperative hands finally separated the sealed sides and removed the sandwich. Lauren watched from the corner of her eye as she opened her own and smelled the delicious aroma of chicken salad. Before she could take a bite, Zoey grasped her hand.

"We gotta say grace, Mom. Dear Jesus, thank You for the food. And thank You that Daisy is going to her new forever home." She laughed softly. "Her new *old* forever home. I know that man will take good care of her."

"Amen." Lauren's eyes burned, but she wouldn't let tears come. Zoey's faith was real and deep and often put her mama to shame. God truly had cared for them these past fifteen years.

Her new job had been a huge blessing and an opportunity to get away from her hometown, where some people still asked her why she'd divorced her husband, as though it had been her fault. Didn't every woman want to be married to Singleton Weatherby Parker? After all, he was the primetime anchor for the local NBC affiliate, handsome beyond words, perfect in his news presentations and a man who managed to skate above controversy without a hint of scandal. Of course those countless admirers didn't know the man off camera. The man who'd rejected his firstborn because of her failure to be perfect and had divorced Lauren because she refused to hide Zoey away in a care home. With the divorce, he'd begrudged the minimum child support the judge ordered. Then he married his pregnant beauty-queen trophy wife, and they now had two perfect children. Good riddance. Except that two years ago, he'd gone to court to request a reduction in his childcare payments, citing financial problems.

Lauren suspected he'd hidden some of his assets, but she couldn't manage the lawyer fees to take him to court, so she'd studied to become a paralegal to combat his scheme. But after earning her certification, she decided to forgo the drama and not to go after him. In fact, she released him from any financial obligation as long as he signed away his parental rights. He was all too happy to do that. Zoey didn't know much about her father, and Lauren deflected her questions as much as she could. She dreaded the day when Zoey demanded better answers.

To make a fresh start, she'd done an online search and applied for several open paralegal jobs. Most wanted applicants with more experience, but somehow she'd snagged a position with Mattson and Mattson, Attorneys at Law, maybe because the two young lawyers were just starting to grow their law office and could only offer a minimal salary. She grabbed the offer like a lifeline.

She and Zoey had packed up and driven west to start their new life, leaving the Sunshine State of Florida for the Land of Sunshine. So far, New Mexico was living up to its reputation, but winter was coming. For the first time in Zoey's life, Lauren would have to buy her a winter coat. That would protect her from the cold, but what would protect her from the challenges she would meet at her new school?

THE FOLLOWING MONDAY, Lauren pulled her car up in front of Riverton High School. "You sure you don't want me to go in with you?" She unclicked her seat belt, ready to get out and walk Zoey into the school building.

"Oh, Mom." Zoey rolled her eyes. "Me and Jesus got this." She managed her typical smirk that always accompanied her deliberate grammar mistakes. She opened her door and scooched to the edge of the seat, carefully planting her feet before grasping the door and pulling herself upright. She slung her backpack over one shoulder, wobbled a bit, righted herself, then shut the door and headed toward the brick building with her familiar halting gait among the other countless students. And she didn't even look back.

Lauren shook her head. Zoey had come a long way in learning to control her uncooperative body, and now she faced this new challenge with her usual courage.

Several students watched her awkward trek across the concrete, but no one said anything, at least not that Lauren could hear.

"Lord, please send her a friend."

In fact, Lauren could use one herself. She'd been on the

edge of anxiety since her encounter Saturday with that Matt-son person. What a bully, and so much like Singleton. Now, as she drove toward work, her anxiety grew. What would Will and Sam have to say about her encounter with their cousin? Would they believe his not-so-subtle accusation that she'd sto-len his valuable dog? Would they fire her?

"Lord, please help. You know my savings are almost gone. I can't start over again." And who would hire her if the Matt-son clan turned against her?

Parking in front of the one-story storefront law office, she shook off her dismal thoughts and pasted on her professional smile before entering. Toward the back of the large, open room, newlywed Will sat on the edge of Sam's desk. When she en-tered, they turned her way, and their serious expressions sent a frisson of alarm through her chest.

"Morning, Lauren." Will's baritone voice sounded much like his older cousin's, and their resemblance was undeniable. "Come on over here for a minute."

She stared at them for a second or two, her heart dropping lower. "Sure."

"Let her put her stuff down, Cuz." Sam had many of the Mattson features as well, except that his hair was light brown instead of black, and his eyes more green than blue.

Lauren set her purse and lunch on her desk, then walked across the room on shaky legs.

"Take a look at this and tell me what you think." Sam handed her a few sheets of paper, which she couldn't read for the blurriness in her eyes.

She blinked and finally managed to focus on the pages of architectural drawings. "Um, what am I looking at?" Not a pink slip, that was for sure.

"We're trying to decide whether to partition off this room so our clients have more privacy during consultations," Will said, "or find another building already set up that way."

"Or build something new," Sam said. "That'll be pricey, but we're thinking it might be worth the expense in the long run."

"Oh." To her horror, Lauren's voice wobbled.

"Hey, are you okay?" Will stood and grabbed a chair, then helped her sit. "What's going on?"

"Oh," she repeated, scrambling for an intelligent response. "My daughter started at her new school today." She managed a shaky laugh. So much for her claim to Robert Mattson that talking about personal matters was unprofessional.

"Ah," the cousins said in a tenor-baritone duet.

"She'll be okay." Will, ever the optimist, patted her shoulder.

"I know. Thanks." Lauren forced her thoughts away from her unnecessary fears and to the matter at hand. "So, what are the pros and cons of each option?" She fetched a legal pad and pen from her own desk and made columns. "Ideas?"

While they discussed the possibilities, in the back of her mind, Lauren allowed herself some relief. At least for now, her employment wasn't in danger. But how long would it be before Robert Mattson talked to his cousins about Lady and cast doubt on her honesty, a death knell for the job of anyone working in law?

ON HER WAY to pick Zoey up from school, Lauren passed that unmistakable huge black Ram truck with Robert Mattson driving the other direction. Even through his dark-tinted window, she could see the handsome cut of his jaw. Unlike her previous encounter with the rancher, this time he was smiling, which greatly enhanced his good looks, much as a smile did for her ex. And, as with her ex, she had no doubt that behind the smile lurked a devious mind that only looked out for himself.

She pulled in behind the other parents' vehicles lined up in front of the school. Most of them were pickup trucks, which made her little eleven-year-old Honda Fit seem even smaller. On the trip from Orlando, they'd had a few scary moments as they traveled alongside semis that seemed intent on squashing them. But she wouldn't trade this comfy little runabout for anything.

"Mom!" Zoey opened the car door and practically jumped inside. "I've got a new friend. *Two* new friends."

"That's awesome, honey." *And* answered her prayer. Lauren's eyes watered, and she blinked to focus on the traffic ahead as she pulled back into the street. "Tell me all about them and all about your day."

"Well…" Zoey gave her a sly look. "One of them is a boy."

"Okay." This was new. Her daughter hadn't shown much interest in boys yet, maybe because some of them had been her worst tormentors.

"Yeah. I sat next to him in computer class, and we talked a lot. Then at lunch, when I was having trouble with my tray, he came over and took it." Her face glowed. "He took me over to a table with his sister. She's in my English class, and they're twins." She laughed. "But you wouldn't know it. He's real tall, like almost six feet. She's a little taller than me, maybe five-eight. He's got black hair, and she's a blonde. They both have blue eyes. They said they want me to sit with them at lunch every day."

Listening to her happy chatter, Lauren's heart filled with joy. "They sound very nice." More than that, maybe they would be her silent protectors if other students weren't so kind. She gave Zoey a quick, side-eyed glance. "Do they have names?"

Zoey snorted. "Duh. Of course, Mom. They're Bobby and Mandy Mattson, and they live on the Double Bar M Ranch. They want me to come out and ride horses with them."

While she continued to chatter on about her wonderful first day, Lauren could hardly keep her eyes on the road.

Why did her precious daughter's much-needed new friends have to be related to that horrible man who accused Lauren of stealing his valuable dog?

CHAPTER TWO

"EVERYTHING LOOKS GREAT, Mom." Rob helped himself to a large portion of his favorite beef stew and grabbed two biscuits from the basket in front of his plate. The spicy aroma of the stew made his mouth water. "Nobody can cook like you, right, kids?"

"Right," the twins said in unison as they filled their plates.

"Can I have a peanut butter sandwich?" Eight-year-old Clementine frowned at the stew Mom had served her.

"Sorry, Clementine." Rob chuckled. "We're cattle ranchers. Gotta eat beef at least once a day."

She huffed out a dramatic sigh and wrinkled her nose as if the food on her plate smelled like something other than mouthwateringly delicious.

"Gramma, what are we gonna eat after you leave?" Bobby asked before shoveling a large spoonful into his mouth. Lady, who lay beside his chair, watched him but didn't beg for a bite.

"And who's going to teach my brother good manners when you're gone?" Mandy smirked at Bobby. "That was an awful big bite."

He returned a goofy glare and again shoveled a large spoonful into his mouth.

"I'm sure y'all can manage," Mom laughed. "Back in the

day, cowboys learned to cook for themselves. As for their manners, well, everybody had better manners back then." She set her fork down and sighed. "I'm starting to feel guilty about leaving you all."

"It's not too late to change your mind." Mandy's hopeful expression was mirrored on her brother's face.

"Yeah, Gramma." Clementine's voice was edged with a whine. "Not too late."

"Hey, now." Rob couldn't let their pleading get to Mom, no matter how much he wanted her to stay on the ranch where she'd lived for forty-five years since marrying Dad. "Your grandmother needs a break from taking care of you mavericks. Besides, Phoenix isn't that far. We'll have lots of visits."

"Yes, we will. Especially at Christmas." Mom picked up her fork. "Now, you three, how was your first day back to school?"

"It was fun." Clementine was always the first of his kids to speak up. "I saw all my friends, and I like my teacher."

"That's good, honey. It's real important to like your teacher." Rob eyed his older daughter. "Mandy?"

Her blue eyes twinkled. "We saw all our old friends, too, and we met a new girl and invited her out to ride this coming Saturday." She looked at Rob, raising her eyebrows as though she'd asked a question, not stated a plan.

"No problem. Just be sure you practice your own barrel racing. You need to keep that up so you'll be ready for the Miss Riverton Stampede next spring."

"Oh, Dad." Mandy rolled her eyes. "Been there, done that. Isn't it time to let somebody else wear the crown? I mean, I really enjoyed being Junior Miss Stampede, but I'd rather—"

"Aw, come on, sweetheart." Rob tried to keep his voice light, but she had no idea how much this meant to him. "It's a family tradition, and people expect the ladies in our family to compete. First Gramma, then your mom." He could finally speak about Jordyn without choking up. "See where it got them? As rodeo queens, they caught the attention of some pretty high-profile cowboys." He grinned playfully, but it was true. Mom had married Dad right after her reign as Miss Riverton Stampede ended, and Rob had put off proposing to Jordyn until her reign was almost over so she could keep her crown. "Right, Mom?"

"Don't put me in the middle of this." She held one hand up like a stop sign. "I loved being a rodeo queen and all the opportunities it gave me. But you have to let these kids find their own paths."

With that kind of support, maybe Rob would have an easier time influencing those paths once Mom moved out. No, that wasn't true. He might do all right raising Bobby, but Mandy and Clementine needed Mom's womanly influence. Still, he wouldn't fight her move.

"I want to be Miss Riverton Stampede." Clementine gave Rob a hopeful smile.

"Very good, sweetheart." He winked at her. "You just keep up with your riding lessons, and when you're old enough, you'll get your chance." He eyed Bobby. "Okay, enough about the women. How's it going with Lady today? You spend any time working her with the steers?"

"Yessir." He reached down and patted Lady's head. "I think she remembers some of her training, but she's not real enthusiastic about it. She mostly wants to hang out with me, not work the cattle with the other dogs."

He blew out a sigh. Just what he'd feared. That Parker woman and her daughter had ruined the best natural cow herding dog he'd ever had. "Well, keep at it." Maybe he'd have to work with Bobby and Lady himself.

He still hadn't decided whether or not to tell Will and Sam about his encounter with the Parkers. He didn't feel right letting his cousins continue to employ a dishonest woman in their law office. On the other hand, if they fired her, how would she support her daughter? Besides, Rob didn't have any actual evidence to prove Mrs. Parker stole Lady, except that the chip had been removed from Lady's shoulder. He should have gotten the name of that Santa Fe vet who treated the dog so he could check her story, but he wasn't about to ask her for it now.

"So, tell us more about your new friend," Mom said to the twins.

"Well, she's really sweet and really cute." Mandy shot a look at Bobby, but he didn't react. Good thing. It was way too early for his son to get interested in girls.

"Yeah, she's real nice and super-smart at computers." Bobby grinned. "A real computer geek, like me."

Geek? Rob hated that word but stifled the urge to scold his son. How could he raise the next owner of the Double Bar M when his heir apparent preferred computers to cattle?

"And what's her name?" Mom continued her interrogation.

"Zoey Parker." The twins spoke in unison, as they often did.

If a boulder had fallen on Rob's chest, he couldn't have felt more impact. The bite of beef he was about to swallow came near to choking him, but he managed to cough it out before it reached his throat. How could this be happening? How could his own children become traitors unaware?

"And her mother works for Will and Sam," Bobby said.

"Oh, how nice," Mom said. "Do they go to church?"

"I haven't seen them there." Bobby shrugged. "Hey, sis, we should invite Zoey to youth group."

"Sure thing."

As their conversation continued, Rob scrambled to sort out his tangled thoughts and feelings. He wanted nothing to do with Lauren Parker, but by befriending her daughter, his own children had shown what they were really made of. They weren't put off by her disability. In fact, hadn't even mentioned it. He couldn't be prouder of them for that omission. Now he just had to figure out how to help them keep their promise to take Zoey riding without having to encounter her mother. Fat chance of that. It was his responsibility to keep watch to be sure Zoey was safe as she rode, as he did with any guest to the ranch. Which meant, like it or not, he would be there when Zoey and her mother arrived on Saturday.

LAUREN FOLLOWED THE directions on her phone's GPS, wishing for all she was worth that she and Zoey were going somewhere else, anywhere else, this Saturday. Why did she feel like she was headed for her execution, not for a fun and exciting opportunity for Zoey to learn something new, something that would help her develop her motor skills? Would they encounter Robert Mattson, or would his children be in charge of the horse riding?

Not that she had full confidence in two fifteen-year-olds being responsible enough to help Zoey learn to ride. But Lauren would stick close to catch Zoey if she started to fall.

"Look, Mom. There it is." Zoey had bounced with excitement in the passenger seat ever since they'd left their apartment. Now she pointed to the huge redbrick archway set some twenty yards off the highway. Emblazoned ironworks words across the arch announced Double Bar M Ranch.

"Yep." Lauren swallowed hard as she pulled up to the intercom on a post and punched the call button.

"Can I help you?" a youngish female voice said.

"It's me, Mandy," Zoey called out across the car.

"Zoeeeeey!"

Her squeal, followed by a buzzing sound and the whir of the well-oiled gate opening, didn't help Lauren's nerves. Somehow she managed to hide her emotions from Zoey as she negotiated the gravel driveway onto the property, past pastures and up to the beautiful wood frame house on the left. Like a white columned antebellum mansion, it stood on a hill above the Rio Grande. Several other houses and outbuildings dotted the vast property, including a huge red barn off to the right.

At the main house, complete with a white picket fence covered with late summer roses and sweet peas, a teen girl dashed out the door, followed by a tall, lanky teen boy and a little girl...and Lady.

"Park here," the girl called out as she waved a hand toward a spot beside the fence, then hurried over to Zoey's door.

Lauren got out and surveyed the property. With horseback riding their purpose for being here, she would have preferred to park closer to the barn so Zoey wouldn't have so far to walk. But she wouldn't embarrass her daughter by suggesting it.

Zoey was out of the car in a flash, falling to her knees to hug Lady, who wagged all over as she greeted her. "Oh, Daisy, I've missed you so much."

The other kids watched, their faces bright with innocent pleasure.

"Her name's Lady," the little girl said. "How do you know her?"

Zoey looked up at Lauren, her eyes filled with sadness. When Lauren realized they would be coming to this ranch, they'd talked about seeing Lady again, but that didn't mean Zoey would be able to hide how much she missed the dog. And now she could see how much the dog missed her.

"Hi, Mrs. Parker." The lanky boy, getting close to six feet tall, as Zoey had said, was definitely his father's son, at least in looks. "I'm Bobby."

"Hi, Bobby." Cute boy, and obviously much nicer than his namesake dad.

"I'm Mandy." The teen girl, close to five foot eight inches, also as Zoey had said, gently tugged on the younger one's blond ponytail. "This is Clementine."

"Aka Pest." The boy chucked the little one under the chin. "Or Short Stuff."

She grinned but kept her eyes on Zoey and repeated her question. "How do you know Lady?"

"These are the people who found Lady and took care of her," Mandy said. "Right, Mrs. Parker?"

"Right." So her father had told them, at least the older ones.

"I'm glad to meet you. Thank you for inviting Zoey out to ride. She's never ridden—"

"They know, Mom." Zoey scolded her with a look.

All righty, then. This was Zoey's party, so Lauren would try her best to keep quiet.

"Let's go!" Mandy grasped Zoey's hand, not to help her but in a companionable way.

Lauren followed the kids and Lady across the barnyard toward the huge red structure, with Lady sticking close to Zoey. Would that cause a problem? Two other dogs trotted from the barn toward the group, tails wagging, and ate up the affection the kids gave them. A few cats dotted the area, but they appeared content to watch the action rather than take part. Maybe she should get Zoey a kitten, which would be so much easier to care for in their apartment.

"Mrs. Parker," Bobby said, "we're so grateful to you for taking care of Lady. I know you miss her, but we can give you a puppy, if you want one. That is, when she has one."

Zoey shot her a hopeful look.

"Thanks. We'll see." These purebred dogs were way out of her price range, and she doubted their father would just give one away.

As they entered the barn, Lauren fanned herself with her hand, waving away flies and animal odors but welcoming the shade after walking in the August sunshine. The kids didn't seem bothered by the heat or the smells. While they gave Zoey a tour of the huge building, Lauren hung back by the door.

She caught a glimpse of Robert Mattson and another man as they entered the building at the far end. Using broad gestures, he was apparently giving orders to the other man. Scurrying across the dirt floor in a less than dignified manner, she followed the kids into the second aisle. They stood outside a stall where a beautiful paint horse hung its head over the door and gave them an expectant look.

"This is Tripper. He's real gentle. A retired ol' cowpony,

so he's our best ride for beginners." Bobby dug a carrot out of his back jeans pocket and handed it to Zoey. "You can give it to him."

Without missing a beat, Zoey did as he said. The horse lipped the carrot into its mouth and chewed, which involved some serious moisture.

"Ewww." Zoey giggled and wiped her hand on her jeans.

While the other kids laughed, Lauren failed to hide her grimace. Good thing none of them looked her way. Lady moved closer to Zoey, gazing up at her as if making sure she was all right.

"You can't be finicky around horses," Mandy said. "If it's not slobber, it's manure."

"And before you ride—" Robert Mattson appeared around the corner of the aisle "—you muck out the stall. Work before pleasure."

Despite the heat, Lauren felt a chill sweep down her back.

"Hey, Dad." The twins spoke together, and little Clementine hurried over to hug her father. He patted her on the head.

"Hey." He gave Lauren a brief glance, clear annoyance on his face.

A wave of anxiety swept into her chest. Oh, how she did *not* want to be here. "Hi."

He walked over to Zoey, and his expression turned hospitable. "Welcome to the Double Bar M Ranch, Zoey. You ready for some barn chores before you ride?"

"Yessir." From her big grin, Zoey seemed not to remember that their previous encounter had been less than pleasant. "Gimme that shovel, and I'll get to work."

He chuckled, turning his face from stern to undeniably handsome. Lauren had to look away. Her ex had been charming and handsome. Especially when he acted like Mr. Nice Guy around people he wanted to impress.

Mandy put a bridle on Tripper, led him out of the stall and handed the lead to Clementine, who tugged him several yards down the aisle. At Mandy's direction, Zoey picked up the shovel, struggling a bit with its weight.

"I'll do it." Bobby reached for the shovel.

"No. I got this." Shrugging away from him, Zoey worked hard to scoop up some of the soiled straw. After three tries, she succeeded, then dumped it in the nearby wheelbarrow. Only a little spilled off onto the floor. Lady followed her every move, almost like she wanted to help.

"Great job." Mandy grabbed another shovel and joined her.

Robert stepped over to Lauren and tilted his hat back from his forehead. "Is she gonna be all right?"

His whispered words sent an odd little shudder down her side. She looked up into his blue eyes, and his tall, broad-shouldered, very masculine presence tickled her feminine heart. *Oh, my. I'm my own worst enemy.* She looked down and stepped away from him.

"Yes. She's fine." Did she sound as snippy to him as she did to herself?

From his annoyed expression, the answer was yes. But what did he expect? He hadn't apologized for accusing her of stealing Lady. Hadn't really thanked her for rescuing that sweet little dog that clearly favored Zoey today.

"By the way, I have Lady's shot record in my car. I'll leave it with you." She spared him a glance. "You can call the vet and ask about the chip. Or the lack of chip."

He didn't speak for a moment. Finally, he leaned back against the wall and crossed his arms. "I'll do that."

How rude. If Zoey's happiness and much-needed exercise were not at stake, she'd take her daughter home right now and never come back.

After they spread fresh straw over the floor of the stall, Mandy and Zoey handed the shovels to Bobby to put away.

"Ready to saddle up?" Mandy asked Zoey.

"More than ready."

Watching her daughter struggle through the saddling procedure, Lauren had to clench her fists to keep from helping her. A glance at Robert revealed he seemed to have the same problem. At last the job was done.

"Here you go." Bobby half squatted and offered cupped hands to lift Zoey into the saddle.

"Here I go." She cast a nervous grin in Lauren's direction. Lauren returned a thumbs-up.

"Oops. Almost forgot your safety helmet." Bobby straightened and grabbed a black riding helmet from a nearby hook and handed it to Zoey.

"Oh, yeah." She laughed as she put it on and managed to snap the strap without too much trouble. "Gotta protect this crazy head of mine."

The kids also laughed, and Lauren smiled. Her daughter's sense of humor had smoothed over many awkward situations in her young life. She'd stopped wearing her own everyday safety helmet just last year, but today she was willing to wear this one.

Across the aisle, Lauren saw a sign. "Notice: This is an equine facility. All activities on these grounds are subject to the Equine Inherent Risk Law." She would have to check that law when she went to work on Monday. She'd learned a great deal about New Mexico law over the past few months, necessary information for her job. But none were as personally important to her as this one.

Arms still folded across his broad chest, Robert watched the kids like a hawk. Was he proud of their care and skilled instructions to Zoey, or was he sticking close hoping to avoid a lawsuit?

With Mandy on Tripper's opposite side and Bobby lifting, Zoey was soon in the saddle with her sneakers settled in the stirrups. She grinned broadly as Mandy showed her how to hold the reins.

"Okay, let's head out to the corral." Mandy grasped Tripper's bridle and walked toward a broad doorway at the side of the barn.

Lauren followed, and little Clementine skipped along beside her dad, who was focused on the others. Lady trotted close to Tripper, careful to avoid his hooves.

The riding lesson went on longer than Lauren expected. Mandy led Tripper around the corral with great patience, while Bobby and even Robert watched with sustained interest. Zoey was having the time of her life.

"She's a natural." Robert's observation startled Lauren.

"You don't have to say that." Sometimes people tried to be helpful by giving Zoey more praise than was warranted.

"I call 'em as I see 'em." Robert snorted. "You need to have more faith in your daughter."

Lauren swallowed a sharp retort. She refused to argue with this man. Besides, she had plenty of faith in Zoey's can-do attitude. She preferred honest assessment rather than phony praise.

The morning wore on, but the kids were having so much fun, no one seemed in a hurry for the riding lesson to end. Worse still, Lauren had hoped one time on horseback would be enough, but the kids were already making plans for next Saturday.

"Hey, Mrs. Parker." Mandy held up her phone. "My gramma just sent me a text saying she'd like you and Zoey to stay for lunch."

She started to make an excuse, but heard a quiet groan from the big man beside her. How rude, especially since she had no intention of staying on the ranch any longer than necessary.

"You can't say no," Bobby said. "Gramma makes the best tuna salad in the world." He spoke as if it were a done deal.

Lauren scrambled for an honest excuse, but the hopeful look on Zoey's face made it impossible.

"Please, Mom."

She released a long sigh. "That's very kind. Please text back that we accept."

Robert groaned again, and Lauren could almost feel disapproval radiating from him. Which made his large presence almost feel menacing.

"On second thought—"

"No." His voice had a harsh edge. "When my mother invites you, you come. Got that?"

Lauren was too stunned to respond. There was something in his voice that went beyond giving orders. She should pack up Zoey and leave now, but curiosity made her want to meet the woman who commanded such obedience from her forty-something son.

CHAPTER THREE

ROB FELT TRAPPED. Mom hadn't invited anybody to a meal since Dad died two years ago, and her two closest friends had already moved to Phoenix. He wasn't about to deny her the pleasure of having guests, even if those guests included Lauren Parker. So he'd bite the bullet and tolerate her for Mom's sake.

Zoey was another matter. He was glad to have her stay. She was the most uncomplicated teenager he'd ever met, very different from some of the twins' other friends, who clearly hung around them because their last name was Mattson. He'd known that kind of hanger-on in his own high school years, so they were easy to spot. Zoey didn't seem to have an agenda other than to enjoy the twins' company. Even Clementine got some of her attention. How could such a sweet girl be the daughter of a dog thief? It did bother him that Lady seemed glued to Zoey's side, but enough time with Bobby should fix that.

"How can I help you?" Lauren stood at Mom's elbow while Mom sliced tomatoes on the kitchen counter.

"Thanks. You can set the table." His mom nodded toward the round kitchen table. "Plates and glasses in that cupboard." She pointed with her chin. "Fill the glasses with ice from the fridge door. Is sweet tea okay?"

Rob watched from the doorway as Lauren followed Mom's

instructions. The two women chatted like women do, seeming to hit it off right away. Great. Just what Rob needed. His mother being friends with his enemy. Maybe Mom would move to Phoenix before he could prove Lauren's dishonesty. She was waiting for the completion of her condo, so her move-in date was uncertain. Maybe by Christmas. No, that was no reason to want Mom gone. Without her help, he had no idea what he'd do with Clementine while he took care of the ranch and his responsibilities to the Cattlemen's Association and the Riverton Stampede Committee.

The kids kept the conversation around the table going as they rehashed the morning's ride to Mom. She listened intently, while Mrs. Parker seemed more interested in her plate. More important, Lady had settled beside Zoey's chair rather than Bobby's. How was Rob going to break that attachment when border collies were known for their loyalty?

Clementine stared across the table at Zoey. "Why do you talk so funny?"

Rob sucked in a breath. "Clementine, that's rude!"

She winced at his harsh tone, but he couldn't let her thoughtlessness go uncorrected. Mom looked surprised and disappointed, as did the twins. Mrs. Parker appeared unfazed. Maybe other kids had asked her daughter the same question.

"It's okay, Mr. Mattson." Zoey smiled like she'd just received a compliment. "It's natural for kids to wonder about my goofy ways. It's like this, Clem." Zoey had already adopted the nickname Rob hated, probably because it was short and easier for her to pronounce. "Sometimes something goes wonky when a baby is born that makes them have cerebral palsy." She grimaced. Or maybe it was one of her uncontrolled facial movements. As usual, a little hum preceded her words. "When my mom saw I wasn't doing stuff babies are supposed to do—" she gave Mrs. Parker a sweet smile "—she made me exercise, so I can do lots more than I would have if I'd just stayed in bed all the time. Like, I wore braces on my legs so I could learn to walk, but I don't have to wear them anymore."

"One thing's sure," Bobby piped up. "It sure didn't affect your brain." Seated next to Clementine, he tweaked his little sister's nose. "She's the smartest one in our computer class." He faced Zoey. "Which reminds me, can you stay after lunch and help me with my programming assignment?"

"No way," Mandy said. "She's going to help me with my English essay—"

"Whoa. Put the brakes on." Mrs. Parker laughed—an undeniably pleasant sound—and her face took on the same maternal glow Rob had noticed before, which made her pretty face even prettier. Unlike his relationship with his own teens, these two communicated well. How could he think of putting Mrs. Parker in jail when her daughter so obviously needed her? Would Zoey's father step up to take care of her?

"Sorry to spoil your homework fun," Mrs. Parker continued. "But we have some errands to run, then Zoey needs to rest after her busy morning. And, of course, we have laundry." She gave Mom a look women often shared.

"Oh, yes." Mom laughed.

The twins sighed in unison, but nodded their understanding as well.

"Lauren," Mom said, "will you and Zoey come to church with us tomorrow? We attend Riverton Community Church."

"Zoey has to come to youth group with us tomorrow night," Mandy added.

"Whoa." Why had Rob echoed Lauren's word? "I'm sure Mrs. Parker and Zoey have their own church to attend."

"Please call me Lauren." She turned those gorgeous eyes toward him, but without the flirtatious eyelash batting some women sent his way.

Fine with him, but he wasn't about to form an attachment with this woman. "Sure. Call me Rob."

"Or you can call him Big Boss." Bobby smirked, earning

himself a swat on the shoulder from Rob. "Hey, I'm just telling it like it is. After all, that's what our cowhands call him."

"And you may call me Andrea," Mom said. "Now that we
know who everybody is, what about church?"

"Well..." Lauren eyed Zoey, whose hopeful smile let her
opinion be known. "How about we meet you there?"

That settled, they finished lunch, then started in on Mom's
peach cobbler made with her recently home-canned New Mexico peaches and covered with fresh cream from one of their
two milk cows.

"This is delicious, Andrea," Lauren said. "And Bobby sure
was right about your tuna salad. It's the best I've ever eaten.
Will you share your recipe?"

"Thank you." Mom beamed. "Of course you may have my
recipe."

They chatted about Mom's "secret sauce," which generated
more of that female bonding Rob didn't like to see between
these two. If that wasn't enough, as their guests were leaving,
Lady tried to climb into Lauren's little Honda with Zoey and
whined when Bobby pulled her back.

"No, Lady." Bobby held on to her new collar. "You have to
stay with me." He didn't seem as bothered by Lady's new attachment as Rob had hoped.

Zoey seemed to struggle with tears. Then she sniffed and
put on a bright smile. "Thanks for a great morning."

Lauren glanced at Rob with a guarded expression. What
was her problem? "Yes, thank you for a lovely morning."

"Next time *you* have to ride, Mrs. Parker." Mandy offered
her a challenging grin.

"Ha. That'll be the day." Now Lauren smiled. "See you tomorrow at church." She ducked her head and climbed into her
little car, started it, then lowered the window and held out some
papers to Rob. "Here's Lady's shot record and the business
card for that vet in Santa Fe. You be sure to call him, okay?"

Rob stared at the card, which looked like it had been run

over by a truck. Where had she found it? On the roadside?
Maybe that was how she'd concocted the story about the vet.
As for the shot record, it could easily have been printed out
from any computer.

He watched as they drove away, telling himself he just
wanted to be sure the new sensor worked and would open the
front gate as her car approached. Who was he kidding? She
was a beautiful woman with a lovely daughter who, despite
his suspicions *and* determination not to like her, was starting
to get under his skin. Good thing they were going to church
tomorrow. Maybe Pastor Tim's sermon would convict her, and
she would admit she had something to do with Lady's dognapping. Yeah. That was it. She just needed to admit she'd done
wrong, and they could go from there.

EVERY TIME LAUREN took Zoey into a new experience, she
worried about how people would treat her daughter, which
was probably why she'd put off going to church here in Riverton. But from the moment they'd stepped out of the car,
they'd been greeted by friendly folks of every age. Several
teens waved and called out to Zoey, and she responded in
kind. Mandy and Bobby, followed by cute little Clementine,
ran across the church's front lawn, greeting them as though
they hadn't seen each other in weeks instead of spending the
previous morning together.

"You missed Sunday school." Mandy looped her arm around
Zoey's and led the way toward the redbrick structure. "You
have to come earlier next week. Let's sit together for the main
service."

Lauren had no choice but to follow, even when Rob joined
them. Andrea followed Zoey's example and looped her arm
around Lauren's as though they were old friends instead of
new acquaintances. How could such a lovely woman be the
mother of a bully like Robert Mattson?

The music was a blend of praise songs and old standards,

both of which lifted Lauren's heart in worship. The minister, Pastor Tim, gave an inspiring message from II Timothy about following one's holy calling, reminding her to get serious about her own personal Bible study. After the service, Andrea invited them to lunch at a local restaurant, but Lauren declined.

"Zoey's looking forward to youth group this evening, but she'll need to rest this afternoon."

"Another time, then," Andrea said.

Robert sauntered over to them. "What did you think of the sermon?"

This was the first time he'd shown interest in her opinion, and for some silly reason, her heart skipped a beat. "It was very nice. I like the pastor's down-to-earth style and his preaching from God's Word."

"Huh." His soft grunt almost sounded like he didn't believe her. He stared at her for a moment, and she had a ridiculous urge to squirm under his scrutiny. All pleasant feelings disappeared, and she looked away.

"Hey, folks." Will Mattson and his new bride, Olivia, joined them. He greeted Robert with a handshake. "Lauren, I'm glad to see you here."

After all around greetings, Will nudged Robert with his fist. "So, I see you've finally met our very accomplished paralegal."

The teasing look in his blue eyes hinted at matchmaking. Obviously her boss was not reading the room correctly. No way would she ever be interested in a bully like Robert Mattson. In fact, she had no interest in any kind of romance. Her daughter and her job took all of her time and energy, so why complicate their lives by adding a man? But even as she settled on that thought, a wave of sadness followed. She was doing the best she could as a mother, but she would always regret that Zoey would never know a father's love and nurturing. Once Zoey had been diagnosed with cerebral palsy, Singleton walked out and never set eyes on her again. As for Zoey, she'd only seen him on television, never knowing he was her father. And Lauren was happy to keep it that way as long as she could.

THAT EVENING, WHEN they arrived at the church, the gym was alive with activity. Teens had already started playing volleyball, and as they had that morning, they greeted Zoey and invited her to play. Without asking Lauren, she joined Mandy on the court.

Lauren considered stopping her. If someone spiked the ball and it hit Zoey in the head, it could cause serious injury. Even a light hit might cause a seizure like the ones Zoey occasionally experienced. Should she have brought her daughter's helmet? No, unlike yesterday when she was riding Tripper, Zoey would never wear it when she was among her peers.

Lord, please protect her.

Lauren sat on the lowest bench in the bleachers and watched as her daughter stood near the net and kept an eye on the fast-moving ball.

"Mind if I sit here?" The ever-present Robert Mattson parked his large person a few feet away from her.

Really? You're going to sit by me? Glancing at him, she managed a half smile before turning her eyes back to Zoey. "Sure."

"Looks like the kids are having fun." Robert waved a hand toward the court.

She managed a noncommittal "Uh-huh."

"If I know my son, he's keeping an eye on the refreshment table."

Across the gym, a long table had been set up with sodas, bottled water, ice cream, cookies and chips. Should she have brought something to add to the snacks? Too late now.

Recorded praise music wafted through the air and blended with the shouts and laughter of the teens, echoing off the gym walls. Parents watching the informal game chatted in the bleachers behind her.

The volleyball popped over the net toward Zoey, and she managed to lift her hands in time to send it flying toward one of her teammates. As they cheered her good move, Lauren swallowed the lump in her throat.

"She's doing real well." Rob's unexpected praise startled Lauren.

"Yes." Lauren glanced his way again. "Your kids, too."

"Yeah. They're pretty good at most sports."

Why was he being so chatty? Okay, she could do chatty with him. What father didn't like to brag about his kids? With this being the school's fall semester, only one thing came to her mind.

"Does Bobby play football?"

He snorted softly. "More or less. He's not crazy about it, but he manages to keep up the family tradition."

"Let me guess. You were the starting quarterback." She punctuated her cheeky question with a laugh.

He grinned. Actually *grinned*, revealing a dimple on his left cheek she hadn't noticed before. "Guilty. But as a senior, not a sophomore. He's got two years to work up to it."

Poor kid. What did Bobby want to do? "And I suppose it's a birthright for him?"

"Birthright?" Rob shook his head. "Huh. Never thought of it that way." He swiped a hand down his cheek, where a five-o'clock shadow added to his overall handsome cowboy appearance. "It's just what my family always does."

That explained a lot. "And if he prefers to do something else?"

"Huh." His favorite word. "He still has time to get his head on right."

"Zoey says he's into computer programming. What's not right about that?"

He gave her a long look. "He's gonna take over the Double Bar M Ranch one day. I can see computers for the business side of things, but ranching's a hands-on enterprise that takes time and dedication and hard physical work."

"Hmm." Lauren turned her attention back to the game. Just as she'd suspected from their few encounters, this man ruled his family rather than guided them. That was no way to raise kids.

Zoey was doing her best as the ball came her way another time, but Lauren could see she was struggling to keep her arms up. Which meant she was getting tired. Time to pull her out of the game. Before she could act, the ball sailed over the net and banged Zoey in the forehead, knocking her down, her head hitting the wooden floor with an audible thump.

The noisy gym fell silent. The youth pastor and other adults rushed to Zoey.

And Lauren's world stopped.

CHAPTER FOUR

INSTINCT AND EXPERIENCE shook Lauren from the iron grip of panic. She rushed to her daughter. To her relief, Zoey was conscious and blinking her eyes, a tiny grin—or grimace?—forming on her lips as she tried to sit up.

"Lie still, honey." Lauren brushed Zoey's hair back from her forehead, where a red mark was still spreading.

"Oops." Zoey spoke softly. "I missed the ball."

"Yeah, but the ball sure didn't miss you," some boy nearby quipped.

Nervous laughter erupted until a female voice hissed, "Shh."

The same woman knelt beside Lauren. "Ma'am, I'm a nurse. Will you let me check her out?" Without waiting for an answer, she nudged Lauren aside and checked Zoey's eyes and neck.

"Please be careful," Lauren whispered. "She has CP."

Zoey scolded her with a frown. She hated it when Lauren announced her condition.

"I see." The nurse took Zoey's pulse. "Then we'll wait for the paramedics to bring a collar and take her to the hospital for tests."

"Okay, kids." The youth pastor spoke in a cheerful but authoritative tone. "Let's break for snacks while the grown-ups handle this." He herded the twenty or so youths toward the refreshment table.

"Does this mean I won't get any ice cream?" Zoey added a comical whine to her question. As always, she was making light of a worrisome situation. Sometimes it made it hard for Lauren to know how serious her injuries were.

"Don't worry, kiddo." Robert Mattson's words, spoken right behind Lauren, sent an odd feeling down her back. Had he been this close all along? "We'll make sure to save you some. What's your favorite flavor?"

"Strawberry." Zoey sent him a wobbly smile. "Thanks."

While the other adults managed the youth and children, eventually sending them to their evening classes, Robert stayed nearby, though Lauren couldn't imagine why. Despite his twins' objections, he'd sent them with the others.

Minutes later, paramedics arrived and secured Zoey's neck with a collar before lifting her onto the lowered gurney and raising it to transport height.

"I'll go with you," Robert said.

"Thanks, but that's not necessary." Lauren nodded toward Becca, the nurse. "She's going."

"Yeah, Rob." Becca waved him away. "You just take care of my kids for me. We women can manage this."

"I said I'm going." Robert retrieved his Stetson from the bleachers and plopped it on his head. "And you, Becca, can take care of *my* kids."

"Let's go." The lead paramedic pushed the gurney toward the door. "ER's waiting."

Becca gave Lauren an apologetic shrug. "I'll be praying for you."

Lauren had no choice but to follow the paramedics to the ambulance and climb in beside Zoey. A second before the attendant closed the door, she saw Robert get into his monster black pickup. She didn't want this bossy bully to accompany her, but right now she had to take care of her daughter.

In the back of her mind, she could only wonder what went on in this community that required everybody to do exactly what Robert Mattson said. It almost seemed like he said "jump" and they asked "how high?"

AFTER CHURCH THIS MORNING, Rob had decided the best way to uncover Lauren's dishonesty was to stick close to her whenever possible. So he'd sought her out and sat beside her in the bleachers, hoping casual conversation would uncover her true character. But all her focus had been on Zoey, as with any good mother. He'd been as upset as everyone else when the sweet little gal had been slammed to the floor by that volleyball. If either of his daughters had CP, he wouldn't let her go near a volleyball court or any other sport. Not after what happened to his sister and his wife. But try telling a modern woman what she couldn't do, and a man got in plenty of trouble, as he'd learned the hard way.

But he wasn't about to let Zoey miss out on any treatment at the hospital. Had Lauren's health insurance from Will's law office kicked in yet? If not, he'd pay for Zoey's treatments, no matter how much Lauren objected. After all, his kids had invited Zoey to church and encouraged her to play, so he was responsible for her welfare at church as much as at the ranch.

He pulled into the hospital parking lot right after the ambulance and followed Lauren inside through the ER entrance. In spite of the blast of hospital smells striking him—rubbing alcohol, sickness, cleaning solution—all of which reminded him of both Jordyn's and Dad's deaths, he was proud of this little hospital. His family had been its major donors over the years so citizens of Riverton didn't have to drive to Santa Fe or Albuquerque for special tests and treatments. When Dad died, he'd left a large bequest to purchase an MRI scanner and other vital equipment in an area where cowboys sometimes suffered serious injuries in their daily work. Rob knew Dad had done it because of Jordyn's death. If they'd had that MRI scanner when she had her accident, the doctors might have been able to save her, but the X-ray that had revealed her broken neck missed the fatal damage to her brain.

He shoved away the bitter memory, which could still make his belly ache after four years. Time to focus on the young girl being checked by the new ER resident.

"Mom, you'll need to take out her earrings." The doctor handed Lauren a medical form on a clipboard. "While we get that MRI done, I need you to fill out her medical history."

"Yes, of course." Lauren brushed a hand over Zoey's cheek, then carefully removed the jewelry from her earlobes. "You okay, honey?"

"Yeah. I'm fine." Zoey seemed more annoyed than injured.

"Not worried about going into that MRI tube?"

"Been there, done that, Mom."

Brave kid. Rob grinned at her over Lauren's shoulder, and Zoey returned a sweet smile as the orderly wheeled her from the ER cubicle. Lauren looked his way and scowled. Or maybe just frowned.

"You really don't need to stay. I've got this."

That was what Jordyn had always said. Except she hadn't always "got this."

"Not a problem. You'll need a ride back to the church to pick up your car after she's done here."

Sighing, Lauren shook her head. "Whatever." She wandered from the ER to the nearest waiting room, plunked herself down on the gray Naugahyde couch and filled out the form. That finished, she stared up at the mounted TV where a '70s comedy show was playing without sound.

"You want to hear it? It'll make the time pass faster." He reached up toward the controls on the side, but she'd already picked up the remote and clicked off the show. "Guess that answers that."

She grabbed a gossip magazine from the coffee table, wrinkled her nose and set it back down.

Rob chuckled. "Not the best reading material. But they do have a library. Can I get you a book?"

She stared up at him for several seconds. "Don't you have something more important to do than, for lack of a better word, *entertain* me?"

He chuckled again. Not many people in these parts talked to him that way. Against everything that made sense, he liked her spunk. But then, that kind of brashness could be a defense to hide her deceitfulness. Jordyn had always used bossiness as a smoke screen when she went behind his back on matters they disagreed on, especially when it came to the kids. Again, he smothered the unpleasant memory.

"I'll get us some coffee." He walked away, hoping the coffee machine wasn't as bad as he'd heard. Sad to say, it was. But he brought her a cup anyway and set it on the table beside her, then sipped from his own cup.

"Thanks." She took a careful sip of the steaming brew and made a grimace too cute to describe. "You trying to poison me?" She shuddered and set the cup back down.

"This is gourmet stuff." He made a show of drinking more of his own and managed not to choke on it. "You should taste the coffee we have on our cattle drives. Nothing like a little trail dust to flavor your morning joe."

"Cattle drives?" She picked up the cup and drank another sip. It seemed to go down easier this time. "You still drive cattle?" She blinked those gray-green eyes, and a dangerous little tickle threaded through his chest. "Like in the Old West?"

Who didn't know that? Oh, yeah. City women from back East.

"Sure do. Every spring we haul the cattle up into the Sangre de Cristo Mountains in semis as far as the trucks can go. From there, we mount up and drive them farther up to the best summer pasture."

"Wow. All of that so we can eat steak and hamburgers." Her interest seemed genuine.

"Yes, ma'am." He was warming to his favorite topic, and it helped to have an interested audience. Or was she just faking it? Since Jordyn died, lots of women had shown interest in whatever he said, but their real interest was in his wealth and position in the community. He'd have to be on guard with this one. Her natural feminine attractiveness might charm some men, so he'd have to fortify his own defenses.

"Our roundup's in a couple of weeks. I'm hoping Bobby will have Lady trained back into her instinctive herding by then."

A shadow crossed her face, and she looked away. "I hope so, too."

He sat across from her and considered her words. Did she really hope Lady would remember her early training and be worth the investment he'd made in her? The two pups she'd had while she was missing were healthy and strong, but their dad was a mongrel. Rob had let Will and Olivia keep the little mutts for their newly blended family. If nothing else, Lady could still be a good breeding dog. Or not. A mother dog was always an important part of the training, and if she didn't teach her pedigreed pups how to herd, his whole purpose for buying her would be wasted.

"Mrs. Parker?" The doctor entered the waiting room carrying a CD case. "She came through just fine. We'll have the results within twenty-four hours after our radiologist reads the scan, but you can have this for your own records."

"Thanks." Lauren accepted the disk and handed him the clipboard. "Is she ready to go?"

"Yes, ma'am." He read the medical form as he stepped toward the hallway, with Lauren and Rob following. "Hmm. Considering her CP and these seizures she had this summer, you need to keep her activities to a minimum this week to be sure she doesn't have a setback. Just to be safe, I'm writing you a script for Keppra, which she needs to take every day, and one for pain in case she needs it. Make sure she stays hydrated, and keep her at home. Maybe get her teachers to email her schoolwork."

"Oh." Lauren stopped. "You mean she can't go to school?"

Rob didn't wait for Doc to answer. He whipped out his phone and called Will. "Hey, Cuz, you don't mind Lauren bringing Zoey to work this week." He quickly explained the situation. "Great. I'll send over a cot." He ended the call. "There. All set up." To his shock, Lauren stood gaping at him, anger emanating from her entire body.

"Who, just *who* do you think you are?" Hands fisted at her slender waist, she sputtered out the words. "I'm perfectly capable of taking care of my daughter."

Whoa. He hadn't expected this reaction. Most people were glad for help. What was it with this woman?

LAUREN COULDN'T REMEMBER when she'd been this angry. Not even when Singleton announced his rejection of Zoey and his plans to divorce her. Not even when her ex had filed a petition to lower her child support payments. Worst of all, Robert Mattson stood there looking shocked at her outburst when he'd just taken over her life. To her further annoyance, the doctor seemed just as shocked. Oh, right. How could she forget? Everybody treated this wealthy rancher with the utmost respect.

"Take me to my daughter." Lauren looked down the hallway.

"Uh…" The young man had the nerve to look at Robert as if checking to see if he should do as she said. Lauren didn't spare the rancher a glance, but he must have given the okay, because the doc said, "Yes, ma'am. This way."

In the recovery cubicle outside the MRI room, Zoey rested against the partially raised pillows of her bed, her arms crossed in annoyance. "Are we done yet?" She looked past Lauren and smiled. "Did you save me some strawberry ice cream?"

Again, Lauren didn't have to turn around to know Robert was on her heels.

"Sure did. Well, I told Mandy to."

"Thanks." Zoey's sweet smile should have encouraged Lauren, but aimed at Robert, it made her heart sink. Her daughter was getting attached to this man.

"You ready to go, young lady?" a nurse asked as she pushed a wheelchair into the cubicle.

"I can walk."

"Sorry, miss. Hospital policy." The doctor spoke up before Lauren could object. Why was he sticking around? Oh, yeah. Probably to impress Robert Mattson. "Now, you do what your mom says, okay? Keep your activities to a minimum. Take your meds. No school for a week. Then I want to see you in my office on Friday. And no more volleyball, at least for a while. Got it?"

"Got it." Sighing, Zoey teared up.

Lauren felt her own tears coming, but she refused to let them form. "Okay, then. Let's go."

She barely managed to deflect Robert's help as she and the nurse helped Zoey from the bed and into the wheelchair. She had no choice but to accept his ride back to the church and her own vehicle, but that would be the end of it. Somehow she would break free from his hovering presence, or else she feared she would fall into the Mattson trap everyone else seemed caught in.

As he'd told Will, Robert delivered a cot to the law office early Monday morning. Will and Sam had opted for partitioning the current location, and the contractor had already framed in several walls. The cot fit nicely behind Lauren's desk in the reception area and would allow Zoey to nap when needed.

"We'll miss you at school," Mandy said. She, Bobby and Clementine had come with their father, bringing a surprise that didn't appear to please him—Lady. The darling dog greeted Zoey with eager but gentle kisses and furious tail wagging, then nestled beside her on the cot and gazed up into her face with obvious affection.

"We thought maybe you could keep Lady company," Bobby said. "She gets lonely out on the ranch when we're in school." What a sweet boy to make it sound like Zoey was doing them a favor. He must have learned that kindness from his grandmother.

While Zoey exclaimed with delight, Lauren heard Robert's grunt of disapproval but ignored it. Actually, she found his reaction to his kids' generosity oddly amusing. So, not everybody jumped through Robert Mattson's hoops.

No, that wasn't a good reaction. No matter what everybody else did or didn't do, his kids should respect and obey their parent, just as she'd taught Zoey to do. As for her, she had no idea how to stop Robert's interference in her and Zoey's lives when nearly everybody else bent over backward to please him.

CHAPTER FIVE

WHEN LADY JUMPED up on the cot, settled beside Zoey and stared up into her face, Rob knew he'd made a mistake to give in to Bobby. Why was his son so willing to encourage his dog to bond with somebody else? Or re-bond. Lady had already attached to the girl over the summer, and this would only solidify her loyalty and affection.

Rob wouldn't give up though. In less than two weeks when he took Bobby on his first cattle drive, Lady would go, too. A week of being with the herd and learning from the other dogs should restore her training as a pup, when she'd taken to the job like a natural.

"Thank you so much for bringing her." Zoey's bright smile and good color seemed to indicate she was recovering from her accident last evening.

"Thank you for the cot." Lauren didn't look his way as she spoke.

"Mornin', boys." Rob nodded to his cousins, who had come out to the reception area. At twelve and thirteen years younger than Rob, they were used to this old-fashioned cowboy name for them.

"Mornin'," Will said. "I see you and Lauren finally met."

He arched one eyebrow and gave Rob a crooked grin. "I mean other than church yesterday."

Rob ignored the comment and the insinuation that went with it. His newlywed cousin had been trying to fix him up with this woman ever since his wedding, but Rob had managed to dodge the introduction. Time to change the subject.

"I like what you're doing here." He waved a hand toward the framed-in walls. "But if it doesn't work out, you can still use my Fourth Street building."

"Thanks," Sam said. "We'll keep that in mind."

"Hey there, Lady." Will bent down and ruffled the fur behind the dog's ears. "We still need to get you out to my place to say hello to your pups."

"Think she'll remember them?" Clementine petted Lady.

"Or they'll remember her?" Mandy added.

Rob didn't want this to go any further. "Time to get you kids to school. We'll pick Lady up this afternoon. Ma'am." He nodded to Lauren, then herded the kids out to the truck. She'd barely said a word, just mumbled "thank you" when he brought in the cot. No surprise there. She'd been real quiet last evening as they drove back to the church. Was it stubbornness? Pride? Or, to be fair, just a mother worried about her daughter?

He let the twins off at the high school, then Clementine at the elementary school. Before she climbed out, his youngest paused with one foot out of the back door.

"I think Lady likes Zoey. I think we should let her keep her." Before he could explain why that wasn't going to happen, she jumped to the concrete sidewalk, slammed the back door and ran to greet her friends.

No, Lady wasn't going to stay with Zoey, no matter how much they'd bonded. He'd make sure she found her way back to herding, even if he had to take over the training himself.

DESPITE WORKING FULL-TIME, Lauren had kept an eye on Zoey all summer through several daily FaceTime chats. At fifteen, her daughter could stay home alone, and it had helped to have Daisy... *Lady* with her at all times, as well as a helpful neighbor lady who checked on her. But now that she required constant observation in case her fall on the gym floor brought on a seizure, having her here in the office gave Lauren great peace of mind. Even though she'd been offended by Robert's high-handedness in calling Will about the situation *and* deciding to bring the cot rather than asking if she wanted it, she had to admit it was a good plan. Somehow she'd find a way to do more than mumble a weak "thank you" to him. Bake cookies? No. Last Saturday at the ranch, she'd noticed his lovely mother kept the Mattson cookie jar full.

Nothing in Lauren's power or ability could even the score with the wealthy rancher so she wouldn't owe him anything. She'd had a hard enough time at the hospital making sure the clerk in the billing department accepted Zoey's Medicaid rather than Robert's credit card, and she refused his offer to pay for the Keppra prescription and pain medication at the overnight pharmacy. Why did he keep trying to take over her life? Somehow she had to regain control.

For now, she needed to concentrate on the adoption and foster parent petitions on her desk. As she'd told Robert, it was unprofessional to mix personal matters with work. And yet, here she was, bringing her daughter to work, thanks to him.

The prescription from the ER doctor didn't entirely erase Zoey's headache, and the anticonvulsant medication made her vision a little blurry, but she still managed to use her laptop to connect with her teachers through the high school's website. Since the pandemic, the faculty had continued to post their lessons online so students could keep up with their classes. Zoey was good with computers, thanks to her uncle, Lauren's older brother, a software engineer. Most of her family had blamed Lauren for the divorce due to Singleton's charming ways and a few outright lies, but her brother, David, had stood by her.

"Can I bring you ladies some lunch from the diner?" Will

stood by the front door putting on his Stetson. Backlit against the daylight, he looked like a younger version of Robert.

"Yes!" Zoey sat up a little too fast, and her eyelids flickered. Lady went on alert, sitting up to focus on Zoey's face even before Lauren could register alarm. Zoey's expression settled as she added, "Cheeseburger with fries."

Will laughed. "You sound like my neph—my son." He still stumbled over calling the nephew he recently adopted *son*. "He always wants burger and fries. Lauren, how about you?"

"Burger and fries sounds good." Lauren reached for her purse.

Will put up his hand. "I've got this. You ladies have been working hard this morning." He'd given Zoey some envelopes to stuff, a job she'd managed better than Lauren expected. "I'll be back in a jiff."

Before he could go out the door, Robert burst in, his arms full of take-out bags. Lady jumped off the cot and wandered over to greet him.

"Zoey, I brought you some lunch and that long overdue strawberry ice cream. I noticed you didn't feel like eating the ice cream Mandy saved for you last night, so I hope this makes up for it."

He set a soft drink—in a moist plastic cup—on Lauren's desk, barely missing some important papers. She managed to snatch them up just in time.

"Hey, watch it." She couldn't keep the annoyance from her voice.

"Yeah, watch it." Will's tone was more teasing than cross.

"Right." Robert handed a bag to Will. "Put this in your fridge. It's Zoey's ice cream."

"Sure thing." Like everybody else, Will did what Robert said.

"Thanks, Mr. Mattson," Zoey said.

"You can thank Mandy, honey. On the way to school, she reminded me about the ice cream." He opened the second bag. "Now, I hope you ladies like steakburgers, fully loaded. If you don't like the pickles, just put them aside for Sam." He nodded toward his other cousin, who'd come out to greet him.

"I love pickles." Zoey accepted the burger he offered. "Thanks."

"Good." He glanced at Lauren with those brilliant blue eyes, and her pulse kicked up.

She quickly stuffed her silly reaction to his handsome appearance. "Why are you doing this?"

"Yeah, Cuz." Will returned from the back room and smirked at Robert. "Why are you feeding my employees?"

Lauren cringed inwardly. Couldn't her boss see the problem here? She hadn't dared to voice her dislike of Robert's intrusion into her and Zoey's lives, much less mention his hints that she'd lied about finding Lady. For all she knew, Will had no idea Robert had accused her of stealing the dog. Why not? She should be grateful that he hadn't already gotten her fired.

"Shouldn't you be out branding cattle or something?" Sam, who lived in one of the houses out at the ranch, leaned against the unfinished door frame. "What are you doing still in town?"

"My cattlemen's meeting lasted longer than expected. I figured if I was hungry, Zoey must be, too." Robert settled in a chair and pulled a wrapped burger from a bag. "You boys don't mind if I eat here, do you?"

"Make yourself at home," Will said. "I'll go get something for Sam and me." He left the office, grinning and shaking his head.

"Well, eat up, ladies." Robert unwrapped his burger.

"Mr. Mattson, we should thank the Lord for the food." Zoey hadn't even touched a French fry.

Robert gaped for a split second, then rewrapped his food. "Yes, ma'am. You're absolutely right." He closed his eyes. "Lord, thank You for this fine, sunny day. Thank You for Your provision and for our good health. And thank You for the food. May it nourish our bodies to Your service. Amen."

"Amen." Zoey gave him a sweet smile as she picked up a French fry and gave Lauren an expectant look. "Dig in, Mom."

Lauren reluctantly unwrapped her burger and took a bite. Whatever sauce the restaurant used on their steakburgers made her mouth water in appreciation. The fries were thin, crisp and spicy. She looked at the logo on the bags. Mattsons' Steak-house. Of course. The best and most expensive restaurant in Riverton. She'd planned to save up and take Zoey there one day.

How many other ways would this man interrupt her life and her plans before he left her alone?

WHY HAD HE brought lunch to Zoey and Lauren rather than just the ice cream he'd promised? Rob had no idea. As they ate in silence, he examined his actions. When he'd stopped by his family's restaurant for Zoey's promised ice cream, he'd decided to order a take-out burger. It only made sense to pur-chase one for the girl. And of course her mother.

He could see the distrust in Lauren's eyes. The suspicion about his motives. That made two of them. She'd voiced the question he still hadn't answered for himself—why was he doing this?

One glance at Zoey brought it all into focus. The kids. That was why. Bobby, Mandy and even Clementine had adopted Zoey, as Mandy put it, as a "sister of their hearts." For them, it was more than words. They lived it. When they weren't to-gether at school, they FaceTimed on their phones, chatting about movies, music, even homework, as though they couldn't discuss all of that at school. She'd already helped Mandy im-prove her essay writing and taught Bobby some coding tech-niques his teacher didn't seem to know. And that was after just one week in the same classes.

If Zoey were a brat or had bad manners or if she looked down on his kids because she was smarter than they were, he might discourage their friendship. But she was a sweet little gal with a generous spirit and a great sense of humor, especially about her disability. Zoey could be pretty funny in her frank observations about any number of subjects. In the apparent absence of a father, she must have got those good qualities, not to mention her smarts, from her mother. Good thing Lauren hadn't passed on her tendency for untruths about Lady to her daughter.

He hadn't said anything to Will and Sam concerning his suspicions about their paralegal. Best not to until he had concrete evidence. He'd tried to call that Santa Fe vet to check her story about finding Lady, but the call went to voicemail, and he hadn't wanted to leave a message. Since then, he kept putting off a second attempt. Maybe it was an unconscious worry. Learning that his suspicions about Lauren's lack of integrity were right would mean he'd have to tell his cousins that their employee couldn't be trusted in the sensitive legal matters that comprised their business. Worse, he'd have to break off Zoey's friendship with his kids. It was hard enough to raise the twins without letting them hang out with bad influences, however passive or subtle they might be. Although he hadn't been able to put his decision into words as he bought their lunches, he knew deep down it was so he could spend time with Zoey to find out just how much she took after her mother.

If only women always told the truth. If only Jordyn had just admitted she was going behind his back that day…

He'd loved Jordyn with every part of his soul and being, and he knew she loved him just as much. But against his advice, against his *orders*, she'd been determined to train an untrustworthy horse. Years ago, his sister, Ashley, had disobeyed their dad and done the same thing, which was the reason Rob didn't want his wife to attempt it. At least Ashley's resulting broken back had healed, while Jordyn's bad fall killed her. In his experience, women did what they wanted, even going behind the backs of those who knew better, loved ones who only wanted to protect them from harm.

If only Lauren would just admit the truth.

BY THE END of the week, the doctor said Zoey could attend church on Sunday and school the following Tuesday, the day after Labor Day, although he advised against volleyball and horseback riding for several weeks. Lauren was glad not to be the one to forbid Zoey's activities. Her daughter definitely had a "get back on the horse" personality, which sometimes made it hard to protect her from possible injuries.

Despite last Sunday's unhappy ending, Lauren looked forward to church, where she enjoyed Pastor Tim's Bible-based sermon. After the morning service, people lingered on the church's front lawn, and Lauren spoke with several acquaintances she'd met through work. Out of the corner of her eye, she saw Zoey chatting with Mandy and Bobby, as though they hadn't seen her every day at the office when they brought Lady to keep her company. Those two kids were so special. Their genuine interest in Zoey almost made up for Robert's reserve. Almost. While he never failed to extend greetings to Zoey, the way he looked at Lauren always seemed to hold an accusation.

"Mom, Mom." Zoey hurried toward her with Mandy, Bobby and their grandmother close behind. "Mrs. Mattson wants us to come out to the ranch for a Labor Day barbecue. Can we go?"

Lauren cringed inwardly. "Oh, I don't know." She smiled at Andrea as she remembered their lovely chat on the Saturday before last when they'd first met. "Won't this be a family affair?"

Andrea laughed. "Well, yes and no. It's an informal Mattson reunion, so we have about sixty or seventy relatives and shirt-tail relatives come out to the ranch. But nobody checks your ID at the gate." She squeezed Lauren's hand. "Do say you'll come. I enjoyed our conversation when you came out last time. Unless you have other plans."

"Please say yes, Mom." Zoey's grin said she already knew the answer.

Lauren chuckled. "Yes, we'd love to come." With that many people and such a large ranch, she could easily avoid Robert. "What can I bring?"

"How about a relish tray?" Andrea said.

"Pickles, olives, that sort of thing?"

"Exactly."

"Great. I can do that."

At the grocery store on the way home, she and Zoey loaded up their cart with every possible pickled vegetable they could find, along with three divided plastic serving platters and plastic tongs. Their apartment fridge barely held everything they bought.

The next afternoon, they loaded up a cooler and drove to the Double Bar M Ranch. The closer they got, the bigger a knot grew in Lauren's stomach. What was she doing, going to Robert Mattson's home again? She must be out of her mind. Even in a large crowd, how would she manage to avoid him?

CHAPTER SIX

ROB ALWAYS ENJOYED hosting the Labor Day family gathering. The family's long history in the area gave them friendships with many of their neighbors, but nothing was as satisfying as fellowship with family.

Twenty years ago, Dad had remodeled and modernized the two-story "big house," built in 1878, but he'd kept the antebellum look, with its white columned porch overlooking the Rio Grande. Other houses on the property gave evidence of the era in which they were built—a one-story brick ranch style, a two-story clapboard farmhouse, a sprawling adobe hacienda. Jordyn had called the ranch property an architectural crazy quilt.

Rob's cousin Andy, who was Sam's dad, lived in the farmhouse and always managed the barbecue pit. Today, as always, two sides of prime Mattson beef turned on a massive spit down by the barn. Mom had arranged for the countless dishes to be brought by other family members. Rob's only duty was to greet everybody and catch up on family news.

He knew Mom had invited Lauren and Zoey to come, but he still felt a kick under his ribs when the little gray Honda Fit pulled onto the property. Sam, who also lived in the farmhouse, was directing incoming traffic and pointed her to a parking spot by the white picket fence that surrounded the big house. When she stepped out of the little car wearing jeans and a frilly pink blouse, he felt another kick. Why did she have to look so pretty?

Before he could make his way over from the side porch to greet her, Mandy and Clementine ran to meet Zoey, with Lady scampering ahead of them. Zoey knelt and hugged the dog like she hadn't seen her just a few days ago. Rob hated to admit it, but Lady obviously favored Zoey. He released a sigh of annoyance. He never should have let Bobby talk him into taking Lady to the law office last week. It only reinforced their bond. Would the coming week on the cattle drive be enough to break it?

"Hey, Mr. Mattson." Zoey waved, a big smile on her sweet face.

As he approached the car, he returned a smile and touched the brim of his Stetson. "Hey, Zoey, Lauren. Welcome to the Double Bar M Ranch."

Lauren barely spared him a nod before moving toward the back of the car and opening the hatchback. To their credit, his daughters hurried to help her unload her cooler and bags.

"That's okay, girls," he said. "You and Zoey join the other kids." He tilted his head toward the informal soccer game being played in the north pasture. "I'll help Miss Lauren."

"Thanks, Dad." Mandy grabbed Zoey's hand and started in that direction.

"Hey, wait." Lauren set down her bag. "Zoey, you can't..."

Zoey rolled her eyes. "I know, Mom."

"Wear your helmet." Lauren held out the protective gear.

Zoey huffed out a big sigh but obeyed her mom. Poor kid. Helmet on and shoulders slumped, she walked away in her halting gait. Lady kept pace close beside her, but seemed careful not to trip her. As a growing puppy, the dog had "herded" the kids, especially Clementine, when they walked around the property. Now she seemed more companion than shepherd.

Once they got up in the mountains for the roundup, Rob would make sure she remembered her natural instincts.

He turned his attention back to Lauren. "Let me get that." He lifted the cooler. "How's she doing?" He pointed his chin toward the kids.

Lauren eyed him briefly before taking two canvas bags from the car and closing the hatchback. "She's fine."

"No seizures?"

Now Lauren gaped at him. "How do you know...?"

"I couldn't *not* hear your conversation with Doc Edwards at the ER last Sunday."

"Oh, right. You were hovering."

Not sure she was joking, he ignored her smirk. "I did a little reading up on the subject." He took a step toward the front lawn where he and his men had set up long tables in the shade of the cottonwood trees. "So, not everybody with CP has epileptic seizures, right? I'm sorry Zoey, and you of course, have to deal with that double problem. It must be a constant concern for you."

When she just stood there staring at him, he chuckled. "You coming?"

She shook her head but followed him through the open gate in the picket fence.

"Look, I just want my kids to understand CP and epilepsy so they can be sensitive to Zoey." Not entirely true. He was honestly concerned about the girl himself.

"That's very kind of you." There was a slight edge to her tone, but he couldn't decide whether it was irritation or something else.

Mom greeted Lauren with a hug, then helped her unpack. "This is amazing." She laughed. "Did you leave any pickles in the grocery store?"

"Tried not to." Lauren grinned.

No, not a grin. A genuine and very beautiful smile. For a

moment, Rob foolishly wished she would send that smile in his direction.

What was he thinking? He wasn't about to let this woman get under his skin. But as he watched her interacting so well with Mom and his other female relatives, he feared she already had.

LAUREN HAD MET a few of these ladies through Will and Sam, and today they welcomed her like an old friend. Everybody asked about Zoey.

"My niece is a senior." Sam's mother, Linda, was a graying, energetic woman in her early fifties. "When Zoey returns to school, Lizzie said she'll make sure Zoey's okay when they pass in the hallways between classes."

"Thanks." Lauren had to blink away a sudden tear. "All the kids have been so good to her."

"You seem surprised," Andrea said. "What was it like for her back home... Orlando, right?"

"Yes. Orlando." Lauren didn't want to talk about the cruel teasing Zoey had endured since kindergarten. "But this is home now."

Andrea eyed her for a moment before resuming her food arrangements. "Good." She placed protective net screens over the completed trays, then looked beyond Lauren. "Don't you have something to do?"

Lauren turned to see Robert leaning against a tree, arms crossed, a grin on his lips making the dimple on his cheek show up. Why was he hanging around? Did he worry she might steal a bite of food? Or commit some other dastardly deed? Every time he watched her, at church, at the hospital, at the law office, she felt a totally unfounded twinge of guilt.

The sound of an approaching vehicle caught Rob's attention, and he walked toward the newcomers. No longer under his scrutiny, Lauren relaxed and surveyed these beautiful surroundings. Early in her employment at the law office, Will had told her about the first Mattsons to settle here, a couple and their five sons, who arrived shortly after the Civil War. Unlike many cattle ranchers of those times, they'd weathered floods, bitter winters, cattle rustlers and numerous family tragedies to become an established force in the Riverton community. The story sounded like something out of one of those old-fashioned Western movies, with the "good guys" winning in the end.

Sam and Will were definitely good guys. She wasn't yet sure about Robert. At least where she was concerned. As much as she tried not to react, it stung her pride to have someone, especially a man of his prominence and apparent integrity, question her honesty. She'd gotten enough censure from her own family after her divorce, one of the reasons she'd moved so far from home.

An uproar erupted in the vicinity of the informal soccer field. Was that noise a cheer for a goal scored or alarm over an injury?

Zoey! Lauren didn't bother to excuse herself but dashed across the lawn and wide barnyard toward the sound. What was wrong with her that she forgot to watch her daughter? To her surprise, Robert was striding in that direction as well. They arrived at the fenced pasture at the same time.

As though they hadn't just given her a heart attack, the teens and young adults merrily went about their game, with Zoey cheering from outside the fence near the sidelines. Lauren slumped against the wooden railing beside her daughter and breathed out a quiet sigh.

"Good game?" Robert stood on Zoey's other side and bent to scratch Lady behind her ears.

"Yessir." Zoey grinned. "Bobby kicked a goal from over there." She pointed toward the middle of the field.

Robert focused on his son. "That far, eh? That's impressive."

Relieved that the uproar hadn't been about Zoey, Lauren yielded to the urge to tease him. "Wow. If he kicks that well, maybe he should play soccer instead of football. I mean, if *family tradition* isn't allowed to override talent." And expectations.

Robert snorted. "Yeah, right. That'll be the day."

Zoey looked at him, then at Lauren. A sly grin appeared on her lips, and one eyebrow shot up. Lauren frowned and shook her head. Her daughter had never been a matchmaker, so this was new. Lauren would have to stop that thinking before it gained traction.

The ringing clatter of an old-fashioned triangle dinner bell sounded loudly across the ranch.

"About time." Robert chuckled. "That's Andy announcing the meat's ready." He lifted a hand to his mouth and called out to the soccer players. "Head for the chuckwagon, cowboys. Time to eat."

As the fifteen or sixteen young people raced toward the barn, whooping and laughing as they ran, Lauren felt an odd little thrill, but not because she was hungry. This must have been what it was like back in the olden days. She could picture all the ladies in their bonnets and long dresses. As for the men, they'd probably dressed much like their descendants did now—jeans, checkered shirts and Stetson hats. The presence of the many pickup trucks, especially Robert's monster black truck, confirmed the setting was now instead of then.

Guests poured from every part of the ranch and hurried toward the feast. Once the crowd had gathered under the cottonwood trees, Robert put his fingers to his lips and sent out a piercing whistle to get everyone's attention. "All right, y'all, quiet down. Cousin Rev came all the way down from his church up in Alamosa to bless the food, so bow your heads."

While the minister offered a lovely prayer, Lauren tried her best to keep her head lowered. But something urged her to look up, only to find Robert watching her. Why did he keep doing that? Should she leave? No. That would break Zoey's heart. Might as well just try to stay away from him and enjoy the day as much as she could.

With lively country tunes wafting in the air through an outdoor sound system, enjoying herself wasn't hard to do. She'd always preferred country music, one of the many things Singleton had criticized. As his wife, she'd been required to attend highbrow theater events and even opera. But the folksy, down-to-earth sound of country spoke to her soul in ways that even a gifted tenor singing a high C never could.

She helped Zoey fill her plate and sat across from Andrea at one of the many long tables. At the first bite, she closed her eyes and savored the tender beef. "Andrea, this is the best barbecue I've ever tasted."

"It sure is." Andrea laughed. "Since I didn't fix it, I don't mind accepting compliments for my nephew."

"Hey, Lauren." Sam brought his plate and sat next to her. "Cover for me, will you? Ever since Will got married, he's been trying to line me up with a girlfriend. If I'm with you, maybe he and his latest pick will leave me alone."

"Sure, boss. Glad to help." Lauren covered her amusement by taking a bite of coleslaw. Sam was young enough not to realize he'd given her a backhanded compliment.

"Sam, I'm ashamed of you." Andrea scowled at him across the table. "Lauren, you must excuse this rude boy. He should be downright happy to be in the company of a pretty girl like you." She waved a scolding finger at Sam. "And happy to have you working for him. I'm sure you keep those boys in line at the office."

As Lauren tried to think of a humorous quip, a large presence hovered over her like a shadow of doom.

"Mind if I sit here?" Robert didn't wait for an answer, but stepped over the bench and plunked himself down on Zoey's other side. So much for avoiding him.

"Son, do you think there's enough food for everybody?" Andrea glanced around the crowd. "Maybe Andy should have cooked three sides of beef."

"Mom, you know that's never a problem." Robert cut into

his juicy slab of meat. "And we always have plenty of leftovers to take to the church outreach program."

"That's very generous. Most people would tuck away leftovers to feast on for days." Once again, Lauren found something to respect about Robert Mattson. Or at least his family.

And once again, Zoey cast a teasing look at her, adding a nudge with her elbow. When they got home, Lauren would have to sit her daughter down and tell her to stop it.

ROB MADE SURE the band was fed before they set up in the barn. It wouldn't be Labor Day at the Double Bar M Ranch without a good old-fashioned barn dance. Once they started the live music, nobody had to make an announcement. Family and guests crowded the wide aisles of the largest barn to show off their footwork in line dancing, square dancing, even the lively polka Mom had insisted on. Boot scooting in a line dance was more his speed.

When "Achy Breaky Heart" began, somehow he ended up next to Lauren in the second row of dancers. While many folks had begun to wilt by the end of this hot day, Lauren looked as fresh as she had when she stepped out of her car this afternoon. And pretty cute as she struggled to keep up with the tricky moves of the dance. When she bumped into him for the second time, he could see from her shocked expression that she hadn't meant to.

"Sorry." Her face reddened as she stood watching the footwork of the front line, then shook her head. "Nope. Can't do it." She started to move past him.

Without thinking, he touched her arm. "Hey, don't give up."

Blinking her gray-green eyes, she looked up at him, and an odd feeling skittered through him. *Man*, she sure was pretty. *Quit that!*

"Come on, now." He took her hand. "Follow me." He waited for the right beat of the music. "Four steps to the right. Four steps to the left." Gripping his hand, she managed to follow him. "Now heel touches. One, two, three, four. Now four steps to face the right."

As they continued each different movement, her grip loosened, and she seemed to catch on. By the time the song ended, she was smiling.

"That was fun, but I don't think sneakers are made for line dancing." She applauded with the rest of the crowd. "Maybe if I get some Western boots, I'll do better next time."

As she moved away from him, he argued with himself over asking her to dance with him for the next number, a country-western waltz. Being the main host of this shindig, he should also ask other ladies to dance. He hesitated about one second too long. Sam approached her and gave a comical bow.

"Miz Parker, may I have this dance?"

"Why, yes, Mr. Mattson, you may." She took his hand and followed him back to the floor without a backward glance.

Rob stared after them. Was his young cousin falling for his paralegal? After all, he'd sought her out during dinner even though she was somewhere in her late thirties, at least ten years older than Sam. Then Rob saw Will glaring at the couple. Oh, right. Will was trying to set Sam up with the neighbor lady who stood beside him. Rob snorted out a laugh. Since he'd danced with Lauren, maybe his young cousin would consider that particular matchmaking job a success and would leave him alone. Never mind that Rob had no interest in taking up with any woman, especially Lauren Parker. But just in case Will needed more proof of his supposed success, Rob would be sure to ask her to dance at least one more time.

"MOM, THAT WAS so much fun." Zoey sat on her bed brushing her long brown hair. "I just love going out to the ranch." Even though she hadn't tried to dance, she'd enjoyed talking with the other teens. And the entire day, Lady never left her side. Had even tried to get into the car when they were leaving, much to Robert's obvious annoyance. "Can we do it again?"

"Sure. If we're invited." Lauren didn't want to remind her daughter that the riding lessons would have to wait until the doctor gave her the all clear. She also didn't want to mention that Robert treated her with suspicion when no one else was looking. Yes, he'd danced with her twice, the line dance and the last-call slow two-step. But the openness he displayed when talking to his other guests dissolved into a cool reserve when he spoke to her.

"Time for bed, sweetheart. Busy school day tomorrow."

At work the next morning, it seemed odd not to have Zoey *and* Lady on a cot behind her desk. It also seemed odd not to have Robert and his kids bring the dog and come get her after school. She should have been glad not to have interruptions to her work, but she had to admit the addition of a social life felt good. Yesterday she'd made some new friends whose warm welcomes made up for Robert's reserve, at least a little.

"So, Miz Parker." Will set a document on her desk. "Did you enjoy dancing with Big Boss?"

She gave him an innocent blink. "Who? Oh, yes. Robert was very helpful with the line dancing, but I really enjoyed the waltz with Sam. He sure can dance up a storm. Maybe it's the cowboy boots. My sneakers weren't the best shoes to wear."

Will chuckled. "Right. Okay, back to work. Can you input these adoption papers for me and print out four copies? Judge Mathis will sign them on Thursday."

"No problem." She checked his notes to be sure they were legible, then got to work.

At noon, she saw Robert's huge black truck roll by and feared...hoped?...for a moment he would stop by. Why did she want to see him again? Did she somehow hope to prove him wrong about her? How foolish and useless. She'd spent three years trying to please Singleton, but he always found something to criticize. Besides, she had nothing to prove to Robert.

Due to the noontime Main Street traffic, he drove slowly, so she was able to read the new addition to the large truck.

"Double Bar M Ranch" had been painted on the door, with his own name underneath in smaller letters. Did he drive that huge truck through town to show off how wealthy he was?

Oh, dear. Now who was judging? As much as his attitude toward her made her uncomfortable, she hadn't observed any overblown pride. Or maybe he was just good at hiding it. Not that she cared to find out, but working for his cousins, and their kids being friends, how could she manage to avoid the man?

Worse still, deep inside, did she even really want to avoid him?

CHAPTER SEVEN

"BUT WHY DO I have to go on roundup, Dad?" Bobby came close to pouting like he used to do as a three-year-old. "I hate to miss my classes. What about my grades? My programming club?"

"Come on, now." Rob noticed his son hadn't mentioned missing a week's worth of football practice. "Be honest. You'll miss your friends more than your classes." He took a bite of Mom's amazing meatloaf, then waved his fork at Bobby. "I've told you before, there's more to your education than what you learn in the schoolroom. I should've taken you with me last April when we trucked the cattle up to summer pasture. Now, no more arguments. You're going with me this Saturday because you need to see that side of ranching. Remember, these are things you need to know for the day when you'll manage this ranch."

Bobby rolled his eyes. "How could I forget?" He bent over his plate, shoulders hunched. Beside him, Lady laid her head on his knee, and he absentmindedly petted her.

What was wrong with this boy? In his own younger years, Rob had ached for the day when he went on his first roundup. When Dad had finally let him go at fourteen, he'd had the time of his life. It wasn't like Bobby was lazy or scared. He

did his barn chores without complaint and rode like a champ…
though he didn't care about signing up for rodeo events. But
then, not every cowboy felt the need to compete in the arena.

"Dad, if you need another hand," Mandy said, "I could go
instead of Bobby. I want to learn how to do the hard stuff."
She blinked those blue eyes at him, which usually made him
cave. Not this time.

"Me too," Clementine piped up, her expression as hopeful
as Mandy's.

"Thanks, girls. You just take care of your schoolwork.
That's your job."

They ate in silence until Bobby spoke up again.

"I've got a great idea, Dad." His grin warned Rob that he
wasn't going to like whatever bright idea this was. "I won't
argue about going with you if you let me take my tablet so
I can keep up with my assignments, and—" he gave Mandy
a conspiratorial wink "—if you leave Lady with Zoey while
we're gone." Lying on the floor beside his chair, the dog lifted
her head at the mention of her name.

"What?" Rob thought his head might explode. "Where do
you get these ideas? Lady is your dog, and she's going on the
roundup with us so she can reconnect with her herding instincts and remember her early training."

"But—"

"No!" Rob slapped his hand on the table, rattling the silver-
ware and sloshing the iced tea in his glass. Clementine looked
like she was about to cry, and Mandy ducked her head. Bobby
just glared at him.

"Robert…" Mom stared at him with the look that still could
give him pause.

He exhaled a slow breath. "Look, son, I carefully chose
Lady from an exceptional litter, and I spent over two thousand
dollars for her. She's an investment in the future. Your future.
And her job is to herd cattle and teach her future pups to do
the same. This Saturday, she's going on roundup with us."

As he spoke, Lady watched his face. To her credit, she hadn't jumped at his outburst. That proved she hadn't lost the shockproof instincts she'd displayed as a puppy that caused him to choose her out of a litter of five.

"You can take your tablet and work on your assignments in the evenings. If I need to write a note to your teachers, I'll do it. Most of them understand that big ranches around here, including the Double Bar M, go on roundup every September, and they've always made allowances for it."

And what was this about wanting Zoey to keep Lady while they were gone? Even if Rob let her stay home, Mandy was perfectly capable of tending her. No need to bother Lauren by adding dog care on top of her full-time job.

Against his better thinking, a picture of the honey-brown-haired beauty flashed into his mind. When he'd driven down Main Street one day last week, he'd noticed her through the storefront glass of the law office. If he wasn't mistaken, she saw him, too. It had given him that ridiculous kick under his ribs he often felt around her. Yes, she was pretty, but she always seemed to watch him warily, as if she knew one day he would uncover the truth about how she "found" Lady. Maybe when he got back from roundup, he could finally reach that Santa Fe vet.

Why was he putting off trying to call him again? Maybe he didn't really want to know the truth. If she was responsible for Lady being stolen, he'd have to have her arrested, which would lead to problems for Zoey. But if Lauren was as innocent as the look in her soulful eyes seemed to indicate, he just might be the one with a problem. Since Jordyn's death, he hadn't felt the slightest interest in any woman, no matter how much matchmaking Will did or how many women at church tried to get his attention. Then this woman barges into his life, and he can't stop thinking about her. What was wrong with him? Hopefully, nothing that a week of rounding up cattle couldn't cure.

LAUREN DIDN'T KNOW why Mandy had invited Zoey out to the ranch. With laundry and housecleaning to do, she hated giving up another Saturday. But she wouldn't deny Zoey the opportunity to watch the cowboys load up their trucks and drive off to their roundup. She wouldn't mind seeing it herself, like observing a real-life version of the old Westerns her dad liked to watch on television.

As Mandy advised in last night's text, they arrived at the Double Bar M Ranch shortly after dawn to observe all the action. Even before parking, she saw Robert directing his ranch hands as they loaded eight horses into the long trailer attached to the back of his huge black truck. That answered her question about why he needed such a monster vehicle. She hadn't even tried to pull a small U-Haul with her little car, but had shipped their few household goods to their new home. She couldn't imagine the power needed to pull a loaded horse trailer up into the mountains.

With a lot of action happening around the barn, she parked near the picket fence by the main house. Zoey was out of the car before Lauren shut off the motor.

"Zoey, wait." She ran around the car to catch her daughter. To her surprise, Zoey was kneeling with Lady in her arms while the dog licked her face. A leash hung from her collar.

The other two dogs trotted over to greet them, but Bobby called to them, and they raced back to the trailer. Lady stayed with Zoey.

Lauren waved to Andrea and Linda, who were packing another large pickup with boxes and coolers, probably the provisions for the cowboys. Nearby, Bobby lifted a saddle into the horse trailer's front storage area, and Mandy handed him some other tack.

"Mom, it's so exciting." Zoey's eyes sparkled.

Feeling the excitement herself, Lauren smiled. "It sure is, sweetie." As before, she marveled at all the work it took so that people could have steaks and hamburgers and leather purses. And fancy Western boots, of course.

Mandy hurried over and grabbed Lady's leash. "Silly girl. How'd you get away from me?" She gave Zoey a hug. "Hi, Mrs. Parker." A hint of sadness clouded her face.

"Hi, Mandy. Are you okay?" Lauren had never seen this girl without a smile.

Mandy sighed. "Dad's making Bobby go on the roundup, but he won't let me go."

"I wish I could go," Zoey laughed. "But I guess I'd just get in the way." She eyed Mandy. "But you wouldn't get in the way. You'd know what to do, right?"

Mandy sighed again. "Yeah, but Dad doesn't see it that way. He never lets me do any of the hard stuff around the ranch. He's so unfair to me."

"I think it's more than that." Why was Lauren defending Robert? Maybe because she understood it wasn't easy to be a parent. She often had a hard time letting Zoey do challenging activities, such as riding a horse. Or playing volleyball. But while kids should experience new things as they matured, a caring parent knew what his or her child needed. "He's just looking out for you."

"Humph." Mandy reached down and petted Lady. "Zoey, did you ask your mom about keeping Lady for us?"

"What? When did this happen?" Lauren stared at the two girls.

Zoey grinned. "In her text last night. That's why she invited us to come out this morning."

"Well, aren't you two sneaky?" Lauren crossed her arms. "Why isn't she going on the roundup?" She couldn't imagine Robert doing this, not when he still thought she had something to do with Lady's theft. "Wasn't he planning to teach her how to herd cattle?"

"Seems the Lord had a different plan." Mandy glanced toward the busy barnyard, where Robert now strode toward them. "Last night we discovered Lady needs to be kept inside for a while so she doesn't run off and find herself another, shall we say, *inappropriate* boyfriend." She and Zoey giggled. "That's why we have her on the leash, so she can't run away."

As this revelation began to make sense to Lauren, Robert reached them.

"Can you handle this?" His gruff tone underscored his cross expression. "This was a last-minute thing, so—"

"Yes, I'm happy to help. But—" She should ask why Lady couldn't just stay on the ranch, but the hopeful look in Zoey's eyes stopped her.

"Good. Just keep her indoors except for morning and evening walks, and be sure you hold on tight to that leash. She'll be all right alone in your apartment during the day. Also, my cousin Sue is a vet, and she can answer any questions and give you any supplies at my expense." He handed Lauren a business card. "Give her a call."

The way he spoke to her, he was clearly used to giving orders to anybody and everybody and expecting them to obey. She wanted to salute and say, *Aye, aye, sir.* Good sense kept her right hand at her side. Never mind that she and Zoey had taken good care of Lady all summer. "I can do that."

He stared at her. "Yes, I'm sure you can. Mandy, you take care of your sister and grandma while we're gone." He spun around on his dusty cowboy boots and strode away like the Big Boss that he was. An old-fashioned movie hero couldn't have done it any better.

Lauren watched him, her emotions hovering between admiration for the attractive man and annoyance at his high-handed ways. She shook away those thoughts and turned to Mandy. "We're happy to take care of Lady for you, but why can't she just stay here in your house?"

"Mom!" Zoey protested.

Mandy just shrugged. "Have you ever seen my little sister close the door when she goes outside? Never. When we noticed

Lady's condition last evening, Dad thought…well, he agreed with Bobby and me…that she'd make a run for it and get into trouble again. The best solution was to ask Zoey, and you of course, to make sure she's safe and happy." She petted Lady. "Just so you know, Bobby and I and even Clementine can see Lady loves Zoey and wants to be with her."

Lauren resisted agreeing with her, at least in Zoey's hearing. "How do you feel about that?"

Mandy's smile was genuine. "We agree. We love her, of course, but we aren't very attached to her. Besides, we have the other dogs." She laughed. "And more cats than you can count."

Lauren didn't know what to say. Should she offer to buy Lady? No, she couldn't afford such a pricey pet. Besides, she doubted Robert would sell her his expensive breeding dog. It was a wonder he'd allowed Zoey to keep her, but then, he'd been forced to by Lady's unexpected condition. She hadn't been back with the Mattsons long enough for them to predict it.

The sun rose above the horizon as Robert's monster truck rolled past her pulling the loaded horse trailer. He glanced her way and touched the brim of his hat, cowboy gentleman that he was, but didn't smile. Not that he'd ever actually smiled at her. But it wasn't her fault he'd made the decision to let her, well, *Zoey* take care of Lady while he took care of ranch business.

She'd always thought no man could be as controlling and annoying as her ex-husband. But Robert Mattson had Single-ton beat by a mile.

ROB INHALED A lungful of pure, icy mountain air, sensing the imminence of an early winter. He nestled down into his sleeping bag, pleased this roundup was going so well. Back in 1888 and again in 1923, his family had lost much of their herd in early winter storms. After those disasters, they'd learned to read the signs about when to get their steers to market.

He looked up at the countless stars dotting the blackened

sky and whispered, "Thank You, Lord, for all of this beauty. For the ranch. For a healthy herd. For my family."

He glanced toward the one-man tent where Bobby sat hunched over his tablet. How could that kid prefer to stare at a screen instead of enjoying the untamed wilderness pastures that would one day belong to him? This week, he'd done a decent job of scouting out some mavericks under Andy's guidance and with the help of Irish and Scotch. Did he enjoy working with the dogs? Had he caught the cowboy bug yet? If his hurry to get back to his tablet was any indication, the answer was no.

How could he have spent his entire fifteen years on the ranch without loving this life? How many kids his age got to spend the night under the stars and know the satisfaction of a job well done? Some of Rob's best talks with his dad had been right here in these mountains during roundup. The memory gave him an idea.

"Hey, Bobby."

No answer.

"Bobby!"

"Yessir?" The mumbled response revealed his preoccupation.

"Come on out here."

His sigh was deep and audible. "Yessir."

His tablet light went out, and he crawled out of the shelter he preferred to the open air, pulling a blanket around his shoulders and shuddering.

"You need something, Dad?"

Rob was thankful Bobby couldn't see the annoyance that must be written across his face. "Yeah. Go make sure Scotch and Irish have enough water in their pan." The two border collies had worked hard today, although before they left home, it had been tricky to keep Scotch away from Lady.

"I already did."

"Good. Now come over here and sit with me." Rob pulled himself up and crossed his legs. "So, what did you learn today?"

Bobby plunked down on the edge of the sleeping bag. "It's really cool, Dad. I figured out a really cool coding sequence that will help my programming team when we compete in Albuquerque in November." The excitement in his voice gave Rob a chill that was anything but "really cool."

"Good. I'm glad you're doing so well. But how about the roundup? Did Uncle Andy have some good things to teach you?"

"Yessir." Bobby glanced back at his tent. Even in the dim light of the campfire, Rob could see his longing to get back to his tablet.

"Like what?"

Bobby sighed…again. "Well, he showed me how Scotch and Irish use teamwork to herd the steers and how they know which ones of the new calves belongs to which mother and how to keep them together."

"Right." This was good. How could he keep it going? "And Lady will do the same thing once she's back in training. She's got the right instincts. We just need to work with her a little more."

Bobby stared at him for a few seconds. "I don't want to say you're wrong, Dad, but—"

"But you think I'm wrong."

Bobby grinned. "Yessir."

Now Rob sighed. "Yeah, well, I paid too much for her to give up and let her be somebody's pet." Annoyance threaded through his chest over being trapped into letting Lady stay with Zoey and Lauren. But he'd had no choice. Six days ago, they had to get on the road before sunup, so he didn't have time to figure out another plan. With time, he'd have boarded her at Cousin Sue's vet clinic. Too many last-minute decisions prevented that.

Would Zoey be able to keep Lady indoors? Would they be

able to hang on to her leash when they took her out for her walks? Despite his suspicions about Lauren, he had to admit she was a responsible person, although her wary expression when she looked at him kept his suspicions alive.

Why did he spend so much time thinking about that frustrating woman? And why hadn't he just tried to call the Santa Fe vet again to find out the truth?

Simple. He didn't want to know. Feeding his suspicions helped him keep a wall between them, one that those pretty gray-green eyes might just one day pierce through his resolve like a laser beam. And at all cost, he had to prevent that.

CHAPTER EIGHT

LAUREN DIDN'T USUALLY watch the clock, but today she fidgeted in her chair as quitting time neared. Yesterday evening, Robert had texted his plan to come by the apartment this evening to take Lady home. Lauren had mixed feelings about seeing him again. Would he be his usual gruff self, or would he show some gratitude to Zoey at least for taking care of Lady? With that man, she could never guess.

Finally the hands of the antique clock above the door reached five and twelve. Lauren saved her document, closed out the program and logged off of her computer.

"Any plans for tonight?" Will asked Sam as they emerged from the back offices.

"Um, well…"

"Why don't you come out to our place and finally meet the young lady who's renting our art studio? She's—"

"Lauren!" Sam's voice held a hint of panic. "Don't you still need me to hang that shadow box for you?"

She managed not to laugh. Should she encourage Will's matchmaking or rescue Sam from his cousin's plans? In fact, it might be good to have him at the apartment when Robert arrived.

"I hate to spoil your fun, Will, but I keep tripping over the shadow box. It sure would be nice to have it on the wall and out of the way."

He gave her a skeptical smirk. "Yeah, right." He clapped Sam on the shoulder. "Don't think you're going to get out of meeting Lily. She's—"

"Will you look at the time." Sam glanced at his watch. "Lauren, I'll be right over after I grab supper."

"Why not eat with Zoey and me? We're having spaghetti."

Eyes narrowed, Will looked back and forth between them with fake annoyance. "Okay. Have it your way." He plopped his Stetson on his head and walked to the door. "See you two at church on Sunday. Don't forget to lock up."

As he made his exit, Lauren grabbed her purse. "You don't really have to be my personal handyman, Sam. If you have Friday night plans, feel free to change your mind."

"Ha. After you saved me from the clutches of some artsy type woman Will and Olivia think is *just perfect* for me?" He snorted. "And this coming from the guy who resisted romance even when it smacked him in the face. No, I'm more than happy to help you out."

"Okay, then." Back in Orlando, Lauren had managed to avoid several matchmaking attempts herself. Thankfully, no one here in Riverton had signed up for that job. "See you at my place in a few."

The ten-block drive to her apartment complex took longer than usual due to Friday evening traffic. Lauren pulled into her designated parking space and hurried into the building a little breathless. She was met by Mrs. Walston, the neighbor who checked on Zoey every day.

"All's quiet on the Western Front," the retired history teacher said. "I watched as she walked that pretty little dog down to the end of the block and back again."

"Thank you." Lauren hesitated before adding, "I have a guest…two guests coming over this evening. My boss and the man who owns Lady." As kind as Mrs. Walston was, she did have a tendency to gossip, not to mention to go on and on about random topics, so it was best to keep her informed. It was a small thing to put up with her borderline snooping to have a responsible adult who cared enough to keep an eye on Zoey when Lauren was at work.

"How nice." The lady gave her a maternal smile. "Well, you enjoy your evening." She disappeared behind her door.

Entering her own first-floor apartment, Lauren was greeted by a wagging dog and the aroma of onions cooking. She knelt to ruffle Lady's fur and accepted her welcome-home licks, then they both joined Zoey in the kitchen. "I see you've started supper."

"Yep." Zoey beamed with self-confidence. "I'm getting ready to brown the hamburger." She was struggling to pull apart the edges of the package of grain-fed ground beef.

"Here. Let me." Lauren reached for the meat.

Zoey turned one shoulder. "I can do it."

"Right." Letting her daughter struggle was the hardest part of parenting. "I have trouble separating the sides, too. I usually give up and use the scissors."

Zoey rolled her eyes. "Okay. I can take a hint." She took the scissors from the knife block and struggled to cut into the plastic wrap.

Nearby, Lady watched Zoey, tilting her head as though questioning what she was doing. When the scissors slipped from her wet hands, Lauren gasped softly, and Lady let out a little whimper.

"Okay, you guys, stop that." Zoey speared each of them with a cross look before trying again. This time, the sharp blades crosscut through the plastic, and she was able to pull the meat out and place it in the sizzling pan of onions. Only a little grease popped up. "See. I can do it."

"Yes, you can." Lauren gave her a side hug. "Since you have this all in hand, what can I do to help?"

"Make the salad." Zoey reached into the skillet, carefully

pinched off a tiny piece of hamburger and held it out to Lady. The grateful dog licked it from her hand and seemed to smile. Zoey stepped over to the sink and washed her hands, then returned to the stove to break up the meat with a cooking spoon. "Mom? Salad?"

Lauren resisted the urge to suggest a different tool. "Right." She opened the fridge. "Hey, you remember Mandy's dad is coming to pick up Lady?"

Zoey stabbed at the meat. "I remember."

"And Sam's coming over to hang the shadow box, so I invited him to eat with us."

"For supper?" Zoey stared at her, panic in her eyes. "Mom, you take over here." She held out the spoon. "I don't want you to get fired for serving your boss lumpy spaghetti sauce."

"I'm sure he won't fire me for that, but maybe for not having dessert." Lauren accepted the spoon and set it in the sink, then selected the four-bladed meat chopper from the utensil holder and began to break the hamburger into small bits. "How about you whip up some peach cobbler?"

While her daughter assembled the canned peaches and biscuit mix, Lauren filled a stockpot with water and turned on the back burner. A knock sounded on the door just as Zoey put the cobbler in the oven. She hurried to answer, with Lady close beside her.

"I hope you don't mind," Sam said as they entered the kitchen. "I brought my checkers and board to teach Zoey. We talked about it the other week when she was at the office. Is that okay?" Like his cousin Will, and unlike his cousin Robert, Sam had a relaxed, personable way about him. Once Robert took Lady later this evening, it would be good to have something to distract Zoey.

"Sounds good." He might be her boss, but Lauren was still in charge here at home. "Zoey, how's your homework coming?"

"No problem." She grinned. "I finished most of it in study hall."

"Then checkers it is."

While she and Zoey finished supper preparations, Sam mounted the heavy shadow box over the chest of drawers in Zoey's bedroom.

Lauren spread a tablecloth over the battered card table they used for dining, then set up three metal folding chairs. Sam didn't seem to mind bending his tall frame into the chair. At Lauren's invitation, he offered a blessing for the food and added a request for Lady to have an easy transition back to the ranch. Lauren sent him a grateful smile. He and Will hadn't taken sides about the dog, but they seemed to know all about it and still hadn't fired her. Maybe Robert hadn't told them of his suspicions.

"That's quite a collection of doodads you've got in your shadow box, Zoey," Sam said. "Where'd you get all that stuff?" He twirled a bite of spaghetti onto his fork and put it in his mouth.

"We collected them at the truck stops as we drove across the country." Zoey had been proud of the various tiny figurines she'd found. "They're reminders of where we've traveled."

They were halfway into dessert when another knock sounded on the door.

"I'll get it." Sam rose from the table and headed toward the door before Lauren could move. "Hey, Rob."

Lauren had to smother a laugh at the surprised expression on Robert's face.

"Sam." Robert entered and removed his hat. "What're you doing here?"

"Just helping Lauren out and honing my handyman skills. Come on in. I'm sure there's enough of Zoey's peach cobbler for you to join us."

Lauren wanted to punch her boss's arm. What was he doing by playing the part of host? Even so, she quickly laid out a place mat for Robert and unfolded another chair. "Yes, come have a seat. You're just in time. I'm not sure Sam planned to leave any cobbler or ice cream."

Lady wandered over to greet Robert, then returned to her spot beside Zoey's chair. Lauren swallowed the sudden emotion trying to rise in her throat. She would miss Lady almost as much as Zoey. Almost, but not quite. Zoey's eyes glistened with tears, but she managed to smile. After their guests left, they would have a good cry together.

"THIS IS MIGHTY TASTY, Zoey. I sure wasn't expecting this." Rob had been raised never to turn down an offered dessert. Mom insisted a hardworking man could always find room for a lady's homemade specialty, no matter how it tasted, as a goodwill gesture. In this case, Zoey's cobbler was almost as good as Mom's, though he thought maybe she'd used store-bought canned peaches and a biscuit mix, while Mom made hers with home-canned peaches and scratch dough. "Thanks."

"You're welcome. And thank you for letting us take care of Lady." Zoey's eyes seemed a bit teary. No surprise there. "We kept her indoors except for her walks, just like you said. She was used to being here, so I think that's why she didn't try to get away. One time on our walk, when I was daydreaming about my homework and stepped into the street, she pulled me back before a car came zooming past us." She reached down and petted Lady. "I guess she was herding me back to safety." She laughed softly, and her voice broke. Was it from emotion or due to her CP?

Rob grimaced, imagining the dangerous scene. "I don't know which to comment on first. She sure was doing a good job of watching out for you." He chuckled. "But you were actually daydreaming about homework?"

Sam also chuckled, while Lauren sent Rob a grateful smile—a smile he felt deep in his chest.

Zoey rolled her eyes at his teasing, just like Mandy always did. "Yes. I have to write a short story for English class, and I'm writing about how we found Lady. That takes a lot of planning so I can make it interesting."

Rob glanced at Lauren, who ducked her head. Guilt? Would Zoey's school assignment finally reveal the truth about how Lady came into their lives? He doubted the girl would lie, but she might make up a fictional version of the events. "I'd like to read that when you're done."

"Sure." Zoey grinned. "I'd like that."

"And on that note—" He reached into his back pocket and took out his wallet. "We didn't discuss your dog-watching fee. Would a hundred—"

"Absolutely not." Lauren glared at him, then softened her look. "We were happy to help out in a pinch. And Lady was a perfect...well, lady. It was a pure pleasure to watch her. Besides, you don't charge us for Zoey's riding lessons."

At the finality in her tone, he put the wallet away. He noticed she didn't say they'd missed Lady living with them or repeat what Zoey said about the dog feeling right at home here. He had to give her credit for that.

"Okay. Thanks." He noticed Zoey's sweet smile, so apparently she agreed with her mom. "So, when are you coming back out to ride?" What was he saying? He didn't usually speak without thinking, but this time his tongue seemed to have a mind of its own.

"Doc says give it another week, and if I take my meds and don't have any seizures, I can ride a week from tomorrow. I can't wait."

The eagerness in her voice made him smile. "Great. I'll tell the kids, and we'll plan on it."

"In the meantime," Sam said, "let's exercise your strategizing skills with a good game of checkers."

While they talked checkers, Rob took the opportunity to glance around the apartment. The kitchen was a small alcove off of the living and dining areas. Down the short hallway, he could see two open bedroom doors. In the living area, a small flat-screen television sat on a low table across from two well-worn upholstered chairs. On the walls were a couple of stock photo pictures and two homemade cross-stitch samplers of Bible verses. This rickety old card table looked like it came from the 1800s.

Life couldn't be easy for this mom. Zoey wore T-shirts and ripped jeans like the other kids, while Lauren wore the same navy pantsuit he'd seen her wearing at work when he'd brought them lunch. Was that her only professional clothing? They didn't appear to have much in the way of material things, but the room felt like it was filled with love. Truth was, he had to respect that, especially since she'd refused the money he'd tried to offer. He wasn't about to spoil these impressions by trying again to reach that Santa Fe vet. At least not yet.

"Thanks for the dessert." He carefully pushed the uncomfortable metal chair back from the wobbly table. "Time for me to collect my dog and head out." He bent down and ruffled Lady's fur behind her ears. "Come on, girl. Let's go home." He gripped her collar and tugged, only to have her resist his efforts by settling firmly on the floor and whining. Smart dog. She knew what this was about.

Zoey reached down to pet her. "You do what he says, Lady. It's time for you to go home."

Again her eyes...and Lauren's...shone with tears. Rob had to grip his own emotions. "Come on, girl." He lifted Lady and headed toward the door, with Sam following. "You coming?"

"Nope. Just want to tell you something. Like I said, Zoey and I are going to play checkers." Sam followed Rob out of the apartment. "That week Zoey spent at the office gave Will and me a chance to notice how she blossoms with some brotherly, or *uncle-ly*, if that's a word, attention. That's why I thought she might like checkers." He turned away, then back again. "Lauren's a nice lady. You should take her out." He nudged Rob's arm and grinned, then stepped back into the apartment. "See you, Cuz."

Rob shook off his annoyance at Sam's suggestion. As he headed toward his truck, Lady whimpered and wiggled in his arms. Once in the vehicle, she slumped down on the seat, apparently resigned. Her condition had changed, so after he drove through the ranch's front gate, he let her run free. She greeted Scotch and Irish, then followed him into the house.

"Lady!" Clementine greeted them at the door and knelt to give the dog a hug. "Welcome home." Lady licked her face and leaned into the hug. Rob figured Clementine was the dog's second favorite person in the world after Zoey. What would it take for her loyalty to transfer back to Bobby?

Bobby wandered into the front hall munching on one of Mom's giant blueberry muffins. "Hey, Lady." He petted her, then headed for the staircase.

"Hey." Rob couldn't keep the sharp tone from his voice. "This is your dog. You need to keep her with you."

"Oh." Bobby blinked in that "is anybody home" way of his. "Yeah. Come on, Lady."

She looked between him and Clementine and plodded after him with obvious reluctance.

Rob released a long sigh. How was he going to get a return on the investment he'd made in this valuable dog when his son couldn't care less about training her? Worse than that, how could he get his son interested in his own inheritance? Since the late 1880s, five generations of Robert Mattsons had owned and managed the Double Bar M Ranch. It was a hands-on operation, but with Bobby's interest focused on computers and electronics, he'd probably try texting orders to his cowhands. Yeah, that would work for maintaining a healthy herd of cattle. Not.

Rob didn't usually have trouble sleeping, but he lay awake far into the night worrying about his legacy and feeling like he'd somehow failed his ancestors. Lauren's pretty face and the one real smile she'd sent his way that evening came to mind. She had single-parent worries, too. How did she cope with the challenges life threw her way? At least Rob didn't have to worry about providing for his family.

One of the samplers on her wall read, "Trust in the Lord with all thine heart."

Maybe that was how she did it, by trusting in the Lord. When he was younger and life was easier, he'd always believed God had his life under control. Then Jordyn died, and his faith had taken a hit. Maybe it was time to try trusting the Lord again, even in the matter of retraining his valuable herding dog.

LAUREN STARED UP at the ceiling, unable to fall asleep for all the thoughts tumbling through her mind. Robert's large presence in her small apartment had made her feel claustrophobic. Or was it some other feeling she couldn't define? She didn't like the way her feelings for the big rancher had softened. Good thing Sam had stuck around for an hour or so to take Zoey's mind off of Lady's absence. Lauren missed the adorable dog, too.

Should she go to the local animal shelter and get another pet? Maybe a cat, an older indoor kitty that could stay home alone all day and not require twice daily walks. That might be a good Christmas present for Zoey. Besides, if they adopted a dog, it might not have Lady's protective instincts. Zoey hadn't told her about the traffic incident, and Lauren had difficulty hiding her shock. After Sam left, she'd scolded Zoey.

Zoey had just shrugged it off. *I didn't want to worry you, Mom.*

Her daughter wanted her independence, but that incident proved she wasn't ready for it yet. "Lord, please remind her to be more careful. And please protect her when she's not paying attention." The thought of losing her daughter was more than Lauren could bear. Hadn't she suffered enough loss already?

CHAPTER NINE

ON SATURDAY MORNING, Lauren went to the mailbox just inside the building's front door. As expected, Mrs. Walston poked her head out of her apartment. "Good morning, dear." She wore her usual maternal smile. "I don't want to hold you up, but I wondered if Zoey's told you anything about theme week starting Monday and homecoming next Saturday?"

"Theme week and homecoming?" Lauren's mommy-heart dipped. Zoey had been hurt last year when a boy at her old school had pretended to ask her to the homecoming dance, then called it off the day of the dance. At least they'd been able to take the unworn dress back to the store. No wonder Zoey hadn't mentioned the upcoming event.

"Yes, indeed." Mrs. W's smile broadened. "When I was teaching, I loved these events more than all the other student activities, even prom. A theme is posted for each day, and students can wear costumes to match it. Beach Day, Pirate Day, Flower Child Day, Favorite Book Character Day…"

Lauren smiled at the dear lady's enthusiasm. "And Cowboy Day?"

"Oh, no." Mrs. W. laughed. "Most of them are cowboys all year long, so that's one theme they don't bother with." She patted Lauren's arm. "Now, I just wanted you to know that I have several costumes Zoey can borrow for the daily themes. And our church has what we call our Princess Closet to provide formal dresses for special events like homecoming and prom so parents don't have to spend money on a gown their daughter will wear only one time. We have quite a collection of closeout gowns from several bridal shops in the area, and we loan them to the girls for the school dances. No charge, of course. If Zoey would like to come down after school one day this coming week, we can find a special dress for her to wear."

"Oh, wow." Lauren's heart swelled with appreciation. "I know she'll enjoy theme week, but I don't know if she's going to the dance. If she does, a borrowed dress would be answered prayer." And before she even had a chance to pray about it.

"Good." Mrs. W. patted her hand. "A pretty girl like her should have several nice boys lining up to ask her, but sometimes the students go in groups instead of dating. One way or the other, I'm sure she'll want to attend." She turned toward her door, then back again. "Oh, by the way, the school always appreciates parent volunteers who can help out at the dance. You know, serving punch and cookies...and of course keeping an eye on the young people. At these special events, the teachers can't do it all. You may want to volunteer your services."

"Thanks. I'll do that." This woman was turning out to be a good neighbor. A little bossy, maybe, but not in a bad way like a certain other person Lauren knew.

After last year's unhappy experience, Zoey might not expect much of the homecoming dance, but if the small group of friends she'd made at school invited her, Lauren would be sure to volunteer to help so she could drive her there and keep tabs on her. But she would definitely wait for Zoey to receive an honest invitation before talking to her about a dress and the theme week costumes.

She didn't have long to wait. After church the next day, Mandy and Grace, another classmate, joined Zoey and Lauren on the church's front lawn.

"Miss Lauren, homecoming is next Saturday, and after the football game, a bunch of us kids are going to the dance together," Mandy said. "Can Zoey come with us?"

Zoey gave Lauren a pleading look. "Please, Mom." She sounded like she didn't expect her approval.

Thank You, Lord, for preparing me for this.

"Sure. That sounds like fun." She smiled at Zoey's surprised grin. "Who else is going?"

They named two other girls Lauren hadn't met yet. All the more reason for her to volunteer to help so she could see if these girls were acceptable friends for Zoey.

"Want to go for pizza with us now?" Grace asked Zoey.

"Mom?" Again, Zoey pleaded with a look.

"Well, uh…" Lauren and Zoey usually got a burger after church and talked about Pastor Tim's sermon. Was it time to let go a little bit? "Who's driving?"

"My cousin June." Mandy's hopeful expression mirrored Zoey's. "She's twenty, almost twenty-one, and a safe driver. I promise we'll bring Zoey home safely."

Lauren briefly pondered the situation. She'd met June, who taught pre-K Sunday school, and she seemed trustworthy and mature for her age. Lauren didn't want to deny her daughter this chance to have fun with friends.

"Okay." She reached into her purse, dug out her last twenty-dollar bill and handed it to Zoey. She'd have to eat a sandwich at home, but it was worth it to see Zoey have friends. Still… "Just keep your phone handy."

"Thanks, Mom." Zoey gave her a quick hug.

Her emotions mixed, Lauren watched the girls hurry across the lawn toward a blue four-door pickup, where June waited. She waved and smiled, and Lauren returned the gesture.

"It's hard to let them go, isn't it?" Andrea Mattson approached, looking sharp in her lavender pantsuit, with a floral scarf draped perfectly around her shoulders and fancy gray Western boots peeking out from beneath her trouser hemline.

"How about you joining us for lunch?" She tilted her head toward another pickup, this one an elegant burgundy red, where Linda and Andy Mattson stood. "We usually go to the steak house for Sunday lunch."

We? Did that include Robert? The pickup wasn't his black diesel monster, so maybe he had other plans. But she'd given Zoey her last twenty dollars, and she didn't dare use her one emergency credit card. "I'm not sure…"

"Come on." Andrea slipped her arm around Lauren's waist. "My treat."

Could this woman read her mind? Only pride would keep her from accepting such a kind offer, especially when she didn't really want to eat alone at home. "Sure. Thank you. I'll meet you there."

"Nonsense. Ride with us in the truck. We'll bring you back to get your car later." She tugged on Lauren's arm. "Let's go. We don't want to miss our reservation."

Did they have to make a reservation at their own restaurant? "O-okay." She let Andrea guide her across the fading lawn. To her shock, Robert also walked in that direction. How could she get out of this situation without offending Andrea?

"Hey, Lauren." He opened the front passenger door. "Here you go, Mom." He gave Andrea a hand up, then opened the back door. "Hope you don't mind sitting back here with the hired help." He nodded toward Andy and Linda as he assisted Lauren to climb in.

"Hey, watch it, Cuz." Andy sent him a phony glare, while Linda laughed.

Lauren laughed, too. Maybe this wouldn't be so bad after all. "Where's that big black truck of yours?"

He shut the door and walked around to the driver's seat. Once he'd punched the ignition start button, he spoke over his shoulder. "That's just for heavy ranch work. This is my everyday ride." Everyday ride? With its gray leather seats and a lit up computer dashboard resembling big city lights? Pretty fancy for every day.

The restaurant, located near the center of town, already had a parking lot filled with more trucks than Lauren could count. Most people around here drove them, whether they lived in town or on one of the many ranches in the area. Robert pulled into a parking spot marked Reserved. No surprise there.

Inside, they were greeted by various patrons and numerous other Mattsons, including newlyweds Will and Olivia and their two cute little children. Sam sat with friends, some of whom she recognized as clients of the law office.

"Order whatever you like. This is my favorite." Andrea pointed to a picture of a center cut ribeye on the menu.

What a gracious way to help Lauren order a juicy steak rather than search the menu for the cheapest item, as her parents had taught her to do when someone else was buying. "Thanks. I'll get it, too."

Robert and Andy sat across the table talking ranch work, while Linda and Andrea traded news about their grown children. With Linda and Andy being Sam's parents, Lauren listened politely. She'd learned in a previous job that it wasn't wise to learn too much about one's employer, but these ladies didn't seem clued in to that insight. With this being a rather tight community, she supposed everybody knew everybody else's business anyway. All she could do was pretend not to pay attention. But when their orders arrived and Robert said, "Let's pray," she had to admit knowing this was a family of faith reassured her about Zoey's involvement with their kids.

"Is Bobby slated for the starting lineup for the homecoming game?" Andy cut into his steak and took a bite.

"Not sure," Robert said. "He's big enough to mix it up with the guys, but as a sophomore, I wouldn't be surprised if Coach had somebody else in mind to start. Sad to say, we've got a pretty weak lineup this year since several of our best players graduated last year."

"Speaking of football, Lauren," Andrea said, "I heard you say Zoey has your permission to go to the homecoming dance."

Robert snorted. "Mom, only you can connect football with a dance."

The others, including Lauren, laughed.

"Humph." Andrea snatched up a dinner roll and buttered it. "It's a homecoming tradition. Do you think everybody returns home just for the game? Nonsense. They come back to watch the parade and the game, but also to socialize at the dance."

"That's so true." Lauren spoke without thinking, then took a bite of steak to keep from saying more. She really shouldn't intrude in this family conversation.

"So what event did you like best when you were in school?" Robert stared at her with those startling blue eyes. "The game or the dance?"

Heat flooded her face, and she looked down at her plate. Oh, how she hated her feminine response to his all-too-appealing good looks. "Well…"

"Did you have a brother—" he raised one eyebrow in a teasing way "—or a boyfriend who played on the football team? That's usually what draws a girl's interest to the game." He looked at Andy, who nodded and grinned his agreement.

"Surely you jest." Lauren laughed at the chauvinistic comment. "Actually, my brother was into computers, so he was on the programming team rather than playing football."

Frowning, Robert stabbed at his steak. "Huh. Just what I didn't need to hear."

How rude. "I'll have you know not one of those boys who played at our school grew up to have NFL careers or even went on to play in college." To hide her annoyance, she tried to keep her tone cheerful and teasing. "On the other hand, my brother has had a solid career as a software engineer and even coaches the programming team at the university."

After a moment of quiet, during which Robert chewed his last bite of steak, Andrea spoke up.

"Your family must be so proud." She waved to the server. "Shall we order dessert?"

Still annoyed, and a bit confused, by Robert's attitude, Lauren decided to indulge in the chocolate cheesecake on the menu. She'd worry about the calories later. Maybe run some laps around the block. Maybe never come out to Sunday dinner with the Mattsons again.

ROB LEARNED LONG ago to just go along with whatever Mom planned, at least in the social realm. Count on her to invite Lauren for lunch since Mandy had taken Zoey for pizza. Everything was going fine until she had to bring up her brother's programming career. Good thing Bobby had opted to hang out with his friends rather than come to the steak house for lunch so he didn't hear her comment. Rob could only hope his son never learned about it. Rob didn't know much about Lauren's upbringing, but he doubted her parents had a business they'd spent a lifetime building so they could pass it on to their son.

Of course Lauren had no idea why her brother's success should bother him. He could tell she'd been hurt when he'd dismissed her proud declaration as something he didn't need to hear. He couldn't fix that without exposing his own pain over Bobby's disinterest in the future he should love.

Besides, why did Lauren refuse to look directly at him most of the time? A man could discern a lot about another person who never looked him straight in the eye. Was it guilt? Months before Jordyn's death, she'd started hiding something he couldn't figure out and rarely looked at him square in the eye. It wasn't until after her accident he learned what she'd been up to. By then it was too late to protect her...from herself.

Maybe the best way to solve his confusion over his unwanted attraction to Lauren would be to avoid her whenever possible. Not that Mom would understand and cooperate. She seemed to have adopted this single mother as her latest cause. Andy might be the one to help. That was it. When Zoey and

Lauren came out to the ranch for Zoey's next ride, Rob would ask his cousin to oversee the lesson. That would reduce the time spent with her. Problem solved.

But if that was true, why did the plan cause an ache in his belly that had nothing to do with the salty caramel cookie he'd foolishly eaten for dessert on top of the sixteen-ounce steak and loaded potato he'd devoured? No, Rob wouldn't shirk his responsibility to make sure Zoey stayed safe when she came out to ride his horses, even if it meant he had to be around Lauren, too.

"You LOOK SO BEAUTIFUL, honey." Lauren fussed with the puffy sleeves of the dusky pink tea-length formal Zoey had chosen from the Princess Closet.

"You're not so bad yourself." Zoey eyed the years-old basic black dress Lauren had dressed up with a purple scarf and the amethyst earrings she'd inherited from her grandmother.

"Thanks." Lauren refreshed her lipstick, then noticed Zoey copying her. They'd always done everything together, but one day soon, this baby bird would fly away. Best to treasure these precious mother-daughter moments while she could. "Did you enjoy the game?"

"Ugh. No." Zoey rolled her eyes. "Our guys were pitiful."

"They weren't so bad." She and Zoey had sat with Robert, Mandy, Andrea and Clementine for the nail-biter competition, with the girls cheering their lungs out and Robert calling plays from the stands. The Riverton Golden Eagles did their best to hold the line against the Española Sunrays, to no avail. The Golden Eagles' disappointment as the score mounted against them was palpable. "They tried their best. That's all any of us can do."

"Yeah." Zoey gave her the side-eye. "You know what I liked best about the game? It was before it started, when Savannah Reese rode into the stadium on her horse carrying an American flag in front of the cheerleaders and the team and all of them carrying American flags running after her. I just love to see the flags waving in the wind, especially when a rider carries it on horseback. Every year a senior girl gets to do that." She took a deep breath after her long speech.

"That *was* exciting and very inspiring. The parade was—"

Zoey faced her. "I want to do that."

"What?" Lauren held her breath.

"When I'm a senior, I want to carry the flag and ride into the stadium on Tripper in front of the team."

Lauren's eyes burned, but she wouldn't let the tears come. "Well, we have two years to work on that, don't we?" She managed a laugh. "I'm not sure good ol' Tripper would be able to gallop around the field fast enough to make the flag wave, but maybe—" She had to stop. It wouldn't do any good to encourage her daughter's dream about such a dangerous activity she'd probably never get to do.

A frown crossed Zoey's forehead. "Mom, I'm nervous about the dance. I'm glad you're going, too."

Whew. Fast change of subject. "Me too, honey. We'll have a good time."

"Uh, no. *We* won't have a good time. You just stay behind the refreshment table and serve the punch." She gave Lauren a cheeky grin. "And *I* will pretend I don't know you."

This was new and a tiny bit hurtful. The baby bird truly was getting ready to fly away. But an hour later when she took up her post behind the large glass punch bowl, she noticed it was typical of the kids whose mothers were also volunteers. It was like they were saying, *Be there for me, Mom, but I'll pretend you aren't.*

In the dimly lit gymnasium, the boys wore Western-style suits and bolo ties and the ever-present cowboy boots. Many of the girls also wore boots with their formal gowns, something that gave Lauren a chuckle. A floral archway stood at the entrance of the gymnasium, and the country-western band struck up a fanfare to announce the homecoming court. Among them were Mandy and her escort as the sophomore attendants. Years ago, Lauren had that honor as a junior at her high school, and she would much prefer Zoey to run for that office instead of aspiring to ride a horse at breakneck speed around the stadium. Across the room, she saw Robert watch his daughter with obvious pride. Surely Mandy would be chosen to carry the flag when the girls were seniors.

After the homecoming court and queen and king were introduced, the music began again, and the older students paired up and began to dance. Zoey and her friends clustered together by the folded bleachers, keeping time with the lively music and trying for all they were worth not to look at the cluster of boys, who were also trying not to look their way.

At last, Bobby broke from the herd and headed toward the girls. To Lauren's relief and joy, he held out his hand to Zoey. Lauren couldn't hear what he said, but Zoey's sweet smile spoke volumes. She and Zoey had practiced some steps at home, and it showed in the way she managed to follow Bobby's surprisingly smooth leading. Robert must have taught him.

As she watched her daughter partner with other boys in various numbers, Lauren's heart could hardly contain the joy at the way these young people accepted Zoey. For all of her worries and prayers about her daughter's future, it seemed she was on her way to a normal life. As normal as it could be.

ROB LEANED BACK against the gym wall, arms crossed, watching the events unfold. He usually didn't mind being a prominent presence at any public gathering. It came with the territory of being a community leader and the owner of the largest cattle ranch in the area. But he'd promised Bobby and especially Mandy that he'd keep his distance so as not to embarrass them. So, after letting them out of the truck, he'd waited five minutes before going into the gym.

Then, as he'd walked down the dimly lit hallway, he could hear some male students talking around the corner.

"She's such a freak," a familiar voice said. "I'd like to see her fall flat on her ugly face." He'd spoken in a mock-halting voice, mimicking Zoey, including the slight hum that often preceded her words. "Let's go see what we can do to make that happen." His two companions had laughed.

Rob had peered around the corner. Just as he'd suspected, it was Jeff Sizemore and two of his gang. Sizemore came from a disreputable family that had caused grief in this community for well over a century and, worse, were proud of it. Jeff and his friends obviously planned to harm Zoey. No, that wasn't going to happen.

"Hey." Rob had strode toward them and grasped Jeff on the shoulder. "You cause trouble, and you'll have me to deal with."

Jeff twisted away, sneering. "You and what army?"

Rob stepped up close and personal to tower over the skinny boy of medium height. "No army needed, son. I've dealt with your sort all my life without any help."

To his satisfaction, fear flooded the boy's eyes and his friends', too. They broke away and slunk into the gym just as the music began.

Rob had followed. He'd keep an eye on them…and Zoey, to make sure they didn't trip her or embarrass her in any other way. He'd had to subdue his anger over such cruel plans because it had been time for his own daughter to make her entrance along with the rest of the homecoming court. He was proud of Mandy for being chosen to represent the sophomore class. She looked so much like her mother, who'd been homecoming queen their senior year. Would Mandy aim for that honor in two years? Or would she say it was enough to have been in the court this year? He should be proud of her willingness to let others be recognized by their peers, but it was hard for him not to want her to repeat her beautiful mother's success.

After the court had been introduced and the dance music began, Rob had found a corner to watch from, keeping his distance as he'd promised the twins.

"Hey, Rob." Rex Blake, with his sweet wife, Annie, joined him. "Looks like the kids are having a good time." As always at formal high school events, Rex wore his dress uniform to remind rowdy kids to behave themselves.

"Yep. Say, I'm glad you're here." Rob gave his good friend a brief report on what the Sizemore kid had planned.

"That's so cruel," Annie said. "From what my kids have told me, Zoey is such a sweetheart. Why would anyone want to hurt her?"

"Maybe her popularity and their lack of it makes 'em jealous." Rex shook his head. "We'll keep an eye on them *and* her. In the meantime, I'm gonna dance with my lady." He and Annie took to the floor alongside the students.

Rob hadn't planned to dance. Then he noticed Lauren serving punch at the refreshment table. As the evening wore on, he wondered if anyone would ask her out onto the floor, but no one approached her. Maybe the married male teachers and fathers of students thought partnering with the beautiful lady would cause their own lady to be jealous. He resisted as long as he could, because this fascination with a possibly devious woman was dangerous to his sense of wellbeing. Then she started rocking around keeping time with the two-step song the band struck up. Before Rob could tell his feet what to do, they did it on their own, skirting the edges of the basketball court to avoid bumping into the couples crowding the floor. He reached the refreshment table just as Rex arrived from the other side.

"Ms. Parker, would you do me the honor—" Rex extended a hand.

Rob didn't let him finish. "Lauren, I believe this is our dance."

Looking at Rob, then Rex, she blinked, and her jaw dropped. "I…oh, here." She grabbed up the ladle, filled a disposable cup with pink lemonade from the large, glass punch bowl and thrust it across the table toward a short, brown-haired boy. "Here you go." After receiving his polite "Thank you," she stared back and forth between Rob and that pesky sheriff who used to be his friend five minutes ago. Didn't this guy still have a wife somewhere in the room?

Lauren looked awful cute in her confusion. "I'm really supposed to stay here or some of the kids might decide to spice up the punch."

Rex snorted out a laugh. "You go on and dance with that varmint." He hooked a thumb toward Rob. "I'll watch over the refreshments."

"Oh, thanks. You're so sweet." Here came that smile of hers that could knock Rob back a few feet. She sent it to Rex, then Rob.

Somehow he managed to keep his cool as he led her onto the dance floor. What was wrong with him? He'd only asked her to dance because nobody else had. In a way, he was copying Bobby, who'd set the standard by asking Zoey out to the floor. But now that Rob had his hand on Lauren's waist and his other hand holding hers, he could barely get his feet to move to the music. Finally, he forced a step, and more followed. As she had at his Labor Day celebration at the ranch, she followed smoothly, almost like she belonged here in his arms.

Whoa! This has to stop. He wasn't about to fall for her, no matter how pretty she looked as she stared up at him with that gorgeous smile. No telling what she was hiding behind it.

"I believe it's customary to have some conversation while we dance." She punctuated her statement with a laugh.

He noticed she didn't look directly into his eyes but seemed focused on his chin. With him being a head taller, maybe she didn't want to get a crick in her neck. Yeah. That was it.

"Okay." He smirked. "What do you want to talk about?"

"So you want me to start?" She laughed again, a pleasant, feminine sound. "All righty, then. How about them Golden Eagles?" Her pretty lips formed a saucy grin.

"Ugh." He winced. "You sure know how to hurt a sports fan's feelings." He shook his head. "Not to mention a father's.

Coach and I are counting on Bobby growing into his natural inherited leadership abilities any day now."

"Oh, right. That's the expectation, isn't it?"

They moved around the floor for several moments before she spoke again.

"You know, kids need to find their own futures, not become what we want them to be. Zoey tells me Bobby's really good at computer programming. Maybe football's just not his thing."

Rob noticed she didn't mention ranching, and he wouldn't, either. If forced to let Bobby choose, he might be able to let football go after his son graduated, but as long as he lived, he'd never let Bobby give up his responsibility to continue the family ranching legacy.

The music ended, and he gave her a slight bow. "Thank you, ma'am." Before he could escort her back to the refreshment table, the band director announced a line dance. Rob grasped Lauren's soft hand, which had felt so good in his larger one. "Want to try line dancing again?"

"Thanks, but I should get back to my job so Sheriff Blake can dance with his wife." She nodded toward the table where Annie had joined her husband.

"Okay." He walked her across the floor and released her with another bow. "Thank you for the dance."

"Thank you." Again, she didn't look directly into his eyes. Could he really attribute that to hiding a secret? Or was it just shyness? He'd never spent time with women near his own age because Jordyn had been his one and only sweetheart since eighth grade. So he'd never learned to read all the signals women sent out. But until he knew the truth about Lady's abduction, he wouldn't be able to trust Lauren. Maybe he'd try to call that Santa Fe vet again on Monday. Or maybe he'd put it off *again* so he wouldn't have to deal with his ridiculous growing admiration for this woman.

CHAPTER TEN

WITH THE WORDS to "I Could Have Danced All Night" from her favorite musical, *My Fair Lady*, singing through her brain, Lauren could hardly sleep. What was wrong with her? While Robert Mattson might try to mold his children's lives through his cowboy version of Henry Higgins, she was no Eliza Doolittle. Hadn't she spent the last thirteen years since her divorce refusing to accept attentions from bossy men like her ex-husband?

Not that Robert had said anything controlling to her last night. In fact, she'd enjoyed the firm grip of his calloused hand in hers as he guided her around the gym floor. Had enjoyed the gentle touch of his other hand at her waist. What would it be like to be protected by such a strong, upright man? From the vantage point of her spot behind the refreshment table, she'd noticed he didn't ask anyone else to dance. Why had he singled her out?

Honestly, Lauren, you have officially lost your mind. Can't you see you're contradicting yourself? Besides, it was one dance, not a lifelong commitment. She rolled over and pulled the covers up over her ears to shut out the ticking of the wall clock above her bed. But the music in her mind refused to be quiet. She truly could have danced all night.

To her relief, she woke on Sunday morning to the words of another song Zoey was singing while she got ready for church. The worshipful words of "Great Is Thy Faithfulness" lifted her heart and seemed to promise this would be another beautiful fall day at church. Last night, she'd accepted an invitation from another single mom to attend her Sunday school class before the main service, so they would be leaving for church an hour earlier than usual. And she always looked forward to the wisdom of Pastor Tim's sermons and the biblical truths he shared. Would Andrea ask her to lunch at the steak house again? She tried not to get her hopes up. After all, Robert's mother might want to treat someone else to lunch today.

After making sure Zoey found her own class, Lauren joined her new friend, Trudy, in the adult class, which included fifteen single parents with children of varying ages. Lauren looked around to see if Robert was here, then scolded herself when she was disappointed not to see him. The other attendees welcomed her, and the lesson was inspiring, so this might be the perfect place to make more new friends who understood the struggles of raising a child alone, especially the part about when to let go.

During the break before the main service, she joined Zoey in front of the sanctuary building.

"Do you want to sit with your friends?"

Zoey shook her head. "No. I'll sit with you." She offered a weak smile. "Don't want you to get lonely."

Lauren brushed a stray strand of hair from Zoey's cheek, a ploy for checking her temperature without annoying her. No heat emanated from her skin. "Do you feel all right?" Or had something happened in her class?

"I'm just tired from last night." Her weary voice supported her words. "It just caught up with me."

"Want to go home?"

Zoey shook her head. "Oh, no. I love Pastor Tim's sermons."

Lauren sighed. "Me too. Let's go in."

The sanctuary was filling quickly, so she found room in the back pew. Several rows down and across the aisle, she saw Robert and his family. As though he felt her gaze, he looked back at her and smiled, and her traitorous heart skipped. *Oh, my.* She was her own worst enemy.

Halfway through the sermon, Zoey stiffened, then stared ahead blankly. Lauren grabbed her purse and dug out the midazolam nasal spray Zoey hadn't needed since last summer. But she couldn't use it until Zoey was awake.

"Excuse me," she whispered to the woman on Zoey's other side. "My daughter is ill. Please help me lay her down on the pew."

"Of course." The middle-aged woman helped Zoey lie down, even took off her own denim jacket and rolled it up to support Zoey's head. "Shall I call 9-1-1?"

"No. Not yet." Lauren forced down her rising panic and followed the procedure she'd memorized years ago after Zoey had her first seizure. Lay her on her side. Loosen her clothing. Don't put anything in her mouth. Time the seizure. If it was more than five minutes, call 9-1-1. She glanced at her watch. At times like this, five minutes felt like an eternity.

Last summer, Zoey had blanked out twice, both without the mild muscle spasms that had accompanied her childhood seizures. Each time, Lady had warned them of what was coming by crowding up to Zoey and urging her to sit. Oh, how Lauren missed that sweet dog. She chided herself for not realizing Zoey's tiredness was a warning this could happen.

Two ushers hurried over to help. In whispered tones, Lauren explained the situation. This wasn't an emergency...yet. Zoey would be fine as soon as she woke up. No need to cause an alarm or disturb the service. But the minutes were ticking by.

At last, Zoey blinked and focused on Lauren, then tried to sit up.

"Lie still, sweetie." Lauren set a hand on her upper arm to hold her in place.

"Sorry." Color rushed to Zoey's cheeks, not of illness but embarrassment.

"Shh," one of the ushers said. "No need to be sorry."

The final hymn was announced, and the congregation stood to sing. Lauren grabbed this opportunity to leave without causing a scene, which would only embarrass Zoey further. She would hold off on using the midazolam until they spoke to Zoey's doctor. "Can you bring a wheelchair?" She'd seen one outside in the vestibule.

The usher made quick work of fetching it and helped Lauren take Zoey out to the car. She buckled her in on the passenger side, then hopped into the driver's seat and hurried out of the parking lot before it became crowded with others leaving the service.

"You're going the wrong way, Mom."

"We're going to the ER."

"I'm okay now." Zoey didn't usually whine like this. "Just take me home."

Lauren reached over and patted her hand. "Sorry, honey. We need to be sure."

Zoey's deep, weary sigh assured Lauren she was doing the right thing.

"LET'S INVITE LAUREN to lunch again, Robert." Mom followed Rob from the pew. "I think she enjoyed herself with us last month."

"Sure." Rob would be glad to spend time with Lauren after last night. She'd refused a second dance with him, but he wasn't sure whether the line dance scared her off or that she didn't want to dance with him again. "I'll find her." Her reaction to his asking her to lunch would tell him what he wanted to know.

His height gave him the advantage of seeing over the heads of most other people leaving the sanctuary. To his disappointment, he couldn't locate Lauren and Zoey near the back pew.

Maybe they were already outside. As he stood in line to shake hands with Pastor Tim, he heard Jake, one of the ushers, speaking to the clergyman.

"Her mother said she'd take her to the ER. Poor kid. She didn't look well at all."

Rob stepped closer. "Are you talking about Lauren Parker?"

"Yes," Jake said. "Her daughter had some sort of seizure—"

"Oh, no." Mom stood at Rob's elbow. "We should go."

"I'll go. You collect the kids and get them fed."

Mom had driven her own pickup today, so Rob didn't give her a chance to answer. Putting on his hat and clutching his Bible, he jogged from the church to his truck. Of course the entire congregation was leaving church at the same time, so traffic slowly wended its way from the parking lot and out onto the street. Rob drummed his hands on the steering wheel. His father had taught him Mattsons never used their position to push ahead of other people, but sometimes, like today, he sure did want to drive over the lawn and curb to get around this congestion.

He didn't even understand the anxiety flooding his chest. When had he decided it was his responsibility to take care of Lauren and Zoey? Did Lauren even want his help? And hadn't the pastor's sermon emphasized being still and knowing God was in control? That all things worked together for good for His children? He had to choose to trust the Lord for whatever was happening with Zoey, but it sure was hard right now.

Finally, he managed to maneuver out onto the street and head toward the hospital six blocks away. He pulled into a parking space next to Lauren's little Honda and made his way inside through the ER door.

"Hey, Mr. Mattson." The receptionist focused her attention on him. "Do you need to see the doctor?"

"Hey, Marie. I'm here to check on Zoey Parker." He removed his hat and took a step toward the ER ward.

"I'm sorry, but you can't go back there." The dark-haired

thirtysomething woman gave him a stern look. "Family only, unless they invite you."

This was new. People usually made way for Rob rather than block him. "Can you find out what's happening for me?"

"I can do that." Marie made a quick trip through the swinging doors and soon returned. "You can go on back. Cubicle four."

As he made his way down the curtained ward, worry crept into his mind. What was he doing here? How would Lauren react to his intrusion? He peered around the partially open curtain.

"Hi." Questions written across her pretty face, Lauren sat beside the bed where Zoey lay.

"Hey, Mr. Mattson." Zoey looked tired but not sick. "Come on in. Is Mandy with you?"

As an unfamiliar awkwardness flooded Rob, he turned his hat in his hands. "Sorry. I should have brought her. Just wanted to see how you're doing."

Zoey sighed. "Lots better than Mom thinks I am."

Lauren patted her hand. "It never hurts to be sure."

"What happened?" Nosy question he shouldn't have asked.

"She had a mild seizure."

"Does this happen often?" More nosiness. Why couldn't he keep his mouth shut?

"This is the third one since we moved here," Lauren said. "I should have realized it was coming and taken her home after Sunday school."

"This summer, Lady warned me when I was about to go blank."

"Warned you?" Go blank? A chill swept up Rob's back and made his hair stand on end.

"Yeah. She would snuggle up next to me and make me sit down. Then she'd stay with me until it was over." She emitted a soft laugh. "I usually don't know what's happened, so she was really helpful."

Rob rocked back on his heels. Lady had likely saved this girl's life more than once, and not just when she'd pulled Zoey back from the street. He had to sort through this. What if his valuable border collie had a more important job than herding cattle? What if the dog's obvious affection for Zoey was more than the usual faithfulness the breed exhibited, but a true protective instinct to care for her because of her epilepsy and CP?

No, that couldn't be. Lady was a border collie, born and bred to herd. There were other breeds that had that instinctive nurturing gift. Maybe he could put Lauren in touch with someone who raised those dogs so she could get Zoey one of her own.

"So." Lauren stared up at him, a teasing grin on her lips. "Now that you've checked on us, don't you want to meet your family for your usual Sunday lunch? I think there's a sixteen-ounce steak calling your name."

"Uh, yeah. I should at least let them know what's happening." He grimaced. "So, what *is* happening?"

"We're waiting for the doctor. Since Zoey's not in distress, he's seeing other patients first."

Rob's first impulse was to find Doc and drag him away from whatever he was doing and bring him down here to check on Zoey right away. Instead, he said, "Can I bring you something to eat?"

Lauren traded a look with her daughter. "I think we're okay. Thanks."

"Will you call me after she sees Doc?" Rob paused. She probably wouldn't want to call him. "Or Mom. She was worried when she heard about Zoey."

Lauren blinked in that cute, surprised way of hers. "Sure. I can call Andrea."

"Right." As he'd thought, she'd prefer to call Mom. That should tell him something right there. "We'll be praying for you." Rob put his hat on and left the cubicle. In a wild moment, he stopped by Marie's desk. "If there's any problem with her bill, you send it to me."

Marie, ever the professional, didn't so much as lift an eyebrow. "Thank you, Mr. Mattson." Her dismissive tone suggested she wouldn't be sending him the bill, so he'd have to talk to Edgar Johnson, the hospital administrator, to find out if Lauren needed his help, which she'd no doubt turn down if he offered it to her directly. Edgar wouldn't be in his office on Sunday, so Rob would call him tomorrow.

Still pondering his own motives and actions regarding Lauren and Zoey, he was all the way home before he realized he'd forgotten to go to the steak house for lunch. Parking the truck in the four-car garage near the big house, he didn't see Mom's smaller pickup, so she and the kids must still be at lunch. He did see Lady scampering toward him, so he bent to ruffle her fur behind her ears, only to see her look beyond him toward the truck.

"Sorry, girl. The kids aren't with me right now. They'll be home soon."

Rob waved to Grady, who sat reading a book in front of the bunkhouse, with Scotch and Irish resting on the ground beside him. One of six year-round ranch hands who lived here, Grady was taking his turn to stay home and guard the place. Even before Lady was stolen, it had been a hard, fast rule that one of the hands or a family member would take turns staying home from church to guard against thieves. The practice went all the way back to the days of cattle rustlers in the late 1800s. Before Lady's theft, nobody worried too much that anyone would actually try to steal anything from the ranch. Now everybody here, family or employee, had to be constantly vigilant.

He headed toward the house, and Lady followed him, then lay down on the back porch and watched toward the road.

"Hey, how about a little attention for me? Who do you think pays for your food?"

She gave him a brief glance before turning back to her vigil. She didn't even follow him inside for a treat. Just like Lauren, she wasn't interested in his company. Only in Lady's case, he was in charge, and he was determined to change her mind about her old job. Maybe it was time for him to take both Lady and Bobby in hand and mold them to fit the jobs they were born to do.

What had Lauren said last night? Kids need to find their own futures? But didn't they need guidance toward that future? Didn't they need to have a goal and a coach to push them toward it?

As more memories from last night came to mind, he took some leftover meatloaf from the fridge and didn't bother to heat it in the microwave before taking a bite. Ugh. Should have gone back to the restaurant for steak.

Last night, he couldn't have been prouder of Bobby for asking Zoey to dance. Like all the Mattson men before him, Bobby was a gentleman who did right by his friends. And both he and Mandy had that built-in radar to warn them about kids who tried to get close to them because of their family's place in the community. Zoey wasn't one of those. That was why he encouraged the twins' friendship with her. She had a sweet innocence about her and seemed more concerned about what other people needed rather than using her disability to her advantage. His kids could enjoy her company without worries about being used. Then there was the way she helped them both with their homework. Although they'd only known her for less than two months, she already seemed like an honorary member of the family. He enjoyed interacting with her, and she was friendly to him in return...unlike Lauren, who kept him guessing about her opinion of him.

That was probably best, at least for him. Lauren could have latched on to him like a couple of local women had tried to do after Jordyn died. Instead, she refused his offers of help and didn't seem interested in spending time with him. She'd been reluctant to dance with him last night and refused a second one. Of course she had let him pay for last week's lunch at the steak house. No, she'd accepted it because Mom had invited her. And he had yet to meet anybody who could resist Mom's hospitality.

None of this pointed to a woman who would steal a valuable dog. So why didn't he just try again to reach that vet and get Lauren's story confirmed? Easy answer. Because he just couldn't stand the idea that he might learn she'd been a part of Lady's dognapping.

LAUREN SETTLED ZOEY in her bed, grateful that the doctor had found nothing serious when he examined her. This episode had been similar to those she had this past summer. Doc's main concerns were that Zoey had become dehydrated and that she'd probably eaten too much sugar at last night's dance, thus bringing on this morning's seizure. He did give her clearance to resume her riding lessons, as long as she kept hydrated and took her anticonvulsant medication.

She heated a can of chicken noodle soup and took it to Zoey's room, only to find her sound asleep. And no wonder. These episodes always wore her out. Lauren returned to the kitchen and ate the soup.

She didn't know what to make of Robert showing up at the hospital. Which reminded her, she'd promised to call Andrea. She grabbed her phone and punched the first number under Andrea's name. Surely by now her friend would be home from lunch.

"Double Bar M Ranch." Robert's baritone voice boomed into her ear.

For a few beats, Lauren couldn't speak for the strangely pleasant shiver that swept down her back.

"Um, Robert?" *Duh!* Of course it was Robert. *Oh, no.* She must have called the ranch's landline when she should have called Andrea's cell phone.

He chuckled, sending another shiver down her neck. "Yeah. Hey, Lauren." Pause. "How's Zoey?"

"She's sleeping." Lauren took a breath. "I meant to call your mother. Sorry for the—"

"Don't be sorry." She could hear the smile in his voice. "I'm glad you called here. What did Doc say?"

Lauren gave him a brief report.

"So, does that mean she can come back out to the ranch next Saturday and resume her riding lessons?"

At the borderline eagerness in his tone, Lauren couldn't speak for a moment. "Yes, that would be nice. In fact, he said it would be good exercise as long as she takes her meds and stays hydrated. Do you mind?"

He chuckled. "Not at all. The kids always enjoy having her out here." Pause. "We all do."

Her heart warmed. "Oh. Okay. Thanks. We'll come. Guess that means I'll have to do my laundry on Friday night." Had she actually said that out loud? What was wrong with her?

Robert laughed. "You do that."

"Okay," she repeated. "See you Saturday."

"Good." He didn't hang up, but seemed about to say more.

"Did you have something else to say?"

"You called me, remember?" Another deep, shiver-inducing chuckle. "Did *you* have something else to say?"

At his repetition of her words, Lauren punched the mute icon on her phone and giggled like a schoolgirl. This was so silly. So…so…she didn't know what. She took a deep breath before punching the icon again. "Zoey wants some boots for when she rides. Do you know where I can get a pair for a reasonable price?" Oh, no. That sounded like she was asking for charity.

"Better than that. We probably have a pair around here that'll fit her."

Lauren sighed. Oh, how she longed for her daughter to have more than she could provide. This family had already given her and Zoey so much, but only pride would make her refuse. "Thanks." Then she could see if Zoey could actually wear Western boots without spending any money for a new pair.

"Say," Robert said, "what would you think about joining

me for that new Bible study Pastor Tim announced today? It starts a week from this Wednesday. Don't know about you, but I'm interested in what that Hebrew scholar has to say about Genesis."

Was he asking her out? Or just offering a ride to church? Either way, this was her first such invitation in all the years since Singleton had divorced her in favor of a perfect…and *pregnant* younger woman, so he could have a perfect child. Not many men wanted to spend time with a woman once they found out she had a child with a disability.

Silly tears burned her eyes. She swallowed hard to keep the emotion from her voice. "I'd like to hear him, too." She'd have to ask Mrs. W. to spend that evening with Zoey or at least check in on her. "Yes, I'll join you."

"Great." He hesitated. "Maybe we could have a bite to eat beforehand?" The up tone at the end of his sentence made it a question instead of his usual bossiness. It also made him sound a little uncertain.

Bless his heart, he was nervous! She should meet him half-way. "Sounds good." More than good. Nothing short of exciting.

But after they ended the call, she slumped back in her chair in horror. What had she just done? Yes, she was interested in the Genesis study, but going with Robert might send the wrong signals to…well, to somebody…to *everybody*.

"Mom?" Zoey came into the room rubbing her eyes. "I heard you laughing. What's up?"

Lauren stood and embraced her. "Hungry?" She'd always shared everything with Zoey, but now she had to sort out her conversation with Robert before telling her about it. In truth, she could already see the obvious. Her association with him had just turned a big corner. Whether it would lead to something good or to another heartbreak, only time would tell.

CHAPTER ELEVEN

ROB SCRATCHED HIS head in confusion. What had he just done? He'd never once thought about asking any woman, much less Lauren Parker, to go anyplace with him. Of course, this was a church Bible study, but from her subdued response, she wasn't exactly thrilled. Maybe she'd change her mind, and he wouldn't have to follow through. If he could have seen her face, it would have told him what he needed to know. In the meantime, how was he going to explain it to his kids? To Mom? Not that she hadn't already been silently pushing him toward Lauren since the first time she and Zoey visited the ranch. She'd be as happy as a trout biting on a May fly to know he'd asked the woman to go with him somewhere, but especially to Bible study.

Maybe it wasn't all bad. Getting closer to her should reveal the truth of her character. And he still had this coming Saturday to spend in her company. To say he couldn't wait for the week to pass didn't fully explain his eagerness.

With regular ranch work to oversee, including making sure his prize bull, Buster, was doing his duty by the cows, checking through the hay storage barn to be sure it held enough for winter, not to mention his responsibilities to the Riverton Cattlemen's Association, Rob had plenty to keep him busy. But in the back of his mind, and sometimes right up-front, interfering with what he was doing at the moment, he couldn't get Lauren off his mind. She was beautiful, kind and thoughtful. And fun, at least when she was with the kids. Of course he'd prefer that she responded to him a little more openly, but that was probably shyness on her part. He didn't know much about her ex-husband, only that Sam had told him the man had remarried. How could he have let her and Zoey go? Rob had no idea how big-city folks regarded marriage, but he'd always believed it to be sacred, a commitment not only to his wife, but to the Lord. How did a man justify breaking his marriage vows?

Saturday arrived, bringing Lauren and Zoey to the ranch at midmorning. Remembering his promise to provide boots for Zoey, Rob had dug out several pairs of Jordyn's old ones that didn't fit Mandy. Only after he brought several pairs downstairs did he realize he no longer felt the sharp pain in his heart that usually accompanied anything to do with Jordyn's belongings. It wasn't that he didn't still love her, still miss her, but she would be happy to see her boots going to a deserving girl.

He saw them arrive through the back window. Mandy and Bobby ran out to meet them, with Lady racing ahead to greet Zoey. The way that dog wagged herself silly around Zoey made her preference clear, and the girl obviously loved her in return.

Maybe… No, he had to shut down that train of thought. Lady belonged to Bobby, and that was that. Once football season was over, maybe even before, Rob would work with them before and after school every day to train them both for the jobs they were born to do.

He stepped out on the back porch and waved. "Mornin'. Had your coffee yet?"

Lauren walked through the gate. "Yes, but I can always drink another cup."

Her smile hit him right in the chest. Wow, she was beautiful. "Great. Come on in. You too, Zoey. I have some boots for you to try on."

"For me? Really?" She gave him a big grin.

Once they were inside and Mom had served coffee to Lauren, with the kids opting for sodas, Zoey tried on the boots, finally settling on a weathered tan-and-brown pair. "These feel good. Thanks."

Rob noticed Lauren's sneakers. "How about you? Want to try these on?" He held up a red, white and blue pair Jordyn had never gotten around to wearing.

"Oh, I don't know."

"It won't hurt to try them on." He pushed them toward her, and before she got the wrong idea, he added, "They're lots better than sneakers for walking around the barn and corral."

"Oh. Okay. Thanks." Again, her beautiful smile stirred up that pesky tickle in his chest.

She sat on a kitchen chair and pulled off a sneaker, then stuck her foot into one of the boots. And took it off with a laugh. "Well, it's a bit big. I'd need some mighty thick socks to be able to wear them. Just call me Footloose. Or Bootloose. Or something like that."

Rob laughed, as did Mom and the kids. It felt good, like they were all one family.

No, that was *not* what he meant. Or was it?

LAUREN LIKED TO hear Robert laugh. It was a melodious baritone chuckle that emanated from deep inside him and made her smile. He was proving not to be the grouchy old bear she and Zoey had met less than two months ago. Apparently he'd forgotten their introduction came about when he'd accused her of stealing Lady. That was a relief.

While driving out here, she'd felt some moments of trepidation before remembering the day wasn't about her, but Zoey. What little girl didn't want to ride horses? Lauren sure had. But even with numerous horse farms in Central Florida, she'd never had the opportunity to visit them or even climb into a saddle. Now her daughter had a chance to ride. And maybe one day she could, too, if she could drum up enough courage to try. Daydream pictures of taking lessons from Robert came to mind, but she quickly dismissed them as flights of fancy.

In the barn, Zoey did her share of stall mucking before helping Mandy put a bridle and saddle on Tripper. The old gelding had perked up the minute they approached his stall, as though he was as eager for a ride as the kids were. Lady greeted Tripper, meeting him nose to nose in a friendly gesture. And, as before, Robert leaned against the wall, arms crossed and watched, which Lauren appreciated. Bobby and especially Mandy were clearly competent in caring for Tripper, but it was good for their dad to be available. From the pleasant look on his handsome face—yes, she admitted to herself again, he was handsome—he enjoyed this as much as the kids. Which revealed his generous heart as much as letting Zoey wear his late wife's boots. And being concerned about her own footwear, even though the pair he offered hadn't fit her.

"By the way." Robert moved closer to Lauren and spoke in a low voice close to her ear. "The Bible study this week starts at eight at the fellowship hall. Can I pick you up for supper around six?"

As before, a pleasant shiver swept down her side. This time she didn't try to stop it. "Sure. That works for me." Did she sound breathless?

Lady was as involved in the morning's riding lesson as the kids. She sat at the ready just inside the corral fence, her eyes on Zoey's every movement as she rode Tripper. When Zoey tipped to the side, Lady stood and took a step toward the horse. But with Bobby and Mandy walking on either side of Tripper, Zoey soon regained her balance, so Lady settled back down.

Watching from outside the fence, Lauren resisted mentioning to Robert the way Lady focused her protective attention on Zoey. His attention was focused on the kids, which she appreciated. To think that this busy rancher took time to be concerned about her daughter should be enough. Yet it would give her so much relief if Zoey could have Lady with her all the time, especially when Lauren couldn't be with her.

The morning went by all too fast. Once again, Andrea insisted Lauren and Zoey must stay for lunch. Her tuna salad had a delicious flavor Lauren hadn't been able to replicate even when following Andrea's recipe.

"Lauren," Andrea said from her end of the table. "I hope you'll sit with us in church tomorrow."

Zoey and Mandy put their heads together and whispered something, then giggled. Lined up with Clementine on the other side of the table, the girls looked like mischief waiting to happen.

Lauren studiously avoided turning toward Robert, who sat at the other end of the table. "Thanks. We'll see how the morning goes."

In truth, she preferred to sit at the back in case Zoey had another episode. If she did and they were seated in the middle of the sanctuary, they would interrupt the service and embarrass both of them.

She needn't have worried. Zoey took her meds and kept hydrated. On Sunday morning, she eagerly met up with Mandy. Seeing her daughter have such a good friend at last was an answered prayer, but what were these two girls up to? Was it just chatter about boys? Probably.

Invited to after-church lunch again, Lauren found herself seated next to Robert due to Andrea's maneuvering, with Linda and Andy making up the rest of the party. Robert's pleasant spicy aftershave only added to his manly presence, and she had to still the fluttering in her heart. This was ridiculous. She had no intention of falling for this man, no matter how kind he was to her and Zoey.

After they'd put in their order, he leaned close and whispered, "I think our girls are up to something. What do you think?"

As she tried without success to quell the pleasant shivers

going down her arm, she looked across the restaurant dining room where the girls sat with Bobby and some other kids.

"Oh, probably just the usual teenage chatter." She smiled up at Robert. At his intense, blue-eyed gaze, she had to look away. He was the classic ruggedly handsome cowboy. The kind who rode in and saved the day, then, like a true gentleman, tipped his hat to his leading lady before riding off into the sunset. She'd fallen for a perfectly handsome, well-mannered man once before and had her heart broken. If only she could tell that heart to be more careful with this one, but she didn't seem to have control over it at the moment.

She cleared her throat. "You know how kids like to dramatize everything."

He chuckled in his warm, deep-voice way, and her heart took another dip. "I've noticed that."

"What are you two whispering about?" Linda gave Robert a little smirk. "Let's not have any secrets."

He shrugged. "Just talking about how to raise our kids. Y'all did a fine job with your two. Maybe you have some advice for us single parents as we navigate these teen years."

"Oh, now, let's don't go there." Andy shook his head. "You know the trouble we had with Sam as a teen. He was a handful—"

"Hey, wait a minute," Lauren interrupted. "Better not speak ill of my boss. You don't want me to lose respect for him. That would undermine his authority with me." There she went, speaking up when she should have kept quiet.

The others laughed, so she persuaded herself to relax.

"I admire your loyalty, Lauren." Robert's baritone voice once again stirred her emotions. "And your discretion. I'm sure my young cousins are glad they hired you."

The server arrived with their dinners, and Robert offered grace before they all dug in. Lauren stirred the toppings into her loaded baked potato and took a bite.

"Most of us cattle folk start with our steak." Robert took a bite of his, as if to prove his point. "Yours okay?"

"I'll let you know." Lauren followed suit. "Mm. Delicious."

"On another topic," Linda said to Andrea, "how's your condo coming down in Phoenix?"

Lauren glanced at Robert, who frowned and stabbed into his steak a little more forcefully, his disapproval of his mother's upcoming move apparent.

"It was close to being finished, but hit a snag." Andrea responded to Linda, but gave her son a sympathetic smile. "James says he had to send back the—"

"James?" Robert almost growled the name. "Who on earth is James?" He might have been interrogating one of his kids rather than his mother.

Andrea sat up straighter and glared at him. "He's my contractor." She paused and took a breath. "And I'll warn you, I've invited him up for Thanksgiving so you can meet him."

Even without knowing this family for very long, Lauren could see Andrea's announcement made clear she had special feelings for the man who was completing her future home.

"You have, have you? Thanks for letting me know." Robert's gruff tone revealed his reaction to his mother's possible romance.

The conversation moved on to other things, but Robert's earlier compliment about Will and Sam being glad they hired her stayed with Lauren and still had the power to lift her heart when he picked her up on Wednesday evening. As always, he looked sharp in his black Western-cut blazer, blue shirt, bolo tie and classic black Stetson hat. He could definitely be a movie star.

"What sounds good?" he asked as he helped her climb up into his red pickup.

She adjusted her denim skirt on the leather seat. "I assumed we'd go to your steak house."

He chuckled, that warm sound she had come to like all too much. "Let's try something different."

"Sure."

He drove them to a cute little old-fashioned diner several blocks from the church, where the aroma of grilled onions dominated the room, country music played softly in the background and six or so other patrons occupied the tables. He greeted the middle-aged waitress like an old friend, and after she gave Lauren a quick once-over, she sat them in a back corner.

"It's nice and quiet in here." Robert took off his hat and set it on the seat beside him. "Makes it easier to have a conversation."

Uh-oh. Lauren's stomach turned, and not just because she was hungry. What did he want to talk about?

After they ordered, he settled his vivid blue gaze on her and smiled. "You know, we haven't had much of a chance to really get acquainted. I'd like to hear your story. What brought you to Riverton? Other than working for my rascally young cousins, I mean."

She blinked and stared down at the paper placemat in front of her, which advertised the diner's specialty milkshakes. Why did this suddenly feel like a job interview? Or some sort of interrogation? All of her former confidence that he had forgotten the unpleasantness of their first meeting fled. But she had nothing to hide. Might as well spill it all and be done with it.

"MY STORY?" LAUREN widened her eyes, which looked turquoise tonight, matching the pretty button-up blouse she wore. "If you want to know why I came out here, I should start with what I left behind." Her expression became guarded, and she shrugged. "It's not pretty."

Rob hadn't meant to put her on the defensive. Just wanted to know more about her and what made her tick besides raising her remarkable daughter. "Hey, we all have stuff in our pasts." He chuckled apologetically. "Didn't mean to intrude."

She gave him a half smile. "That's okay." Another shrug. "As you know, I'm divorced. Not because I wanted to be, but because my ex…" She chewed her lip. "It's always easy to make him sound like the bad guy, but—"

"But he was?" Rob grinned.

"Well…in my view, he was." She sighed. "The split was his choice. He already had a pregnant girlfriend waiting in the wings and married pretty quickly after the papers were signed."

A protective feeling stirred in his chest. "Did you have any custody problems?"

"No." Her voice sounded weary, making him sorry he'd started this. "He wasn't interested in raising a child with a disability."

What a rotten man. Rob tamped down his flash of anger. "He doesn't know what he's missing. Zoey's one terrific kid."

"Yes, she is. Thank you for seeing that. But I'm sure he's happy with his trophy wife and their two perfect kids. I rarely think about him anymore." She smiled at the waitress, who'd just set down her plate. "Thanks."

After they'd prayed for their dinner, she resumed her story between bites. "Singleton is a—"

"Singleton?" Rob snorted. "What kind of name is that?"

She laughed, a real laugh, accompanied by a twinkle in her eyes that hinted she might agree it was a ridiculous name. "Singleton Weatherby Parker. It's a family name. He's been the main news anchor at the NBC affiliate in Orlando for about fifteen years. He has an image to maintain, so having a child with a disability didn't line up with that." She huffed out a breath. "Anyway, after years of running in place in my hometown, I needed to try something new. So I applied to Mattson and Mattson online, and was so grateful that your cousins were willing to hire me even though I'd just earned my paralegal license." She gave him a cute little grin. "And just to let you know, I happen to think your 'rascally' cousins are pretty terrific young men."

He chuckled. "Yeah. It runs in the family."

"Along with a skosh of pride, at least in some of you?"

"Goes with the territory of being terrific."

Her second bout of genuine laughter dispelled his concerns that he'd made a mistake to ask about her past. It was good to know how badly she'd been treated and yet managed to survive and be an exceptional mother.

As for that Singleton Weatherby Parker—he couldn't quite get past that pretentious name—from what Rob had seen in his forty-two years, men like him were more concerned about their own wants and needs rather than taking care of the families the Lord had given them. How could any real man so easily divorce a wife he'd promised to love, honor and cherish? How could he ignore his precious child and go off to make a new family even before the divorce?

"So, what about you? What's your story?" Lauren asked before popping a bite of broccoli in her mouth.

Again, he was sorry to have opened the topic. But fair was fair.

"It's kinda boring. Raised on the ranch, took over management when my dad wanted to retire." A soft pang hit his chest. "I wouldn't say this to Mom, but I don't think he should have retired. He just didn't know what to do with himself. After sitting around twiddling his thumbs for more than a year, he died a little over two years ago."

"I'm so sorry." The sweet sympathy in her eyes made her even more beautiful. "And to lose your wife, too. That's so sad. It must have been hard for you and the kids."

"Yeah." Again, fair was fair. "She had a riding accident four years ago and broke her neck." He coughed to keep from groaning at the memory. "The fall also caused a brain bleed the doctors didn't find in time."

"Oh, how awful." Now her eyes reddened. "She was a rodeo queen, right? A good rider?"

"Being a good rider, even the best, can't save you from a horse that doesn't want to be tamed." Rob didn't want to say more, especially since Jordyn had kept her attempts to train Rowdy a secret after he'd forbidden her to work with the horse. "On that topic…" He forced a cheerful tone into his voice. "You don't have to worry about Tripper. He's a good ol' horse and hasn't ever thrown anybody. He's extra careful with kids and inexperienced riders. Just seems to have that instinct."

"Just like…" She looked down at her plate and bit her lip.

"Go on. You mean just like Lady." He should have figured they'd come around to talking about his dog.

"Yes." She looked up, and her beautiful eyes pierced him. "How's her training, uh, *re*training going?"

Rob took a bite of his Reuben sandwich to keep from answering right away. At last he said, "Not so good."

"I'm sorry. We didn't—" She stopped. "I'll pray she finds her calling again."

He stared into her eyes, loving the way they caught the light and the color of her blouse. "Thanks. I appreciate that."

How could that Singleton dude have let this woman go? Rob never would have abandoned Jordyn, even if he'd found out about her foolish attempts to train an untrainable horse. Marriage was until "death do us part." Somehow they would have worked things out.

As if to support his thoughts on the subject, the Hebrew scholar who presented the first lesson on the book of Genesis spoke at length about God's creation of man and woman and how He had given them to each other in a beautiful garden. In particular, Rob was moved by the teacher's explanation of God's interaction with Adam. When God called to Adam, he responded, "Here I am." The Hebrew word conveyed more than physical presence. It was an awareness of Adam's deeply spiritual communion with his Creator.

To think of being in the physical presence of God and then to succumb to temptation and break that connection seemed the very definition of sin and depravity. And stupidity. Adam not only broke his relationship with God, but he didn't do right by his wife, blaming her for his failure in leadership.

The man spoke simply, quietly, but his words held his audience's attention. Rob glanced at Lauren to note her reaction, glad to see her soft, receptive expression. Maybe they could talk about the lesson later. For now, he was reminded of how many times marriage had come to mind in the past few days, weeks. And always when he was around her.

So what made a good marriage? His relationship with Jordyn had always been open and honest from the beginning when they were in middle school. He didn't know when or why or how their communication broke down. He only knew she'd started keeping secrets from him. That it was about her determination to train Rowdy and his forbidding her to do so only came to light after her tragic fall and death.

As he had many times since she died, he wondered what he would do differently if only he could go back and fix it. Adam probably thought that more than once in the years after he and Eve were thrown out of the Garden of Eden. In Rob's case, maybe he'd been too heavy-handed with Jordyn, while Adam had been too willing to, as Pastor Tim often said, *go along to get along*. Either way it didn't lead to a good marriage.

By the time Sunday rolled around again, Rob admitted to himself that spending time in Lauren's company was becoming a habit, and a good one at that. Before the Sunday evening service, he and Lauren settled in the gym bleachers next to each other while the kids played their games and burned off some energy. The twins joined in the volleyball game, and Zoey played foosball with another student. Her coordination appeared to be improving because she held her own against the boy.

"Has Bobby mentioned the computer programming event

at the University of New Mexico next month?" Lauren sipped coffee from a Styrofoam cup.

Rob ground his teeth. "Yeah."

Lauren watched him for a moment. "What do you think?"

"He has a football game that Friday night, so that takes priority."

She stared at him for a moment, then shook her head and looked away.

"What?" He didn't want to ask, but did anyway.

"Oh, nothing." She gave him a little smile. "Zoey signed up for it." She sipped her coffee again. "If Bobby signs up, we could ride-share. It would make it more fun for her." Pause. "Plus making it easier for her in a new and unfamiliar situation."

"Maybe Mandy could go." Rob waved a dismissive hand. "Bobby needs to be with his team."

"As a benchwarmer? Like at the homecoming game?"

"What? No. He'll get to play." He wasn't being honest. Coach always put his seniors and juniors on the first string. Sophomores only went in when the Golden Eagles were winning by plenty of points. "Even a few minutes on the field is good training."

"But if he goes with the computer team, he'll be first string." Her cute grin held a hint of teasing.

He returned a smirk. "Right. Listen, Lauren, I know you're proud of your brother's computer programming job, but Bobby doesn't need that. His future is on the ranch. After he graduates from high school, he'll get his degree in agriculture and animal husbandry, then come back to work in the family business. He doesn't need to waste time on the intricacies of software programming."

"Seems like you have it all planned out. What does Bobby think?"

He didn't answer for a moment. "He'll come around when the time comes."

"Hmm."

Rob ignored her smug look. Maybe she just didn't understand family legacy, how each generation needed to respect and follow the path their ancestors set before them. Maybe if he took her on a tour of the ranch next Saturday and explained that history, she'd jump on board and help him encourage Bobby to quit fighting the path he was supposed to follow.

[faint mirrored text from facing page, illegible]

CHAPTER TWELVE

"It's so beautiful." Lauren gazed down the hill toward the Rio Grande. "That natural earthen levee is a lot prettier than the concrete levee where the river runs through town." She couldn't guess why Robert offered this tour of his ranch, but she was enjoying every minute of it, especially when he talked about his family's history. "I guess it protects the lower fields from flooding, right?" The levee, maybe fifteen feet high and overgrown with grass and trees, stood as a barrier next to the lower pasture where around thirty cattle grazed.

Robert chuckled. "First of all, it's not natural. My ancestors build it by hand, one shovelful at a time." He grunted, as though considering that laborious task. "It took several years to finish, and each year, floods would wash away part of the previous year's work. So they had to rebuild before they could add on."

"Oh, my." She inhaled a deep breath of the cool autumn air, along with the usual smells of cattle that she was somehow getting used to. "I can't imagine all that work by hand."

"Right. Today we'd just use the backhoe and have the whole thing repaired in a matter of days. Maybe hours." He took a step down the hill, and she followed. "A man had to be pretty tough and strong in those days."

"A woman, too. Your mom's told me about some of the women who helped settle this land. Oops!" She stumbled over a hidden rock and grabbed his arm to keep from falling.

He gripped her hand and helped her regain her balance. "You okay?" The concern in his gaze sent a silly tickle through her heart.

Heat rushed to her face. "Sorry."

"No problem." He smiled, revealing his dimple. Another tickle spiked in her chest. "Even after a hundred and forty years, we still have lots of fieldstone working its way to the surface. We have to be careful riding the horses out here so they don't break a leg."

He hadn't released his gentle grip on her arm and continued to gaze down at her in his intense way. Somehow she managed not to look away, as she usually did. Maybe she was getting used to having this gorgeous cowboy stare at her like he thought she was special.

No, she must not think that way. He was only being hospitable. The twins had given Zoey her riding lesson, and after another of Andrea's delicious lunches, she was helping them with their homework. So Robert had invited Lauren for a tour of the ranch. How could she turn him down? She loved the history of this area. Loved learning about the women whose portraits hung in the hallways and great room in what they all called "the Big House." Loved hearing about his ancestors' struggles and their successes.

When he continued to hold her arm, continued to stare at her without saying anything, something inside her shifted. What did he want? What did *she* want?

He took a breath, as though about to speak, and her heart hitched up another notch.

"Daddy! Miss Lauren!" Clementine came running down the hill, waving a piece of paper.

Robert exhaled a long breath and shook his head. "What is it, Clementine?"

Lauren couldn't blame him for the hint of annoyance in his voice. Whatever he'd planned to say was lost, perhaps forever. Still, she managed to turn a bright smile toward the little girl.

"What do you have there, sweetheart?" Lauren reached out a hand and pulled Clementine into a side hug.

"It's a picture." The child proudly thrust the page at her. "I drew it for you, Miss Lauren."

"Oh, my." Lauren wished she could hide the picture from Robert, but he was looking over her shoulder at his daughter's artwork. It depicted surprisingly good representations of their family members, plus two. Andrea, easy to spot with her graying hair, the twins, Clementine, Robert. And Zoey. And Lauren. And Lady. "Oh, my" was right. What would Robert think about this? "It's just lovely. You're an artist, sweetie. I'll take it home and put it on my fridge."

Clementine looked up at Robert. "Do you like it, Daddy?" Hunger for his praise beamed from her blue eyes. "Do you like it?"

As he often did, he patted her head, almost absentmindedly. "Sure, honey. Nice job. Now you run along. Miss Lauren and I were—"

"Miss Lauren is about to collect her daughter and go home." Lauren gave him a teasing smirk. "Laundry."

He snorted out a rueful laugh, his disappointment clear. "You and your laundry. Okay, let's go back to the house."

As they trudged up the hill, with Clementine clinging to Robert's hand, Lauren felt a different kind of tug in her heart. This darling little girl was so desperate for her daddy's attention. Didn't he realize she needed as much love and care as his older children? It might not be Lauren's place to tell him, but she could pray he would see it for himself without something drastic happening.

AFTER RETHINKING CLEMENTINE'S ill-timed interruption to his conversation with Lauren, Rob decided it was for the best.

He had no idea what he'd intended to say to this woman who was becoming all too important to him. Did his youngest daughter's picture foreshadow a future blended family? No, he couldn't say that yet, couldn't even say he loved Lauren. He'd have to think about it. One thing he knew. He liked her more and more every time they were together. Just as he'd hoped, she ate up the stories about his family's history. Had spoken with admiration for the pictures of the strong, tough men…and women, of course…who'd laid the foundation for this ranch and made it a success. Whether it helped Lauren understand why Bobby needed to follow in their footsteps, Rob couldn't say. But her interest, untinged by the covetousness he'd seen in other women, was open and encouraging. Or maybe she simply loved history. He'd have to spend more time with her to find out.

He and the kids walked her and Zoey to their car, with Lady sticking close to Zoey like she expected to go with her.

"No, Lady." Bobby held on to his dog's collar as she tried to climb into the little Honda. "Stay."

She struggled against his grasp until Lauren nudged Zoey's arm. "Tell her to stay."

Zoey held up a hand. "Stay, Lady."

Instantly, Lady sat on the ground by Bobby. But when the car drove out through the front gate, Lady trotted after it for a few yards until the electric gate clanged shut. Then she lay there looking like she'd lost her best friend. Only time would fix that, time in Bobby's company and with his training.

As he watched Lauren drive her little car beyond the front gate, another thought came to mind. Maybe he could have suggested they should see where their friendship was going. No, that sounded too much like teenagers in the throes of their first crush. Maybe without addressing the subject, he could simply come up with more excuses to spend time with her.

Yeah, that was it. He always had some errand or another in town. It would be easy to drop by the law office and ask her to lunch. Or make some excuse to chat with his cousins and include her in the conversation.

In the meantime, he'd see her at church tomorrow. For some reason, she usually preferred to sit at the back, but maybe he could enlist Mandy to get Zoey to sit farther down in the middle pew where Rob's family had sat for a hundred years. Then he'd ask Mom to invite them to lunch again. He doubted she'd turn down another steak dinner.

With those plans in mind, the next morning he took special care to look his best as he got ready for church. The aromas of bacon and waffles reached him as he came down the stairs. But the scene he expected of his family seated around the breakfast table wasn't what he saw. Mom was huddled with the twins beside the stove, and they turned as one when he entered the room.

"What's going on—"

"I'm so sorry, Dad." Bobby looked like he'd been crying. "Lady's missing."

Rob's old doubts slammed into his brain, but he quickly dismissed them. How foolish to think Lauren had anything to do with this. After all, she'd reminded Zoey to tell Lady to stay. He really needed to reach that Santa Fe vet, but his second attempt the other day had been met with an outgoing voicemail message that the clinic was closed for vacation. Maybe the Lord didn't want him to reach the man.

Mom and the twins were staring at him, bringing him back to the present.

"Okay, let's eat breakfast. Lady's probably just hanging out with Scotch and Irish by the barn." He pulled out his chair and sat down. "Come on. We don't want to be late for church." He reached out a hand to Mandy, who sat on his left beside Clementine. "Let's pray. Lord, You know where Lady is and You know how much we love her. Please bring her back so she can fulfill the purpose You've given her. Amen."

Mom cleared her throat.

Rob winced. "And, Lord, thank You for Your bountiful provision for this family. May we always be mindful of all You've given us."

While he ate Mom's delicious waffles covered with butter and maple syrup, he considered staying home from church and searching every inch of the ranch. Surely Lady was hiding in some corner of the barn. Maybe she was in the lower pasture with the yearling steers practicing her herding. Yeah, no. That was unlikely.

After breakfast, he told Grady to pass the word among the ranch hands to keep an eye out for Lady, then drove the family toward town.

Halfway along the five-mile drive, he saw Lauren's unmistakable little Honda driving toward them. She must have recognized his truck from a distance because she came to a stop on the side of the road, as he did.

She rolled down her window. "Hey, cowboy. Did you lose something?"

Seated on the passenger side with Lady in her lap, Zoey grinned and waved.

If a heart could burst with happiness, Rob's would do so right now. While Mom and his three kids exclaimed their joy over seeing Lady, he hid his excitement and relief with a laugh. His suspicions about Lauren were definitely unfounded. Exiting the truck, he crossed the highway and bent down to speak to her through her open window.

"Thanks for bringing her back, Lauren. Don't know what I'm gonna do with that little gal." He could see her guarded expression. After his unfair accusations when they met, he didn't blame her. "Where did you find her?"

Lauren stepped out of her car. "We found her curled up outside our apartment building door when we came out to leave for Sunday school. Want to take her now? Or I can leave her at the ranch."

A quick consultation with Mom gave him a better plan.

"We'll take her. Can you fit the kids in your car? Don't want them to be late to Sunday school."

"Sure."

The shuffle of bodies on the side of the road was more chaotic than it should have been, with each of his kids insisting on welcoming Lady back to the family, and Lady trying to wriggle free and get back to Zoey. In the truck, Mom finally had Lady in hand, more or less, so Rob shut the door to keep her from jumping out, then crossed the road again to make sure Lauren could manage the kids. Bobby had folded his lanky frame into the back seat of the Honda, and Mandy climbed in beside him, with Clementine squeezing into the space between them.

"Y'all okay back there?" Rob chuckled as the siblings squirmed and pushed to get comfortable.

"Yessir." They spoke all at once, with Clementine making it a trio.

"Okay, see you at church. Thanks, Lauren, Zoey."

He waited until Lauren made a U-turn and headed back to town before climbing back in the truck and doing the same in the other direction.

"Well, that's something." Mom petted Lady, who had slumped down on her lap. The dog had a few burrs stuck in her coat, and her feet and legs were dusty. Otherwise she looked okay. He'd have to check her out once they got her home.

"What's something?"

"You just sent your kids off with a woman who, a few months ago, you had no use for." She grinned in her annoying way. "Are we seeing a little, um, *romance* developing?"

Rob wasn't about to discuss his confused feelings about Lauren with Mom. "The only *romance*—" he shuddered as he said the word "—I see developing is between you and that James person." He slid a quick glance toward her. "Don't think I haven't overheard you talking with him on the phone. And it's not all about wallpaper and landscaping."

"Ah. Redirecting the topic, I see." Mom chuckled. "Not to mention eavesdropping."

He returned a cheeky grin. "How else can I find out anything about my family?" He was teasing, of course, but he did have some concerns about this contractor. Maybe he should hire a private investigator to check the man out. Or maybe he could just trust his mother's judgment and let her live her own life.

No, not when he got that thread of worry weaving through him every time she mentioned the man. If James drove up to spend Thanksgiving with them as planned, Rob would grill him like a police detective to be sure he wasn't out for Mom's considerable money. He had a responsibility to guard his family. All of them.

CHAPTER THIRTEEN

SEEING ROBERT PARK his truck in front of the law office, Lauren couldn't keep the grin from her face. He was smiling, too, as he hopped out and walked toward the front door. This was the second time this week he'd asked her to lunch. Was that why he was here? Over the past two weeks, they'd gotten closer to each other, usually over a meal before Bible study and on Saturdays while the kids were riding.

He poked his head in the door. "Hey. Want to go to lunch with me?"

She inhaled quietly to keep from sounding breathless. "Sure. Give me a minute to finish this document." She forced her concentration back to her computer. She didn't dare make a mistake that would trip Will up when he took this custody case to court.

"No problem. I'll go pester my cousins and check out the improvements in this place." He disappeared around the corner into the new hallway the builders had finished last week.

Lauren's hands refused to cooperate as she continued typing. Which was silly because she'd attended their regular Bible study with him just last night. She needed to get control of her involuntary responses to his presence, even when he surprised her like today.

Eyes on her computer, she heard another person enter the front door. She looked up and briefly couldn't figure out where she'd seen him before. As realization struck, she felt herself moving her rolling chair back toward the wall behind her desk.

"Hello, Lauren." Her ex-husband stood before her, a sardonic grin on his face. "Well, don't you look professional in that granny hairdo and frumpy suit. Looks like the years haven't been all that good to you." He spoke in a low voice, his tone full of intimidation.

After all these years, he still used insults to try to dominate and control her. Heat rushed up her neck and filled her face. Struggling to gather her wits, she swallowed hard and fought against the urge to take out the clip holding up her hair to let it fall over her shoulders. Because he'd always wanted her to wear it that way. His coming here could not be good. But what could he want? Hadn't she already torn out her heart and given it to him on a platter years ago? As she looked closer, she could see he'd had work done on his face, because his skin was altogether too tight for a man his age. But as much as she was tempted to return an insult, she managed to contain it.

"Singleton." She scrambled to recall her old battle plan of how to maintain her self-confidence under the onslaught of his insults. Not one idea came to mind. But then, no matter what she'd ever done, he'd always managed to win. "What brings you here?"

"Right to the point. That's my girl." He smirked, and one corner of his lips lifted in a sneer.

I am not *your girl!* "How did you even find me?" Her voice sounded thin, weak. Oh, how she hated not being able to exhibit strength in the face of this invasion.

"Ah, there you go, proving your ignorance. Did you forget I got my start in investigative journalism? I can still find anybody, anyplace." He laughed in that evil way of his.

"If you have anything to say to me, you could have written a letter. Sent a text. Why did you come all the way out to New Mexico?"

"Get real, Lauren." He glanced toward the hall to the back offices, then placed his fists on her desk and leaned toward her in a menacing posture. "Only a fool would create a paper or text trail. This is between you and me, *Lauren*. Nobody needs to know about our business."

"But—"

"Listen, I don't have time for chitchat." He spoke in a low, threatening tone. "I'm here to tell you I'm running for the US Senate, and I need you to clean up the mess you made of my reputation. Some smart-aleck reporter dug up info about our divorce, so I need a statement from you saying you instigated our separation and abandoned me. Took our poor, disabled child and left for parts unknown. For the sake of my campaign, I need to take Jody—"

"Jody? You don't even know your own daughter's name." Terror smothered her, making it hard to breathe. "You signed away your parental rights—" She had the paperwork packed away in a locked file box back at the apartment, but would that be enough? With Singleton, she had no idea what devious tricks he might pull. He certainly knew the right people to back up his claims, and he could afford the best big-city lawyers.

"Lauren?" Robert returned to the reception area, with Sam and Will right behind him. Lined up shoulder to shoulder, the three formed a formidable group. "Who's this?"

Singleton's entire demeanor changed. Suddenly he was the affable news anchor and, apparently, the budding politician. He stepped over to the Mattson cousins and reached out to Robert, but Robert pulled back instead of shaking his hand. That didn't faze Singleton.

"Singleton Weatherby Parker. Glad to meet you. Nice little place you have here." He waved a hand around the modest office. "Just right for a small town. Clean and tidy and not too showy."

"What do you want?" Scowling at him, all three cousins seemed to speak at once.

Singleton took a step back. The shock on his overworked face made her laugh, releasing the tension in her chest almost on a sob.

Robert stepped over to her and put his arm around her waist in a brotherly way, much like Pastor Tim did with the older folks he wanted to encourage. "You okay?"

For a single beat, she longed to melt into his protective arms. But this was her battle. The only way to win it was to fight it herself. Before she could speak, Sam posted his fists at his waist.

"Yeah, Lauren," he said. "Is this dude bothering you?"

"No. Yes." She struggled to speak, to be very careful of what she said. If she played this wrong, Singleton might actually find a way to take Zoey away from her. "This is my ex-husband. He wants to take Zo…my daughter."

"Yeah, I heard." Robert gave her another little side hug, then moved toward Singleton and towered over him. "Listen, buddy, you need to back off. Her daughter's not going anyplace, especially not with a man who doesn't even know her name and who's denied her existence for the better part of fifteen years."

Singleton collected himself, as Lauren had seen him do many times when he felt threatened, and straightened to his six-foot height, which still fell short of Robert's imposing stature. "Do you have any idea who I am?" This was new. He rarely let his carefully constructed facade slip.

"Yeah, I know who you are," Robert drawled, sounding like the legendary TV Western marshal getting ready to throw the shady gambler out of Dodge. "The question is, do you know who *I* am?"

"Sure, cowboy. You're this woman's latest boyfri—"

Robert grabbed Singleton's shirt and tie and pulled him up nose to nose. "This *lady* is a decent, hardworking single mother who this community cares deeply about. So you need to high-tail it back to your little television station and don't bother to come back *or* try to contact her again." He gave Singleton a little shove. "You got that?"

Singleton straightened his tie and tugged at his shirt cuffs. Lauren could practically see the steam coming out of his ears. She didn't know whether to laugh or cry. "Robert, I—"

"Don't worry, Lauren." He held up a hand. "I've got this." He faced Singleton again. "I said, you got that?"

Still working his cuffs, a nervous gesture Lauren had never seen before, Singleton said, "I hardly think you have anything real to threaten me with—"

Robert held up his hand, palm out like a stop sign. Singleton flinched and stepped back.

Robert pulled his phone from his pocket and punched it. "Rex, I've got some fella here at my cousins' law office who's threatening Lauren. I think he needs to cool his heels in your jail. I'll hold on to him until you get here. Good. See you soon."

Lauren glanced at Will and Sam, whose expressions showed the same determination as Robert's, like a posse of good guys staring down an outlaw. Singleton's artificially tanned face turned white around the edges, and his jaw slackened.

Somehow Lauren managed to hold in the giddy laugh trying to escape her. Nothing about this scene was funny. But why couldn't her resolve gain any traction? Why was she letting Robert and her bosses manage the situation? Didn't they realize Singleton would only come back at her when she was alone? She had to fight this herself.

Robert punched his phone again. "Hey, Marty. Rob Mattson here. Listen, I need you to get Zoey Parker down to the school office and keep her there with our school resource officer. Don't let anybody, any strangers, talk to her. Tell her everything's okay so she won't worry. Good. Thanks."

Zoey *would* worry! She'd be terrified! Lauren tried to protest, but the words wouldn't form.

Rob punched his phone a third time. "Hey, George. Rob

Mattson here. I need you to bring your photographer over to the law office. We've got a good story for the front page of the *Riverton Journal*. Good. See you soon."

He disconnected the call and gave Singleton a warning look. "Does that answer your question about who I am?"

Singleton glared at Robert, then Will, then Sam, finally settling an arrogant grin in Lauren's direction. "You haven't heard the last from me." He walked toward the door. She didn't have a single doubt that he meant it.

Sam reached the door first and placed his palm against it. "Just cool your heels, pilgrim." He did his best imitation of a famous Western movie hero. "The sheriff'll be right over, along with the editor and photog from the paper."

"You have no right to hold me here." Singleton's voice sounded a little reedy, not at all like his eloquent on-screen news delivery. "And no authority."

The next few minutes proved him wrong. Sheriff Blake arrived, sat him down and questioned him, with Robert correcting him when he tried to lie, while George took notes and Bill took photos.

"Now, Mr. Weatherby Parker—" the sheriff spoke in a paternal tone "—you just skedaddle back to your little television job and your political campaign. I can't wish you well in either because you ain't the kind of man we should have in the news service or in public office." He cleared his throat. "And if you decide to cause any more trouble for our Miss Lauren, you can be sure we'll let everybody, and I do mean *everybody* here and in Florida, know exactly what sort of man you really are."

"Aw, Sheriff," George grumbled, "do you mean I can't run this story on the front page tonight and send it out to all the news services?" There was a twinkle in his eye as he spoke.

"Naw, better not. At least not yet. Let's give ol' Singleton here a chance to do the right thing and get outta Dodge with his tail between his legs. But we'll hold on to that story and those pictures in case he tries to cause Miss Lauren any trouble in the future." The sheriff eyed Singleton up and down. "You got that?" At Singleton's weak nod, he added, "You can go, Senator Wannabe." Sheriff Blake opened the door and shoved Singleton's shoulder perhaps a little too forcefully.

Trying to regather his dignity, he strode from the office, but was clearly shaken, because he stumbled on the uneven pavement and barely managed to regain his balance before hurrying away toward a fancy new car parked out front, no doubt a rental.

While her protectors guffawed at Singleton's awkward retreat, Lauren dropped into her chair and covered her face, finally surrendering to tears.

Robert knelt beside her. "Hey, honey, don't cry. He can't hurt you. I'll...we'll make sure of that."

She barely registered his use of *honey*. He didn't have a clue what she was thinking. Couldn't he see that he was just like Singleton? Taking over her life and making decisions for her? But it wouldn't do to alienate him, not when he must be seeing himself as some sort of hero. Oh, she was so foolish. He *was* a hero. Just one she didn't want in this situation.

She looked up at him and gave him a wobbly smile. "I know. It's just that—" *Think fast, Lauren!* "—just that I've never told Zoey very much about her father. Now I'll have to tell her everything. She's going to be devastated."

FOR MAYBE THE second time in his life, Rob had used his family name and position in the community to take control of a bad situation. If he'd given in to his first impulse when he heard Lauren's ex belittling her, he would have pummeled that narcissistic manipulator into the ground. But that would have reduced Rob to Parker's level and probably reduced him in Lauren's eyes. The sweet smile on her pretty face, if a little strained right now, made his self-control all the more rewarding.

"Don't worry, sweetheart." He couldn't seem to keep from

using fond names for her. If she didn't like it, she didn't show it. "Zoey's a smart girl. She'll understand."

"You don't know that." She mumbled the words.

He couldn't blame her for having natural concerns about her child, but he'd make sure Zoey was safe. Behind him, he heard the others start to disperse, their part in rescuing her complete.

"Thank you." She looked around him. "Thank you all for your help."

Rex touched the brim of his hat, which he'd probably kept on to reinforce his authority in front of Parker. "You're welcome, Miss Lauren. You let us know if he even calls you—"

"Or texts you," said George, a younger man. "Or tries to contact you on any social media."

"Right." The sheriff nodded. "You'd know about all that stuff."

"Rob, Lauren, I'll text you the pictures." Bill held up his camera. "After I download them."

"Thanks, guys." Rob stood and shook hands with the three men who'd come running at his call. "Let me know if I can return the favor."

Will and Sam had already gone back to their offices, but soon emerged wearing their hats and winter vests.

"Let us take you to lunch." Will beckoned to Lauren.

"Oh, I—"

"She's going with me." Rob took her fleece jacket from the coatrack in the corner behind her desk and held it for her. Glancing down, he noticed the jacket's frayed cuffs and worn sleeves. Maybe he could get Mom to pick out a new coat for her. Or maybe he should take her over to the mall and buy one for her right now. "You should give her the rest of the day off so she can see about Zoey, okay?"

"I don't need the day off." Sounding annoyed, Lauren stepped back, not accepting his help into the coat. What was that all about? "I'm going to the school now to bring Zoey back here." She looked at his cousins. "Is that okay?"

"Sure," Will and Sam said together. Funny how these guys were almost like the twins. Probably because they were close in age and grew up together. Now, if they could just catch his drift that he had this under control.

"We should have lunch first so you can have a chance to get past all this stuff before you talk to Zoey." Rob again lifted the coat for her. "Here. It's pretty cold outside."

"No. I'm going to the school." She snatched the coat from him and put it on herself.

He couldn't quite read her expression, but it sure didn't look like gratitude. "Don't you want some backup?"

Lauren glared up at him, and a memory flashed through his mind. That was the way Jordyn had looked at him when he forbade her to train Rowdy. *Uh-oh...*

"Time for us to make our exit." Will headed for the door, Sam right on his heels. "Lauren, don't forget to lock up."

Once they were outside, she huffed out a cross sigh. "As if I would forget." She grabbed up her purse and walked to the door. "You going?"

Rob stared at her for a moment. "Yeah. You sure you don't want me—"

"No." She held the door open, despite the brisk wind sweeping in, and tapped her foot on the floor. "Any time, cowboy."

Ouch. "Are you mad at me?"

"Yes. No." She gave his arm a little shove. "I really need to get to Zoey."

"Sure." He stepped out the door. "Are you sure you don't want me—"

"No. Thank you." She shut the door and punched in the lock code, then marched toward the parking lot beside the building.

Rob stared after her. *What in the world just happened?*

ROBERT IS NOT SINGLETON!

Lauren tried to hammer that thought into her brain, but it wasn't working. Of course she wasn't being fair. Despite his earlier suspicions, Robert had never, not even once, belittled her. Then again, Singleton hadn't, either, when they'd first met. Not until she'd fallen for his charming romantic advances did he start criticizing everything she did, said or wore. Her brother had warned her to drop him, but their parents thought Singleton was perfect in every way. And Lauren had been so enthralled with the up-and-coming news anchor that she refused to heed her brother's warnings.

Not that Robert was making romantic moves toward her. Their lives simply intersected in many ways. She worked for his cousins. They attended the same church. Most important, he'd been helpful with Zoey, letting his twins teach her to ride and sticking around to make sure she was safe. Yes, they'd gone out to lunch and dinner a few times. Yes, they'd found a common interest in the Bible study. But that didn't mean they were in a relationship, as she'd been with Singleton all those years ago, when it had been a terrible mistake to rely on her youthful feelings.

The best way to avoid making another mistake was to avoid Robert Mattson…if only she could do that without putting an end to Zoey's riding lessons or the other times she spent with Mandy and Bobby. After all of the challenges Zoey had faced and did face, Lauren couldn't bring herself to cut off the first real friendships her daughter ever had. She also didn't want to stop attending the Bible study because what she learned was deepening her faith. But she could go by herself.

Zoey was waiting for her in the office with shaking hands and stuttering speech that revealed her anxiety. "M-Mom, wh-what happened?"

"Don't worry, honey." Lauren signed the sheet offered by the school secretary. "Thanks, Marty. Let's go, Zoey." She then nodded to the school resource officer, a muscular, sixty-something man. "Thank you."

"Just doing my job, ma'am." His paternal smile reminded her of Robert's warm concern for Zoey.

She drove through the fast-food restaurant and bought lunch and milkshakes for both of them. She would make chicken and dumplings for supper, more comfort food, probably more for herself than for Zoey.

They arrived at the office before her bosses. Inside, she spread out their food on her desk and managed to say a feeble prayer of thanks. She looked up to see Zoey staring at her.

"Mom, what's going on? Why'd you have me called to the office?" She sniffed back tears. "I was so scared something happened to you."

"As you can see, I'm fine." Lauren forced a cheerful tone. "Eat your chicken nuggets." She dunked one in the honey mustard sauce and took a bite. "Mm. Delicious, as always."

"Mom..." Zoey leveled her gaze on Lauren, a new maturity shining in her eyes. "Don't treat me like a baby. Miss Marty got me out of class and made me sit in the office with Deputy Garrett. She didn't tell me why. You think I'm not going to worry?"

Lauren exhaled a long sigh. This was Robert's fault. Didn't he know nobody could take a student from the school without a parent's signed permission? Zoey had been safe at her classroom. But then, who knew what Singleton could have done? Might still do? Now Lauren was forced to tell her daughter the whole story about her father, something she'd dreaded for years.

At twenty-three months, Zoey failed to meet the usual milestones of healthy infant maturing and was subsequently diagnosed as having cerebral palsy, so Singleton wanted to put her in a care home away from public view. When Lauren refused, he left them. And ever since the divorce, which she did not contest, well-meaning people who thought Singleton hung the moon had warned her never to criticize him to Zoey. Because, everybody said, that would unfairly alienate the child from the absent parent. Or, on the other hand, cause the child to defend him even though she never knew him. So, how could she give her daughter an accurate picture of Singleton?

"Sweetie." Lauren took Zoey's hand. "A man came here to the office today." She inhaled deeply. "He's your father."

Zoey gasped, and her eyes widened with fear. "Wh-what did he want?"

This wasn't the response Lauren had expected. "He…he wanted to meet you and take you back to—"

"I don't want to meet him." Uncharacteristic hurt and a hint of anger shone in Zoey's eyes.

"I'm glad to hear that. Can you tell me why?"

Zoey rolled her eyes and gave her that teenage look questioning her mother's intelligence. "Mom, do you think all last summer when I stayed home alone I wouldn't look through your stuff?" She gave Lauren a cute little grin. "I figured you were hiding something from me, and I found your divorce papers." Her expression shone with hurt again. "And I found those papers my father…*that man* signed saying he gave away his parental rights so he didn't have to pay child support. And that was just two years ago. Now I understand why we didn't have much money since then." She smirked. "What kind of name is Singleton, anyway?"

Lauren chuckled. That's what Robert had said. And she couldn't be cross with Zoey for snooping. She should have realized her natural curiosity would prompt this search. And she should have told Zoey about Singleton long ago rather than deflecting all of her daughter's questions about who her father was. Instead, she'd arranged all the paperwork to be finalized while her daughter was in school. She never told Zoey her father was ashamed of her, that he wanted to deny her existence until it became politically expedient for him to trot her out for show, all the while making Lauren the villain.

"My sweet girl, I wish I could tell you he had some redeeming quality, but…" Lauren stopped before she said something really bad that might come back later and hurt them both.

"You know what I figured out?" Zoey snickered. "After I read all that stuff, I thought, hey, even Genghis Khan had kids. The important thing is Jesus loves me and accepts me just as I am. I'm His child. Knowing that, believing that is what's important."

Count on this remarkable girl to turn to God, whatever the situation.

"Hey, did Mandy's dad tell you about the Riverton Fall Festival two weekends from this Saturday?"

Zoey was ready to move on to another subject, so Lauren let the matter drop. When it was convenient, she would explain more about Singleton's political plans and how he'd wanted to use his rejected daughter to ramp up his social and street cred...at Lauren's expense, of course.

"Yes, I think it was mentioned." Recalling how she'd acted toward Robert after he sent her ex packing, she knew an apology was in order. "Want to go?"

"*Duh.* Corn dogs, cotton candy, pumpkin pie–eating competitions, carnival rides. What's not to like?" Zoey giggled. "This Saturday after my riding lesson, Bobby's gonna show me how Lady's doing with her herding lessons. They practice before and after school every day, and his dad wants him to enter in the calf herding competition."

"That'll be fun." For Robert's sake, and Bobby's, Lauren hoped, even prayed, Lady could be retrained for the job she was meant to have.

But even as she lifted her silent prayer, she knew her real hope and dream was that Zoey could adopt Lady as her companion and, after Singleton's threats, her protector.

Yeah, that wasn't going to happen.

CHAPTER FOURTEEN

"DAD, YOU KNOW I can't whistle." Bobby scowled at Rob as they stood inside the pasture fence, with their three dogs sitting nearby and a dozen or so yearling steers grazing on the autumn stubble of grass. "How'm I supposed to signal Lady when my lips won't cooperate?"

Before Rob could answer, Mandy piped up from her seat on the top fence rail. "It's easy." She put her fingers to her lips and let out an ear-piercing sound, and all three border collies perked up their ears and looked at her, waiting further instructions. "See?" She jumped down and grabbed Bobby's left hand. "Just hold your fingers like this." She tried to show him, but he pulled away. Shrugging, she repeated the shrill sound, and the dogs stood up on the alert.

Bobby glared at her. "Sis, you know I've been trying to whistle since we were kids. It just comes out like a sick wheeze."

Since we were kids? Like you're all grown-up now. Rob chuckled despite his annoyance. This exercise wasn't working according to plan, although he had to give Bobby credit for trying to master the skill even though his heart wasn't in it. But given enough time, he was bound to change his mind.

"Okay, son. Tell you what. I'll dig out my old whistle, and

we'll try again this evening after football practice. You need to keep working with Lady before the contest so you can at least make a showing." Rob's hopes of his son being a champion dog trainer would have to wait, but maybe entering the herding event would stir up a sense of competition in Bobby, something oddly lacking considering his heritage. "You two go flag down the school bus to get to school. I'll work with Lady for a little while." He escorted them out through the gate.

While Lady followed the kids out of the pasture, Scotch and Irish trotted over to him, their tilted heads asking why he wasn't putting them to work with the steers. The two older dogs didn't need practice, but Lady would require some serious work. At the rate Bobby was going, Rob would have to spend a lot of time with her himself, then turn her instruction over to Bobby.

"How about me, Daddy?" Clementine climbed down from the fence. "Do I get to stay home today?" She gave him a sassy grin.

"Hey, kiddo. Didn't see you there." He patted her head, careful not to mess up the ponytail Mom had arranged. He'd have to depend on Mandy to take care of her little sister's hair after Mom moved to Phoenix. He'd miss all the help she'd given him with the kids since Jordyn's death, but mostly he'd miss her. He wasn't looking forward to meeting that fella she kept talking about who was working on her condo. He still might hire a PI to investigate him.

The kids grabbed their backpacks from beside the fence and dashed toward the front gate as the yellow school bus rounded a distant curve. He watched as they flagged it down and climbed aboard, then returned to the pasture. They were growing up too fast, but not so fast that he didn't want to keep an eye on them. Wasn't that the job, the privilege of every parent? Well, maybe not *every* parent.

The memory of Lauren's ex threatening to take Zoey away from her brought a burst of anger to Rob's chest. Then he remembered her angrily dismissing him, making clear her feelings for him. Okay, he could deal with that. He could back off and let her be. On the other hand, after learning about and meeting that Singleton dude, Rob figured her ex was the dark secret he'd thought she was hiding. Another doubt about her character fell away. He hadn't known her for long, but the walls were coming down. Not that she'd ever shown interest in him beyond friendship.

It'd been different with Jordyn, the only woman beside his mother and sister he'd ever been close to. They'd grown up together and gone steady since middle school. No matter how much Rob examined his memories or beat himself up over this, he would never understand why she'd gone behind his back and tried to train Rowdy. What had she needed to prove? And to whom?

Forgive.

The word seemed to come out of nowhere.

Forgive.

It grew louder in his mind, and he slumped against the pasture fence. "Lord, is that what I need to do? Even if I'll never have the answers about Jordyn's deception?"

Forgive.

"All right. I get it." He lifted his gaze to the clear blue morning sky. "Lord, I don't know if Jordyn can hear me, but if not, please pass this on to her. Darlin', I'll never stop missing you, but I forgive you." More conviction grew in his chest. "I know you're with the Lord, so you've probably already forgiven me for failing you." A rush of memories came to mind.

Jordyn on their wedding day, too beautiful for words. Jordyn on bed rest until the twins were born, then pushing through exhaustion when they came down with childhood illnesses. Jordyn weeping over the two babies that didn't make it to full term. Jordyn when Clementine came out all red and howling and determined to live. Mostly, Jordyn, sweet, understanding and supportive as Rob endeavored every day, every hour to live up to his family's hundred-and-forty-year legacy. But what had she done for herself?

Daughter of a world-class bull-riding champion, she'd been a fierce, fearless barrel racer and beautiful rodeo queen. After they married, it took several years for the kids to come along. When they did, at Rob's insistence, she'd given up her own pursuits to stay home and take care of them. Had she longed for something more? If so, no wonder she didn't tell him what she was doing. Yes, she'd disobeyed his orders, something none of his ranch hands would ever do. But she wasn't a hired hand. She was his wife. His partner. His equal. If he'd been less heavy-handed, maybe she would have trusted him enough to tell him she wanted to train Rowdy so she could get back into barrel racing. If only they'd talked. If only he'd listened. He could have helped her choose a different horse. He should have— Then it hit him. Her death was as much his fault as hers.

For the first time since Jordyn's funeral, Rob broke down and wept, leaning his arms on the top fence rail and resting his head on his forearm as tears dampened his long shirtsleeves.

Scotch and Irish lay on the ground nearby and watched him, heads still tilted in their questioning way. But Lady nudged up against his leg. When he reached down to pet her, she licked his hand. He knelt and pulled her into his arms. This little gal sure did have a special instinct for human needs. She licked his cheek, then rested her head against his chest. With that contact, he felt a comfort, a brief respite from his grief. He held Lady close, and she let him.

He'd always had dogs, had been close to several of them. Only one had responded to his emotions this way, but she hadn't been a border collie, just a bedraggled mutt that wandered in off the prairie when Rob was about ten years old. He'd nursed Lottie back to health, and she'd been devoted to him. Had waited by the front fence every day until he came home from school and followed him everywhere around the ranch.

No wonder Lady wanted to be with Zoey so much that she'd followed her back to the apartment two weeks ago. Last spring, Zoey and Lauren rescued Lady and nursed her back to health. She'd bonded with them in a way she never had with Bobby, even as a puppy.

Rob released a long sigh. Did that mean he had to give up on Bobby and turn his expensive herding dog over to Zoey? Could Lauren even afford the healthy dog food Lady required? And what about Lady being shut up in that apartment every day while Zoey went to school and Lauren worked?

No, that wasn't a good idea. He needed to stick with his plans. He would work with Bobby and Lady before and after school every day until the Riverton Fall Festival competition. He didn't want Lady to lose her nurturing skills, but she could learn to do so much more than be a lay-about companion. On a ranch, everybody worked, even the barn cats, so Lady simply had to learn how to do her job.

"HEY, COWBOY." LAUREN sidled up to Robert as he supervised the kids while they tacked up Tripper and two other horses. Ready to eat humble pie, she wasn't sure how to begin.

"Howdy, ma'am." He touched the brim of his hat and gave her a welcoming, teasing smile, dimple and all, which almost threw her off course.

She could stare at this good-looking man all day. Instead, she managed, "Look, I'm really sorry for being cross with you the other day."

"Hey, no problem. You were worried about Zoey." The soft, understanding look in his eyes warmed her heart and dispelled her anxiety about the situation.

"And thanks for sticking up for me, Marshal Dillon." She enjoyed his deep chuckle for a moment. "And for chasing the bad guy out of Dodge." She glanced at the kids, but they weren't paying attention to this conversation.

"Wellll," Robert drawled, "truth be told, I can't take all the

credit, Miss Lauren. It was Sheriff Blake who made that varmint skedaddle."

She loved this new banter. "That's true, but not till you
rounded up a posse to back him up."

"Aw, shucks, ma'am—"

"Ready to go, Dad." Mandy had Zoey up in the saddle, and
she and Bobby were ready to mount their own horses. "Miss
Lauren, is it okay for us to ride around the ranch a bit? We
won't go far or fast."

"And we'll stay on the flat land," Bobby added.

Her focus swiftly shifting, Lauren walked over to Tripper
and studied her daughter's smiling face. "You okay up there?"

"Yes, ma'am. Are you?" Zoey glanced at Robert and
smirked.

So she'd been paying more attention than Lauren had
thought. "Yes, smarty-pants. I'm fine. You be careful. Let
Mandy or Bobby know if you sense anything happening." She
gave her a meaningful glance.

Zoey rolled her eyes. "I know." She reached up and adjusted
her helmet strap. "I don't want to fall even more than you don't
want me to, y'know."

Lauren squeezed Zoey's hand. "I know."

Oh, how hard it was to let go of her not-so-little girl. As the
kids rode out of the barn at a slow pace, with Lady trotting
alongside Tripper and keeping her eyes on Zoey, she sent up
a silent prayer for their safety.

"Want to saddle up and ride with them?"

Robert's question in her ear sent a nice little shiver down her
side. She had to inhale a quick breath before she could answer.

"Let's just watch from here."

He chuckled. "Still not ready to ride?"

She glanced up, enjoying his teasing grin. "Nope."

"Okay, then. But one day."

"Uh-huh." In truth, she would like to give it a try. But what
if she fell off and broke an arm? How would she take care of

Zoey or work at the law firm? No, that kind of fun would have to wait until Zoey no longer needed her. Besides, Robert's attention should be on the kids, not her…although she didn't mind in the least the dimpled smiles he kept sending her way.

SEATED IN THE bleachers at the Riverton Fairgrounds arena the following Saturday, Rob watched as Bobby entered the field with Lady. The dog had been excited to greet Zoey when she and Lauren arrived at the fairgrounds. But once Zoey sent her back to Bobby, he managed to keep her at his side. Now Zoey and Lauren sat with Rob and his family, waiting for their boy and his dog to compete. Before and after school, Bobby had practiced diligently with Lady, using the whistle Rob provided, and now he could command his dog by varying the pitch and length of each signal.

Bobby's pal Josh Moberly, from a neighboring ranch, put his dog through his paces. Scout ran close to the ground and stared into the face of the steer he was to cut from the herd. At Josh's signal, he ran to its left side to direct it to the right. The steer tried to go left, but Scout was all up in its face, getting between it and the other animals. Within seconds, the steer ran toward the chute at the end of the arena with Scout chasing all the way. The dog then ran back to crouch by Josh's side and await his next command.

Rob's excitement grew as he waited for Lady to perform just as perfectly. They stepped into position and waited for the judge's signal as the crowd grew quiet. Except for one voice… Zoey's.

"Go, Lady!"

Lady perked up her ears, then dashed away from Bobby, squeezed through the end of the gate and headed for the stands. Before Bobby could figure out what was happening, Lady was at Zoey's side, wagging her tail and looking for a treat.

"Oh, no, Lady." Zoey laughed, but her face was flushed. "Go back to Bobby. It's your turn to herd those cows." She tried to wave her away. "Oh, I'm so sorry, Mr. Mattson." She cast a worried glance at Rob. "Lady, go back to Bobby." Tears started to form in her eyes.

"Don't worry, kiddo." Rob didn't want her to get too upset over this. "There's always next time."

"I'm sorry, too." Seated beside him, Lauren gave him a sympathetic smile. "We shouldn't have come."

"Don't say that." Rob squeezed her hand. Bobby should have grabbed Lady's collar when she started to bolt.

He glanced toward the arena, where his son was jogging toward the gate. Despite Lady's breaking form and thereby disqualifying them both, he didn't look disappointed. No surprise there. Rob had enough disappointment for them both.

"Hey, don't worry, son. A little more work, and you and Lady will do better next spring."

"Thanks, Dad." Bobby petted Lady. "Good girl." He dug a treat from his pocket and gave it to the dog.

Rob groaned inside. He shouldn't be rewarding Lady when she hadn't done her job. No, that was wrong. Depriving the dog wasn't the way to train her or win her allegiance. Besides, Rob could see Lady had no idea she'd done something wrong.

After others competed, Josh and Scout won the blue ribbon. With Mom, Lauren and the kids all chatting about the other Fall Festival events, Rob had no choice but to set aside his disappointment about Lady and try to enjoy the rest of the day. It was time for him to have a serious talk with Lauren, so he'd invited her to dinner this evening. A nervous thread wound through his chest. When the time came, would he have the courage to tell her what he'd been thinking about?

"ARE YOU SURE you'll be okay?" Lauren resisted the urge to hold on to Zoey as her daughter prepared to climb into Andrea's truck. She'd never been on a sleepover, and Lauren had been reluctant to let her accept Mandy's invitation.

"Mo-o-m." Zoey whispered her complaint. "I'll be fine. Just go."

"She'll be fine," Andrea echoed as she gave Lauren a side hug. "We'll swing by your apartment and get her pj's and Sunday clothes. Oh, and her meds. I can call you if she needs anything else. You just enjoy your evening out." She glanced at Robert, who was leaning against the side of the pickup, arms crossed. "Go on."

Zoey had already climbed into the truck and made herself comfortable beside Mandy and Lady. The dog plunked her head down on Zoey's lap as though the day had worn her out. They'd been inseparable since the herding competition, with Lady walking beside Zoey around the midway and Clementine tagging along beside them. Lauren had noticed Lady seemed attached to the little girl, because she wouldn't let her stray far from the family group. If only those judges could see the way Lady "herded" these two kids, they'd give her a ribbon.

"Ready?" Robert gave her one of his gorgeous, dimpled smiles. "Don't know about you, but all this walking's made me hungry."

Lauren returned a smile. "So those four hot dogs and all that cotton candy didn't hold you?"

"Hey, I only had two hot dogs and one stick of cotton candy." Robert took her elbow and guided her toward his pickup, parked several spaces away. "Anyway, I always have room for a steak."

He seemed pretty happy despite Lady's disappointing behavior. Lauren wouldn't bring it up though. That would ruin this lovely evening before it started.

"After all that walking, I could eat, too." She gave him an impish grin. "But I'm hungry for grilled salmon or maybe chicken Alfredo."

He put a hand on his chest. "Wow, you sure know how to hurt a cattleman's heart." He opened the front passenger door and helped her climb in. "Might as well do drive-through and get chicken nuggets."

Before she could respond, he shut the door and jogged around to the driver's side like a man half his age. Once behind the wheel, he again gave her that smile that tickled her heart. "So, what'll it be?"

"Oh, well." She exhaled a long sigh. "Guess it'll have to be steak."

His warm chuckle rumbled clear down in his chest. "Smart lady."

Truth was she loved the steaks at his family's restaurant. So that's what she ordered once they were seated across from each other in a back booth. As always, the aromas of grilled steaks and freshly made bread wafted through the air, inciting her appetite.

"So, how did you feel about—"

"I wanted to talk with you about—"

They spoke at the same time, then laughed.

"You go first." Lauren doubted he wanted to discuss Lady's behavior, so she was glad he spoke up. "What did you want to talk to me about?"

"Not *to* you." He nodded to the server, who'd just brought their sweet tea and complimentary rolls and cornbread to the table. "*With* you."

"Oh." Must be something about the kids. "Okay. Shoot."

He buttered a piece of cornbread and took a bite, so she followed suit. The spicy morsel, seasoned with onions, corn and jalapeño peppers, melted in her mouth.

"Wow. This is so good." She buttered another bite. "What did you want to say?"

He took a deep breath, almost like he was gathering courage. What on earth?

"Lauren, at the risk of sounding like an awkward teenage boy, I—I'd like to know where you see our relationship—" he cleared his throat "—our *friend*ship going."

A crumb of cornbread stuck in her throat, and she coughed so hard, Robert came around the table to pound her back.

She held up a hand. "I'm okay." She took a long drink of her tea, then laughed. "Whew! That was not a commentary on the cornbread."

"Glad to hear it." He took his seat again and gazed at her, his question still in his eyes.

"So, you want a DTR conversation?" She managed not to laugh at the confusion on his face. "Define the relationship?"

"Ah." Another smile. "Yeah. That."

She could look into that handsome face all evening and never tire of the way the candlelight reflected in his ice-blue eyes. "Well, where do you think it's going?"

Her ex's domineering behavior notwithstanding, she still held on to the old-fashioned idea that a man should state his feelings first.

"I like being with you. You're easy to talk to. Good with the kids. Get along with my mom. That's a big one." He chuckled as he reached across the wide table and briefly touched her hand. "I like *you*, Lauren. A lot."

She swallowed hard, and it had nothing to do with the cornbread. "I like you, too, Robert."

He continued to look at her expectantly. What else did he want her to say?

"I like your whole family. You've all been so kind and generous to Zoey. And me."

He gave a little shrug. "You and Zoey are special to us."

"Thanks." Even though a warm feeling blossomed in her heart and spread up to her face, she was glad he hadn't said he loved her. Especially since she couldn't quite define her own feelings for him. "You're all special to us, too."

"Y'know, since this afternoon, I've been thinking." He buttered another bite of cornbread. "Maybe Zoey should start training Lady to herd cattle. I could teach her."

Wow. This was a rapid change of subject. But she didn't mind. Robert was offering to help her daughter develop her motor skills in a new and challenging way. Almost like a father would do. No, she must not think of it that way.

"How would that work? I mean, doesn't Lady need someone to practice with her every day? I'm not sure we could get out to the ranch that often." Even as she said the words, she tried to think of ways to make it happen.

"Have you noticed that little pink adobe cottage next to Andy's house?"

She lifted one eyebrow. "You mean that large, gorgeous hacienda?"

"That's the one." He grinned. "Nobody's living there right now. Maybe you and Zoey could move out there. It's fully furnished." His grin softened into a warm smile. "Rent-free, of course, because Zoey would be working for us." He paused while the server set their steaks in front of them. "Thanks." Then to Lauren murmured, "Let's pray."

He touched her hand again and bowed his head. "Lord, thank You for Your provision and for the many blessings You bestow on us. Thank You for Lauren and Zoey coming into our lives. Please give us wisdom as our friendship grows."

Lauren had difficulty swallowing her first bite of steak. It was tender and delicious, but her heart was already in her throat. *Yes, Lord, please give wisdom.* Would she be foolish to move out to the ranch? Would it even be proper, with Andrea moving to Phoenix after Christmas? And rent-free? Despite his claim that Zoey would be earning their keep, it sounded too much like charity. It had been one thing for her dad to charge her a reduced rent back in Orlando, but he was family, while Robert was… Hmm. They still had yet to define their relationship. Just how far did he want this to go?

How far did *she* want it to go? The last thing she and Zoey needed was for her to make another poor choice in the romance department. Moving out to the ranch might be the best thing that ever happened to them. But it also might be the worst decision she'd ever made since marrying Singleton.

CHAPTER FIFTEEN

WAY TO KILL a conversation, Rob. He wanted to kick himself. He'd wanted to get closer to Lauren through a friendly conversation, but he'd gotten off track, something he rarely did. This lady did that to him. Made him forget what he was doing. Was that good or not so good?

He could see her surprise and maybe a hint of alarm when he brought up moving out to the ranch. He hadn't even thought it through. The words just came out, the idea seeming like the logical solution to having Zoey train Lady. But was such a move wise? What if their relationship didn't grow the way he'd begun to hope it would? Having Lauren live so close could get awkward. But he wouldn't retract his suggestion that Zoey should train Lady. Whatever the logistics of the plan, he felt sure she'd do a good job, and maybe it would be good for her, too.

As for Bobby, Rob could no longer ignore the fact that his son would prefer to play with the dogs rather than train them. Now Rob would need to interest him in some other important part of running the ranch before it was too late. Once he went off to college, he'd major in whatever he wanted, no matter what Rob's plans for him were. In grade school, both he and Mandy had raised steers as their 4-H projects, but he'd lost interest while Mandy continued. She was the one who knew all the ins and outs of the ranch. Took to it like a duck to water. Maybe—

"Would you like some dessert?" Their server stood beside their table, dessert menus in hand.

Rob shook off his musings and looked across the table at Lauren to see she'd finished her small ribeye steak. "Dessert?"

"Sure. I can just hear that chocolate cheesecake calling my name." She smiled in her cute, teasing way. "How about you, cowboy?"

He felt a little kick in his chest every time she called him cowboy. Just one more appealing way she affected him. "I'll take the salty caramel cookie. With ice cream. Make that vanilla."

"Coming right up." The server, a senior from the high school, glanced between Rob and Lauren, then sent him a sassy grin and a quick lift of her eyebrows. "Y'all behave now, Mr. Mattson." She dashed away before he could respond.

Okay, if even a teenage server, who was probably into romance books and movies, could see something was happening here, maybe Rob could get the conversation back on track with his original plan.

"Lauren—"

"Robert—"

"You go first this time. Wait. Why do you always call me Robert? Everybody else calls me Rob."

"Not your mother." She shrugged. "And she was the one who named you."

"Nope. I come from a long line of Robert Mattsons. She didn't have a choice."

"Ah. I see." She flashed him a teasing grin. "Okay, I'll call you Rob."

He chuckled. "No. I like that you call me Robert."

She rolled her eyes like Mandy often did. "You're so funny. Make up your mind."

This wasn't going the way he'd hoped. "Can we get back to, what did you call it, our DTR?"

She blinked. "O-okay. So, how do you define our relationship? Our friendship? Whatever you want to call it."

"I think I'd like for you to be part of my life. Well, you already are, but... I'm not saying this too well." Jordyn used to fill in what he couldn't say, but they'd known each other since childhood. Knew what the other one was thinking without saying a word until she... No, better not go there.

He hadn't known Lauren for long. How did he learn more without being intrusive? Might as well give it a try. "I want to know you better. To know what makes you tick beyond being a really good mom to a very special daughter. And, apparently, an outstanding paralegal for my cousins."

She shrugged. "What you see is what you get." Her face reddened. "I mean I am what you see. Nothing more."

"I like what I see." He gave her what he hoped was an encouraging smile. "The problem I'm having is I think I like you too much."

She stared at him for a moment, her pretty lips quirking to one side. "I don't know whether to be flattered or insulted."

"Ugh. I told you I'm not saying this well." He inhaled a deep breath. "I sure don't mean to either flatter or insult you. Just telling you how I feel." He offered a sheepish grin. "Do you think this clumsy-tongued cowboy has a chance of—" What? What did he want from her? "—of seeing where this all goes?"

The sweet smile on her beautiful face gave him the answer he was hoping for.

LAUREN'S HEART HICCUPED. She already loved spending time with this cowboy. But what if they were rushing things? She didn't dare make another mistake.

"I think we can do that, as long as we don't take it too fast."

"Right." His doubtful expression bloomed into one of pure happiness. "Whew. Glad we have that taken care of."

"There." The server set their desserts in front of them. "That wasn't so hard, was it?"

Lauren eyed her doubtfully. Had she been eavesdropping?

"Hey, kiddo." Robert gave her a stern look. "You better keep this to yourself if you want to keep your job." Then he grinned. "Or maybe I should bribe you with a big tip."

The girl giggled. "Aw, Mr. Mattson, you always give us big tips. But I'll try hard not to say anything. You two just look so...so..."

"Thanks—" Robert looked at her name tag "—Stacy. Keep up the good work."

"Yessir." Grinning, she took a step away.

"And mind your own business."

Still grinning, Stacy left them in peace.

"Well, that was fun." Lauren couldn't imagine what it was going to be like having her name, and Zoey's, linked to the most prominent rancher in the state. "And interesting."

"Yeah." He reclaimed Lauren's hand across the table. "Are you okay?"

"Are you kidding?" Unexpected tears sprang to her eyes. "The man whose company I enjoy so much just told me he feels the same way. I don't think I could be any better."

"Me, either."

Chocolate cheesecake had never tasted so good. Even the much richer caramel cookie Robert fed her across the table only added extra sweetness to the evening, as much for the endearing gesture of sharing as for the taste.

Robert Mattson V wanted to explore their relationship. Was she foolish to imagine a future with him? He was fond of Zoey and interested in helping her develop new skills. Did Lauren dare to dream? A tiny, uncomfortable thread of doubt wound through her mind. She'd lost big-time in the romance department. Did she dare hope for a better result this time?

"So, how do we do this?" She took her last bite of cheesecake. "I mean, what do we tell our families?"

He smiled and shrugged. "If they're anything like Stacy, I don't think we'll have to tell them anything."

At her apartment building, he walked her to the outside door. "Shall I pick you up for church tomorrow?"

"I should drive. Zoey will be tired from the fair and spending the night at your place, and I may need to bring her home right after the service."

"Okay." He kept staring at her as though he wanted to say more.

"I should go in."

"Right." He opened the apartment building's front door, then closed it and gently enfolded her in his strong arms. "Lauren," he whispered into her hair.

Oh, it felt so good to be held that way. So comforting. So... romantic.

He lifted her chin and gazed at her lips. "May I—?"

As much as she longed for him to kiss her, her best instincts said no, not when she still needed to examine that bothersome thread of doubt. Instead, she rose up on tiptoes and kissed his cheek. "Good night." She pulled away and hurried inside before he could say more.

As always, she second-guessed her actions. Should she have let him kiss her? For some reason, as nice as it might have been, she was glad she hadn't. A kiss was a seal, a promise. And they definitely weren't ready for promises. Did he understand that?

Still, his words about their server observing their growing feelings for each other were spot-on. The next day at church, everybody seemed to give them the same knowing smile. Or maybe they smiled because she and Zoey sat with Robert and his family in the middle pew, as though it was something they'd long expected.

Zoey reported that she'd had a great time sleeping over with Mandy. Mandy said it was like having a twin sister to add to her twin brother. Clementine hung on to Zoey's hand and insisted on sitting beside her. Andrea gave Lauren and Robert that special maternal smile that said at last everything was right in her world. Even Will, along with his wife, Olivia, and Sam and Andy and Linda and the whole Mattson clan seemed to treat her and Zoey with a special warmth. Or maybe that warmth had always been there, and she was just now letting herself feel it.

But she must listen to her doubts. Could she ever truly be a part of this wealthy family? Did she want to be? Or would her relationship with Robert somehow fail just as her marriage had?

MONDAY MORNING, BEFORE heading for his meeting with the Riverton Cattlemen's Association, Rob sat at his desk for his daily Bible reading and prayer time. As he prayed for Lauren, he remembered after church she'd seemed a little down, not like the happy lady who'd agreed to explore their relationship the night before. She and Zoey hadn't shown up for evening church, with Mandy saying Zoey had texted to say she needed to rest. Had Lauren changed her mind about him? Or did she just need a little cheering up?

He noticed the worn business card she'd given him from the Santa Fe vet sticking out from under the edge of his desk blotter. Maybe that was it. They'd never resolved the whole thing about Lady, although he'd tried to fix it last night by suggesting Zoey should train the dog. He should have apologized first and told Lauren he knew she couldn't have stolen Lady. To put a nail in the coffin of his earlier accusations, he would try again to reach that vet.

He punched in the number listed on the card. The call connected on the second ring.

"Vargas Veterinary Clinic. How may I help you?" The cheerful voice of the young woman sounded like someone who liked her job.

"May I speak to Dr. Vargas?"

"May I say who's calling?"

"Robert Mattson from the Double Bar M Ranch." Not that he needed to say that last bit. Everybody in New Mexico knew who he was. But it wouldn't hurt to add a little clout to his inquiry.

After a short pause, the woman said, "I'm sorry. Dr. Vargas is…is in surgery. Can I have him call you back?"

"Maybe you can answer my question. Do you remember last May when a lady brought in a dog she'd found and asked the doctor to check her over?"

Another pause.

"Yes. She wanted us to take the chip out of the dog's shoulder. Of course, Dr. Vargas refused, but he did give the dog they called Daisy the shots she needed. I don't know where she went after that."

Rob felt like a two-ton bull had just rammed into his chest. Barely able to speak, he managed to say, "Okay. Thanks." He disconnected the call and set his phone down.

As the numbness from the shock wore off, his first reaction was grief. Like Jordyn, Lauren had been lying all along, even dragging her sweet, innocent daughter into her deception. Anger moved in, replacing his grief. How could he have been so stupid? He'd been drawn to her beauty and sugar-sweet personality. Felt sorry for her for being a single mother with a deadbeat ex-husband and a kid to raise on her own. What a sob story. A trap that had all too easily ensnared him.

He shut his Bible and grabbed his phone and his hat. He'd have just enough time before his meeting to get to the law office and settle this once and for all. If Lauren lost her job, it was no more than she deserved. But as he sped toward town, he couldn't help but regret what would happen to Zoey once her mother was exposed as a liar and a thief.

LAUREN GLANCED OUT the storefront, surprised to see Robert parking his truck and heading for the door. Her heart lifted with excitement. But instead of his usual gorgeous smile, he wore a dark frown. He burst into the reception area like an angry bear.

"Hi, Robert."

"Don't 'Hi, Robert' me, Lauren." He stood there, fists at his waist, and stared off for a moment, like he was trying to control his anger. At last, he set his fists on her desk, just like Singleton had over two weeks ago, leaning toward her in an almost threatening pose. "You lied."

"What?" She gulped down sudden fear. "What are you talking about?"

"You stole Lady and had her chip removed and—"

"Hey, Rob." Sam appeared from his back office. "What's going on?"

Robert straightened. "You should know that this woman isn't who she claims to be. She's a thief and a liar."

"Now, just a minute." Lauren stood and glared at him. "I didn't lie about finding Lady. Which you will find out if you will simply call Dr. Vargas."

"I just did." Robert huffed out a cross breath. "And you know what I found out? I found out you asked him to remove Lady's chip, but he refused."

If he'd slapped her, it couldn't hurt any more than his false accusation. "That's not true. Dr. Vargas scanned her and told me she didn't have a chip." She couldn't stop her sudden tears. "We had a big discussion about it. Surely he remembers. Why would he lie to you?"

"Because you're the one who's lying."

"Hold on a minute, Cuz." Sam touched Robert's shoulder. "Let's go back to my office so you can cool down."

"Don't bother." Lauren couldn't stay here. Not another second. Grabbing her coat and purse, she rushed out of the building and drove home. She'd been smart to listen to her doubts. Just as she'd suspected, she would never find happiness with Robert.

In the dim first-floor hallway at her apartment house, she made out a black-and-white object in front of her door.

"Lady! How did you get inside?" A helpful neighbor must have let her in after seeing her here all last summer. Lauren knelt and petted the dog, who looked past her expectantly. "No, Zoey's not here. And you shouldn't be, either." Now Robert would never believe the truth. Not that she should care what that bully thought.

She took Lady inside and gave her some water, then found the brush Zoey had used to clean her last summer. From the dirt and burrs on her coat, she'd obviously come from the ranch, as she had several weeks ago. Lauren would have to take her back right away. Except, in her state of mind, she shouldn't drive anywhere. She would just have to endure whatever cruel words Robert threw at her.

In the quiet of her apartment, she fell on her bed and wept with great, gulping sobs. A happy life with Robert had just been too much to hope for.

Lady jumped up on the bed and snuggled against her, looking into her eyes with what seemed like understanding. Lauren hugged her close. "You're such a good girl, Lady."

Tears spent, she sat on the edge of her bed and considered what to do. She'd saved a little money over these past few months, so maybe she and Zoey could go back to Orlando. Dad had said they were welcome home anytime. But taking Zoey back into Singleton's sphere of influence was too dangerous. What could she do? Where could she go?

Of course the first thing she had to do was take Lady back to the ranch. Robert's face came to mind. He'd reminded her of an angry grizzly. Well, now she was angry, too. Angry with herself for not heeding her internal warnings that he was a bully, just like Singleton. Angry that he'd wooed her with all of his cowboy charms, and she'd begun to fall for him. Today was a blessing in disguise because now she saw him as he truly was, and she wouldn't make the mistake of getting involved with the wrong man again.

But what if he had her charged with theft? Would she go to jail? What would happen to Zoey? Lauren would be forced to rely on her parents to take care of her. Then Singleton could make use of this to further his political plans and take their daughter away from her for good.

Her tears renewed, and she wept long and hard, then fell asleep, not waking up until she heard Zoey unlocking the apartment door. Lady jumped off the bed and dashed from the room. Lauren hurried to the bathroom, shut the door and tried to lessen the puffiness of her face with cold water.

"Mom?" Zoey stood outside the door. "What's Lady doing here? Why are you home this early?"

Lauren couldn't respond for the renewed tears clogging her throat.

"Mom, are you okay?"

No, I'm not okay. "Be out in a minute." Somehow she managed a cheerful tone. "Go fix yourself a snack."

What could she tell Zoey about this horrible situation? The temptation to invent a lie, to pack up her daughter and run away from Riverton and all its inhabitants, was strong. No, she had never lied to Zoey, and she wasn't about to do so now. Despite what Robert Mattson V thought, she was not a liar.

"You GONNA TELL me why my paralegal just ran out of the office like a scared rabbit?" Sam waved Rob to a chair beside his desk in the back office.

Rob huffed out a long breath. "Yeah, I'll be happy to." *No, not happy. Downright miserable.* "You know that story she told us about how she ended up with Lady?" At Sam's nod, he continued. "Well, it was a lie. I just called that vet clinic and learned Lauren took Lady there to get her chip removed."

"Hmm." Sam scratched his chin. "That doesn't sound right. Exactly what did the vet say?"

Count on a lawyer to want details.

"I didn't talk to the vet. His receptionist answered the phone. She remembered Lauren bringing Lady in and trying to get Dr. Vargas to—" Rob narrowed his eyes. "You look like you don't believe me."

"'Course I do, Cuz." Sam chuckled. "But I have a strange feeling about this. Lauren is painstaking in her honesty. She's saved Will and me from countless mistakes in our work. I can't see her lying about a dog."

Rob felt an odd fist of doubt grip his chest. "She's just got you fooled, like she did me."

"Fooled? I don't think so." Sam offered him a sympathetic smile, which Rob didn't appreciate. He wasn't the one in the wrong here. "I don't think you do, either. From the looks on both of your faces yesterday at church, I can see your relationship's growing pretty well. We're all real happy about that."

Rob snorted out a laugh. "Yeah, that was before I called the vet."

Sam regarded him for a full ten seconds. "Tell you what. Let me call that vet and see what I can find out."

"Sure. Here's my phone."

"No, I'll use mine. Give me the number." Sam copied the number, then put his phone on speaker.

"Vargas Veterinary Clinic. How may I help you?"

"Yeah, hey there, ma'am. Can I speak to Doc Vargas?" Sam spoke with a cowboy drawl.

"May I say who's calling?"

He paused. "Samuel Andrew."

Rob frowned. Why didn't his cousin give his last name?

"One moment, please."

After a click, a man answered. "Dr. Vargas here."

"Yessir. I wonder if you can help me. Do you remember last—" Sam glanced at Rob, one eyebrow raised in question.

"May," Rob mouthed.

"Last May," Sam continued. "A woman and her daughter

brought in a dog they'd found and asked you to check for a chip so they could find her owner."

Rob's heart was in his throat. *Lord, please...* He didn't even know what to pray.

"Sure do. A sweet little black-and-white border collie with a white heart-shaped marking on her chest. Poor little dog was dehydrated and undernourished. I checked for a chip, but she didn't have one. Gave her shots and..."

"No chip?" Rob burst out. "Are you sure?"

"Look, I know how to do my job. There was an infected scar where it looked like one had been removed." The vet sounded on guard. "Who am I talking to?"

"I'm the dog's owner." Rob's pulse kicked up. "She's home with me now."

"Glad to hear it. I'd like to hear how she got there. For the record, you owe that lady and her daughter a big debt of gratitude. In another day or two on the prairie, that little dog probably would have died without them rescuing her."

Rob rocked back in his chair, for the second time today feeling like he'd been slammed in the chest by a two-ton bull. Lauren hadn't lied. She *had* saved Lady. More than that, she was every decent thing he had come to believe she was. And he'd just destroyed any chance of their relationship growing deeper.

Still on the phone, Sam launched into the story about how Lady had found her way home to the ranch. Rob grabbed his hat and waved to his cousin. "Thanks."

Now what? The memory of the fear on Lauren's face made him sick to his stomach. She'd looked that way when her ex had threatened her, and Rob had proved himself to be no better than that scumbag. How could he make it up to her? Would she ever forgive him? And if she didn't, would he ever be able to forgive himself?

CHAPTER SIXTEEN

AFTER STRUGGLING TO find words to explain the situation, Lauren couldn't come up with anything that wouldn't alarm Zoey. Maybe the less said, the better.

She went to her room, where she found Lady gazing up into Zoey's face with her usual affection.

"Come on, you two. Time to take this little rascal home."

Zoey sighed. "Yes, ma'am." She put her jacket back on. "Let's go, Lady."

Once they were on the way, Zoey said, "Mom, I don't know how we can keep her from coming to see us."

"I don't, either, honey." Right now, Lauren's main concern was how to sneak Lady onto the ranch without running into Robert. If he saw them with Lady, he might have her arrested on the spot, as he'd wanted to do that August day when they first met. Or, rather, when he'd accosted them.

Lord, You know the truth. Please protect us from Robert's anger and...and vengeance.

After she pushed the intercom button by the gate, Andrea answered.

"Lauren, what a nice surprise. Come on in."

The gate swung open, and Lauren drove toward the house. Robert's red pickup was parked near the barn. If he was down there, maybe they could avoid seeing him. Or being seen by him.

Mandy, Bobby and Clementine met them at the back door. Along with their grandmother, they all had a good laugh over Lady's misbehavior. Despite her panicked urge to flee the premises, Lauren managed a smile.

"Yes, she's a handful. Well, we'd better get going. Zoey has homework."

"No, I don't, Mom. I finished it in study hall."

"Good," Andrea said. "You can stay for supper."

While the girls squealed their joy and Bobby grinned his approval, Lauren's heart sank again. "No, I'm afraid not. Come on, Zoey. Bobby, please hold on to Lady."

She headed out the door, practically dragging Zoey to the car. As she was about to climb in, she saw Robert striding toward her across the barnyard like Marshal Dillon coming to arrest a cattle rustler. Hands shaking, she managed to get the key in the ignition, start the car and drive quickly toward the gate, gravel flying from beneath her wheels and her heart pounding in her chest.

"Look out!" The panic in Zoey's voice brought her to her senses.

She managed to stop before reaching the busy highway, where a huge semi tractor-trailer truck roared past them. If she hadn't stopped, the truck would have hit them. Her heart raced.

"Mom, what's wrong?"

"Nothing, sweetheart." Well, there she went, telling a lie to her precious daughter after all. But what else could she have said?

ROB DIDN'T BLAME Lauren for hightailing it off the ranch property. He must have scared her bad, when all he wanted to do was take her in his arms and beg her forgiveness. Now he'd have to wait to tell her how wrong he'd been. No, it was worse than just being wrong. He'd believed the lies of a stranger rather than believing the good he saw in her with his own eyes. Worse still, he'd laid on her the blame for Jordyn's deceptions. But he'd already forgiven Jordyn and asked the Lord to forgive him for his failures as a husband. With Lauren, there was nothing to forgive. The only thing she'd stolen was his heart, and now he'd deeply wounded hers by believing a lie.

Sam had called this afternoon and reported the rest of his conversation with Dr. Vargas. Seemed the receptionist had been mistaken about the chip, although when Rob talked to the girl, she'd been adamant about remembering Lauren's visit to the clinic. Even remembered they'd called his dog Daisy. Why would a stranger in a responsible position at a veterinary clinic lie like that about someone she'd just met?

That would have to remain a mystery, but Rob no longer cared about that young woman's motivation. He only wanted a chance to make things right with Lauren, to possibly gain her forgiveness. His guilt only compounded when he found the family gathered around their wayward border collie. Once again, Lauren had proved herself to be honorable. A thief would have done her best to hide Lady to repay him for accosting her this morning. Rob hadn't told Mom about that disaster, so he did his best to act like everything was okay. But when Mom said Lauren had turned down her invitation to supper, it struck another blow. Of course she wouldn't want to face him, because she didn't know he'd finally learned the truth—the real truth—from the vet. So what was a chump cowboy to do to regain his lady's trust?

After the kids went to bed, Mom casually mentioned something about flowers. Had her radar picked up the signal that all was not well between him and Lauren?

Sam hadn't offered any advice on how to fix the situation, but what did his young bachelor cousin know about relationships when he rarely even dated? One thing was sure. If Rob approached Lauren, he'd better take flowers—as Mom had slyly suggested—along with a large helping of humble pie, and not stride toward her like a lawman out to arrest an outlaw. He had some time-consuming work to do on the ranch that couldn't wait, so he'd give her time to cool down and see her at Bible study on Wednesday evening.

Except she didn't show up at the church that evening. As worry ate a hole in his chest, Rob couldn't concentrate on the lesson. After the final prayer, he beat a hasty retreat before anybody could question him about Lauren's absence. What could he say? What could he do?

Mom's idea of flowers came to mind. That was it. First thing tomorrow, he'd go to Cousin Jenny's florist shop and buy every red rose she had, then head over to the law office. But Jenny had only a half dozen red roses, not enough to show Lauren how serious he was. While he waited, Jenny called her supplier in Albuquerque, who promised to ship them right away, but they wouldn't arrive until tomorrow, Friday. Rob hated to wait another day, but, coward that he was, he needed those flowers for a shield when he went to see Lauren.

The next day, he took a two-dozen red rose bouquet, all fancied up with greenery and little white flowers, and made his way through town to the law office. To his disappointment, Lauren was not at her desk, and no coat hung on the rack in the corner.

"Hey, Rob." Will came out to greet him. "Wow, those are beautiful roses. Um, I assume they're for Lauren, right?"

Rob had never liked humbling himself before his younger cousins. After all, he'd always been like a big brother to these two guys, someone they'd always looked up to. But right now he had no cause for pride. "Yeah. Is she coming in? I sort of owe her an apology."

"You sure do." Sam joined them. "Those flowers might just get you a hearing, even though you don't deserve it."

"Thanks a lot." Rob exhaled crossly. "Did you tell her about our phone call to the vet?"

Sam held up both hands and backed away. "No way. That's

between you and Lauren. I learned long ago not to involve myself in lovers' quarrels."

"Thanks for nothing." Rob scowled at him. "All right, then. When will she be in?"

"Don't you remember?" Will gave him an odd look. "This is the weekend Zoey's competing in the computer programming contest in Albuquerque. They won't be back until late Saturday."

Rob stared at his cousins for several moments, not at all helped by their amused smiles. Didn't they know how serious this was? Finally, he thrust the flowers at Will. "Here. Give these to Olivia. If you don't owe her an apology now, you will one day." He strode out of the building to the sound of their laughter. But for Rob, this was anything but funny.

That evening, he ate pizza with Bobby's football team, Coach Johnson's attempt to cheer them up after losing their final home game of the season. As a second stringer, Bobby hadn't played, of course, but he didn't look as dejected as the other boys on the team. Probably because his heart had never been in the game. Lauren had been right. Bobby should have gone to the programming meet where, with Zoey's help, he would be on the team's first string.

LAUREN HATED DRIVING in the dark, but they'd had supper in Albuquerque before the drive home. Zoey rode in the front passenger seat of their little Honda and chatted over her shoulder with her teammates, Grace Martinez and Jeff Sizemore, about the success of their strategies in the competition. They'd done pretty well for sophomores against some more experienced teams and were now making plans for the spring programming meet. Their coach and the other team of three Riverton students followed in a pickup behind her car.

Occasionally, Lauren caught a hint of ridicule in Jeff's voice mimicking Zoey's pronunciations and the way she often had to push her words out on a hum. Lauren hadn't been around the boy long enough to know whether he was teasing or being mean. She had to trust Zoey to choose her friends, but if the boy wore down her daughter's hard-won self-confidence, Lauren might have to turn Mama Bear and have a word with him.

They arrived at Jeff's house around ten o'clock, and she helped him sort his bag out from the pile in the back of the car. From inside the small wood frame house came yelling, at least one barking dog and a few loud thumps.

"Jeff, do you want me to help—"

"No!" He grabbed his backpack. "I don't need nothing from you." He trudged away across the patchy, unkempt yard, shoulders slumped, like a reluctant soldier going into battle.

Poor kid. His homelife must be difficult. No wonder he'd begged Coach Smith to let him fill in for Bobby on the team, even though his poor grades in other classes should have disqualified him.

After taking Grace home, Lauren drove to their apartment. She and Zoey were both exhausted from their busy two days. Should they go to church tomorrow or stay home and rest? Zoey answered that without a word when she woke up Sunday morning with a headache. Although Lauren would never wish her daughter to have any pain or illness, and although neither one of them wanted to miss church, she was more than glad not to have to face Robert and his accusations. Or watch his friends side with him and write her off as a dog thief.

At least Sam and Will hadn't fired her. Which seemed a little strange after the scene Robert created last Monday. In fact, on Tuesday when she'd returned to work, Sam hadn't even mentioned it. She didn't know whether to be grateful or fearful that the ax might yet fall any day now, and she sure wouldn't bring it up.

After a day of rest, Zoey felt well enough to go to school on Monday. "Mom, are we going to the ranch for my riding lesson on Saturday?" The worry in her voice told Lauren she'd picked up on her broken relationship with Robert. Since he hadn't made a move to arrest her and her bosses were surprisingly quiet about the scene he'd caused, Lauren decided she would risk it for Zoey's sake.

"Sure. Pretty soon it'll be too cold for riding, and I know you appreciate the exercise."

What was the worst that could happen? No, better not try to guess.

ON FRIDAY, SEATED in a hard chair in the final meeting of the state cattlemen's association, Rob fidgeted and resisted the urge to check the time on his Apple Watch…again. Thoughts of Lauren had dominated his mind this past week, but he'd been stuck here in Santa Fe, tending to his responsibilities to the ranch and to the larger cattle raising community. As president of the local cattlemen's association, he'd come to the capital to present to the legislative committee a new proposal for controlling river pollution. Before that, he'd had to put out some fires with the Riverton Stampede Committee because the provider for the livestock had backed out due to overcommitment to other rodeos. While these were important affairs he enjoyed managing, nothing would be right in his world until he settled things with Lauren. After his rotten, unfounded accusations, if she never spoke to him again, it was no more than he deserved.

When she hadn't shown up for church last Sunday, he should have just gone to her apartment and made his apology, even without flowers, but decided it was better not to intrude if Zoey wasn't feeling well. Now he'd been stuck here in Santa Fe since Monday, unable to solve the problem hammering at his heart and soul and starting a heartburn fire no over-the-counter medication could put out.

Once the meeting was dismissed, he declined invitations to lunch and headed back to Riverton. Ten miles down the road, he made a U-turn. Time to find out why that receptionist lied to him about Lauren. He took the tattered business card from his wallet and punched the address of Vargas Veterinary Clinic into his navigation system, then drove there. And took a few minutes to quiet his temper before entering the building.

Inside he approached the reception desk, where a dark-haired, middle-aged lady sat at a computer.

"May I help you?"

With her deep alto voice and Hispanic inflections, she clearly was not the woman he'd talked to when he and Sam called here last week.

"Yes, ma'am." He glanced at her name tag. "Howdy, Miz Vargas. Last May a friend of mine—" if only he could still claim that relationship with Lauren "—brought in my lost border collie for a checkup. She'd found the dog beside the road, and she was pretty thin. I wanted to drop by and thank Dr. Vargas in person for taking such good care of Lady... Daisy."

The woman's face blossomed into a smile. "Oh, that's so kind of you. My husband will be happy to hear that." She punched an intercom. "*Querido*, can you come out here a minute?"

While they waited for him, Rob looked around the reception area, where several people sat with their cats, birds and other critters in small cages.

"It must be nice to work with your husband." Rob considered his next words carefully. "Was that your daughter who was working here when my friend brought Daisy in?"

"That one? Humph. Juliet Sizemore is no daughter of mine." Mrs. Vargas scowled. "She was trouble from the start. My husband is a kind man, but even he had enough of her giving out diagnoses over the phone, sometimes outright telling lies to people. He let her go last week."

"Juliet Sizemore, eh?" Rob blew out a long breath. That explained everything. If memory served him, and it did in this case, Juliet was Jeff's older sister. That troubled family caused nothing but grief for themselves and everybody who knew them. Once he told her his name, she probably figured she could create mischief by lying about Lauren. And she sure had.

Dr. Vargas emerged from the back hallway, and Rob shook his hand and thanked him for contributing to "Daisy's" return to health. After several moments of friendly chatter about the animals they both worked with, Rob took his leave. Tomorrow was Saturday. Would Lauren bring Zoey out to the ranch for a lesson? And would she give him a chance to apologize? To repair the damage he'd done to their growing relationship, maybe even shattering it forever?

WITH FIFTEEN YEARS of practice, Lauren managed to keep her emotions subdued in front of Zoey as they drove out to the ranch on Saturday morning. She parked in her regular spot by the picket fence gate near the big house and walked across the barnyard with her daughter. Lady raced from the barn to greet Zoey, and after receiving the necessary hug, walked beside her the rest of the way. Mandy, Bobby and Clementine awaited them, along with shovels and wheelbarrow ready for the usual mucking of the stalls. As always, laughter and teasing filled the air. And, as always, Lauren watched in amazement while they did a chore most people would consider disgusting. Obviously the love of horses and riding made it, if not a pleasure, a necessity worth doing for the reward upon its completion.

While she hovered near in case Zoey needed help in saddling Tripper, she felt Robert's presence before she saw him emerge from the back of the barn, leading a saddled horse.

"Hey." He had the nerve to smile at her, as if their last encounter less than two weeks ago hadn't been the second worst event in her entire life.

"Hi." She moved closer to Tripper's head and held the bridle while Bobby helped Zoey lift the blanket and saddle to the horse's back. Lady was in the middle of it all, as though she was making sure Zoey was okay.

"I'm glad you came." Robert paused several yards away.

She slid him a doubtful look.

"I wanted to tell you—"

"Daddy, can I ride with you today? Pleeease?" Little Clementine's pleading stirred Lauren's heart. It also cut off whatever Robert started to say, for which Lauren was grateful.

He blew out a breath. "No, kiddo. I've already told you you're not ready to ride out with the big kids."

Tears streaming down her cheeks, Clementine ran from the barn. While the twins didn't appear to notice, Zoey did. She knelt beside Lady. "Go play with Clementine. I'm gonna ride Tripper now."

Instead of obeying, Lady grabbed the hem of Zoey's jeans and tugged.

"No, Lady. Don't do that." Zoey tried to retrieve her pant leg, but Lady held on tight and even growled softly. "No, Lady, not now. I'm gonna ride. We can play later." She looked at Lauren. "Mom, will you hold her?"

"Sure." Lauren gripped Lady's collar, and the dog whined. "As soon as you're up on the horses, we'll go find Clementine."

Her heart aching for the little girl, Lauren looked over to see Robert staring at her, but in the shadowed aisle couldn't make out his expression. Why didn't he go ahead and say whatever Clementine had interrupted? Maybe he decided this wasn't the time to air the unpleasantness between them.

He stepped closer. "I thought I'd take the kids down by the river, if that's okay with you. When we come back, I want to talk to you." His whispered words had often given her pleasant shivers, but this time, the shivers held a foreboding.

"No, thank you. You've already told me everything I need to know."

Sudden tears slipped down her cheeks, so she held on to Lady's collar and walked from the barn to keep the kids from noticing. And Robert, of course. She strolled toward her car to wait for Zoey, and noticed on her left the pretty adobe house he'd offered to her so Zoey could live here and train Lady.

That he would give up his idea about Bobby training the dog showed he was willing to change his mind about important matters. Now if only he would change his mind about her. That wasn't likely to happen. After his horrible accusations, did she even want it to?

Once he and the kids rode out of the barn, down the hill and out of sight, she let Lady go. "Go find Clementine, Lady. That's a good girl."

Lady sniffed the air, as if undecided which way to go. Finally, she scampered away, so Lauren settled in the front passenger seat of her car, hoping Andrea wouldn't look outside and notice her. No doubt Robert had told his mother about accosting Lauren, and of course she would take her son's side, just as Lauren's parents had always believed Singleton's versions of their conflicts. For now, she would try to enjoy this beautiful though chilly day, knowing at least Zoey was having a good time. Cattle mooing in the front pasture had become familiar to her. She would miss that soothing sound when she and Zoey no longer came out to the ranch.

ROB FOLLOWED THE kids as they rode beyond the levee to the trail down by the river. The flow of water had slowed since summer, so they had a smooth, solid path for easy riding. As much as he wanted to enjoy this time with the kids while he planned a way to apologize to Lauren, he kept thinking about Lady's odd behavior in grabbing Zoey's pant leg. Was she just playing or—

"Dad, look!" Mandy pointed toward a calf entangled in tree branches and river debris.

Before Rob could grab the rope from his saddle horn, Mandy already had her lasso in hand. With skill he didn't know she possessed, she lassoed the maverick and, with a quick command to her horse to stand, jumped from the saddle to free the calf. Rob could only watch in amazement. When had his young daughter developed a calf-roping skill worthy of a grown-up cowboy in rodeo competition?

"Good job, Mandy." Bobby dismounted and ran to help. He whipped out his pocketknife and began cutting away at the smaller branches entangling the calf.

"Wow, you guys are amazing." Zoey sounded a little tired. "I wish—"

Rob watched in horror as her eyes closed, and she rocked to the side. He spurred his horse up close and put an arm around her waist, just as her head lolled back.

"Lord, help me. Bobby, grab Tripper's bridle." He gently tugged Zoey from the saddle onto his own horse and cradled her in his arms. "You two take care of the maverick. Get him back up to his mama. And bring Tripper. I'm taking Zoey to the house."

Riding slowly back up the trail and over the levee, he now understood Lady's actions. She'd sensed that Zoey was about to have a seizure and didn't want her to ride. What an incredible dog. Maybe…no, he couldn't think beyond taking care of this precious girl he'd come to love almost as much as he loved his own kids.

LULLED BY THE sun's mild warmth, Lauren dozed off, until a distant shriek sounded from the front pasture. Clementine! She shook off her stupor and hurried across the barnyard. Another shriek sent her into a run. Inside the fenced pasture, the crying little girl sat on the ground all too near the milling cattle. Lady barked at them, herding them away to the other side.

Lauren had always avoided getting close to these big animals, but she pushed away her fear and opened the gate and ran to Clementine.

"What happened, honey?"

"I tripped on that." She pointed at the offending rock. "And hurt my leg. Oww!" Her loud sobs broke Lauren's heart.

Several of the steers, possibly stirred up by her noisy wail-

ing, milled around nervously, with Lady continuing to bark
and drive them back.

Lauren gently touched Clementine's leg, which brought on
another scream. Again the cattle moved closer. Lauren needed
to get her out of here.

"Honey, I'm going to pick you up. Hold on to my neck."

She managed to lift her and stagger toward the gate. The
child laid her head against Lauren's upper arm, sobbing.
Maternal love and protectiveness surged through her chest.
"You're going to be okay, sweetheart." She managed to close
and lock the gate behind them.

Lady trotted along beside them, casting anxious looks at
Clementine.

To Lauren's surprise, Robert's horse was tied to the fence
near the gate, and he was hurrying toward the back door with
Zoey in his arms. Lady darted ahead to join them.

"Zoey!" Alarm for her own daughter gripped her, but she
held on to Clementine even tighter.

"Robert, what happened?" Had Zoey fallen off of Tripper? Or—

He paused, trying to open the back door. "She—"

"I'm okay, Mom." Zoey looked weary, as she always did
after a seizure. "You can put me down, Mr. Mattson."

"When we get inside—" He turned toward Lauren, and
his eyes widened. "Clementine! What happened?" His tone
sounded accusing.

Did he think his daughter's accident was Lauren's fault?
What else would he blame her for?

"Daddy, I wanted to get Lady to herd the cows. I thought
if I did, you'd be happy with me. Ow!" she cried again. Lady
gave her an anxious look.

"Honey, I'm happy with you." His voice broke in a tone of
tender regret Lauren hadn't heard before. "I love you, punkin."
He glanced at Lauren. "Let's get these two inside."

His quick cooling of his anger surprised her. Maybe he'd just been upset when he saw Clementine in her arms.

As they settled their girls on the couches in the great room, Lady glanced between them as though trying to decide which one needed her most. She sat beside Zoey, as did Lauren.

Robert pulled out his cell phone and punched it.

"I'm okay, Mom." Zoey gave Lauren a sad smile. "Just a little weak. I forgot to take my Keppra this morning."

Lauren brushed a hand across her cheek. "Oh, honey, I should have checked to be sure you did. I think we need to have the doctor check you."

"Oh, my poor baby." Andrea sat beside Clementine and gently removed her sneaker, which caused more wailing.

"We'll be there in ten minutes." Robert disconnected his call. "Mom, can you make sure the twins are okay? They're coming up from the river. I'm taking Clementine to the ER." He looked at Lauren. "And Zoey?" At least this time he asked instead of telling her what he planned.

"I'll take her."

He sighed. "Lauren, please go with me. I need you to hold Clementine while I drive."

"I—I…wouldn't she prefer her grandmother?"

"I need Mom to help the kids with the horses." He gave her another pained look. "Please. Maybe Zoey can lie down in the back seat?" He glanced at Zoey.

She gave him a weak smile. "I can do that."

"Okay. Sure." Lauren bit her lip.

During the trip to town, the silence in the truck was broken only by Clementine's hiccuping sobs. Careful of her injury, Lauren held her close, treasuring the feel of the sweet child in her arms and wishing it were under very different circumstances. At the ER, the orthopedic specialist took charge of Clementine, and Doc Edwards checked Zoey's vital signs. Once he'd cleared her daughter, Lauren eyed the door, eager to leave, but her car and even her purse were still at the ranch.

X-rays completed, pain shots administered, the orthopedist proclaimed only a hairline break above Clementine's ankle and, with his nurse's assistance, proceeded to apply padding and a plaster cast. With the painkiller taking effect, Clementine giggled as the doctor made jokes and silly faces. She also demanded that Lauren should still hold her hand during the process. Zoey sat in a chair, her color returning by the minute. Robert watched from the corner where he leaned against the wall, arms crossed.

"Can I get you some coffee?" His question surprised her.

"From the machine?"

"That's the only kind available on the weekend." From his slight grin, maybe he was remembering their previous coffee disaster when Zoey had been here the first time. She'd enjoyed their joking about the undrinkable brew.

"Ugh." She grimaced. "No, thanks."

He chuckled. Oh, how she had missed that sound.

What was she thinking? This man had accused her of stealing and lying. Now he was all nice and *Please help me*? No thanks to the coffee *and* to him.

On the way home, Clementine fell asleep in her arms, and Zoey dozed in the back seat. Again, Lauren's maternal instincts kicked in. She'd loved being a mother from the moment she'd discovered her pregnancy. Had loved Zoey through every childhood illness and accident and especially her triumphs over her CP challenges. She would have loved having another child or two, but it hadn't been the Lord's will for her. Just as marital happiness had eluded her.

Halfway back to the ranch, Robert interrupted her musings. "Thanks for your help."

"No problem." Not that she'd had a choice, but she was glad she'd come to help with Clementine. To avoid looking at him, she stared out the passenger side window.

"It's good that Zoey's resting."

"Uh-huh."

He must have taken the hint because he quit trying to engage her in conversation. At the house, Robert carried still-sleeping Clementine, and Lauren helped Zoey inside. Andrea and the twins gathered around to be sure both girls were all right. Lady nuzzled Zoey's hand, then sniffed Clementine's cast and looked into the child's face, her sweet way of checking on her humans.

"Is Clementine's leg broken?" Mandy asked.

"Can we sign her cast?" Bobby grabbed a Sharpie from a side table drawer.

"Shh," Robert said. "Let's let her sleep." He looked at Lauren. "Will you wait while I get her settled? I want...need to talk to you."

"No, Zoey needs to rest, and I have laundry to do." Lauren beckoned to her daughter. "Come on, honey. Bobby, please hold Lady so she won't follow us."

Even though Zoey was tired during the drive home, she talked about her ride by the river. "Mom, I wish you could have seen Mandy lasso the stray calf. She was awesome."

"That *is* awesome." If only Robert would admit his older daughter was a true cowgirl.

"I'm not afraid to ride again." Zoey laughed softly. "But I'll listen to Lady next time. And I'll make sure I take my meds."

Lauren sent her a rueful smile. "We'll see."

Her daughter was brave. Lauren, not so much. She couldn't escape the thought that she'd been a coward for running away rather than having a final confrontation with Robert. Why not deal with it once and for all?

Easy answer. Her heart was still broken from his unfounded accusations, and she couldn't bear to face any further censure.

CHAPTER SEVENTEEN

MOM PULLED BACK the covers so Rob could lay Clementine in her bed. Once settled, she looked at peace and oh so sweet. Doc said she'd experience some pain once the painkillers wore off. Rob sat on the chair beside her bed, intending to be there for her when she woke up to make sure she understood how much he loved her. It cut real deep that she'd preferred Lauren's support while the doctor applied the cast. What hurt worse was she thought she had to earn his love. Had he been that neglectful of his youngest? It sickened him to think she'd entered a pasture with a herd of unruly yearling cattle and could easily have been trampled. If not for Lady's protection and Lauren's quick action, she might have been.

He'd been wrong about Lauren. Neglectful of Clementine. Totally missed the mark with Mandy. Man, who would have thought she could lasso a struggling calf on the first throw? What other ranch chores did she do well? Yes, Bobby could do it all, however reluctantly. But he'd been a bench warmer on a losing football squad when he could have earned some points on the school programming team if Rob hadn't been so stubborn about his activities.

"Daddy, where's Miss Lauren?" Clementine rubbed her eyes, only half-awake.

"Hey, sweetheart. She and Zoey had to go home." To do her laundry, her overused excuse for escaping his company. "But here's Lady."

Lady put her paws on the edge of the bed and touched her nose to Clementine's hand. Clementine petted her. "You saved me, Lady."

"Punkin, you know I love you, don't you?" He brushed her hair back from her face.

"Uh-huh. I love you, too." She gave him a teary smile, then drifted off to sleep again.

"Robert, I can watch over her now." Mom touched his shoulder. "I don't know what happened between you and Lauren, but why not go after her and settle it? Don't let the sun go down on your wrath."

His wrath? That was the whole problem summed up in one short scripture verse. He'd wanted to deepen his relationship with Lauren, but had all too easily believed some stranger's lie. In truth, Lauren had rescued Clementine and showered her with tender care, just as she did her own child. She was everything he could hope for in…in what? Friendship? Relationship? Wife? Had he been using fear as a shield not to love her when all the while his heart was telling him something different? He'd finally gotten around to reading Zoey's essay about how they found Lady, and it had doubled his grief over his terrible treatment of Lauren. She'd been telling the truth all along.

"Thanks, Mom." He grunted. "I have more than one fire to put out tonight."

He made his way to Mandy's room and stuck his head in. She was bent over her homework. "Hey, cowgirl, that was some pretty fancy roping this afternoon."

"Thanks, Dad." She grinned at his praise.

"Yeah, I've been thinking. If you want, you can help with calving in the spring. What would you think about that?"

Her grinned broadened. "I'd love it!"

"Good. Maybe we can put you to work on more of the ranch chores. You up for that?"

"Yessir." Her eyes filled with tears, the happy kind. "I won't let you down, Dad."

"I know you won't, honey. Now get that homework done." He turned from the doorway before she saw his own eyes tearing up. Next problem to solve, Bobby. He went to the room across the hall from Mandy's.

Bobby sat on his bed, propped up on pillows, his computer resting on his knees and a headset covering his ears.

"Hey, kiddo." Rob walked over and glanced at the laptop. The screen showed some complicated coding way beyond Rob's comprehension. He removed Bobby's headset. The boy blinked in his preoccupied way.

"Oh, hey, Dad."

"Hey." Rob sat on the edge of the bed. "Looks like you're working on some interesting stuff."

"Yessir." Bobby's expression grew guarded. "I'm not goofing off. It's homework."

"Sure. I believe you." Now the tough part. "Look, I've been thinking maybe you should spend more time with the programming team. That's where your talents seem to lie. What would you think of that?"

"You mean it?" Bobby grew animated. "What about football?"

"Well, you still have two years to go." This was the hardest for Rob to let go of. "If you still feel the same way next fall, you...you don't have to play."

"Wow." Bobby gave him his goofy grin. "Thanks, Dad. I won't let you down."

That's what Mandy had said. Had he been such an exacting dad to these two? That needed to end. Today. "I know you won't, son."

With one more score to settle, he told Mom he was leaving. The sun was nearing the horizon, and as she'd said, he wasn't going to let it go down until matters were settled with Lauren. He'd planned to buy more flowers to use as a shield when he apologized, but Jenny's shop would be closed by now, and he couldn't delay this any longer. He stood by the pickup for a moment. "Lord, what can I do to show her how sorry I am for being a beast? For believing the worst about her?"

He knew the answer right away and went back into the house to fetch the only gift that would solve this problem once and for all.

AS MUCH AS Lauren had often longed for a happy, stable marriage, she'd learned over the years such happiness wasn't meant for her. Then Robert came into her life...rather, *barged* into her life, and she'd begun to dream again.

What should she do now? Today he seemed to have softened toward her, probably because they were with the kids. Could she trust him not to blow up at her again? At least her job was safe. Probably. Over the past week, Sam and Will had left subtle hints about how much they depended on her, and on Friday, proved it outright by giving her a significant raise in salary. Now she could buy Zoey some much-needed winter clothes.

Robert had let Zoey ride today, had saved her from falling off Tripper when she had her seizure. He'd been so gentle to dear little Clementine, proving he truly was a loving father. Indeed, he was kind and caring...to everyone but her.

Zoey had taken a short nap and now sat in the living room folding laundry, so Lauren started supper. Hands deep in chopping salad greens, she grabbed a carrot stick to nibble, which only made her stomach rumble with hunger. A tasty steak came to mind, but she couldn't afford that luxury.

A knock sounded on the door, reverberating throughout the small apartment.

"I'll get it." Zoey walked across the room, her broken gait showing her weariness from the day. "Lady!"

"What?" Lauren dried her hands and walked to the living room. Her heart seemed to stop. "Robert."

Zoey was down on her knees receiving wet doggy kisses and laughing. "Did you come for a visit, silly girl?"

"No." Robert gazed at Lauren as he answered. "She's come to stay."

"Now, just a minute—" Heat rushed up Lauren's neck, but she tried to tamp down her anger.

"I mean, would you please take care of my, *this* dog, who clearly wants to be with Zoey?" He shuffled his feet in true shy cowboy fashion. "Lauren, I'm sorry for—"

"Zoey, take Lady to your room and close the door."

Zoey looked between her and Robert and grinned. "Yes, ma'am." She quickly obeyed.

Lauren fisted her hands at her waist. "Now, what's this all about?"

He took a step toward her. She held up her hands palms out to stop him, then crossed her arms.

"I'm so sorry for not trusting you. I was so wrong to believe that woman at the vet clinic. She told me you asked Dr. Vargas to remove Lady's chip, but he refused to do it. But when I called back, I mean, when *Sam* called back, the doctor himself said there was no chip and that you and Zoey saved Lady's life."

That was a big speech for this cowboy, and the sorrow in his face, in his entire demeanor, backed up his words.

"Please forgive me, Lauren. I don't deserve it, but—"

"Do you have any idea how much you hurt me? How you, a prominent citizen of this county, this *state*, cast aspersions on my character? I work in a law office. How would it look to clients who trust your cousins if their paralegal isn't honest?"

"I know." He nodded, and his eyes reddened. "If it's any help, my cousins were smarter than me. Like I said, Sam followed up my call with one of his own. He didn't give his last name to the woman who answered, so she had no way to connect us. Turns out she's related to the Sizemore family. They've caused trouble for the Mattsons since the late 1800s. When I gave her my name, she must have decided to cause more trouble." He seemed to realize he was still wearing his hat, because he took it off and turned it in his hands, a gesture she would have found charming once upon a time. "Is there any way I can fix this? I mean, between you and me? Lauren, I love you, and I'll do whatever it takes to make it right."

He loved her? Her eyes burned, and she took a deep breath, trying not to cry. It was no use. She burst into tears and turned away from him. She felt his big, calloused hands gently touch her shoulders. A pleasant shiver swept down her entire being.

"Lauren." He spoke her name so softly, so lovingly. "I love you," he repeated. "Please forgive me. Please tell me what I can do to make things right between us."

She turned around and gazed up into those gorgeous blue eyes. "I think you just did." She tilted her head toward Zoey's closed door. "Bringing Lady to visit Zoey means more to me than you can imagine."

"Not just bringing her for a visit. I meant what I said. I'm giving her to Zoey to keep." He brushed tears from her cheek and gently pulled her into his arms. For several moments, they gazed at each other. Lauren could hardly breathe.

"I love you," he said again.

As warmth flooded her heart, she sighed. "I love you, too, Robert."

"Oh, go ahead and kiss her, Mr. Mattson." Zoey's sudden appearance startled them from their daze. "You have my permission."

"Zoey." Robert sent her a playful scowl. "Don't you have some laundry to do?"

"So, James, how's my mother's condo coming along?" Rob stood in the great room with Mom's contractor...and whatever else he was to her. "Did you get those problems with the plumbing ironed out?"

"Yep." Dressed in jeans, boots and a checkered flannel shirt, the graying man in his sixties looked more like a cowboy than a big-city businessman. "We had to switch companies to get the job done to Andrea's satisfaction."

That usually meant more money. How did Rob go about making sure this dude wasn't bilking her out of her savings? "How much did the change cost?"

James chuckled. "Not a dime. In fact, we got a full refund and applied it to the new fixtures."

"Huh." While Rob considered what his next question should be, he glanced through the archway into the kitchen.

Lauren and Linda were helping Mom put the finishing touches on the Thanksgiving dinner. The kids were playing UNO at the kitchen table, with Lady lying on the floor between Zoey and Clementine. The aromas of roasted turkey, spicy crown roast beef and apple and pumpkin pies filled the house.

"Rob, I'm glad we have a chance to talk. I know you probably have a lot of questions." James looked directly into Rob's eyes, as he had when they met earlier and he gave Rob a firm handshake, both signs of an honest man. "I want you to know Andrea is very special to me, and I'd like to spend the rest of my life with her." He glanced toward the kitchen. "I can show you my financials, if you want. We plan to set up separate accounts so her grandkids will inherit from her, and mine will inherit from me." He inhaled a deep breath as though gathering courage. "So, if that settles the concerns any dutiful son should have, I'm asking your permission to propose to her."

With a proposal of his own in mind, Rob could feel the small box in his jeans pocket. He still hadn't figured out how to get Lauren away from the crowd. When he'd called her dad back in Orlando and asked to marry her, Dan had been surprised. Said nobody did that anymore, but he was fine with whatever Lauren wanted to do. Not the best beginning for their relationship. No wonder Lauren often doubted herself. Rob would make sure he did better by Mom...and James.

He stuck out his hand. "I'm happy to say yes, you have my permission." As they shook hands again, he added, "Welcome to the family."

He prayed his proposal to Lauren went just as well.

Sam and Andy came in from doing chores, and everyone gathered around the table. James offered a prayer of thanks that further encouraged Rob about his spiritual condition. Conversation flowed around the table along with the food. Toward the end of the meal, with desserts calling their names, James stood up.

"Folks, I appreciate your kind hospitality. Now, if you'll indulge me, I'm about to ask Miss Andrea to be my wife—"

Laughing along with everyone else, Mom stood up beside him, clearly not surprised. "Yes!"

"Hold on a minute, honey. Let me ask you." James took a little box from his shirt and opened it to reveal a shiny, pricey sapphire-and-diamond ring. "Not gonna make a big speech, just gonna say I love you, Andrea. Will you marry me?"

Mom answered by planting a kiss on his lips. While Bobby groaned and everybody else cheered, Rob felt a small jab in his chest, but quickly dismissed it. He knew Dad would be pleased that Mom had found a good man to spend her senior years with.

Mom turned to him. "Robert, don't you have something to say to Lauren?"

"Now, Mom." He wanted to do this in private, but that maverick just broke loose. No herding it back into the corral. "All right, then. Lauren, honey, I'm crazy about you. Will you marry me?" Ugh! He'd meant to say something flowery. Too late now. He pulled out the ring he'd chosen from among the many family heirloom jewels, Great-Grandma Mattson's legacy engagement ring, a large ruby set in gold and surrounded by emerald-cut diamonds.

"Sure. Why not?" She winked as she stood and stuck out her left hand. "Oh, Robert, it's gorgeous. Yes, I'll marry you." Once he put the ring on her finger, she cuddled up under his arm and looked up at him with those beautiful gray-green eyes.

He glanced around the table. "Y'all excuse us a minute." Then he planted a kiss on her sweet lips that lasted longer than he could count. He couldn't be sure, but he thought he heard a few more cheers and plenty of laughter from the people who loved them best.

LAUREN HESITATED TO open personal mail at work, especially a letter bearing the return address of an Orlando law office. But, not able to concentrate on the document on her computer, she opened the ivory envelope and pulled out the letter. As she'd suspected, it was from Singleton's lawyer claiming she had pressured him into signing away his parental rights and demanding that she must grant him immediate and open visitation with Zoey. In the midst of planning her December 19 wedding, she just couldn't deal with this now. That didn't keep her from shedding a few tears.

"Hey, Lauren, what's wrong?"

Count on Sam to always be sensitive to her feelings. She handed him the letter. "What can we do?"

He grunted. "This guy just doesn't quit, does he?" He scratched his chin thoughtfully. "The easiest solution would be for you and Rob to get married right away. You've already got your wedding license, right?" At her nod, he said, "Good. Once you say 'I do' we can finish Rob's adoption petition and have Judge Mathis sign it so Zoey's last name will be Mattson. The judge is already on our side about this because your ex signed away his rights in Florida, and we can prove you didn't pressure him. Besides, under New Mexico law, deadbeat fathers can't renege on their parental responsibilities. Also, if you want, we can get a restraining order so Parker won't be able to approach Zoey without getting arrested. This should be easy-peasy."

And so, two days later, Lauren found herself standing beside Robert in the Riverton Community Church sanctuary in front of Pastor Tim, with Zoey and the kids…and Lady…as their supporting posse. They would still have their planned December 19 reception here at the church so all their friends and many, many relatives could enjoy the festivities. But now Zoey was safe with her new dad, one who wanted to be a true father to her, not use her as a political pawn.

After the brief ceremony, the new family piled back into Robert's pickup and headed toward the courthouse, where they met Sam at Judge Mathis's office. With all the proper paperwork signed and sealed, they hit the road again, first stopping at the steak house for lunch, then back in the truck, with the kids singing silly camp songs. When Lady tired of the noise, she lifted her voice in plaintive howls that somehow added harmony as they drove home toward the Double Bar M Ranch.

Home. That sounded so good. Lauren could hardly wait to begin her new life as Mrs. Robert Mattson.

ROB CHUCKLED AT the noise the kids and Lady were making. It was sweet music to him. They pulled into the barnyard, and he parked near the picket fence. The kids hopped out of the truck and raced toward the house, with Lady right behind them. Rob took a little longer helping Lauren from the vehicle. He pulled her into a hug for a sweet kiss before sweeping her up in his arms.

She squealed in surprise and laughed. "What are you doing?"

"Gotta carry my new bride over the threshold, right?"

She laughed again. "I guess you do."

He felt a paw on his jeans and looked down to see Lady eyeing them both with concern.

"It's okay, girl. Go find Zoey."

Lady tilted her head.

Lauren looked down. "It's okay, Lady. Go find Clementine."

As the dog raced off to obey them both, they shared a laugh.

"I hope she doesn't get confused," Lauren said.

"She'll get it sorted out." Of that, Rob was certain.

Lady was back home, back where she belonged. But with a new job—taking care of Rob's youngest kiddo, Clementine, and his much loved new daughter, Zoey. And all was right in his world.

* * * * *

MILLS & BOON